Advance praise for

IN THE
PENALTY
BOX

D0112898

"A delightful, fast-paced, heart-skipping, super-fun read!"
—**Jennifer Brody / Vera Strange, award-winning author
of the 13th Continuum trilogy**

"This novel is pure joy. A sweet romance, engrossing characters, and intense hockey action. Reading it was like sitting in a chilly ice rink, wrapped in a fleece blanket and sipping hot chocolate."
—**Rob Shapiro, author of *The Book of Sam***

"A flirty, sweet figure skater vs. hockey player romance with an adorable twist."
—**T.H. Hernandez, author of *Prom-Wrecked***

"Lynn Rush and Kelly Anne Blount have created characters you will fall in love with and cheer for—and you might even consider strapping on your own skates."
—**Fiona Simpson, freelance editor**

"A heartwarming story of perseverance, love and friendship. Rush and Blount do an amazing job of weaving depth into this feel-good story. I enjoyed it from beginning to end."
—**Noreen Bruce, RespectYourShelves blog**

IN THE
PENALTY
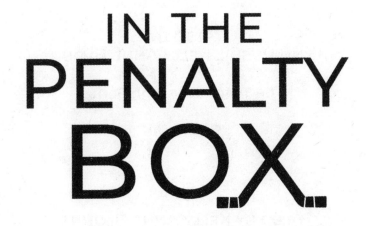

Also by
Lynn Rush & Kelly Anne Blount

The Twin River High Series

Gutter Girl

Also by Kelly Anne Blount

I Hate You, Fuller James

IN THE
PENALTY
BOX

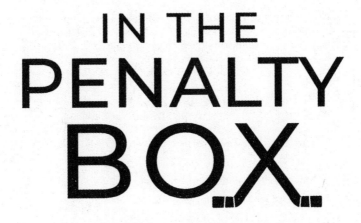

NYT & *USA TODAY* BESTSELLING AUTHOR
LYNN RUSH
USA TODAY BESTSELLING AUTHOR
KELLY ANNE BLOUNT

Entangled Publishing, LLC
10940 S Parker Road
Suite 327
Parker, CO 80134
rights@entangledpublishing.com

Entangled Teen is an imprint of Entangled Publishing, LLC.

Visit our website at www.entangledpublishing.com.

Edited by Stacy Abrams
Cover design by LJ Anderson, Mayhem Cover Creations
Cover images by
Vasyl Dolmatov/GettyImages and
karych/Depositphotos
Interior design by Toni Kerr

ISBN 978-1-68281-576-2
Ebook ISBN 978-1-68281-583-0

Manufactured in the United States of America

First Edition January 2021

10 9 8 7 6 5 4 3 2 1

entangled teen
an imprint of Entangled Publishing LLC

CHAPTER ONE

Willow

Ten months of physical therapy and grueling pain was about to pay off. Clutching my arms to my chest, I spun through the air.

I *had* to land this jump.

My skate made contact with the ice. *Yes!* I felt fine. Finally, I—

Pain exploded up from my heel: a cruel reminder of the injury that crushed my Olympic dreams and threatened to decimate my future as a champion figure skater. My jaw clenched as I balled up my fists.

I flailed like a newbie, then turned my left skate at an angle and came to a stop in the middle of the rink.

A vise cinched around my chest, and a wave of nausea stormed through my stomach. I'd failed. Again. My shoulders slumped.

The muscle in my ankle seized, and it felt like a steel baseball bat had rammed my calf. I bent over and clutched the area as hot tears burst from my eyes and seared a path down my cold cheeks. I'd been fanatical about my physical therapy exercises. Spent hours in the pool keeping up my cardio. But it'd been almost a year now, and my progress had been so unbelievably slow. Rupturing an Achilles tendon was one of the worst injuries a figure skater could endure.

And the hardest to recover from.

Coach's words echoed in my mind. *"Everything's going to be just fine. You'll be back on the ice before you know it."*

Lies.

Everything she had said on the ride to the hospital was a lie.

The sound of laughter yanked me back to the moment, and I shifted to see what was going on behind me. Three hockey players lined up outside the rink, near the door. When they glanced my way, they shook their heads. Hockey players always hated getting rink time after figure skaters. I'd been chewed out more times than I could count for roughing up their smooth ice with my toe picks.

I wasn't surprised they were chomping at the bit to get on the ice. This rink was really nice, and that was coming from someone who'd spent the last nine years in Colorado, skating at a first-class training center that had top-notch ice.

The large clock mounted on the wall showed I still had three minutes until the Zamboni came out, so I pushed off, gaining some speed.

One more try. You can do this, Willow!

Hearing the scrape of my blades on the ice and feeling the breeze against my skin as I picked up speed kicked me into the zone. Everything else faded as I drank in the burn in my quads, my heart racing.

If I could just land one more jump today, I'd be happy.

A fluttery feeling spread from my chest to my fingertips.

Holding out my hands, I pushed off with my back skate and snapped the opposite knee around the front. My heart hammered as the near-perfect rotation threw me into a spin that felt as natural as breathing.

I was weightless. I was free. This was what I lived for.

And I was going to land this jump.

My skate hit the ice. My leg buckled, and in the next breath, my butt slammed into the frozen surface. The momentum sent me sliding, but the boards stopped me with a breath-stealing *crack*.

"Damn it!" I slouched to the side and slammed my fist on the ice.

Heat rushed up my face as some of the hockey players snickered. I pounded the ice one more time, then scrambled to my feet, fighting back the tears. From the stands, Jessa smiled and gave me a small wave.

She was the best friend in the world to be sitting here, watching me like this. My biggest cheerleader, she wanted to see me landing these jumps nearly as much as I wanted to land them. As I *needed* to land them. I had to get back to competition strength ASAP, or any chances of making it onto the Olympic team would be gone, gone, gone.

My breath hitched in my chest as I slowly stood. Jessa was the only person I'd stayed in touch with here in Woodhaven after my family had moved out to Colorado. My parents came back two years ago when Gramps got sick, but I'd only returned a couple of weeks ago.

At the sound of the Zamboni roaring to life, I made my way toward the exit. Glancing down for a moment as I brushed the ice from my sore butt, my shoulder rammed into something hard.

"Son of a puck," a guy shouted. "Watch out!"

I spun but couldn't jab my skate into the ice to stop me. And for the third time in mere minutes, my tailbone slammed against the unrelenting surface.

A hot jolt of pain shot up my spine, so I sat there a second to collect myself.

The guy I'd collided with loomed over me. He pushed his helmet back, and floppy, dark brown hair spilled out around his sun-kissed face. Swirls of amber flashed through his brown eyes, and his lips curled into a smile.

Just like that, my heart started banging in my chest and heat pooled at the apples of my cheeks.

He bent toward me, his hair shifting forward, framing his face. He was tall, broad shouldered, and from what I could see beneath his tight, form-fitting long-sleeve shirt, muscular as hell. He was wearing black hockey pants and elbow guards, but his shoulder pads were splayed on the ice beside him. A small scar on his chin marred his otherwise smooth, flawless skin.

Mouth going dry, I let out a fake cough and cursed myself for not bringing a water bottle down to the ice with me.

I planned to say something witty, but my words were failing me. "Did you just say 'son of a puck'?"

The guy rubbed the back of his neck. "It's a hockey thing." All of a sudden, a teasing glint lit his eye. "Guess a *figure skater* wouldn't understand."

"Riiight." I stretched out the long vowel, smirking right back at him. Despite sitting on the cold ice, heat coursed through my body.

Who did this hockey player think he was, anyway?

He held out his hand. "I am sorry. I thought you saw me."

I waved him off. "Today is *not* my day."

"Come on, let me help you up, Toe Pick," he insisted. "You hit the ice pretty hard out there."

Tingles shot through my body as our fingers met.

Damn, this guy is cute!

He hoisted me up, but I missed stabbing my toe pick into the ice to stabilize myself, and I fell forward, my knee making direct contact with his crotch.

"Shit!" I let out a gasp as my stomach cramped, and I hit the ice knees first.

"Omph!" He grunted, then fell backward onto the ice, landing right beside me.

"Oh my gosh!" Talk about first introductions gone terribly wrong.

Wide brown eyes zeroed in on me. This guy had the longest black eyelashes I'd ever seen; any girl would pay good money for a set of those.

"I'm so sorry!" I pushed off the ice and got back onto my blades, heat fusing my cheeks.

"My bad." He rolled over and hopped onto his skates.

"Is your— I mean. Are you okay?"

He grinned, his face turning a shade of red. "Hockey players wear protection. So I'm good."

"Oh," I said, then with a giggle, "guess a *figure skater* wouldn't understand, huh?"

He chuckled and leaned on his stick as he looked at me. "You're not half bad, you know. On your skates, I mean. Well, at least when I'm not within three feet of you."

"Should have seen me before," I muttered.

He arched an eyebrow.

"Long story," I said as I pushed away on unsteady legs. What the hell was wrong with me today? "Anyway, I don't want to intrude on your ice time, *hockey player.*"

"Maybe I'll see you out here again?" His voice sounded hopeful, and his smile made my knees go weak.

"Probably will," I said with what I hoped was a flirty smile, temporarily forgetting about my throbbing Achilles.

"See ya, Toe Pick," he called out.

"See ya, Puck Head," I yelled, not turning back as I made my way to the exit.

I turned around and snuck a quick glance at the hockey player who'd helped me to my feet. He was fully geared up now and warming up with a few laps around the rink. *Not too shabby of a skater, either…*

I stepped over the threshold from the ice to the flooring and plopped onto the cold metal bench.

Defeat crushed my lungs and made it difficult to take a deep breath. Everything felt heavy on me. My legs. My arms. My heart.

The hockey players made their way toward the team bench as the Zamboni entered the rink and began zooming around the ice, clearing away the work I'd put in out there for the last hour.

Work that felt pointless for how much my Achilles hurt. Seemed like I'd never get over this injury.

My fingers met my temples. I made small circles for several seconds before I packed up my stuff and limped to the bleachers where Jessa was sitting. She'd asked if I'd stay and watch the hockey scrimmage with her, since her best guy friend Preach was playing. It was the last thing I wanted to do—I'd much rather take a shower and bust out my physical therapy exercises—but she'd hung here watching me for more than an hour, so it was only fair.

Plus, there *was* some nice eye candy out there to admire.

"Great practice, Will," my best friend said as she clomped down the steps, carrying a cup of hot chocolate.

"Thanks for hanging out," I said. "You look adorable, by the way." Her long, blond hair spilled from beneath a silver and maroon stocking cap. It really made her gray eyes stand out against her pale skin.

"Thanks. How's your ankle?" Jessa slid in beside me.

"Eh, not great."

Understatement of the year.

"I thought you did awesome. I don't know how you do all that spinning without getting dizzy." Jessa took a sip of her drink.

I chuckled. "On another topic, did you see that puck head plow into me?" I slipped a sweatshirt over my head and a pair of jogging pants over my leggings to chase away the chill of the rink. Didn't help that I'd spent most of my time on my ass out there. "I totally kneed him in the crotch. I wanted to die."

"That's Brodie 'Wind' Windom." Jessa grinned.

"Windom. As in…the name on the sign in front of the rink?" I leaned forward and covered my face with my hands, then peeked through my fingers at Jessa. "Oh great, I totally just ice-accosted a Windom?"

She laughed, her eyes lighting up. "Yeah, you did." She chuckled some more. "Brodie's family is loaded. They remodeled the old rink, spent three million dollars or something."

I kept my eyes on this "Wind" guy as he skated across the fresh ice. "It's a really nice rink."

"Yeah, the boys' hockey team at Woodhaven has won State like ten times in the past twenty-five years. Brodie's dad played pro for a while, so I guess it made sense to give the guys a nice rink."

"Wow." No wonder he looked so confident on the ice.

"His family owns the new apartments off High Street. They have a bunch of properties in Minnesota, too."

"Must be nice." My chest tightened. I couldn't help but find myself feeling jealous. My family had never had an excess of money. "Why can't I remember him from elementary school?"

"They moved here after you left," said Jessa, staring out over the ice. "You would have loved playing street hockey with him down on Heron Lane, though. He was always out there with at least twenty other kids."

My lips curved into a smile as nostalgia warmed my chest. "Those were the good old days…" I'd spend my entire summer break in rollerblades. Racing toward the net, stick in hand, ready to score on whatever kid was brave enough to fill the goalie position.

"Remember when you took down—"

"Heads up!" someone yelled.

Adrenaline surged through my chest, nearly stealing my breath as I whipped my focus to the ice. I never did understand why people yelled that, since something was obviously coming at them. Shouldn't they say *duck*?

It happened as if in slow motion, but not.

The puck pinged off the upper part of the crossbar; the goalie had totally missed the shot. It cracked against the polycarbonate barrier but hit the corner rail and blasted out of the rink.

My heart hammered so wildly, I thought it might burst out of my chest.

"Watch out!" someone else screamed.

I stood in horror as the puck sailed over the wall and hurled through the air directly at Jessa and me.

I snatched my bag from beside me and dove forward. With an upward thrust, I swung the bag in front of Jessa. Even through her scream, I heard the puck smack into it. The momentum had me staggering back into a sitting position beside her.

"Oh my gosh!" Jessa yelled. The puck flopped onto my best friend's lap, and she screeched again.

A loud exhale escaped my lips, and goose bumps prickled the back of my neck.

"Holy crap," someone said behind us, but I was too rattled to look at who it was. "Did you see that?"

A few gasps sounded from around me.

"Shit!" someone from the rink said as Brodie and a couple other players sprinted toward us.

I turned my attention back to my best friend. "You okay?" My hands were shaking from the adrenaline coursing through my body.

Jessa looked at me, her face white as the ice. "I—I think so?"

Her jaw tensed, and her eyes widened. I wasn't entirely sure she'd blinked yet.

I picked up the solid black disc from her lap and tossed it into the air. It flipped twice before it landed in my palm.

I turned my attention back toward the ice and arched an eyebrow at Brodie. "Lose something?"

CHAPTER TWO

Brodie

"**S**weet skills, Toe Pick." I dropped the puck to the ice before me, then lifted it to my stick. "Josiah, you think you could have stopped that?"

Our stocky goalie grinned and shook his head, then looked down at his skates.

Mystery Girl's dark eyebrows quirked up, and her lips curled into a mischievous smile that sent a jolt of lightning right down my spine.

I had no idea who she was, but she was hot. Her tight body was now covered with long sweatpants and a hoodie, but I'd seen her out on the ice earlier, landing some sweet jumps. She had nice, lean, but really strong legs and long black hair in thick braids that went to the middle of her back. The thing that stole the show, though, were her eyes. Bright blue, and even through the three feet separating us, I saw the green flecks shimmer within them. Her skin was smooth and flushed at the apples of her cheeks.

"I wonder if that was a one-time thing or if you actually have some hockey in ya," Preach said from beside me.

I backhanded him, still watching Mystery Girl in complete

shock at how she'd knocked my rogue puck down.

"Oh, it's not, and I do," the girl said with a grin, then turned to me. "But I wouldn't want to embarrass you. I mean, with your name being on the front of the building and all."

Shit. She knew who I was because of the sign. I'd much rather her know my name from the three banners hanging on the wall near the clock for lead scorer. Or because she and Jessa were talking about me. But no, Dad had to put "Windom" on the front of the building when he renovated the place.

"Um…yeah, nice block there." I gulped through the sudden dryness in my mouth.

Jessa stood beside her, and she nudged Mystery Girl. "My girl isn't too shabby with a stick in her hand."

A couple of the guys next to me burst out laughing.

Mortified, Jessa slapped a hand over her mouth.

"Thanks for that." The girl chuckled, her cheeks reddening. "I'm Willow, and I've held my own on a hockey team before. I mean, it was street hockey, but how much different can it be on the ice?"

So her name was Willow. It had to have been the first time I'd ever seen her here before, because I would have noticed her for sure. Not that I would have done anything about it. I'd had enough experience with Ice Princesses after dating Sydney last year. I needed to steer clear of that type of drama—and heartache—for sure.

But seeing this Willow girl knocking down my wild puck, then dishing out the sarcasm right back at me, she didn't come off as the Ice Princess type. She was all kinds of sexy… and tempting.

I pushed back, easing away from the wall, and moved the puck back with me. "Thanks for batting that down. I'm glad you didn't get hurt, Toe Pick."

I flipped the puck up onto my stick again and nodded

at her, then hustled toward the center line. My heart was hammering, and my hands were sweating under my gloves. It was like I could still feel her gaze on me, piercing through my hockey pads.

"Look at you, *Wind*—a cute little figure skater blocked your shot. You *must* be getting rusty." Pax smacked my butt as he skated by. "Are we playing or what?"

With my helmet cradled against my hip, I snuck another glance at Willow and Jessa. They leaned into each other, like they were whispering.

Probably laughing their asses off at my complete ineptness. First, I'd rammed smack into Willow, totally not meaning to. Then she completely kneed me in the balls when I was helping her up.

Third, my wild puck almost killed her and Jessa.

Damn, I was off my game.

Sure, it was only the first of August—I had time to get in shape these last couple of weeks of summer town league—but still. I had to stay focused. If I didn't get onto the Boston College hockey team, I'd be the first Windom in three generations to not make it.

"Dude." Preach sprayed me as he came to a stop, inches before ramming into me. "I think you have some drool…"

I punched his shoulder. He was my best friend, knew me better than anyone, so he could probably tell I was intrigued. "Shut it, man." My cheeks suddenly felt like they were on fire.

"She is hot, though," he added.

"She's probably an Ice Princess." I tapped the ice at my feet. "Look what her toe pick is doing to the ice! It's all chopped up."

Preach chuckled, and through his hockey mask, I saw him roll his eyes. "Sure, Brodie. Whatever."

"She's friends with Jessa, huh?"

"I guess," Preach said. "I can ask Jessa what's going on with our mysterious skater friend Willow if you want…"

I shoved him and jumped into some fast-feet drills to get my blood pumping for our pick-up game. I needed to stay focused. Only two weeks left until the town's Fall League started, which meant hardcore practices and training.

I huffed and zeroed in on the ice before me. Her bright eyes, smooth skin, and sexy smile flashed in my mind. Distractions were not an option for me right now. My last two girlfriends had messed with my head *and* my hockey stats.

Not this year.

I had to nail this season.

Senior year was coming up, and I had to stay on Boston College's radar. Coach Raymond was the best in college hockey as far as I was concerned. He'd reached out a couple of times, calling my dad and asking how I was doing, but I was sure it was only because of the family name. He hadn't shown up to any of my games last year or talked to Coach directly about my stats. An awesome season and a State win would definitely get me back on his agenda.

I sprayed ice at Preach, Teddy, and Nathaniel as I came to a stop by them, then coasted to my left wing position. "Not getting any younger, guys."

"Dick," Teddy Cook said as he readied himself to drop the puck.

"Hey, Wind!" I didn't have to look up to know that had been Amanda Fert calling my name.

"Looks like your *girlfriend* is here," Nathaniel Baker said as he leaned forward, ready to slap the puck once it landed.

Amanda *so* wasn't my girlfriend. She was a total puck bunny and only into me because I was team captain last year, highest scorer, and my name was on the front of the ice arena. She didn't give two craps about me.

Preach snickered as our left defenseman, Pax Hunt, dropped the puck, then bolted to his normal position. Nathaniel slapped the puck, using my momentary distraction to his advantage.

Case in point, no girls.

I tore after the puck, easily beating Nathaniel to it, and took off. A quick pass to Preach, and then I dodged around Nathaniel and picked up Preach's return pass. Curling the puck around, I spun, tapped it, then deked and blasted left, leaving our defenseman sophomore, Trevor, in the dust.

"You ass," he yelled.

"Eat it." I faked right, then slapped the puck.

Nothing but net.

I shoved my arms up, my stick in the air, and hollered.

"Nice one, man." Teddy rammed into me, and I landed on my stomach, the wind knocking out of me. I curled inward as I slid across the ice, bringing my knees to my chest as I tried to gasp some air in, but none came. Heat flooded my body, and my neck hairs prickled.

That Teddy sure could double as a left tackle on our football team for how big he was.

Nathaniel slid to a stop beside us, coating us with a layer of ice. "Damn, Teddy! Roughing the player much?"

I hopped up and got lost in the pick-up game, falling into my zone. My safe place. Nothing mattered when I was on the ice with my guys. The sting of loss and missing who was right in front of me—all of it was gone. Vapor.

Only the chill of the ice, my teammates, and the puck existed.

"Yo," Teddy yelled.

I caught his flip pass, and I attacked the zone. Two guys

chased me, but I had them. I took the shot, slapping the hell out of that puck.

Pax mimicked the sound of a horn, signaling a score. Clapping and whistling echoed through the arena from the handful of spectators who always showed for our pick-up games. It was a sound I lived for.

And if everything went right this year, hopefully a sound I'd hear as a third-generation Boston College hockey player.

CHAPTER THREE

Willow

The ping of a skate blade hitting metal rang through the arena, and the bellow that followed sent my stomach lurching.

The goalie on the side closest to Jessa and me crumpled into himself and fell to the ice, curled up in a ball. I couldn't see beyond his goalie mask, but I could imagine the pure anguish contorting his face as he desperately clutched his right knee.

Another bellow sliced through the chilly air. Brodie flew across the ice over to the guy rolling in agony.

Crap. Seeing an athlete go down that hard was tough for anyone to watch, but it instantly brought me back to the disastrous fall that had caused my Achilles tendon to snap like an overstretched rubber band.

The back of my heel ached with sympathy pains as the rest of his teammates skated over to him.

"Josiah," a woman behind us yelled and hustled down the bleachers to the door leading to the rink. Her open jacket flapped as she ran.

"His mom," Jessa said.

"Josiah. Goalie. Got it." I hadn't met many people since I'd gotten to town, but hopefully that would all change once school started. Even if my plan was to only be here for a few months while I rehabbed my injury, I was excited to meet more of Jessa's friends. Maybe even reconnect with some of the kids I knew in grade school.

Jessa hadn't talked about many people while I was living in Colorado, other than Preach and a few others. I had a hard time believing that they never hooked up, but she swore they were only friends.

When the goalie finally pulled off his mask, I winced — pain twisted his face. This wasn't a small injury. Poor guy. As Brodie and Preach helped Josiah to his feet, it was clear he wasn't putting any weight on his right leg and he held it at an angle. Another teammate raced to open the door leading off the rink.

Holding up his gloved hands, Josiah tried to shake off Brodie and Preach's help as they approached the wall. What the heck was he doing? He couldn't even skate, and he was obviously hurt. With a sharp downward motion, Josiah pulled away. Preach and Brodie reluctantly backed off as their teammate limped away from the ice.

After Josiah left the arena, the players met in the middle of the rink. I couldn't hear what they were saying, but all of a sudden Preach stood tall and waved in my direction.

My heart started beating faster.

I glanced over my shoulder, then back to the group. He couldn't be waving at me, could he?

Preach and Brodie pushed away from their teammates, waving me to the rink.

"Dude, come on!" Jessa exclaimed. "Let's see what he wants."

The adrenaline that had faded after I'd gotten off the rink

started to course through my veins again.

We made our way down the bleachers and toward the hard plastic walls surrounding the rink. Even from this distance, I could see the determination in Brodie's eyes. I knew it because I'd seen that same intensity staring back at me from my mirror before each competition. From what I'd seen so far, the guy did skate like the wind, but what I was most intrigued by was his clear compassion for his teammates. A lot of the girls I trained with were focused on advancing their own career, even if it was at another teammate's expense.

"Want to come over to the dark side for a hot minute?" Preach asked with a grin. "We need someone to cover goalie."

"You want *me* to play *hockey*?" My stomach clenched. As if I'd risk getting hurt. Well, hurt even worse.

"Just to fill in for the rest of our ice time," Brodie clarified.

A few more skaters came up behind Brodie and Preach.

A guy with blond locks flopping out from beneath his helmet stopped a few inches shy of ramming into Brodie. "The way you shot down my boy Brodie's wild puck earlier, you gotta fill in."

The twang of his voice made it sound like he belonged on a surfboard riding the waves in California more than skating on ice.

"Yeah, yeah, Nathaniel." Brodie smacked the guy in the chest. "Like you haven't sent one flying before."

Nathaniel coughed from Brodie's punch, then shoved off him, coming closer to where I was standing. "Wait a second..." He pulled up his helmet and nailed me with a stare. "You used to play street hockey with us a billion years ago. You're Willow Covington?"

Oh my gosh...I'd forgotten. A warm feeling spread through my chest at the thought that I'd know a few more people than Jessa at Woodhaven High. "Nathaniel! That's right."

"Your grams used to bring us orange slices when we played…and Kool-Aid. The red flavor." Nathaniel laughed, his dark blue eyes flickering. I remembered those eyes now, and his blond hair. It was whiter back then and closely shaved. I totally hadn't recognized him standing here now, a strapping six-foot-tall guy.

He was so shy back in the day, hardly said a word to any of the girls playing with us.

"Dude, did you just call red a flavor?" Brodie laughed.

"Yeah, everybody loves red Kool-Aid!" Preach backhanded him.

I laughed.

"See, she thinks I'm funny," Brodie added. My cheeks felt piping hot.

Another guy skated forward. His eyes shifted from my face to my chest. "Give it a shot, Twinkle Toes. I mean, you can obviously skate."

Ugh, what a jerk. "Hey, asshole, my eyes are up here." I ground my teeth and fisted my hands as I stared him down.

"Don't worry, we'll take it easy on you." The guy winked at me, and I kind of wanted to punch him in his sexist face.

I opened my mouth to respond but stopped when Brodie shoved him. "Don't be a jerk, Pax."

The Neanderthal skated away, chuckling, but Brodie stayed where he was and nodded toward me. "I know you're all about the triple axels, not the five-hole, but it's only a pick-up game. What do you say? You in?"

That was a great question. My heart rate ticked up a beat at the idea of getting back on the ice, but it was definitely a risk. I wiped my sweaty palms on my jogging pants and let out a breath from my tight chest.

One of the guys, still wearing his helmet, left the group to retrieve Josiah's stick from inside the goal. Instead of heading back toward his teammates, he punched the goal. The anchor released, and one side swung back violently.

The guys all turned toward him.

"You okay, Trevor?" Preach called over his shoulder.

He offered a nod but ripped off his helmet and threw it across the ice.

"It's fine. Give him a second to cool down." Preach's jaw tensed, then he said, "Josiah said he wanted us to keep playing and we have an hour left, so are you in?"

Before I could answer, the kid Brodie had called Pax huffed and shook his head. "She wouldn't last five minutes in goalie gear. It's not *sequined* enough."

My nostrils flared, and that hot anger that jerk had ignited in me before when he was staring at my chest flared to life again.

"You scared of a figure skater kicking your ass, Pax?" Brodie said with a chuckle.

Oh, it was on! That Pax guy needed to be shown a thing or two.

Drops of sweat beaded on my brow.

Brodie locked eyes with me, and I almost got lost in the pools of dark brown and amber. "Come on, Willow. Are you really just a figure skater or can you throw down?"

Scared? Me? I wiggled my fingers in anticipation as my heart started pounding out a rhythm.

"We saw you skating. You've totally got this," Preach said, a smile filling his face. "We'll track down some gear for you."

"Yeah, you totally used to own Heron Lane," Nathaniel added as a fluttering sensation spread across my stomach.

"I have my little brother's old stuff in my trunk. We were going to drop it off at Goodwill." Jessa bolted up the stairs, adding, "I'll be right back."

"Go get 'em, Champ." I heard a new voice add to the mix. I spun around, my gaze landing on Gramps. "Show those boys what you're made of."

My heart soared. "Gramps!" I grinned. "What are you doing here?"

"I wanted to see my Snowflake skate." He smiled back at me as he took a seat behind where Jessa and I had been. "I got here a little late, but it looks like I may see you on the ice after all."

"Okay, fine, guys," I said with a smile. "Let's do this."

CHAPTER FOUR

Brodie

"**D**amn, girl, you need to turn your skates down," Nathaniel said from the middle of the rink as he shaded his eyes. "Those things are way too bright!"

Willow stepped through the half door wearing Jessa's little brother's crappy hockey equipment.

And those white skates were a sharp contrast to the dark goalie gear. I bit back a chuckle and glanced at Preach. He'd rested his helmet atop his head and was covering his mouth with his hand, more than likely holding back a chuckle, too.

Leave it to Nathaniel to make a comment, though.

The pads were a little too big, and—

"I can't see!" Nathaniel had one hand over his eyes and was reaching out in front of him with his other. "It's…like the sun…"

"After I show you up on this ice, you'll want a pair just like mine," Willow responded.

I let out a chuckle and nodded at Preach. "Go deal with that joker, will ya?"

He pulled his helmet down, then sped at Nathaniel and didn't stop until his shoulder rammed into Nathaniel's stomach. They landed in a heap. Pax, Teddy, Eric, and Trevor jumped onto the pile as well.

It appeared that Trevor had worked through his frustration over Josiah getting hurt, so that was good.

Jessa clapped her hands and laughed. "Thank goodness for Dillon's growth spurt."

I remembered Jessa's little brother, Dillon, from Saturday morning youth league. He was an average player but too small and had gotten knocked around pretty harshly out there. Now that I thought about it, Willow wasn't much bigger than Dillon. Sure, this was a pick-up game, but we still hit pretty hard. What if she got hurt?

I know I'd been teasing her, but maybe this wasn't such a good idea after all.

Jessa put the helmet on Willow's head but couldn't get the chin strap fastened.

"For the love of ice." I playfully slapped her hand away and grabbed the strap.

"Well, if this ridiculous thing wasn't so cumbersome, I could snap it." Willow narrowed her eyes at me, but even through the full-face mask she was wearing, I saw a smile.

"And maybe put a little glitter on it, Ice Princess," I said, unable to hold back my grin.

"Be nice, or I won't goalie for you."

"Maybe that's a good thing. I don't want you getting hurt."

"You think I can't do it?"

"No. Not even." I gave the chin strap one more tug. "But even this stuff is too big on you."

"Oh please. I got this."

I chuckled. "You ever play goalie during your street hockey days?"

"Well, kind of, but not exactly. We rotated spots back then. Otherwise, all we'd have were a bunch of right and left wingers." She cleared her throat and rolled her eyes at me. "But I stopped your sad attempt at a goal earlier—you know, the one that almost clocked my best friend—so it'll be fine."

She kind of reminded me of my little brother, Caleb. Even at eight years old, he was always making smart-ass remarks, and he didn't back down from anything. With his health issues lately, the poor kid had been forced to grow up way too fast.

His severe asthma kept him off the ice, but I was okay with that. I didn't want him getting hurt. The town, on the other hand…they figured he should be like me.

Top scorer. Fastest on the ice.

That was pressure he didn't need.

"Here," Jessa said, handing me a pair of mitts. They were frayed and had a hole at the top.

"Seriously?" These were crap.

I picked at the worn leather, and my finger went right through the lacing—I wasn't even pushing very hard. There was no way she could be in the goal with these.

"A puck could break through this and nail you in the head. Let's use Josiah's spare gloves. His other gear is too big for you, but maybe those would work."

"I dunno," Willow said. "Would he be cool with that?"

"Yeah." We swapped gear and sticks from time to time during practice, but a sinking sensation in my stomach told me it would be a long time before Josiah needed any of his gear.

I snagged Josiah's extra gloves from the team's bench, then hustled back to Willow and Jessa. "Here. Give these a try."

Jessa shrugged. "She'll be fine with whatever you give her. She legit has Spider-Man reflexes."

"I'll block anything you shoot at me." Willow's massive blue eyes flared with an excitement I recognized. This girl loved the ice.

I tightened the mitt over her left hand. "That'll happen."

Jessa giggled, then cleared her throat. They looked at one another like they had a secret joke, and I was the butt of it.

"Bet you a coffee you don't get one past me," Willow said.

I glanced at Jessa to see if Willow was serious, and she was nodding.

"You do know that I hold the county record for goals in a game, right, *figure skater*?"

Willow glanced at Jessa. "That might have been nice to know."

"You didn't ask!" Jessa laughed and hugged Willow from the side. "Doesn't matter. Go get 'em, girl!"

Willow eased onto the ice, nice and slow. Her legs were bent slightly, and her arms were out, as if she were testing the waters.

"County record, huh, Puck Head?" she said, studying the ice around her as she got her bearings.

I skated beside her toward the goal, in case she faltered, and said, "Yep. You going to challenge me to a shootout?"

"Um, no." She chuckled. "Maybe tomorrow."

"Tomorrow, huh?" I winked. "Let's just see if you can survive today."

"Bring it."

I drew in a deep breath, the cool air settling me down. I wasn't sure we should keep playing after Josiah's injury, let alone have someone in goal who was trained in spinning and twirling, not catching and blocking. But she seemed determined enough. And she could seriously skate—like she was as comfortable on the ice as I was. Then again, I'd learned to skate about the same time I learned to walk, and I'd been practicing here since I was nine. My initials were engraved beneath the players' bench.

My first goal was here.

My first championship was here.

Hell, even my first kiss was here.

A familiar and calming sensation settled over me, like a blanket right out of the dryer. I loved being here. It was my second home. My church.

Willow pushed off, gaining a few feet of distance from me. "Okay, let me give this a try." A few more pushes and she got a little speed going.

"Nice. You're doing—"

She turned to spray a stop, but her shin guard shifted down. She flopped onto her stomach and skidded headfirst into the net.

"Goal!" Nathaniel yelled, then fell back onto the ice laughing.

"Ufff." She pushed herself onto her back. "Dang it."

"You good?" I asked around a laugh.

"I'm good." She scrambled to her feet and drifted back toward the goal. "Are we gonna play or just stand around?"

"Oh yeah. It's on!" Nathaniel yelled as he and the rest of the team positioned up.

"Gotta love her determination," I said as I skated up to Preach.

"Yeah, yeah, yeah," he said, his massive smile fading some. "Let's go."

Landen threw the puck down, and I snatched it. I zig-zagged around Preach, Jason, and Trevor, then spun, shoving the puck between Trevor's skates.

"You're going down," he said, chasing after me.

I slapped the puck to Nathaniel, and he dished it back a little ahead of me. I was right on target for the goal.

Willow stood there, totally not in the ready position at all, her five-hole wide open. Practically begging for me to slap the puck through.

Nudging her mask up, she made eye contact. Her eyes

widened, then narrowed, immediately focusing on the puck.

With amazing accuracy from what I could tell.

I picked up the pace, moving the puck as fast as I could, but she kept it in her sights.

There, she finally sat, readying herself. The too-big stick slapped the ice, covering a little bit of her five-hole.

I raised my stick, setting up to slap the puck home, when a force of nature rammed into me from the side.

Preach.

I planted my skate, spraying the glass to the left of the goal, and spun around.

Laughing, he pushed off me, having stolen the puck. "Not today, buddy."

Oh, he was so toast.

I gave Willow a quick look and didn't miss the relief brightening her blue eyes.

"You got lucky," I said. "I almost won a coffee off you."

She nudged her mask up and stuck her tongue out at me.

Seriously, the girl stuck her tongue out at me. Other than my eight-year-old brother, who does that?

Damn if it wasn't cute, though.

I battled Preach and came away with the puck again. This time, everyone was down at the other end, and there was no way they'd be able to catch me in time.

My nickname wasn't Wind for nothing.

It was just Willow and me—no chance for a check. I couldn't help but grin. Each stride burned through my quads; the scrape of my stick across the ice and the smell of the frozen water energized my soul. Everything blurred into nothingness. Sounds muffled.

The goal. The net. The puck.

I drew in a deep breath as I pushed two more times. A quick fake left, then right, and I slapped the puck.

Willow squeaked but raised her mitt. Her skates shifted as she reached up and kicked her leg a little. Almost like her arm and her leg were joined, they went out together to deflect the shot.

The slap of the puck landing in the middle of her glove rang out in the arena like a bell, and it felt like a puck had hit me square in the chest. I froze, coasting across the ice, as the sound of the puck hitting her leather echoed in my mind.

With her hand still up in the air, she fell into the splits.

Two guys behind me groaned.

She just sat there, though, in the splits, holding up her glove.

"Yes!" Jessa yelled from the bleachers.

I came to a stop before Willow and met her gaze. She'd freaking stopped my shot. The surprise must have shocked my vocabulary right out of my brain, because I couldn't formulate a word.

Willow tossed me the puck, then pushed herself to her feet. I reached down and grabbed her to help her up the rest of the way.

She patted my chest and grinned. "You, *hockey player*, owe me a coffee."

CHAPTER FIVE

Willow

"**D**id you see me stop that goal from Brodie?" My face hurt from smiling so much. Though I'd let a few goals in, I'd also blocked at least five shots during my hour with the hockey players. "I know I'm not going to be the next Wayne Gretzky right off the bat, but I think I did pretty well."

Gramps chuckled. "Gretzky wasn't a goalie, but you did remind me of Andrei Vasilevskiy…"

"Oh, right. Yeah, that guy." *Note to self, Google Andrei Vasilevskiy when I get home.*

I still couldn't quite believe it. *Me…playing hockey.*

Funny thing, though, I hadn't felt this good about myself in months. Talk about a spectacular debut at the Kenneth Windom Ice Den, only it wasn't with my figure skating.

"You did a great job, Snowflake." Gramps clicked his seat belt into place. "You're a natural."

"Thanks, Gramps." I looked down at my phone. Jessa had already messaged me with some action shots she'd taken while I was geared up.

I tapped a message open to Ericka, my host home sister

back in Colorado, to send her a picture.

ME: Check me out...

ERICKA: No. Freaking. Way.

ERICKA: Figure skater turned hockey player?

ME: No no no. Just having some fun.

ERICKA: I miss you. It's not the same here without you.

An ache stabbed at my chest. I missed her, too. She was an amazing speed skater with a bright future ahead of her, plus I missed having someone as close as a sister to talk athletics with.

"It was just like when we used to play on Heron Lane! Remember how Grams always used to bring us orange slices?"

"Those were fun times, weren't they?" My grandpa's voice choked with emotion.

Hearing his voice crack felt like a skating blade to the chest and brought a fresh wave of burning tears to sting my eyes.

I smiled at him, but my heart pinged with pain. When she'd passed, our whole family had struggled with the loss.

Accepting the challenge Brodie threw down at me today sure was an unexpected pick-me-up. Competing on the ice again made me remember just how much I'd missed it. Granted, it was hockey and not a solo program aiming for a gold medal, but it still fueled my competitive fire.

For a few minutes, I managed to forget about my Achilles. It was sore from the attempted jumps earlier, but the exhilaration and adrenaline from the game had numbed the pain. I might have to find out when they scrimmaged again and see if they needed help.

No. They probably had a backup goalie, and I shouldn't do it. I couldn't risk another injury.

"How do you feel about grabbing a hamburger and fries with your ol' gramps?"

"Sounds great." I clicked the lock button on the side of my phone and set it on my lap. I low-key wanted to ask Gramps to take me to Walgreens so I could get some prints of me tearing up the ice. Granted, it was in the wrong sport, but if I kept working, I'd get past this injury and back to my skating program in Colorado in no time.

"It's nice to see you on the ice again, and see you with Jessa, too."

A flutter shot across my belly.

"It's good to be back," I said, even though it might not be 100 percent true. Having to move back to Woodhaven from Colorado had hit me hard. As if it wasn't bad enough that I'd seriously injured my foot, my sponsors had frozen their support a few months back, and my parents couldn't afford the training program and rehab expenses without the money my sponsors contributed. Living with a host family out there helped with the cost, but it wasn't enough.

Being back in Gramps's house reminded me of Grams so much, which was both nice and painful. I was going to miss him when I moved back to Colorado once my rehab was done.

Ten minutes later, we pulled up to an A&W.

A guy wearing white roller skates with bright orange wheels made his way to the side of our car. "Hey, there. I'm Jake. Can I interest you in a couple of root beer floats?"

"Definitely. Two, please." Gramps and I placed the rest of our order, then settled into our seats.

"Car service is so underrated." I unclicked my seat belt. "As are roller skates."

Smiling, Gramps reached over and patted me on the shoulder. "You're such a great kid. You know that, right?"

"Thanks, Gramps."

"I know these past few months have been really tough with rehab, losing the sponsors, moving away from Colorado..." He pressed his lips together and rubbed his open palms against the steering wheel. "Snowflake, I have some news to share with you."

My hunger pangs instantly morphed into pangs of dread. "Are you okay? Are Mom and Dad okay?"

Memories of Gramps getting sick two years ago flashed through my mind. Mom and Dad were struggling to make ends meet, so financially it made the most sense for them to move back here to help Gramps. The first two years I was out in Colorado, I only had one sponsor, which meant racking up major debt. Luckily, my third year up until a few months ago, I had enough sponsors and a host family, so my costs of living in Colorado were mostly covered. To this day, I felt guilty about not doing more. Even if I'd been making minimum wage, it would have helped.

"Everyone is fine." Gramps brought his hands to his lap.

"You scared me for a minute." My heart was still pounding, but I felt slightly better.

His brow pinched as he turned toward me. "Willow, we heard from Dr. Nolan today."

Breath whooshed out of my lungs. Dr. Nolan was my physical therapist in Colorado. She'd been checking in with my PT in Wisconsin every day for the two weeks I'd been here, keeping track of my progress. But more importantly, she was the only person who could sign off on my return to the skating team.

"Did she tell you when I can go back?" Maybe I wouldn't be stuck here as long as I'd thought. I'd been following everything to the T, so—

"It wasn't good news, Snowflake." Gramps's shoulders slumped.

My mouth opened, but no words came out. It felt as if a wave of arctic air stormed through the car when a shiver rattled down my spine. My stomach churned as I replayed what he'd said. Not good news? I was getting better. I mean, I knew I was struggling making jumps, but everything else was coming along fine. My leg strength had improved significantly these last couple of months.

"She said that you're not making progress quickly enough to return to the team."

"But I'll get there. They said they'd hold my spot while I rehabbed out here." I squeezed my eyes shut as the tears burned. "They said they'd give me until December. I'm getting better. Stronger every single day."

Bile stung the back of my throat, and I couldn't get enough air in my lungs. Darkness curved my vision as I focused on my breathing. In. Out.

"I know you are."

Gramps's voice was calm, but it didn't help. My breathing hitched. This wasn't happening. There must be a misunderstanding. Today was the first day I'd tried jumps on the ice, and while they didn't go super well, it didn't mean they never would. I just needed more time. How could they do this to me?

He let out a slow breath. "I'm sorry, Willow. They've filled your spot."

Black spots dotted my vision. Gramps continued to talk, but the words melted into nonsense.

"Willow?" Gramps squeezed my hand. "Are you all right?"

I couldn't respond. My heart thumped so hard, it literally stole the words from my mouth. I could feel my pulse in my ears. They filled my spot? I bet freaking Sasha Abbott weaseled her way in front of Coach while I was away. I'd only been gone two weeks—two freaking weeks. I should have stayed in Colorado for my rehab, then I could have been at the rink each day...

Shit. I balled up my fists, my nails digging into the palms of my hands.

Our waiter skated out of the restaurant and toward the car. "Here are your root beer floats. I'll be right back with the rest of your order."

Gramps thanked him and set the floats in the cupholders between us.

"This can't be happening. It has to be some kind of mistake." I hid my face behind splayed fingers and rocked back and forth in my seat. "I—I need to call Dr. Nolan. Figure this out. There's no way they'd cut me."

I'd brought home more gold than any other skater on that damn team. I'd sacrificed so much. My family had, too.

I felt light-headed. This couldn't be happening.

Oh, God. Mom and Dad. Everything they'd given up for me to skate. To live at the training center. A wave of nausea cramped my stomach, and I leaned forward in my seat. Everything. Everything I'd worked for had all been for nothing.

No. No way. I sat up straight and drew in a deep breath, willing the burning tears away. It was not going to end here. I'd get back there, or I'd find another training facility to take me. I only had until January to get back in shape so I could pass my level assessments and get picked up by a new skating program.

Pain ripped through my chest. Hot searing pain. Like someone was burning my skin with a hot poker.

Jake returned with the rest of the food, but before he could clip the tray on to the side of the car, Gramps whispered something to him. He gave a quick nod and skated away with the tray underhand. He came back a few minutes later with our food in to-go bags.

"Snowflake, I know it's overwhelming right now, and I

know it's hard to see them, but you do have options. You could go to college next year. Get into coaching..."

"Skating is my life, Gramps," I finally said, breaking the silence.

Gramps set the food on the backseat floor. "Is there anything your old Gramps can do to help you?"

"Thanks, but no." The team I'd given my life to had abandoned me. They didn't believe in me. They didn't think I could do it. My hands trembled as I ran them through my hair.

Hot tears welled in the corners of my eyes, threatening to spill onto my cheeks at any moment. But I couldn't move. I couldn't blink.

I couldn't breathe. I was done skating?

Hell no, I wasn't.

I fisted my hands and rested them on my thighs as a wave of warmth blanketed over me. My heart rate calmed down a little as I focused on the goal. No matter what I had to do, I *would* return to skating.

This was not the end of my dream to be Willow Covington, Olympic gold medalist.

Somehow, I'd make sure of it.

CHAPTER SIX

Willow

"**C**an you please pass me a can of diced tomatoes?"

"Sure thing, Hana." The director of the Helping Hands Homeless Shelter had promised the residents she'd make them their favorite chili recipe tonight.

The shelves in front of me were barely stocked, leaving a twinge of guilt in my gut. Feeling upset about losing my spot on the training team in Colorado seemed a lot less relevant when there were people with nowhere to live and nothing to eat. Just like Gramps had said when I'd told him I didn't want to come today.

I'd found out I was cut from the skating team two days ago, and I'd felt like a lump ever since. I didn't want to go anywhere or talk to anyone. I'd finally told Jessa this morning, and she was as sweet as could be.

Being here reminded me that I'd relied on the kindness of strangers for the past three years, considering the only way I'd been able to train and go to school in Colorado was due to sponsorship from a private donor. It had been awarded to me when my parents weren't able to pay for my skating anymore. The sponsorship was based on skill and financial need. Skating was expensive.

Back when I was five, my parents nearly had to pull me out of lessons because they couldn't afford proper skates. Luckily, someone at the rink had donated a pair that fit me. It had been a struggle from that point forward, but my parents had given everything they had to help me reach elite status.

That was why losing my sponsorships had been an even bigger punch to the gut. Everything my parents had sacrificed over the years and the money people had donated with the hopes that I'd end up at the Olympics...it was all in the garbage until I could get back into championship shape.

I pushed a sack of potatoes to the side. "We're running low, but we have two big cans of diced tomatoes with garlic and oregano or one with green chilies."

Hana smiled, her silver ponytail swinging over her shoulder and her gray eyes sparkling. "I'll take one of each."

"Gramps said as long as he's feeling up to it, we'd be able to pick out a few things this weekend when we go grocery shopping," I said, glancing back at the nearly empty shelves. "What's at the top of the list?"

Gramps always put the needs of others before his own well-being. According to my dad, he hadn't blinked when my dad asked if he and my mom could move in. And then when I needed to move in, too, he was genuinely excited about it.

It was supposed to be temporary, until Mom found a job closer to Woodhaven. But secretly, I enjoyed living with Gramps. He made me laugh, and there was always a hot meal on the table. Things were so much more relaxed at his house than at the training center.

The only time there was tension was when Mom and Dad talked on the phone. Their terse conversations in hushed voices were starting to worry me. Dad always brushed it off, but it didn't take a genius to know things weren't going well between them.

"Anything is helpful, but canned vegetables, oatmeal, and rice always go a long way. Fresh fruit and vegetables are great, too. They don't last as long and cost a bit more, but they are always appreciated." Balancing one oversize can in each hand, Hana smiled. "I'm so glad you're here, honey. Your grandfather talks about you constantly."

Her smile warmed my chest. She really was sweet. I never would have guessed she was in her mid-sixties by her energy and enthusiasm, and she always wore something pink, too, whether it was clothing, something in her hair, or her painted nails. She said the bright color made her smile.

"Thanks. I'm glad I'm here, too." I checked over the sparsely filled shelves one more time. "I've put everything away. Is there anything else I can do before I leave? My dad isn't picking me up for twenty more minutes."

"If you want to help me prep for dinner tonight, that would be great." Hana motioned with her shoulder toward the hallway.

Nodding, I folded up the paper bags the donations had come in and set them on the lowest shelf. This was only my second time volunteering here, but I was finally starting to get to know my way around the place. Gramps had only been out to visit me in Colorado twice, but the first time, he made sure that I was volunteering at least five to ten hours a week somewhere. He said volunteer work not only helped others, but it built strong character.

Gramps usually spent every morning at the shelter, but he mentioned he wasn't feeling well yesterday, so he was at home resting. Hopefully he didn't get bronchitis again. Last time he had it, it landed him in the hospital for a couple of days.

"Hey, Hana! Sorry I'm running late," a voice called from around the corner where the front door was. The voice sounded familiar, but I couldn't picture the face it belonged to.

"Don't worry, Preach! That busted pipe is still waiting for you in the basement," Hana said with a chuckle as she shut the closet door behind me.

Preach? I froze. Part of me wanted to melt into the wall. Sure, he was a nice guy and all, but I didn't really want to face anyone right now. Then again, he didn't know I'd been cut from my skating team. Unless Jessa had told him already. Which would be fine, I guess, but still.

My heart ramped up a couple of ticks per minute, and my hands went sweaty. I wasn't sure why I was suddenly nervous, but I was. The word would get out soon, considering it was probably blasted all over social media by my not-so-favorite ex-teammate Sasha Abbott. So I needed to toughen up.

"Everything all right, Willow?" Hana asked, arching an eyebrow.

Preach stuck his head around the corner. "Toe Pick?"

"Toe Pick?" Hana said, laughing. "Now what kind of greeting is that, young man?"

"Nickname of affection, right, Willow?" He grinned, and his dark brown eyes flashed with mischief as he stepped into the hallway.

I chuckled at his playfulness and said, "If you say so."

"I didn't know you volunteered here." He shoved his hands in his pockets.

His flawless skin and perfect smile that triggered a slight dimple on his left cheek were hard to ignore. He stood about six feet tall, and his floppy, dark brown hair framed his face in a perfectly messy fashion. Brodie was much more my type, but damn, Woodhaven had a lot of hot guys…

I'd watched him play hockey, and he was good, but he didn't come off as cocky like a few of the other guys in that pick-up game. According to Jessa, he not only served here at the mission, but he led the school food drive every year, and he single handedly raised over $2,000 for a kid whose family needed help paying for his leukemia treatments.

"Willow?" Preach said my name and waved his hand in front of my face. "You still with us?"

"Oh. Uh, y-yeah," I stammered. "Just thinking about something."

"How do you two know each other?" Hana asked.

"Willow joined our pick-up game the other day. She's really good." Preach smiled. "She even stopped one of Wind's shots."

"Yeah, I heard about that while I was grocery shopping yesterday." Hana grinned and nodded. "I didn't know that you played hockey."

Heat pooled in my cheeks. "Uh, no. I don't. I was practicing my jumps, and Preach invited me to join their game after their goalie got hurt."

Preach leaned against the wall, beside the painting of the founder of the mission. "You know we have another pick-up game tomorrow... You interested?"

"Hockey isn't really my thing," I said, my palms starting to sweat. Had he really asked me if I was interested in playing with them again? "Anyways, uh...I've got to get in the kitchen to help Hana with dinner. I'll see you later."

Me play hockey for real? Impossible.

CHAPTER SEVEN

Brodie

"Careful, Limp Lungs, or you'll have another attack," I said as Caleb tackled me around the waist.

For an eight-year-old with severe asthma, he was impressively strong. He couldn't participate in sports or many outdoor activities, yet here he was almost knocking me over on the living room floor.

If I'd been on the ice, he wouldn't have even budged me, but on land I wasn't as coordinated.

"Dork face." Caleb tightened his hold around me as my butt thumped against the carpet. I twisted at my waist and easily flipped him onto his back. He grunted and let out a wheeze.

I froze.

He punched my stomach.

And then *I* started wheezing.

"Ha." He pushed off me. "Sucker."

"That was dirty." I rolled onto my stomach and planted my elbows in the shag carpet.

He flopped onto his back, laughing. Sprinkled in the laughs, though, was an all-too-familiar cough. His lungs were filling up again. Third cold in as many months.

Damn asthma. One minute we could be messing around, having fun, the next he was almost suffocating from horrible coughing and wheezing. Mom had always hated when we'd wrestle, but the kid deserved a little bit of normalcy, so I made sure not to push too hard. But there was always the underlying worry that we'd get a little too rough and we'd be making another trip to the emergency room.

If I lost him, I wouldn't survive it. I'd barely survived Mom dying. An image of Mom's face flashed before my eyes, and I flinched at the impact. She'd died just under two years ago, but sometimes it still felt like yesterday. My chest ached at the memory of Dad—

No! I shook my head, dislodging the memories from my mind. My stomach churned, but I fixed my focus back to Caleb. He needed me to be strong. Be here with him.

When his last cold had turned into bronchitis, it landed him in the hospital for three days—and I'd almost completely lost it.

"You boys settle down out there," our maid, Rita, called from the kitchen. "And Brodie, quit calling your brother Limp Lungs!"

"Rita!" Caleb smacked his forehead, then got up. "Haven't you seen *The Goonies*?"

"Is that one of your video games?"

I chuckled as my little brother rolled his eyes.

"No! We've gone over this a million times!" Caleb stood in the entryway to the living room, and I could see her shadow against the wall near him. "These friends and one of their older brothers go on an adventure to find One-Eyed Willy's long-lost treasure. The older brother always calls the little brother Limp Lungs because he has asthma, like me!"

"It's still not nice." She peeked her head into the living

room and smiled at me. "Enough roughhousing."

"Yes, ma'am," I said.

"Suck up!" Caleb hopped onto the couch and stuck out his tongue.

Just like Willow had stuck her tongue out at me at the rink a couple of days ago. Right before she stunned me with her goalie skills.

I shook my head. *No, no thinking about Willow.*

"I hate Rita's food." Caleb stuck his finger in his mouth as if he was trying to gag himself or something.

"Whatever Rita's making, you'll eat it and say 'thank you.' Or I'll start making dinner and then you'll *really* be sorry."

He rolled his eyes, then leaned to the side and dug out his phone. The kitchen was at the end of the hallway, but I could hear pots and pans clanking. Rita *was* a horrible cook, but I was way worse.

Unless it was corn dogs and Tabasco sauce. I could totally nail that.

We'd eaten plenty of those meals after Mom died, before Rita came to take care of us. George, our house manager, and a couple other staff members helped her, but it was mostly Rita.

I was glad for them, though, because over this last year Dad was constantly away for work, so we needed the help. Not to mention, it got pretty lonely here with only me and Caleb in this huge house.

My breath hitched in my chest. Damn, I missed my mom.

Guess Dad really didn't know how to take care of us or himself after Mom died. She'd been killed by a drunk driver, and now when Dad was home, he was usually drinking.

"Who's Willow?" Caleb asked as he sat up, staring at his phone.

Wait a minute, that was *my* phone.

"What the hell, man?" I shot up and went to grab it.

He pulled it out of reach and laughed. "You're quick on the ice, but off the ice…not so much. Should we get you some skates? Would that help?"

"You're so dead." I hopped up to tackle him, but he leaped over the back of the couch and darted behind the dining room table, holding my phone out to tease me.

I stood at the head of the table, and he stood at the other end, a grin filling his face. His shaggy brown hair was a shade darker than mine, and even though he had the same brown eyes as me, they appeared darker, because his skin was so pale all the time.

He really did look like a mini-me, only sickly.

"That's the new girl from the pick-up game. The figure skater?" He looked at me with wide eyes. "Why are you on her Instagram profile? I'm *so* posting a comment."

"You better not!" My heart shot up into my throat at the thought of him commenting on her stuff. Talk about mortifying.

I darted around the corner, but he did the same—and how the heck did he do that while looking at my phone? The kid was a ninja.

"You loooove her. You want to kiss her. You—"

Picking up my speed around the table, I almost caught him, but he bolted through the doorway into the main living room where we'd been watching a movie. He scrambled over the back of the leather couch, landed on the cushion, and jumped onto the coffee table.

I did the same but stopped on the cushion, towering over him more than I normally did, since the coffee table was short. I stared him down and held out my hand.

His grin vanished, his chest rose, and he let out a deep cough that about rattled *my* lungs.

He handed my phone to me mid-cough. "I'm okay." *Cough.* "Here." *Cough. Cough.*

"Dude." I stepped down.

"I'm good." He plopped onto the center of the coffee table and sat cross-legged, still coughing.

"Hey, guys, Rita let me in. Didn't you hear the doorbell ringing?" Preach said as he hurdled the couch and flopped onto the chaise part.

"Sorry, man. Too busy chasing this little turd down," I said.

"What's— Dude. You okay?" he asked Caleb.

"Stop asking me that." He pounded the tabletop. "You should ask Brodie why he's scoping a *figure* skater's Insta."

"You are—" I went to reach for Caleb, but he scrambled away, laughing.

"Rita. I need food," he yelled.

"Manners," Preach said to my little brother.

"Yeah, dude. Manners." I shook my head and tapped my phone as I flopped onto the couch near Preach, breathless. That little kid was fast.

"*Pleeeeeeeeease*," Caleb yelled.

Sure enough, Willow's profile filled the screen. I had to find out more about her, so I'd Googled her. And there was a lot out there. She was big-time in the figure skating world. I wasn't surprised, though, because she sure had looked at home on the ice.

"I knew you liked her." Preach shoved my shoulder. "I still can't believe she blocked one of your shots."

"Shocked the hell out of me, too." I scrolled through her feed. "Did you talk to Jessa? What's the tea?"

"Yep, but if I tell you, you'll be pissed."

I glanced up from my phone. "What do you mean?"

"'Cause you're gonna totally fall for her, and I know you're—and I quote—'never dating again.'"

"Can you blame me? I mean, damn, Sydney and Gretchen." Just mentioning their names made my heart sting with phantom stabbing pains.

"True." Preach nodded. "They messed with you hard. But Willow—"

"Whoa, whoa, whoa." I waved my hands. "There will be no dating. No Ice Princesses. No…talk of dating. Nothing."

"Fine. Whatever you say." Preach's face turned serious. "So how's Josiah?"

The air whooshed out of my lungs, and it felt like a fifty-pound weight sat on my chest. "He's done, man. He'll be lucky if he can even try out for the regular season."

Preach's head fell back against the leather cushion, and he let out a labored breath. "What about Izan? You check in with him about filling in?"

"You and I both know he isn't ready." I shook my head. "Do you think the figure skater would actually be up for it?"

Preach arched his brow and eyed me for a few beats. "She was pretty awesome, huh?"

I gave a noncommittal shrug, scrolling through her Insta feed.

"But it's a no-go anyway. She's rehabbing to get back to figure skating. She's not going to want to play hockey." Preach stretched out and propped his feet on the coffee table as he focused on the TV screen. "Jessa said she's heading back to her training center as soon as she's strong enough."

"And we don't need another person coming in and getting everyone's hopes up and then leaving again. Remember when Mitch did that? We were screwed for a right wing and almost didn't have a replacement in time." A flash of anger burned through my gut remembering how that had really hurt our team.

"She's big-time out in Colorado, primed for the Olympics,

right?" Preach said. "But she blew out her Achilles. That injury is serious. It'll take her awhile to get better. It's not like she needs to be doing triple axels to stand in goal."

"Shit, she blew out her Achilles?" I said, sagging into the leather couch as if I suddenly weighed a million pounds. Achilles injury to a skater? That had to suck for her, yet when I saw her on the ice, she was strong. Sure, she hadn't landed the couple of jumps she'd tried, but it seemed like she was close.

A car was bursting into flames on a glacier, and a sub shot through the ice. Best. Movie. Ever. But even cinematic genius couldn't distract me from getting more info on Willow.

"Sure did," Preach said. "She was out in Colorado, living at the training center. Got injured almost a year ago and was rehabbing on site, but then she lost all her sponsors and had to move here to finish."

"Holy shit, her sponsors bailed?" Damn, that girl had suffered a lot, hadn't she? "Sponsors…she must be really good." I tapped my YouTube app to life and typed in her name. Now we were getting somewhere.

"Yeah, Jessa said it was her first day trying some significant jumps since the injury. And it didn't go well." Preach leaned back in his seat and closed his eyes.

"Until she got into the goal." I bit back a chuckle at the image of her tripping over her goalie pads right into the net.

"Exactly! She'd be great on our Fall League Team."

"She's good, but really? A figure skater?" I scrubbed my face with my hands. "As a goalie?"

"What's wrong with that?"

"Nothing. I just can't imagine she'd want to do it, and there'd be a learning curve, man. I mean, if she's that big in the skating world, she'll get back into it." I held up my phone to show an article that popped up. "Google says she's trying to be back in time for next year's competitions."

"Jessa just texted me." Preach turned in his seat, his dark brown eyes serious, his jaw tense. "Willow got the news that her team cut her."

My stomach churned. I couldn't imagine getting dropped from the hockey team. Hockey was my life, and judging by the look of determination in her eyes, figure skating was the same for her.

"If she's that good, another squad will pick her up," I said.

"Sounds like the percentage is pretty low for figure skaters returning to that level of competition after an injury like hers." Preach smiled. "But Jessa says she's determined, so who knows? Still, wouldn't having her for a few months be worth it?"

I could see that about Willow, and I'd only known her for about five seconds. She radiated determination and talent. But hockey? She'd never be satisfied with anything that wasn't figure skating, would she? She'd leave as soon as she got the chance.

"I saw her at the shelter today," Preach said, pulling out his phone. "She didn't mention getting cut from the team."

That caught my attention.

Serving at the Helping Hands homeless shelter was pretty impressive. So she was a phenomenal athlete, good-hearted, and the way she bantered with me made her seem pretty laid back.

"She's nice. Hana, the director, was all up with the praise for Willow for blocking your shot."

Dang, the whole town was in my business again. It was like they didn't have anything else to do other than watch us play hockey. "It was luck."

"Yeah, right." Preach chuckled.

I pulled out my phone and checked her IG feed again.

Looked like she had lots of friends back at the training

facility, but almost all the pictures were of her on the ice or at an ice arena. No boyfriend from what I could tell. Not that I should be thinking about that anyway.

It was my senior year; I'd been decimated by my last two girlfriends. I was not going down that road again to get all attached to someone, then have them ditch my ass when things got tough or a better offer showed up.

Gretchen had been like a puck cracked through my chest and had pulverized my heart. And right after Mom. That was messed up. And then Sydney. She was a figure skater, and supposedly we'd had a lot in common, but she was only interested in me because my name was on the Ice Den.

"Earth to Wind…"

"Huh?" I sat up.

Preach looked at me, his head bobbing and his hand up as if he was waiting for something.

"What?"

"Willow's got family in town. Used to live here as a kid."

"Yeah, she used to play hockey on Heron Lane. I heard her mentioning that."

"Her family moved in with her grandpa."

Scents of spicy fajitas rolled in, and my stomach growled. I needed to curb this Willow discussion because potential hockey player or not, I couldn't afford to have another girl on my brain.

Preach huffed. "She was coordinated, even in that oversize goalie stuff."

And really cute, though I didn't admit that to Preach.

I tossed my phone to the couch and stood. I wasn't really sure where I stood on the idea of Willow playing hockey with us. If she even wanted to. "I'm hungry."

"Hello!" Dad's voice echoed through the hallway. Sounded like it came from the kitchen.

"Daddy!" Caleb screeched.

I glanced at Preach, and his eyes were wider than I'd seen them in a long time. "I thought your dad was in London?"

"Me, too. You better go."

Preach nodded, and I hustled down the hallway. He'd find his own way out, and I needed to see what Dad was doing home. The ping of shattering glass rang from the kitchen, and I picked up the pace right along with my heart.

Shards of jagged glass covered the floor. Dad stood in the middle of the kitchen, holding Caleb with one arm and a pizza box in the other. He was balancing it like he would a serving tray.

"It's okay!" Rita scurried out of the kitchen. "I'll get the broom."

"What happened?" I grabbed the pizza box from Dad, and he settled Caleb on the countertop beside the fridge, but Caleb didn't let go of him.

"Brought some food…" He stumbled to the side slightly and palmed the counter beside Caleb. "To have dinner with my boys."

Shit. He's drunk. And Dad wasn't a particularly nice drunk, either. Never physically violent or anything, but venom often laced his words when he'd had too much alcohol.

"Rita already cooked," I said. "I thought you were in London for a week."

"Canceled." He planted a kiss on Caleb's forehead, then peeled out from my brother's embrace. "Let's eat!"

He made his way to the kitchen island I'd set the pizza box on, glass crunching beneath his shoes. He was tall like me, but his brown hair had sprinkles of gray throughout. His normally tanned skin was wan and a little pasty beneath the lights.

"Here, buddy." He handed Caleb a slice of the pepperoni.

Rita rounded the corner, holding a broom and dustpan, but I met her and grabbed them. "Thanks, Rita. I can do this."

She narrowed her eyes at me. "Are you sure?"

"I can take care of things the rest of the night."

She nodded, then glanced at my dad and back to me. "Call if you need me."

"Thanks, Rita," I said and gave her a one-armed hug. She didn't need to take care of Dad when he was like this. "You're the best."

I faced the kitchen, prepared to clean up the broken glass, when I saw Dad sitting on the barstool at the center island, pouring himself a tumbler of vodka over ice.

It was going to be a long night.

CHAPTER EIGHT

Willow

"I think it's great that you're getting more skating time in." My mom checked over her shoulder before switching lanes.

It'd been three days since Gramps had given me Dr. Nolan's devastating news, but I was done sulking. Yesterday's time at Helping Hands really put things into perspective. It helped me formulate a plan, too, and that meant as much time on the ice as possible.

The car slowed as we approached a stop sign. "I'm sorry I can't watch you practice today."

"I understand." No one needed to remind me about my family's financial situation. Taking off more than two days wasn't an option for my mom; she could lose her job. Her contract work as an ER nurse had kept our family afloat when the Woodhaven Hospital had closed and she lost her job, but it also meant she had to live more than two hours away for months at a time, and the distance and time apart messed with my parents' relationship. They bickered constantly.

I turned toward the window and let out a long exhale.

My mom's phone buzzed. She slid her finger across the

screen and brought it to her ear without looking. "Hello?" She let out a frustrated sigh. "I told you I couldn't take any more time off."

Speaking of bickering about her job and money...

"Hal, we've already gone over this."

She shot me a quick smile, as if she was trying to reassure me everything was fine. A fake smile couldn't settle the unease creeping into my gut at the sudden shift in mood as Mom talked to Dad, though.

"Listen, we can revisit this later. I'm about to drop Willow off at the rink, and then I've got to hit the road."

A knot formed in my left shoulder, and I realized I was squeezing the door handle with all my strength. I released my death grip and let out a breath. Digging into the tightness in my left shoulder with my fingers, I shifted my focus to the scenery instead of listening to Mom. Tall aspen trees towered over the road, blocking out the sun, which was trying to peek from behind dark rain clouds. It almost felt as if we were driving through a tunnel. I sure had missed the green trees of the Midwest.

My phone buzzed with a text.

ERICKA: Hanging in there?

ME: Barely.

ERICKA: Your Colorado coaches are a bunch of jerks!

ME: Thanks.

ERICKA: Seriously, as soon as you're landing your jumps again, they'll come calling.

ERICKA: Mom and Dad haven't touched your room.

ERICKA: We know you'll be back before the end of the year.

ERICKA: It's a given!

ME: I totally needed to hear that.

ERICKA: ♥ Love you, sis.

ME: Love you more!

I rested my head back and let out a long breath, the heaviness in my chest almost too much to bear. Ericka really was like a sister to me. I missed her so hard and would kill for one of her hugs.

"I said we'll talk about this later." Without another word, Mom pulled the phone from her ear and chucked it in the backseat. "Sorry, hon."

"It's okay. I know how important this job is to you, for us." I cracked my knuckles. A habit my coach in Colorado used to get on me about. My gut twisted at the thought of my coach. Who wasn't my coach anymore. She'd abandoned me. Didn't have faith in me.

Tears stung the back of my eyes, but I blinked them away. I was done crying. I was about action now.

"It's nothing you need to worry about, sweetheart. I hate that I can't stay longer, but remember, you can call me at any time if you're feeling down or need someone to talk to. I'm always here for you."

My fingers slid over the handle of the skating bag propped on my lap. "Thanks, Mom. I love you."

"I love you, too, honey." She smiled, as if the fight with my dad had never happened. "So, what are you going to work on at the rink today? Will you join another one of those hockey pick-up games? Gramps said you did a great job at the last one."

"Not sure. Those guys are pretty serious."

"That they are. This town's all about hockey." Mom shook her head. "They've won State a few times, I think."

Holy crap. Mom even knew about hockey. "Yeah, so I hear. I was just helping them out the other day. I'm sure they have a stellar backup."

"Okay, but be careful if you do decide to join them. I don't want you getting hurt."

"No worries, Mom. Goalies wear tons of pads. It's the safest position on the team."

"All right, just as long as you're safe." She smiled.

The arena parking lot came into view, and I said, "Oh, hey, you can drop me here. I'll walk through the parking lot to the front door. It'll help loosen things up before I start."

"Have a good practice session, honey," my mom said. "I'll be home again soon."

After one more hug and a kiss on the cheek, I stepped into the muggy summer air and watched her drive away. She really was working hard for our family; I understood that. But I missed her. I'd been away in Colorado training so much, I didn't get to see my parents a lot. For some reason, I thought that since I was back, I'd see them more, but I didn't. All they did was work…or fight.

The taillights of her car faded from my sight as she drove away, and I faced skyward and closed my eyes. The thick, damp air stuck to my skin like a wet blanket. I drew in a long breath, then turned around.

The rink stood before me.

I will fully heal.

I will land my jumps again.

I will get my spot back on the team.

My phone buzzed.

JESSA: What are you up to?

ME: Heading into the rink.

I started the trek along the outskirts of the lot toward the front doors.

JESSA: Nice!

JESSA: You sticking around to watch the hockey scrimmage?

ME: When is it?

JESSA: In about a half hour or so.

Crap. I thought open ice time was for the next two hours. Well, a half hour was better than none.

ME: You coming up here to watch?

JESSA: Totally.

Might be fun to hang out with Jessa and watch the game. It wasn't like I had anything else to do for the next two hours. Dad wasn't scheduled to come get me until then anyway.

ME: Yeah. I'll stick around.

JESSA: Maybe you should play with them.

ME: Yeah, right. LOL

JESSA: You did good out there the other day!

JESSA: Like you were having fun.

Fun?

While playing hockey?

Never thought in a million years those words would have been used to describe me. Well, not since I was eight.

JESSA: See you soon!

ME: Sweet.

A fat drop of rain splattered against my nose. I glanced up to see dark gray clouds hanging low in the sky. I tucked my phone back into my pocket just as the sky totally and completely opened up, drenching me as I headed toward the front doors of the rink.

Screeching tires skidded against wet pavement. I whipped around, my bag sliding off my shoulder and crashing to the concrete. A massive black Tahoe with a chrome grill swerved directly toward me.

And I froze.

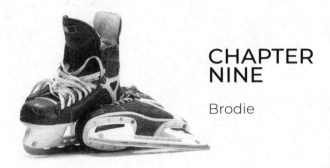

CHAPTER NINE

Brodie

Piercing blue eyes cut through the rain and sliced my chest. Willow stood there, my bumper inches from her leg.

Rain poured over her, but she didn't flinch.

Just stared.

I let out a long breath to try and calm my body. It felt like I'd touched a live wire, my skin buzzing with the adrenaline rush.

"You almost hit her," Caleb whispered from the backseat.

He'd distracted me with a coughing attack. I should have pulled over to check on him, but I was anxious to get to the rink. I needed some ice time before the pick-up game, so I just glanced over at him to see if he was okay.

I'd looked way too long. Especially in this wicked rainstorm.

I could have killed Willow.

I sagged against my seat, suddenly feeling weak as the quick burst of adrenaline at the near miss dissipated. A car accident had ruined my life a year and a half ago, and that pain and grief swarmed through me in an instant, stealing my breath.

Willow grabbed her bag from the ground and then sprinted to the rink entrance.

Caleb smacked my arm. "Park," he said, but his voice cracked, and it wasn't a puberty type crack, either. I'd scared him, too.

"Sorry for freaking you out, little man. I shouldn't have been going so fast." I parked the car, and Caleb went to bolt out, but I grabbed his arm and tossed him his raincoat.

"Brodie," he whined as he put it on.

"It stays on if you're outside, Limp Lungs." Sitting in a cold rink after getting soaked in the rain could be deadly for my asthmatic little bro.

He stuck his tongue out, then hustled toward the entrance. He hated coming here with me because he was stuck on the bleachers watching a sport he could never play. But it was either that or leave him at home with Rita. That didn't seem fair, either.

At least here he was around friends, and he could pig out at the concession stand and play in the video arcade.

With thoughts of Willow's huge, scared eyes rattling around my mind, I hustled into the locker room, threw on my gear, and found myself on the ice. I didn't see her out here or in the bleachers, though. I really needed to apologize.

A few people filled the benches behind the goal. Woodhaven fans *always* showed up, even for pick-up games. Despite how much I didn't like the small town up in my personal business all the time, I sure appreciated their support.

I tossed my bag down next to a wooden bench that stood outside the door to the ice. Hands still shaking, I kicked off my shoes and slid on my skates. Going through the routine usually calmed me, but after the close call a few minutes ago, I was struggling to focus.

After lacing my skates, I got up, shook out my shoulders,

and entered the rink. I drew in a deep breath as I pushed off for my second warm-up lap. The cool air washed over me, finally calming my racing heart.

Caleb slouched on a bleacher a few rows from the top, staring at his phone, totally ignoring the group of giggling girls at the end of the bench.

Zeroing in on the ice, I leaned forward so I could sit into my stride more. My legs were still sore from the workout yesterday, but I pushed through the burn. Needed to flush that soreness out so I could really get moving.

The chilly arena air bit at my cheeks and energized my blood. This was exactly what I needed.

The scrape of someone skating behind me floated into my consciousness. I glanced over my shoulder and met two blue eyes.

Willow's blue eyes.

They were etched into my brain forever because of almost hitting her, but now…wait…she'd kept up with me?

"You might want to watch where you're going." She peeled off.

Just as I smacked into the boards.

I bounced onto my butt and slid to the side. "Damn it."

She turned around and faced me, continuing to skate backward. "You skate like the Wind, but…"

I scrambled to my skates and faced off with her, skating forward while she kept going backward. "But…?"

"But I'm faster!" And with a quick swoosh and a flip of her braids, she turned around and was off.

Naturally, the only thing I could do was chase after her. It only took a few strides, and I came up alongside her.

"Oh no, you don't!" She sat deeper into her stride and darted ahead of me again.

I chuckled and picked up the pace with a few quick steps.

This time she stayed with me, her chest heaving.

"Listen," I said when I finally was right next to her. "I'm sorry for almost hitting you."

"Lucky for me you're not as spot-on with a car as you are when you slap a puck." She flashed me a grin. "It's fine. I'm fine." She'd gone from fear stricken to calm, relaxed, and fast.

Really fast.

Maybe the ice did for her what it did for me.

"Hey, so what are you doing here?" I asked.

"Got the open ice times mixed up, so I figured I'd get my half hour in quick before you guys took over." She pushed off and nodded for me to follow. "I really needed some time out here."

I understood needing ice time, for sure. I came out here to skate quite a bit, especially after Mom died. A familiar ache settled in my chest as I pictured her face.

I followed after her, and we skated in silence for another lap, calm and quiet, listening to the scrapes of our blades. We passed by Caleb, and I gave him a wave, but his focus was still zeroed in on his phone.

"Who's that?" Willow asked.

"My little brother. Likes to come and watch me play sometimes."

"Ah, so the puck head has a softer side," she said with a playful nudge. "How old is he?" She leaned into another curve, and my shoulder brushed hers again.

It didn't even phase her. She was solid on those skates. Strong. Confident, and if that wasn't the sexiest thing I'd seen in a long time…

"Brodie?"

"Oh, um, he's eight. Caleb." I waved to him again as we zoomed by, but still he didn't look up.

"He's adorable. What happened to *you*?" She laughed,

then took off.

"Oh, you did not…" I bolted after her, and it took me nearly a lap to catch up.

She raised her hands in surrender. "I was kidding! Don't check me into the boards."

I tapped her shoulder and laughed. "So, you're saying I'm adorable?"

"Maybe. For a hockey player." She kept her attention straight ahead, but I could tell she was smiling.

She looked absolutely tempting wearing tight workout pants and a white, fitted long-sleeve shirt. Her quads flexed with each stroke as she effortlessly glided over the ice.

"So why'd you need the ice time? Did something happen?"

"Got some pretty sucky news the other day, needed to process it."

"Oh, right, that. I heard."

"You did, huh?" She slouched, but only for a second, then fell back into a nice, solid stride. "Bad news travels fast."

"Joys of a small town. It sucks sometimes." I glided beside her quietly for another lap, then said, "This place is my church, too."

"Everything falls into place when I'm on the ice." She straightened up a little, slowing the pace. "I can't think clearly anywhere else."

"Same," I said.

She drew in a deep breath, gave me a glance, then stared out ahead of her as we neared another curve on the rink. Behind the short wall, I saw the Zamboni guy getting loaded up to clear the ice before our pick-up game.

Her long, black hair flowed out behind her as she moved, but she didn't shift her focus.

"What are you going to do? I mean, about…well, the bad news."

"Show them they made the biggest mistake of their

life. I'm going to spend every free minute I have on the ice, getting stronger and stronger each day." She drew in a deep breath. "I'll get back on an Olympic training team, even if it's a different one."

"So it's a team?"

"Well, kind of. It's not a team in the same sense as hockey, but we all train together at the same facility, with the same coaches. But we all compete individually, trying to place as high as possible all the way through the Olympics."

"And you go to school at the training center, too?" I asked.

"Yep."

"So, it's kind of like Xavier's School for Gifted Youngsters."

"Only I'm not a mutant and Professor X didn't show up at my house." She winked. "But we train as much as they do, at least eight hours on the ice every single day."

Talk about grit. This girl had it. "How do you get into one of these training programs?"

"First, I have to land these damn jumps." Her jaw twitched. "January is coming fast. I need to be a hundred percent by then if I have *any* chance of getting picked up by a coach at one of these programs."

Damn, Willow was intense, and it was the sexiest thing I'd seen in a long time. Chasing her around the ice before school might be the perfect thing to whip both of us into shape.

"I think I can help you."

She stood up straight and glided for a few feet, watching me. "What do you mean, help?"

"Training. Ice time. I mean, I—this Ice Den." Oh my gosh, could I sound any more bumbling right now? "I have a pretty intense training program for hockey. Some of it could help you, I'm sure. And I have extra access to this place, so I could get you more ice time."

"Because of your dad?"

I nodded, warmth creeping up from my chest. "But there's also hockey. You…you could play hockey."

She let out a huff. "Yeah, right."

"Fall League. Tryouts are soon. We need a goalie."

She stumbled two steps, her blades tapping across the ice. "Whoa."

I reached out to steady her by the elbow, and she got her bearings again. "You good?"

"Um, yeah. But goalie? Me? I…I'm not sure that's a good idea. And besides, you must have a backup for Josiah."

"Izan Hernandez. He's good but…" I glanced over my shoulder and found the rink empty, then faced her again as we came to a stop. "Honestly? You're better."

Her mouth fell open, and she said, "Me?" Her voice cracked, and she cleared her throat. "Really? A little Ice Princess *figure skater* as your last line of defense between the puck and the goal?" She batted her eyes exaggeratedly.

"Ha-ha. Very funny."

"Doesn't matter if I'm funny. I can't do it. What if I got hurt?"

"What happened with Josiah was a fluke. You're strong, and unless you plan on ripping off your helmet and getting into fights, you'll be fine. Plus, I'll show you a few things that'll help keep you safe." I nudged her good-naturedly with my shoulder. "You've got killer instincts. Izan is only a freshman and just isn't there yet."

Her cheeks flushed, and she cracked her knuckles, as if she was genuinely thinking it over.

My heart started pounding as the idea of her being on the team started forming in my head. "I need the best people out there, Willow. Winning Fall League, getting to and winning State… Without a good goalie, we're toast. It'll help your figure skating, too."

"How?" She planted her fists on her hips.

"Weights and cardio program, time on the ice, growing strength back in your ankle, honing your balance and reflexes…you name it. Will you at least try out?"

"I don't know…" She rubbed her hands together, then blew on them. Her fingertips were a little red, as was her nose. It looked perfect on her, though. "I can't believe you have to try out for a Town League."

"It's basically the high school team, really. But regulations prevent us from practicing, you know? Town League keeps us all sharp and working as a team during the off season, but we lost a few seniors last year, so there will be a few people trying out."

"I guess I'll think about it." She blew into her hands again. "You know, you do still owe me coffee from the other day. Don't forget I blocked your shot."

"As if I could ever forget. Why do you think I'm here asking you, a 'little Ice Princess,' as you called yourself, to try out?" I reached out and grabbed her hands, then brought them to my heart in a supplicating gesture.

She froze, her eyes wide.

What. The. Hell. Was. I. Doing?

"Oh shit." I dropped her hands. "I'm sorry."

"It's fine." She smiled, her cheeks three shades redder. "No biggie."

"I can't believe I did that. Total invasion of—"

"It's fine, Brodie." She patted my chest, her gaze lingering on mine.

I loved that she called me Brodie. Everyone else called me Wind, for the most part, but her using my given name, it was refreshing. And the way she bantered with me. It was like she didn't think I was a big deal because my name was on the building, which was very cool. I wanted to be known for my talent, not my name.

Warmth from her hand lingered on my chest and seeped through my shirt, kicking my heart rate up another notch as the heat crawled into my neck and my face.

Time stopped. Neither of us breathed, but neither broke eye contact. Everything else but her stunning eyes blurred out of focus. She was at the end of a tunnel.

Only her.

Those lips.

A spray of ice settled over us, and I jerked away from Willow's touch.

"Willow!" Preach put his fist up for her to knuckle bump. "You here to play? We need an extra goalie with Josiah being out. Izan has one of them covered. Not that we're begging or anything, but if you don't say yes, we're going to have to put Pax's sorry butt in the other one." He chuckled.

"And Pax hasn't been able to touch his toes in five years," Nathaniel said, skating by us.

She looked at me, then Preach, and then around the arena. A few of the guys started filing onto the ice. I'd lost track of time.

"I…still don't know," she said.

I tilted my head down, giving her a knowing look. She was intrigued, I could tell. "Come on, Toe Pick. You know you want to…"

CHAPTER TEN

Willow

I didn't know what the hell I'd been thinking. I was a *figure skater*, not a goalie.

"Ouch." I brought my hand to my cheek and clenched my teeth, looking around my gramps's basement.

Brodie sprang to his feet. "I'm so sorry."

"It's okay. Totally my fault for missing it." I waved him off before bending down to pick up the tennis balls he'd been whipping at me for the last thirty minutes. He'd pegged me with at least five, and I'd let way more than that go sailing past me. "I think I was lucky at the rink, blocking a few shots."

I needed to face the facts. Nobody picked up a new sport their senior year. This was a complete waste of time.

Brodie scooped up a few balls that had rolled back toward him. "Let's take five."

We plopped down on the cool cement floor in the middle of my basement. There was one window, about the size of a shoebox, so it was pretty closed up in here.

Sweat dripped down my back. Even though the temperature usually hovered right around sixty-five, it felt like we were in one of those hot yoga studios. I grabbed my shirt by its hem and whipped it off. Sitting in my sports bra and a pair of shorts, I let my head fall into my hands, and I propped my elbows against my knees.

A crashing sound behind me had me whipping around. The bucket of tennis balls Brodie had been holding was on the floor, sending the neon green missiles rolling in every direction across the cement.

"Shit," he said as he frantically gathered them up. His skin flushed along his neck and up to his cheeks as he looked every direction except mine.

"You good?" I asked, watching him stumble around. He normally wasn't like that. Funny how it coincided with me taking my shirt off…

"First of all, your stopping those shots at the rink wasn't luck," Brodie said as he chased the last ball down. "You've got natural talent, and you're better on your skates than a lot of the guys out there. Plus, you've played before—it's just been a while."

I glanced up. "What about Izan?"

"You saw him the other day—he's not ready yet. He can't hold his own in the net."

"Isn't he going to be pissed if I swoop in and become goalie?"

"Does that matter?" Brodie squatted beside me, resting on the balls of his feet, and his closeness demanded I look at him. "If you had the chance to take your spot back on your skating team right now, but there was someone else who wasn't as good standing in the way, would you just give up?"

"No." My heart cramped at the thought of being on a skating team again.

"Exactly." Brodie placed his hand on my back. "So, enough with the pity party. Let's get back at it."

He wasn't kidding when he said he'd train me. Today was the first day we'd been able to connect since he'd offered to help me two days ago, and we'd been down here for three hours already.

. I still couldn't believe he'd asked me to try out for the team. I'd practically made a fool of myself by falling over, I was so shocked. But the thought of getting more ice time and some good cardio and strength-training opportunities sealed the deal. Plus, if I made the team, it was only for a couple of months.

Then again, for how much I was sucking at blocking tennis balls today, I probably wouldn't even make the team.

"Yo, Toe Pick!" Brodie clapped his hands. "Let's go. Or I'll make you play fifty-two puck pick-up."

"Hmm, that's funny. I don't see a single puck down here." I held my hands out and motioned around the basement.

"Oh…I'll show you a puck!" The corner of his mouth quirked up into a sexy half grin.

My face was instantly on fire. As in, molten lava hot. "Um, yeah, I'm going to pass on that offer, but we better get back to it." I crossed my legs and stood.

"How'd you do that?" Brodie asked, still on the floor.

"Do what?"

"Get up like that, without using your hands?" He tried, but he only made it a few inches off the floor before thudding back down on his butt.

"Good balance and strong quads?" I laughed and extended my hand.

Instead of trying again, he grasped my hand and rose to his feet. Only when he got up, he didn't release my hand.

My heart started racing, and my mouth went dry. Suddenly conscious that I was half naked, I wrapped my arm around my torso and released his hand.

Brown and amber swirls stared back at me, unflinching. "You can do this, you know." His voice was lower than normal, and it tickled across my abdomen like a feather.

"I—I know," I whispered.

"That's believable." He grinned, taking a step back.

The intensity that'd been filling those dark orbs knocked me sideways for a second. At first, I thought he might be checking me out, but no, it was focus. He was driven. Competitive. Like me.

Yes. That was what I needed to focus on. Skating. Getting strong.

"Do you kids need a snack?" Gramps called from the top of the stairs, and I heard the creak of wood beneath his weight as he started making his way down the steps.

I wiped the sweat from my brow and drew in a deep breath. "That would be great, Gramps. Thanks!"

He came down the stairs with a tray of orange slices and two glasses of Kool-Aid in hand: exactly what Grams had always brought me as a kid when I was out playing street hockey. A knot formed in my stomach, and my eyes stung at the sudden memory.

"How's it going down here?"

"Good. He's kicking my butt." I accepted the tray and set it on an old desk we'd brought down a few weeks ago and shoved in a corner. "This looks great, Gramps. Thank you."

"Thank you, sir," Brodie said, coming up alongside me, eyeing the fresh fruit. "Orange slices? I remember Nathaniel mentioning something about orange slices when you guys used to play street hockey."

"It was my grandma's thing." I grinned, my heart warming at the memory.

"Why orange slices?" he asked, then bit into one.

"She always used to say they'd help keep our muscles and bones strong." I bit into a slice of the juicy fruit. "Oh man, this brings me back."

"I bet you were feisty at the Heron Lane hockey games."

Gramps snagged one of the stray tennis balls from the floor and grinned as he tossed it to Brodie. "My little Snowflake is one heck of a skater."

My jaw dropped, completely mortified that he'd used his nickname for me in front of Brodie.

"She'll be making headlines again in no time."

I'd told him my plans to get my spot back on the team or a new team, which included my trying out for Fall League hockey, and he'd fully supported me. The thought of leaving him someday made my chest ache, but I'd make him proud. Get back on the podium. Take home more gold.

Brodie took a swig of Kool-Aid. "She sure is talented."

"That she is. You just make sure she's trained up well enough so she doesn't get injured again."

A phantom ache shot down my Achilles, and I reached down to rub it.

"You got it, sir."

Grandpa gave Brodie a firm look, then winked at me. He'd been a little worried that I'd get injured if I'd made the hockey team. But I was strong from skating, and Brodie was showing me how to be safe in the net, so I'd reassured Gramps that I'd be fine.

"Well, I'm going to leave you kids to it." Gramps gave us a quick nod and then disappeared back up the stairs.

Citrus filled the air. I leaned against the desk and bit into another orange slice. Juice dribbled down my chin, so I wiped my face with the back of my hand, forgetting for a moment that Brodie was sitting next to me. My cheeks flushed as I snuck a glance his way, but he was grabbing another orange slice and looking in the opposite direction.

"Your grandpa is pretty cool." Brodie snagged a few more slices and popped one into his mouth.

"Yeah. He's great."

"And your grandma?" He stood still, watching me with those brown orbs. He actually looked interested in me, my story. It was cool.

"Yeah, um…" I bit into another orange. "She died a few years back. Um…cancer."

"That sucks. I'm sorry." He shifted his weight and glanced around.

"Are your grandparents still here?"

"No. It's just Dad, Caleb, and me. Mom and Dad are both only children." He snagged a rogue tennis ball from the floor beside the desk and bounced it on the ground. "Up for round two?"

I wanted to know more, but it seemed like he was done talking, and I didn't want to push it.

"Hell yeah." I assumed my position a few feet in front of the wall as he made his way toward the other side of the room. "Don't hold back!"

"I wouldn't dream of it." Without hesitating, Brodie whipped a ball toward my feet. Shifting my weight, I lunged to my right and managed to connect with the ball, batting it off to the side.

"There you go!" He lobbed another ball at my feet, and I blocked it with my tennis shoe and then kicked that one away.

"Ready position. Right away. Don't hesitate." He whipped another one at me.

Then another.

"Nice!" Brodie grinned. "There's no way Izan would have blocked that shot."

A smile finally returned to my face, and a jolt of positive energy shot through my body.

An hour flew by, and toward the end, I'd managed to block more shots than I missed. Of course, it was nothing like being on the ice, covered in goalie gear, but it was definitely helping my reflexes.

Brodie wiped his brow with the back of his hand and let out a long breath. He pulled the thin shirt over his head, then balled it up and dabbed at the sweat glistening along his neck. But what really caught my eye was a stray bead of sweat making its way over the distinct curves of his corded abs. The guy didn't have an ounce of fat on him, so I could make out each and every groove of his six pack.

Our eyes locked on one another's, and everything around us faded away.

Damn.

He is so hot.

No! My cheeks started burning. *Stop it. Don't even look at his sexy-ass body! He's helping you, not trying to make out with you in your freaking basement!*

I shook the thoughts from my head and focused on my shoes like they were the most important thing in the world right then. Actually, they might be, because if I looked at him much longer, I might self-combust.

"Want to do some strength training?" he asked.

"Oh, ah. Definitely. Start with planks?"

I hustled over to the far wall and grabbed two rolled-up yoga mats. They were pretty thin, and I usually doubled them, but one would have to do today.

Brodie accepted the dark blue mat from me and rolled it out on the ground. "So, your plan to get your spot back on a team. What exactly is it?"

I let the mat fall to the ground before I kicked it open with my toe. "Continue with my PT, cardio on even days, strength training on odd days, and spend as much time on the ice as possible." I balanced on my forearms and positioned my feet behind me.

"Fall League gets ice time after school four days a week," Brodie said, copying my position.

"Please tell me the rink will be open an hour or two before school?"

"Unfortunately not."

"Seriously?"

He winked. "But remember? I can help with that."

CHAPTER ELEVEN

Brodie

"It helps having your name on the building sometimes," I said, clicking on the lights.

"I should say so." Willow cinched her skating bag to her shoulder and turned a circle as she looked around the arena. "Lucky you."

"Most of the time, I hate it."

"Wait, you hate what?" Willow asked.

I cleared my throat. "That my name is on the building."

"Why?"

"It's just so pretentious, don't you think?"

She quirked an eyebrow and tilted her head to the side, watching me. She did that a lot lately. That morning in her basement was two days ago, but I hadn't gotten it—or her—out of my mind since.

Her sweaty body, flying everywhere to stop my shots.

Wearing just a pair of shorts and a sports bra.

She was so hot, I thought she was going to catch me drooling.

But it wasn't only that… She was working so hard.

Focused.

Her dedication and determination radiated off her to the point it was almost palpable. And it was pretty much the sexiest thing I could have imagined.

"I figured you'd *want* to flaunt the name, the money, stuff like that. I mean, we wouldn't be here without it."

"No offense taken." I huffed, then hiked my own bag up over my shoulder more.

"Sorry. Didn't mean it that way." She smiled. "I was actually…trying to pay you a compliment."

"A compliment, huh?"

She shrugged as she inched closer to me. "Put it this way—growing up on the rink with all the richies and being an athlete who couldn't be there if she wasn't sponsored…I met some real snobs."

"I bet," I said, hoping she didn't put me in that category. I never wanted to be like that, neither had Mom, and she made sure Caleb and I appreciated everything we were given.

I finished flipping on the lights, letting them get warmed up to full brightness. "Come on."

I led her through the bleachers and hopped the wall onto the bench. The single bench down the middle of it was empty except for a few hockey sticks and a bag of pucks. I'd asked Coach Kurt to leave some stuff for me, so I was glad he'd done it.

"Should I be scared?" Willow dropped her bag on the bench and picked up a hockey stick. "This one isn't a goalie stick."

"This one is, though." I hoisted up the new stick I'd purchased for her.

"Oh sweet." She reached for it, then pulled back.

"What?" I held it out to her as I stepped over the bench, so I was on the same side as her, but she'd pulled away from the stick, like she didn't want it or something. I knew she needed it, she'd got her goalie equipment and skates from Jessa's brother, but the stick hadn't fit her well enough to keep using. Not if she wanted to *really* do this.

"Is this yours?"

"I have lots of sticks lying around." I thrust it toward her more. "You can have it."

"Really?" she asked, gently taking it from my hands as if I was passing her a golden skating boot.

Warmth blossomed in my chest.

I nodded, stepping away from her to unzip my bag to get my skates out. She stood there, holding the stick horizontally in her hands, looking at it. She flipped it over a few times, and her face lit up.

It wasn't the lights above us finally warming up, either. It was happiness. And I loved how it made her face glow. She wasn't even a hockey player, but it was like she gave her all to whatever she was focusing on.

That stick in her hand was pretty fucking hot, too.

"Are you going to stare at it all morning or actually use it?"

She chuckled, then glanced at me and held up the stick slightly. "Thanks. For this."

"Sure."

"Can I ask you something?"

I nodded as I sat on the bench, readying my skates to put them on.

"Why are you doing this?" She glanced at the stick in her hand again. "The training, the equipment. The…time."

"You're our best shot at winning the Fall League." I let out a breath. "I need the win, and you're the shit."

"Oh. Yeah. To win." She nodded and shifted her weight. "You want to win."

"And it'll help you with your comeback." I jammed my foot into my skate. "Get you back to what you love."

I had to remember that she was leaving. She. *Would*. Leave.

"Perfect." She sat beside me and pulled out her borrowed hockey skates. "When will Josiah be better? Because I don't want to be around you stinky hockey players any longer than needed."

I playfully elbowed her. "Like us hockey jocks want to play second fiddle to a bunch of sequins and twirls anyway. "

She chuckled and shook her head. Her long black braid flipped around her shoulder and rested along her chest. Her back was straight, her shoulders wide, and she looked at me with open blue eyes. It was like she saw right through me or something.

I threw on my skates and was on the ice skating a couple laps as she finished putting on all her equipment.

I had to get out of that space, being so close to her. She would leave eventually, jump back into figure skating as soon as she was strong again. I couldn't get too comfortable with her. Couldn't risk that.

She was our best chance for winning the Fall League. That was my focus. That had to be my focus.

"Hey, Brodie, are you gonna skate around all morning or are we going to actually practice something?"

I skidded to a stop across from the bench I'd left her in to get suited up. She was standing in the goal, in the classic position, her shiny new stick out in front of her, and I could see the grin through her mask.

I sped to the center line where I'd set the bag of pucks, then dumped them onto the ice and scattered them around. Taking one, I dribbled it to my left, focusing on my fast feet, and then I zigged left and right. With a quick flip, I slapped that puck in her wide-open five-hole.

She kicked out to block it but missed by a mile. I curved around and went to the next puck and did the same.

"Shit," she said.

A third time, I came in from the other side. She got a little stick on the puck, but not enough to block it.

"Shit!"

"You're leaving your five-hole wide open, Willow!"

"Like I know what a five-hole is!"

We were going to start on some vocab ASAP. I coasted up to her and said, "See how your knees are together?" I tapped her legs and outlined that triangle opening left unguarded. "Put the heel of the stick on the ice."

She did, watching my stick outline the little hole left unguarded.

"I'm sneaking the puck in there every time. That's what you're trying to stop. Guarding your five-hole. It's huge."

"Guarding my five-hole. Got it," she said, nodding. "Try again."

I snatched the pucks I'd gotten by her and brought them to my stash. "Ready?"

"Bring it!" She tapped the ice with her stick, and I couldn't help smiling.

I brought it. Four more got through before she finally blocked one.

And then another.

Six more got through with her throwing out a few cuss words after the last two. I sped toward her, stick handling the puck left, right, then left, and slapped it by her.

"Damn it!" She dropped her stick.

"Different from tennis balls." I sprayed her with some ice as I stopped beside her.

"Gee, you think?" She sagged to the ground and pounded the ice.

"Let's take a break."

She ripped off her gloves and flopped onto her back. I

ditched mine, too, and sprawled out, resting my head near hers. She turned, so I got a good view of her face. Her cheeks were rosy, her eyes were closed, and her chest was heaving.

"Harder than it looks, huh?" I said.

"That'd be a yes."

"You'll get it."

"Sure, just like you'd get a single axel down in a few days."

"Is that one of those fancy jumps you've been working on?"

"Yup." She grinned.

"Tell you what. I'll get you ready for the goalie position—"

"In time for tryouts in seven days?"

"Yes," I said, fairly confident she would. She was strong, coordinated, and talented.

She opened her eyes and pinned me with a grin. "And in return, I'm going to teach you how to do a toe loop."

CHAPTER TWELVE

Willow

"How's a Toe Loop or whatever going to help me with hockey?" Brodie quirked up his eyebrow, eyeing me with his amber-flecked brown eyes.

"It's all about balance, core strength, and grace." I stood and playfully pushed off him, gliding across the ice away from him, shedding my goalie gear with each stride. I felt so light and free now.

I couldn't wait to try a jump. But first, Brodie. "By the end of my lesson, you won't make a figure skater joke ever again. You'll be kissing my bright-white skates."

He stayed quiet, but he grinned as he flicked off his gloves and threw them onto the bench.

"You're, like, the fastest guy I've ever seen on the ice, and you can take a check, but I can help you have even more balance out here while you're skating circles around everyone."

"Oh, my balance is fine. Don't forget, I was the first junior team captain the hockey team's ever seen." He wasn't wearing any other hockey pads since he was doing drills with me, so there he stood, wearing a tight black long-sleeve grippy shirt, snug in all the right places, jogging pants, and his skates.

His brown, floppy hair was perfectly disheveled, framing his flawless face.

And it stole my breath. Not only his looks, but his comfort level on the ice. It rivaled mine how he stood confident and sure, as if he was just walking down the street.

And damn if it didn't tickle my insides with a delicious tingle of electricity.

"Willow?" Brodie's voice sliced through my daze.

"Oh yeah. Balance. We'll see." I motioned for him to follow my lead to the center of the rink. Heat steamed up from my chest. He'd totally busted me scoping him out.

"I'll nail any jump you throw my way."

"You're going to need a pair of ice skates to jump." I pointed to his hockey skates, which were at least a size twelve. "Those aren't going to cut it."

"Figure skates?" He burst out laughing. "Hard pass."

"Oh, I'll get you in a pair of figure skates before tryouts, but I'll let you stay in those for now." I motioned to his hockey skates with my eyes. "But first, spirals." I turned and started skating backward.

Brodie shrugged. "Spirals it is."

I flipped back around and glided forward. "So, skates have an inside and outside edge. We're going to start with the inside edge. Take a few strokes forward, put your arms out for balance, lift your left leg up behind you, and try to make a straight line. Watch."

Picking up speed, I put my arms out to the sides and lifted my left leg. Doing a full arabesque, I reached up and grabbed hold of my blade with my hands. "Ta-da!"

Brodie waved and exhaled. "Easy peasy."

As I came to a stop several feet in front of him, Brodie pushed off his right skate. He glided forward, but instead of putting his arms out first, he lifted his leg. It only made it about two feet off the ice. Wobbling to the left and then right, his arms shot out, but it was too late. Taking two short strides, he tripped and face-planted into the ice.

I stifled a laugh. "Looks like Mr. Junior Team Captain needs to work on his flexibility *and* balance."

Brodie scrambled to his knees. "I'm just getting warmed up."

He took off, brushing the ice off his chest along the way.

"Arms out, then leg up." I caught him and skated a few feet to his left.

Brodie extended his arms and then slowly lifted his leg.

"You're like one of those little propeller planes on a windy day. Keep your arms straight," I instructed with a giggle.

Straightening his arms, Brodie lifted his leg a little higher. "Start playing me some Celine Dion; I got this!"

"Very nice, but just so you know, no one has skated to one of her songs since like 1990." I slowed and grabbed his leg, then hoisted it up another few inches. The tight muscle flexed beneath my touch, and a streak of heat shot through my stomach.

"Whoa!" He hopped a few times on his skate to stay upright. "You trying to knock me over?"

"It shouldn't…if you have balance and good core strength."

"Ohhh," he chuckled. "I see how you are. It's *get back at Brodie* time for chucking tennis balls at you."

"Well, you did nail me in the face a couple times." I laughed. "Use your arms for balance."

Extending them even farther, he reached out and flexed his fingers.

"Nope, fingers together." I released his leg, then ran my hands along his arm, up to his shoulder, as I skated beside him.

I was so close, the warmth from his body filtered into mine. Or I was combusting because I was touching him. Strength and confidence radiated from him in tangible waves. It filtered into my body, warming it from the inside out. A sweet, woodsy scent emanated from him as we glided, creating a subtle breeze that shifted his hair, and I had to refrain from leaning in to steal another breath of it. He smelled like he'd just come off the ice after skating the outdoor rink at Jackson's Pond.

"Like this?" he asked, snapping me out of my thoughts. Holy cow, I needed to focus.

"Shoulders up and chest out." I tightened my grip on him to guide his movement.

He puffed out his chest and squeezed his fingers together.

"There, you got it! Now you look like an elegant swan," I said with a cheeky grin as I let him glide away from me.

He *was* doing it. Maybe more like an ugly duckling, but he'd get there.

Brodie shot me a glance over his shoulder as he continued to move across the ice. "Like I said, easy."

"Watch out for the boards."

"Huh?" He snapped his head forward, losing his balance in the process.

He toppled over, landing on the ice with a grunt and bringing his knees into his chest. A few seconds later, his right side smacked into the boards with a crack.

"Shit!" I shouted. The hairs on my neck prickled as a jolt of adrenaline scorched through my body. He'd hit the boards pretty hard. I hadn't realized he was moving as fast as he was.

I got to him as quickly as my skates would take me and dropped down beside him, out of breath. "Brodie? Brodie, are you okay?"

He remained silent, his eyes closed as I rolled him onto his back. Had he hit his head? We'd taken our helmets off to do this, but that might have been a mistake. My heart hammered so hard, it made my chest ache. I could just see the small town news headlines: *"Local figure skater takes star hockey player down with a concussion."*

His lips started to twitch, the corners curving into a smile.

"Brodie?" I kept my hands on his chest, scared to move. Was he smiling? As in—

His eyes flew open, and a grin filled his face.

"You Puck Head!" I punched him in the stomach and fell back onto my butt beside him, my heart clamoring to get out of my chest. He'd scared the shit out of me. I don't know what I would have done if he'd gotten hurt.

"Gotcha!" He pointed at me.

The amber flecks in his eyes flared to life as his laughter echoed through the empty ice rink. He held his stomach and rested on his back, still laughing. The sound curled around me, and I couldn't help but smile as a wave of relief washed over me.

"You're a jerk," I said, trying to sound mad, even though seeing him roll around the ice, laughing, made it difficult.

I turned over to get up and skate away, but Brodie cuffed my good ankle and gave it a tug. "Takes a lot more than a little fall like that to knock me out of the game. Like Celine says, my heart will go on."

And then I burst out laughing. "So, this is a game, huh?" While laying on my stomach, I propped my elbows against the ice and rested my chin in my hands.

He held my gaze for a beat or two, not saying a word. But those eyes, they spoke volumes.

The amber flared to life, and his cheeks flushed as his gaze slowly slid over my face. Heat prickled up my neck and pooled in my face as I drank in his attention. Heat and desire replaced the playfulness I'd seen, and it tickled something way deep down.

Back in Colorado, with all the training and competition,

we didn't have much time for guys and dating. Especially hockey players, even though we'd come into contact with them more than other guys thanks to having to share ice time. Everyone on the squad wrote them off as puck heads with no grace. But Brodie, he had that. He was an amazing hockey player, sure, but he had a little finesse in his actions, too.

Not many guys would be secure enough to try learning these moves, especially rough and tough hockey players, but he wasn't pretentious like that. Even though he easily could be, since he was the hometown star, he was just another guy who loved the ice almost as much as I did.

He was kind, too. Helping me like he was. Giving me hockey equipment and spending all this time with me, and it didn't seem like he wanted anything in return, other than for me to join the team and help him get his win. But that wasn't a bad thing. I got the whole needing to win thing.

Kind of made me want to see what else made Brodie "Wind" Windom tick. Then again, I'd be out of here soon, so it wouldn't be worth it to start something up, even if he wanted to. But still—

"You good?" Brodie asked.

He was sitting up now, wiping away the tears of laughter. I hadn't even noticed we'd been lying here for a while. I'd gotten lost in my mind again, thinking about Brodie. Thinking about him a little too much.

"Oh. Ah…yeah." I sat up.

"Got any more fancy moves to show me?"

My fingers twitched. "Watch this."

I got up and started skating around the rink. Ice scraped beneath my skates as I picked up the pace. *You've got this, Willow!*

Closing the space between my ankles, I moved my hands in front of me and shifted my weight to the outer edge of my skate. I exhaled and picked up my right knee and pushed upward. As my hands snapped downward, my body flew through the air. My body turned counterclockwise one and a half times before I landed on my left skate, facing the opposite direction.

"Yes!" Adrenaline rushed through my veins and goose bumps shot down across my arms.

"Holy shit! You did it!" Brodie exclaimed from the other end of the ice.

"I can't believe it." I raced across the rink, my heart pounding. "I haven't landed an axel in a year. My Achilles doesn't even hurt. I mean, it's a little stiff, but that's it."

My hands flew into the air in celebration. I came to a stop just in front of Brodie and did a victory dance.

"Very impressive." He smiled, but his gaze didn't meet mine.

"So, you ready to give that a try?"

Brodie's eyes widened as he looked up at me from the ice. "Uh, yeah, no. I'll stick with shooting pucks, thank you very much."

I laughed and took a seat next to him. "I'm just joking. But I do have one more move for you to try. It's pretty easy, and it will help with your balance."

"What do you have in mind?" he asked.

"Well, since you're so comfortable on your butt, let's try to shoot the duck." I grinned.

He scrunched up his nose. "Shoot the duck?"

"It's a weird name, but it's a pretty easy move. I'll show you." I got to my feet and pushed off my right blade and then my left. Once I'd picked up enough speed, I crouched and stuck my right leg out. Balancing, I put my right hand under my calf and my left hand on my knee. After traveling twenty-five feet, I tucked my leg back in and then stood up from the crouched position.

The ice sprayed beneath my blades as I spun around. When I came to a stop, I said, "Let me guess. Easy peasy?"

Brodie got to his feet and shook his arms out. "Totally."

He raced across the rink, squatting down about halfway.

"Put your right hand under your right calf. Then straighten your right leg out," I shouted. "Good! You've got it! Left hand on your left knee for balance."

Brodie held the position for about four seconds before the blade on his extended skate caught the ice and sent him flying.

Arms and legs out, he looked as if he was making a snow angel.

He grinned up at me. "Nailed it."

"Oh yeah, you're the next Alysa Liu." I put my hands on my hips.

"Lookit these two," a voice called from the bleachers.

Snapping my head around, I saw Pax, the sexist one who had stared at my chest during the first pick-up game, standing there. Beside him was a stocky guy with dark hair, long on the top and shaved on the sides. He was laughing and pointing in our direction.

Pax cupped his hands around his mouth. "Brodie, does this mean we need to get you fitted for a skating tutu?"

CHAPTER THIRTEEN

Brodie

"**F**all League tryouts are in two days, so why are we running bleachers?" Willow said, her shoulders slouching as she approached me on the track.

The early morning sun spilled its colorful rays over her, giving her long black hair a tint of pink. The braids curled over her shoulder and rested on her chest. She was wearing a tight red tank top that dipped low on her chest, giving me a subtle view of her wicked curves. Her black spandex shorts went to her mid-thighs, and each step she took toward me, her toned muscles flexed, demanding my attention.

A flash of heat streaked down my spine at the sight of her making her way to me. She yawned and leaned her head side to side. I heard it cracking even from ten feet away.

"That's gross," I said, shaking my head to get myself focused on the task. Training. Training. Training.

"Yeah, well, I'm still waking up. And once again, I ask, what's up with the not being on the ice two days before Fall League tryouts?"

"Oh, we'll get there." I winked. "But first, butterfly."

She checked behind her and over both her shoulders.

"What? Where?"

I laughed. "No, the hockey term, butterfly, what does it mean?"

"That I head to Mexico for the winter while wearing my hockey pads?"

"That is single-handedly the worst answer of all time," I deadpanned.

"Okay, Hockey Yoda, your ways, teach me. Listen, I will."

"The movie Force is strong with you, young Padawan, but the definition of butterfly is when a goalie drops to their knees to cover the lower part of the net with their legs."

Willow tapped the side of her head. "Got it. See, I wasn't that far off."

"Mexico, really?"

She laughed, and I joined in until my belly hurt.

I finally stopped long enough to grab my Hydro Flask and take a sip of water.

She held hers up that was looped around her left forefinger and grinned. "Let's see what you got on yours."

I took a sip, then showed her my stickers.

"Hockey pucks. *Fast and Furious*." Her eyes widened on that one. "Nice. I love me some *Fast and Furious*." She grabbed my flask. "What else do you have on here? Wolverines. Of course." She turned it. "Cabin Coffee?"

"That's where coffee debts shall be paid." I laughed and grabbed her flask.

Mostly skating stickers and a couple of Vin Diesel. "Oh wow. Vin…cool."

"Yeah, well, I'm more than just a frilly figure skater Ice Princess." She let her small backpack slide off her shoulders and to the grassy sidelines of the track. "So what are we doing here?"

"Not everything can be done on the ice." I took a few

steps back from her, wincing through a subtle soreness in my ass from those weird things she had me doing on the ice the other day. Despite the shit I caught from the guys about it, I'd had fun. Not that I'd ever tell them that, but still. "Let's loosen up first."

She grinned, eyeing me as we made our way onto the track. A slight smile curved her lips, and it looked like she knew a secret she couldn't tell me or something.

"Arm circles first." I held my arms out to my side. "What are you smirking about?"

She mimicked me as I started a set of arm circles and said, "Moving a little gingerly there, *Wind*."

"Nice bruise on your cheek." I switched arm circle directions.

"Guess we're even."

"Hardly. I'm not…that sore."

She chuckled. "Sure you're not."

I couldn't help but laugh. "You are one tough chick, Willow Covington."

"First, I'm not a chick." She winked. "Second, you bet your ass I am."

There weren't many girls who would laugh off getting pegged in the face by tennis balls while training for a sport they hadn't played in a decade. She'd barely flinched. And here I was, sore from doing a couple figure skating tricks.

I led us through some arm swings, trunk twists, and active stretching, then waved her to follow me to the track. "Come on, just a couple laps, then we're hitting some speed work."

"It's a goalie position. Why speed?" She jogged beside me.

"Tryouts are in a couple days, and even though you're goalie, Coach'll run you through some drills with cones, weaving in and out, things like that. It's not so much about making every shot or blocking every shot. It's about technique and comfort level on the ice."

"Okay. I get that."

"You have fast feet from figure skating, but hockey fast feet are a little different."

"And you're teaching me fast feet off the ice?" She rolled her eyes and chuckled.

"Exactly." I picked up the pace for a few strides, and she stayed with me. "See those bleachers?" I pointed ahead to the stands. "They're going to be your best friend for the next hour."

"Yikes."

I chuckled as I picked up the pace again. "To the line there," I said, then took off sprinting.

"Hey!" she yelled then tore after me.

Pumping my arms, I blew through the imaginary finish line several steps ahead of her.

"No fair. You didn't give me any warning."

"Exactly." I took off running again.

I heard her swear at me, but she chased after me again. She was pretty quick, there was no denying that, but was she fast enough? I needed her on this team. Unless Andrei Vasilevskiy suddenly showed up at tryouts, Willow was our best option.

It was weird to think a figure skater was our best option as a goalie. But hey, talent was talent. She was the shit, and I needed her on this team if I had any chance of taking us to a championship.

"Okay, I get it," Willow said breathlessly as she caught up to me. "I take it back, you're wind off the ice, too."

I laughed as I slowed to a jog. One lap here on the track, then she'd really get tested.

"So how'd you get into hockey?"

"Family thing," I said, my chest tightening slightly. The

pressure to keep up the Windom playing hockey at Boston College tradition was legit. But Willow probably understood pressure as good as anyone might. "My dad and his dad, they played for Boston College."

"Wow. Really? Jessa told me your dad was a pro once."

"For a few years." I shook my head.

"You trying to go pro, too?"

"Naw. I mean, well, maybe? Main goal is getting on the hockey team."

"I bet you're a shoo-in."

"Could be, but nothing's guaranteed. I need to prove I can hack it."

"What do you mean? You obviously can." She slowed down a little.

"I just…want to be respected for my talent, not given perks because of my last name, you know?"

"Ahhh…I get it. Because your dad was in the pros and…" She nodded. "I get it."

"He's not in the pros anymore. Now he, well, he has some businesses he runs."

"As in…owns half the town, I hear."

"So you're talking to Jessa about me, then, huh?" I gave her a side glance. Sure, I was teasing her, but the thought of her asking Jessa sent a flash of heat through my chest.

"I might have asked her a…few questions."

Shit. She probably knew my entire life history, then. Couldn't keep anything quiet in this small town. Living here was both good and bad in that sense. Hopefully, she didn't ask about my mom. I wasn't…I didn't want to talk about that with anyone, let alone her.

"But don't worry…" Willow said, playfully slapping my arm as we continued our warm-up jog on the track. "It was just a couple."

"Like what?" I gulped through the nerves thickening in my throat.

"Basics. Girlfriend, grade, embarrassing stories, things like that. So…you showed up to track practice with a cup on, huh?" She chuckled, then took off.

I tore after her.

"I hear the girls got a nice little chuckle out of it."

Heat stormed through my cheeks. "Preach should have told me! He and I came out onto the field together. That jerk."

"Don't worry, you're not alone." Willow laughed. "You know what, though? Once I showed up to a competition; I was so nervous. It was before this snotty girl, Sasha, was on our training team and I was competing against her. Sasha had perfect hair, skin, body, everything. Well, let's just leave it as…I had a major wardrobe malfunction on the ice."

"Malfunction as in…" I glanced at her, and her cheeks were bright red.

"Yeah. A hook busted, and I showed a little more skin than I intended to." She shook her head and covered her face with her free hand. "I was so embarrassed I totally botched the routine, didn't even place."

"Shit," I said, coming to a stop.

"Yeah. So…wearing a cup to track practice…not a big deal." She grinned at me.

Her chest heaved, and she planted her hands on her hips. She wasn't much more than about five-foot-four, but she radiated determination and focus.

"I bet you kicked her ass the next time, though," I said.

"Duh." She rolled her eyes at me, then laughed. "So, where's this wicked-hard workout you were promising me?"

We grabbed our Hydros and made our way up to the bleachers. Standing before the first set of stairs, I nudged her. "Just follow me."

"Running bleachers? That's it?" she asked.

"Oh no. We're doing fast feet drills." I pointed at the stairs before us. "So, you are running bleachers, sure, but you have to touch each step with both feet. Move your arms as fast as you can, because your feet move with your arms."

"Both feet, huh?" She furrowed her brows, narrowing her eyes as she regarded the steps before us. I could almost picture her mind, analyzing what I'd just said, figuring it out, planning out how to do it. And do it well.

"Follow me…and keep up if you can." I jumped onto the first step and started hammering it up the steps, each foot tapping a step as lightly and quickly as I could.

Instantly, my heart ramped up about twenty extra beats per minute. The sound of the tips of my feet tapping the steel stairs echoed around us. The hot morning sun warmed me up enough that sweat started dribbling down my face.

I'd made it to the top before Willow had even reached the middle. "Come on, Ice Princess!"

She grunted, moving her arms even faster. Her feet followed. The front of her foot caught a step, but she recovered, stutter-stepping to compensate. That took talent and balance and coordination. I shouldn't be surprised.

I booked it across the top row of seats to the next set of stairs. I bolted down them, then across the bottom of the bleachers and took a breath. I threw her a glance, and she was on her way down. Dang, she was catching me.

Repeating the same pattern for the entire bleacher section, I stopped at the bottom. Leaning over, resting my hands on my knees, I looked up to see where she was. Only a row and a half behind me. She'd picked up the pace.

With a fluidity that defied logic, she lightly ran up the stairs, her arms gracefully moving. Sweat dripped along her arms, her neck, her face. Her cheeks were flushed and her eyes focused. She looked as graceful here as she did on the ice.

Damn, that's sexy.

I lifted the hem of my tank and wiped the sweat from my face as she started the last set of stairs. She jumped off that final step, arms up in the air. "Yes!"

I slapped her a high-five, and she leaned over, gasping for air.

"Holy shit."

"Tough, huh?"

"It's amazing." She stood tall, resting her hands on her hips as she heaved in air. "We're doing that again, right?"

"Even better, we're going to carioca up the stairs."

"Um. We're going to sing?" She crossed her eyes at me.

A laugh burst out of me before I could stop it. She was so damned cute.

"Laugh it up, chump." She shoved me, then took off running up the steps.

"Hey!" I hadn't shown her the new exercise.

Ah, hell. Who cared? I took off after her. It only took me two sets of stairs to catch her. I reached out to slap her butt because I was about to pass her but froze before doing it. *Holy shit.* Totally inappropriate. I did it to Preach all the time when I passed him on the ice or running bleachers, but with Willow…that'd be a jerk move. I wasn't so sure they did that on the figure skating circuit.

But now, I couldn't get how good her ass looked out of my mind.

I passed by her, focusing on the steps even more so I could get her out of my mind. At least out of my mind in that capacity.

"Damn, I almost beat you," Willow said as she finished up.

"You so didn't."

"Okay, I didn't. But you had to work hard to catch me!"

That I did. "If you say so," I joked.

"What's this carioca drill thing you're talking about?" She stood tall again, drawing in a deep breath.

At the base of the bleachers, I showed her, in slow motion, how to do the drill. "Feet shoulder-length apart. Take your right leg and cross the front, then cross the back, then cross the front." I repeated it a few more steps back to her under her sharp scrutiny.

"Crossover drill," she said as she rolled her eyes. "Oooh… that sounds *harrrd.*"

"That's what she said," I yelled, then took off.

CHAPTER FOURTEEN

Brodie

"You convinced her to try out!" Preach sprayed my skates with ice as he stopped beside me in the center of the ice rink and watched the group of tryouts gather at the other end of the rink.

"Yep. And with nine straight days of training, she's looking pretty good," I said while I rubbed my aching butt. "She's got me doing all sorts of fancy moves that she claims will help my balance and strength. I'm on my ass more than anything, though."

Willow stood a step or two outside the group of people trying out today. She was quite a bit smaller than most of them, but after having trained with her so much, I knew, now, that she was a lot tougher than she looked.

"Brodie Windom, Star Left Wing turned figure skater." Nathaniel tackled me around my waist and laid me out flat. The wind whooshed from my lungs, and I punched him in the stomach. We weren't wearing full pads, so that shit hurt.

He grunted and rolled off me, laughing.

I'd never live down the day they came onto the ice while Willow was showing me a few figure skating moves.

"A girl...trying out for *our* team? I thought you were just *training* her to get in her skating boots." Pax threw his head back and laughed as he coasted by me.

He was my friend, but he sure could be an ass sometimes. "Dickhead."

"Maybe Wind's got a thing for sequins?" Eric said as he passed by, catching up with Pax.

"She's awesome. What's your glitch?" Teddy shoved Pax.

"Josiah is our goalie." He checked Teddy back, but the big guy didn't budge.

"We'll be lucky if he's healthy for school tryouts in October." He pulled Pax's jersey over his head. "You don't just shake off a nasty MCL injury."

"Izan can do it until he's back." Pax flipped his jersey back and charged me.

What the hell? I wasn't the one who'd jersey'd him. I spun out of his reach and sidled up to Preach.

Pax was a junior, and one of the better defenders out there, but his attitude was pretty harsh. I got it a little bit; I mean, his homelife, specifically his dad, was a total mess. It was like Pax had a chip on his shoulder because his dad was a jerk, abusive asshole. He'd been pulled from the home a couple times but was recently placed back there last year.

Preach chuckled. "Izan couldn't make it past second string. He'll be a good backup to Willow."

"A former figure skater as our first-string goalie? The other club teams would never let us live that down." Pax's already almost black eyes darkened even more as he pointed off in the direction of the group Willow was standing in.

"You want to win, don't you?" I shoved him. "Then unless one of these newbies trying out today can beat her, she's in. She's the shit, Pax. Seriously."

"Yup," Nathaniel said. "Guy or girl, it shouldn't matter.

Talent's talent, *bro*."

Even though Fall League wasn't official high school hockey, we still drew the attention of college scouts. And pretty much anyone who made the club team made the school team.

But what mattered was that we had the best possible group of players. We'd almost nailed a perfect season last year; it'd get us noticed for sure if we did it back-to-back.

Coach Kurt stepped onto the ice near the team bench and explained the drills to the group of ten kids trying out for the team today. The guys who were on the Varsity team last year automatically landed a spot.

Willow remained a step away from the group as she listened. She watched everyone but kept most of her attention on Coach. She was focused. Intense.

Really intense.

"Goalies, do this fast-feet drill with your gear on. I want to see how you move in it." He clapped and blew a whistle. "Let's go."

Willow jumped to attention, then worked her mask on with her gloved hand as if she'd done it her whole life. She didn't miss a beat skating, either, even in her goalie gear.

My palms started to sweat.

She'd do great, right?

I didn't need to worry. No, definitely not.

Willow glided across the ice. She looked like she'd always been a hockey player.

Man, she was coordinated.

The line of rookies gathered near the far end of the rink for the next drill. Assistant Coach Paul, clipboard in hand, let the first few go toward us. We were supposed to rush them, see how they handled it, and try and trip them up.

Preach and Nathaniel had the first two, but the fledgling players both tripped on their own clumsy feet, sliding across the ice like the little kids at Mini Mite hockey practice.

Pax and I faced off with the next two. I spun around the first cone, throwing the smaller kid off balance, but he ducked and spun, staying on his skates.

That one had some talent. I hadn't seen him on the ice over the summer, though, must be a transfer.

The next two started off, and Willow was nearing the front of the line. Sweet. She was going to face-off with me.

"Don't go easy just 'cause you have a hard-on for her," Pax said from beside me.

"You're such a dick, man." I shoved him, then zeroed in on Willow.

The whistle blew, and Preach and Trevor took off toward the next victims. The eyes of Teddy's little brother about popped out from his head they got so wide. I could see it from here.

Yeah, that wasn't going to work out so well for him.

I inched up to our imaginary start line as I watched Willow at the other end of the rink. While the ones behind Willow shifted and danced around, she stood calmly, staring at the ice.

Through her mask, I could see her jaw was set and her eyes focused. But on what? I squinted, and it looked like she was staring at her stick. Then she knelt, and as she did, she removed her glove. With her bare hand, she palmed the ice. The guys behind her leaned to the side and glanced over her shoulder.

She didn't seem to notice. She just sat there and held her palm to the ice. Then she gripped the curve of the stick, closed her eyes, and drew in a deep breath.

What the heck was she doing?

Willow slipped her glove back on, then stood tall, and with one push she was at the start line with one other skater.

After a subtle glance at her surroundings, she simply bent her knees and stared at the first cone.

The whistle ripped through the noise, and Willow blasted into action, leaving Lucas in the dust.

I powered toward her. Scrapes of her stick hitting the ice, handling the puck, whispered through the air. A sound I loved.

She'd rounded the first cone with ease, again, leaving Lucas in the dust.

"Lay her flat, Wind. She's got no business being here," Pax said as he peeled off, aiming for Lucas.

He was pretty pissed that a girl was trying out, which was messed up enough. But to tell me to lay her flat? He needed to cut the crap, regardless if Willow made our team or not.

Willow focused on the puck again as she rounded another cone. Then it was open space.

My space.

I shifted to the left as she went right, knowing she'd have to push in my direction.

She was mine.

Leaning on her stick, she deked to the side, then spun, holding the puck close. I cut back, quick-stepped, and jumped into her line. I smacked her stick, then rammed my shoulder into hers.

She grunted but stayed upright as she jumped to her left, squatted as much as she could in her goalie gear, then pushed into a sprint.

Wow. That was a great move.

She was strong.

The small crowd that'd showed up to watch try-outs whooped.

She grimaced, favoring her right leg. But she shot up, still handling the puck. I spun, swiping at the puck, and her stick shot across the ice.

Ha. I had her.

A smile curved the right side of her mouth as she quick-stepped several times, kicking the puck like it was a soccer ball, and she ate up five more feet.

No way.

I went to slap the puck away, but she dug her blade into the ice, stopping herself—and the puck. I found myself on her right side, just as she went to kick the puck forward.

Swinging my stick, I caught the disc before it moved, then slapped it in the other direction. Her skates slipped out from beneath her, and she landed on her butt.

The crack of the stick hitting the ice resonated through the air, and I heard myself gasp. Damn, she'd landed hard. Even with pads, the ice still felt hard as granite.

She grunted as she slid a couple of feet, but then she hopped up and smiled at me like I'd seen so many times during our training sessions together.

"Nice try, Puck Head." And then she elbowed me. Preach burst out laughing as he skidded to a stop beside me.

Then, out of nowhere, Pax skated up and rammed into her, and in the next breath, she was back on her butt.

"Try getting up from that one, *Ice Princess*." Pax grunted, then skated toward the freshman tryout he was terrorizing.

"Nice one, Pax!" Eric yelled from behind me.

"Dick move, man," Teddy said, shaking his head as he chased after Pax.

"Willow!" I skidded beside her, fuming about what Pax had done. "Are you good?"

She let out a long breath as she flopped onto her back. And smiled.

She'd been laid out on her ass, and she was smiling?

Oh yeah. She'd do just fine on this team.

CHAPTER FIFTEEN

Willow

Two days of tryouts for a club team, and every muscle in my body screamed as I sat on the cold wooden locker room bench. I had a newfound respect for hockey players and what they endured.

Too bad that respect wasn't mutual. Even though I'd held my own during tryouts, Pax made it clear that he thought figure skaters were wimpy little girls prancing around the ice in sparkly dresses. I'd made it my personal mission to continue to prove him wrong.

I grabbed my phone from the bench beside me, ready to put it in my locker and head out, but I quickly opened a text to Ericka.

ME: Wish me luck!
ERICKA: You got this!
ERICKA: 💪
ME: I'll text you after.
ERICKA: Love you!
ME: Love you!

Warmth radiated through my chest. Ericka had my back. Besides my family, she was the only one who truly understood how badly I wanted to get back to figure skating at the same level I was when I got hurt. Talking to her always left me feeling hopeful.

Over the last twenty-four hours, I'd replayed every drill, every attempt on goal, and every blocked or missed shot over and over again in my mind. I'd held my own. The countless hours spent training with Brodie had paid off. But Izan, the other guy who tried out, had done well, too.

I needed this more. I had to spend as much time on the ice as humanly possible if I was ever going to get back to figure skating. I already felt stronger from my extra time, even if it was achieved in goalie gear.

I tossed my phone in my locker and slammed it shut.

I glanced up at the clock above the locker room entrance and forced myself to take a deep breath. *You've got this*, I chanted in my head on repeat as I made my way out to the rink.

My hands began to tremble. I cupped them in front of me as my blades carved into the fresh ice.

There had to be close to thirty people, if not more, already sitting in the stands. A bunch of little kids ran around the bleachers, too. Woodhaven only had seven thousand people; if this many of them came to *club tryouts*, how many came to the actual games?

A group of meticulously groomed girls sat in the bleachers right behind the team bench, fawning over the guys. I recognized one as Amanda Fert. She hung around the rink a lot. Jessa had told me that she was what the guys called a Puck Bunny, only hanging around to hook up with the stars. She was pretty with her blond hair, blue eyes, and tall, slender body, but to be nicknamed as a Puck Bunny, I didn't understand why Amanda would be okay with that. It was kind of an insult to female fans. I mean, sure, it meant that they were pretty, but it also meant that they practically worshipped the hockey players. Dating one was like the highest honor they could achieve.

Several guys were on the ice. Some passed a puck back and forth while others leaned against the boards. Everyone had dressed casually, no uniforms or pads necessary for the team announcement.

Coach's whistle cut through the air. "Head to the bench. It's time to announce the team."

The crowd cheered and stomped their feet on the bleachers.

I made my way to the team's bench as the rumble got louder. Most people would look small, standing in the middle of the rink, but not Coach Kurt; he was short but still bulky from years of playing defense on the ice. He lifted the microphone to his mouth and then motioned to his right, where we were all sitting.

"Over the past two days, we've had a great showing of talent. Thank you to everyone who tried out. I'll be announcing the forwards who made the team first, followed up by our team captain. He'll have the honor of announcing the defense."

As Coach began calling out the names of the players who'd made the team, the guys left the box and formed a line on the ice. With broad smiles, they waved to their family members and fans sitting to the left and right of the ice.

I swallowed the growing lump in my throat.

My hands were clammy. I wiped them on my pants and then brought them back to my lap.

"And our starting Left Winger, Brodie 'Wiiiiind' Windom." Coach sounded more like a WWE announcer than a hockey coach. Everyone went berserk.

"Brodie! Brodie! Brodie!" the crowd chanted.

A little girl with pigtails who showed up to every single

practice and pick-up game even threw a rose over the wall.

Memories of hundreds of flowers being thrown onto the ice after my last performance played in my mind like a movie on repeat. I'd won a gold medal.

The youngest girls in our program had taken to the ice, collecting the flowers, teddy bears, and other gifts people had graciously thrown after my nearly perfect performance. Cameras flashed as I waved to my fans and blew them kisses.

A sinking sensation filled my stomach, yanking me back to reality. *What if I don't make it?* I could practically hear the whispers around town. *Who was she kidding? Picking up a new sport at seventeen? She never had a chance.*

No. I could do this. I had to stay strong. Besides, this was a means to an end. And that end involved many gold medals at the Olympics…as a figure skater.

The microphone screeched, snapping me back to reality. Glancing to the right, my heart broke for the six guys sitting with their heads hung low.

"If you didn't make the team, don't give up. I urge you to continue to come to the pick-up games, work on your skills, and try out for the Woodhaven Wolverines Varsity and Junior Varsity teams in October. Remember, as The Rock says, 'Success is all about focus and effort. So keep at it.'"

Coach smiled and then turned his attention back toward the line of guys standing proudly behind him. "Let's give them a round of applause."

People in the bleachers stood and clapped. Several let out loud whistles, and some even held up signs with the player's names on them.

Eventually, Coach held his hand up, and the crowd quieted down. "Now, it's time to announce our team captain."

People in the stands stomped their feet on the bench, the noise ricocheting like thunder through the arena.

"Brodie Windom."

A proud smile spread across my face.

The girls in the front row with the perfect hair and makeup went wild. They literally leaped to their feet and screamed at the top of their lungs. Old guys in overalls and worn jeans pumped their fists into the air.

Brodie raised his hands, acknowledging the praise. Preach, who was standing to his right, patted him on the back. Teddy, who was to Brodie's left, put both hands on his shoulders and shook him back and forth. Brodie flashed the fans behind the team bench a smile that caused my stomach to flip flop.

I thought back to him stripping his shirt off in my basement. The way the sweat clung to his perfectly taut skin and cascaded down his washboard abs. *Ugh, why does he have to be so tempting?*

"Thanks, Coach. I'm excited to lead this team to victory," Brodie said as people in the stands started cheering again. "Now let's see who's going to help me."

Coach handed Brodie a clipboard, and my heart almost catapulted out of my mouth. This was it. My name would or wouldn't be called. It actually surprised me how nervous I was. And how much I wanted to make the team. Maybe it was Brodie's encouragement and excitement about it, but I did feel stronger. All the extra time on the ice and the strength and cardio training with Brodie had been awesome.

Not to mention the fact that I landed an axel that day I showed him how to do some spirals.

Take a deep breath, chill out. If only I could crouch down and touch the ice. My pre-routine ritual had always helped me center myself before performing, but I was seated on the team bench, so I couldn't just get up and touch the ice. Everyone would see and probably make fun of me.

Brodie tapped the microphone. "We've got a great defense this year; let's hear it for: Teddy Cook, Pax Hunt, Trevor Lee, and Eric Smith." Brodie shoved the clipboard beneath his arm and started clapping, a smile filling his face.

The goalie position was next. It was between Izan and me. We'd both done well in tryouts, but Brodie and Preach seemed convinced I was better. I hoped that I'd done enough to prove it over the past two days. I pulled my shoulders back and drew in a deep breath. I needed to stay strong, no matter the results.

I'd done it a million times as a figure skater. I could do it now. Nothing would get to me.

Brodie looked down at the sheet and grinned. My heart shot into my throat, and my hands got even sweatier. Did he see my name on that list? He glanced at Coach, who gave him a nod.

"As many of you know, our goalie, Josiah Brown, got hurt in a pick-up game this summer. Luckily," Brodie said with a smile, "we have someone to stand in until he recovers. Willow Covington—goalie."

Yes! My heart stopped for a beat, then drummed against my ribs. A rush of tingles danced along my arms as I clenched my fist and punched the air, jumping to my feet.

I'd done it. I'd freaking done it!

I hopped over the barrier onto the ice with a loud whoop, but instead of the crowd erupting into cheers, silence echoed through the arena.

My knees weakened, and I grabbed the edge of the plexiglass beside the team bench and gasped. Total and utter silence? Really?

My stomach hardened, and my chest tightened. Guess having the best talent on the team didn't mean much here in Woodhaven.

CHAPTER SIXTEEN

Brodie

'd never heard the arena so quiet, other than when it was just me in here.

Of course the crowd would be shocked. They hadn't seen how amazing Willow had done in tryouts. All they saw was a new person, taking Josiah's spot, and for those thinking Izan would get it…

Coach elbowed me. "Say her name again."

I gripped the mic harder. "Let's give it up for Willow Covington. The Falcons' new starting goalie!"

A few claps trickled through the air. I tucked the mic under my arm and started clapping, then slipped my pinkies in my mouth and let a whistle rip that ricocheted off the walls.

Willow released her hold on the wall and skated toward me. The shock I'd seen in her eyes when the crowd ghosted her pretty much kicked me in the stomach. It was the first time I'd seen hurt flash over her bright blue eyes, and I didn't like it. She'd earned this spot.

As she approached, she kept her eyes locked on me. She stood, her back straight and her shoulders broad. I nodded at her and offered her a smile that hopefully told her to be proud. To own this. She'd earned it.

I knew this was only Fall League, one of the first steps toward getting to and winning State, and she might not be with us the entire journey, but I was glad she was here now. This team was solid. We had a real chance at sweeping the season.

Preach let out a whistle and clapped as well. Teddy and Nathaniel followed suit.

She stopped in front of Coach, and he held out his fist for her to bump, as he had for all the other guys. "Welcome to the team, Willow."

Then she coasted in front of me, fist out.

I bumped that thing and said, "You did it, Toe Pick."

"We're going to kick ass." She laughed and made her way down the line, knocking fists with the other guys.

Pax stood stick straight and refused to look at her, keeping his hands fixed at his sides.

Son of a bitch. Pax did not just leave Willow hanging. Heat stormed through my chest as I glared in his direction. I fisted my free hand so tight my knuckles hurt. He and I were going to have words about this as soon as I found his ass in the locker room.

"Classy, Pax, real classy." Willow flipped one of her braids and turned to skate toward the far end of the line of players.

Another whistle resonated through the air, and then some clapping. I followed the sound directly to my little brother. Right there in the front row, standing up, he clapped and whistled like a wild man.

I whooped a couple more times, then handed the mic back to Coach Kurt.

"Thanks, everyone, for coming out to show your support for these awesome athletes. The first game is next Friday against Twin River, so be sure to come on out and cheer us on to a win."

He waved the team over to him. "Circle up."

I stayed where I was, since I was next to him. Willow was on the other side of the circle, and she leaned forward, eyes focused.

It was as if none of the stunned reaction from the crowd and Pax's abuse had rattled her. She was strong as ice.

And *damn* if that didn't make me respect her even more than I already did.

"Tomorrow, nine a.m., first practice. We've got a week until our first game, so it's two-a-days until then." He clapped. "Now, I know there are questions on how this works with having a female on the team for the first time ever, but it'll be fine. Willow, you'll have to hang with us a bit while we work through how this will work."

She nodded, not appearing upset or phased in the least about Coach saying that. Besides having a separate locker room and moving our pregame huddle out of the guy's locker room, I didn't think there would be much to change.

"She's just going to get hurt and leave us hanging," Pax muttered from somewhere behind me. His voice dripped with bitterness.

"One thing's for certain…" Coach looked at each of us, directly in the eye. "No fraternizing with your teammates. You all hear me? We don't need that kind of distraction or drama. Every person I picked earned their place on this team. Let *that* be the focus."

"And a perfect season!" Teddy yelled.

Pax grumbled and crossed his arms over his chest, glaring at the ice. Willow stood there, face unreadable.

"Go Falcons!" we all shouted, then Pax made a beeline for the locker rooms, followed closely behind by Eric.

"Great job, Toe Pick," I said as I zoomed by her.

I marched down the tunnel, the voices of my teammates

bouncing off the concrete surrounding us. The bright red door to the locker room was propped open, but I yanked that thing shut behind me, and the bang of it closing blasted through the air.

"Pax!" I yelled as he rounded the corner of the first row of lockers.

The echo of doors slamming shut hammered at my mind like a chisel. I darted past Nathaniel and Preach as they watched me with wide eyes.

"Dude," I said as I caught up to Pax. "What the hell, man?"

"We got chicks on our team now?" Pax slammed his locker shut. "We're a freaking joke. We'll be the laughingstock of the league."

"No way, man. This *chick* has more than proven herself." I looked him straight in the eye. "Just stay focused on the goal—she's going to help us win." I jammed my hands onto my hips. "But leaving her hanging out there? Not cool, Pax."

"Yeah, man, can't we all get along? We—"

"Fuck you, Nathaniel, and your stupid la-la let's all be happy Kumbaya crap." Pax jabbed my chest with his forefinger. "And you. Are you all up in her pretty sequined skating skirts? Is that why you're pushing her on us so much?"

I batted his hand away. I had over three inches on his five-foot-eleven height and about a solid fifteen pounds, so I'd put him in his place if I needed to.

I slammed my open palms into Pax's chest. The back of his knees hit the bench and buckled. He went to put his hand down to stop him from tipping over, but he wasn't fast enough.

Shit. I hadn't meant to push him so hard. He was still my friend, but I was pissed. I went to grab him, but his shoulder rammed into the bench, and his body bounced against the floor.

He kicked his feet and used the momentum to sit up. "What the hell, man?"

I loomed over him. "She's good. We need her."

"We do *not* need a prissy figure skater on this team!" he shouted as he rested his elbows on his knees, still sitting on the floor.

"She beat out Izan, Pax. Deal with it."

We'd trained a lot together these past ten or so days. She was laid-back and funny, and I was looking forward to hanging out even more. But I had to remember, it was temporary. She'd leave when she was strong enough to be on her team again. "Josiah will be fine by the time the school season starts."

Pax pushed himself up to sit on the bench. "Izan would have been fine until then."

"Willow's better than he is," Preach said from behind me. "And you know it."

"She's never even played hockey before," Pax stood up and yelled. "She's still tripping over her damn gear!"

Anger coiled in my stomach. "Less than Izan does. Get over yourself, Pax," I said. "You were even more of a dick to her than the crowd was."

I turned and walked by Preach, Nathaniel, and Landen, then flopped onto the wooden bench before my locker.

My knuckles popped as I squeezed my fists.

Preach sat down and leaned into me. "She did good out there."

"Sure did," I said, then glanced at him.

"Pax'll come around."

Heat crept up my neck as I let out a frustrated sigh.

"I'm not so sure." I opened my locker and pulled out my jacket.

"She's exactly what this team needs. Coach obviously saw how good she was, too."

"Brodie?" Caleb's tiny voice had me looking toward the locker room entrance.

There he stood, his scrawny four-foot-two body barely filling the doorframe. He held his backpack in his arms, and he looked at me with big, wide eyes.

"Hey, buddy." I waved him toward me. "You doing okay?"

"What's wrong?" he asked as he shuffled in my direction.

"Hey, kiddo." Preach held up his fist for Caleb to bump.

"Nothing's wrong. Sit down. I'm almost ready."

"Pax is mean." He plopped onto the bench and reached into his bag for his iPad.

Preach frowned. "He can be a real jerk."

"Sorry you saw that, buddy." I ruffled my little brother's hair, a twinge of guilt twisting my stomach. "You're right, Pax was mean. I was mad about how he treated Willow, but I shouldn't have pushed him like that."

"She's a *really* good goalie. And pretty." His eyes widened, and he nodded slightly as he spoke.

"She sure is." Preach gave a quiet chuckle, then coughed when I glared at him.

I'd noticed all too often how pretty Willow was. Training with her, seeing her in those sports bras and all sweaty…it was all I could do to not think of her.

The anger was still bubbling under the surface, but talking to Caleb helped ease it slightly.

Caleb smacked my arm lightly. "Can we go? I'm hungry."

"Burgers at Nikky's?" Preach said.

"Yes." Caleb hopped up and chased after Preach as he strode to the door.

I hustled after them, but Caleb pulled the door shut before I got to it, that little stinker.

He so had a monster wedgie in his near future.

I yanked the door open and bolted out. My shoulder met

something soft, and it squeaked. I stumbled to the side and reached for whoever I'd rammed into.

"Dude," Preach yelled as he lunged forward, arms out toward me.

"It's okay."

Wait, that was Willow's voice.

I looked down, and sure as shit, I was holding Willow Covington up by the shoulders. I'd totally stepped on her foot.

"Smooth on the ice, but a disaster behind the wheel and on land." Willow stared up at me, a slight smile curving the side of her mouth.

The scent of fresh ice swirled around me. It was like a perfume or something. And those big, blue eyes. The determination and perseverance shone through, even now, in this dimly lit hallway.

Willow was exactly the type of girl I needed in my life but definitely couldn't have.

CHAPTER SEVENTEEN

Willow

Ice sprayed across my face mask as I clenched my jaw. *Bring it!*

Matthew Halliday, Twin River's best player, skated toward me, handling the puck with an ease that only came after spending every waking moment on the ice. He played the same position as Brodie but didn't quite have the same record-breaking numbers Brodie had. *Focus, Willow. Stop thinking about Brodie.*

Thirteen days of intense practice and spending four hours a day together had made it tricky to stop thinking about him, though...

I willed myself to turn my thoughts back to Matthew, who was getting closer with every glide across the ice.

My heart thumped as he wound up. He had three seconds to make his shot before the buzzer sounded.

Stop the puck. Whatever you do, just stop the puck.

His stick glided across the ice and slapped the vulcanized rubber disk.

As the puck flew through the air, I pressed my knees together, ignoring the dull ache running down the back of my ankle, and dug my stick into the ice.

Thwack. Glove open, I grabbed the puck before it sailed over my shoulder.

My teammates pumped their fists in the air as I shrugged and cocked my head to the side. "Nice try, Matty."

His emerald green eyes flashed at me. "I can't believe they let a *figure* skater on the guys' hockey team. You're just going to end up ice kill!"

I flipped my mask off and spit my mouth guard out. My braids fell loose and swung against my shoulders. "Aw, are you threatened by little ol' me?"

"Threatened? I feel sorry for your team. They're so desperate they're allowing a delicate little *ice dancer* to be their goalie."

I slammed my stick onto the ice as adrenaline raced through my veins. "I stopped your puck just like I'm going to stop your lips from moving."

"Enough," a loud voice bellowed from the team bench.

I snapped my head to the right and froze. Coach Kurt stood on the team bench with his hands on his hips. He wasn't even five-foot-ten, but with his stocky build and low gravel-like voice, he rarely had to repeat himself and hardly ever yelled.

"This isn't a boxing match."

"Yes, sir," I said, slipping my mouth guard back in and tugging my goalie mask on.

I dropped the puck and passed it to Nathaniel, then shifted into the goal.

Too bad I turned too quickly and lost my balance.

I stabbed my skate into the ice and my stick to the side, and I stayed upright. *Damn pads.*

They weighed about five hundred pounds.

"Nice one, tutu girl," Pax's dad yelled out from the crowd. I shrugged off the insult and the minor padding malfunction, zeroing in on the puck. Nathaniel passed it to Brodie, and he immediately attacked the other team's goal.

Please make it. Please make it.

If we didn't, we'd be tied up, and that meant shootout time. I'd never done one.

My throat tightened, and my stomach flip-flopped as a bead of sweat trickled down my temple.

Preach got the puck. Stick back. *Slap!*

"Just wide," the announcer yelled.

We were out of time.

"You might have blocked my shot earlier, but there's no way I'm going to let that happen again."

I spun around, coming face-to-face with Matthew. "When I stop your puck for the *second* time today, I'm going to frame my stats sheet and mail it to you."

"Never going to happen, Covington."

Rolling my eyes, I made my way to the bench.

"You've got this, Willow." Brodie nudged my shoulder.

"I feel like I'm going to puke," I admitted under my breath.

Flakes of amber sparked in his dark eyes. "This is like any other competition. You've been in this situation hundreds of times. Take a deep breath and focus."

Coach Kurt motioned the team over.

"Willow, they're going to come at you from all angles," Coach said, holding up a small whiteboard with red arrows pointing at the goal. "Their first shooter will probably go for your left side, the second shooter, your five-hole, and the third shooter, he's a wildcard. But you already stopped one of his today, so you know what you're up against. That's only three shots to stop."

"You think you can stay upright for that?" Pax shouted.

"You just earned bleacher running for the next four days." Coach pointed at him.

Oh great. Pax already had it in for me and now he was running because of me…this wasn't going to end well.

"Let's send Twin River packing with a big L," Brodie yelled. "We got this."

We pumped our fists in the air and shouted, "Falcons!"

As the guys assembled in the center of the ice, I slipped off my catcher and knelt down. Pressing my bare palm to the ice, I closed my eyes and focused on the task at hand.

Stop every puck.

Stay calm.

You got this.

I gulped through the nerves and focused on the net as I rose. Our fan's cheers were met with thundering feet being stomped on the metal bleachers by the Twin River crowd. Turning my focus to the first opponent with the puck, all the sounds in the ice rink faded into white noise. Nothing but this game, this second, existed. I would prove I deserved to be here. I would not let this team down.

I blocked the first shot with my stick.

"Yes!" I punched my fist into the air.

Preach was up first for us and scored our first shot. We were off to a solid start.

"Nice one, Preach," Coach yelled from the bench. "Keep up the good work, Willow."

Using the blocker on my left hand, I swatted the next shot into the boards. Nathaniel was up for us. "Come on, Nathaniel! Get it in the back of the net."

He wound up, and the slap echoed through the arena.

It shot wide, and the crowd groaned.

"Good try, Nathaniel," Coach shouted. "Let's go, Willow!"

My mouth went dry as Matthew dropped the puck at the center of the rink. He locked eyes with me and winked. *"You're going down,"* he mouthed.

"Come on, Willow," I whispered. "You got this." I slapped my stick on the ice and bent my knees.

Matthew moved the puck back and forth, effortlessly.

I slammed my stick on the ice and chomped my mouth guard. *Here we go.*

Matthew brought back his stick and slapped the puck so hard, the sound echoed in my head. As it tore through the air, I raised my glove, but it was moving too fast.

I was going to miss it.

I pushed off, making my skate slip.

No!

Pure instinct took over, and I jetted my glove up, punching at that black disc. A sting reverberated through the leather, and the puck bounced against the ice.

I tried to fall on it, but my momentum left me sliding across the ice in the wrong direction.

Damn it!

Roars erupted from the Twin River fans.

Matthew skated up to the net and winked at me. "Framed stats, coming your way."

He grinned at me before heading back to his team on the centerline. But I didn't miss the flash of respect flowing through his eyes or the way his smirk shifted into a half smile.

I wanted to slam my fists into the ice, but now wasn't the time. The goal Matthew had scored on me meant that Brodie had to score on the other goalie or we'd walk away with our first club loss.

On the opposite side of the rink, Brodie pulled down his helmet and tapped his stick on the ice. The rink fell silent. He pressed off his left skate and then his right, handling the puck like a pro.

His stick practically a blur, he slapped the puck even harder than Matthew had. It whizzed through the air and straight past the other goalie. The guy didn't even get a hint of leather on that puck.

My teammates threw their sticks up and pumped their fists into the air.

My hands trembled from relief as I lifted my own stick. We'd won!

I'd almost blown it, but Brodie had secured the win thanks to his wicked slap shot.

The crowd fell into a frenzy.

I joined my teammates skating around the rink. A mixture of pure joy and disappointment swirled through my body. I'd not blocked Matthew's shot when I should have. Thankfully, Brodie covered my mistake, and we'd pulled off a win.

Jessa and Gramps were both on their feet. They had little pom-poms in their hands. I'd never seen Gramps look so proud.

It hit me right in the gut, too. He'd watched me skate plenty of times, but I'd never seen him so excited as I did right now. It sure felt good to be out here again, with cheering crowds, the energy of a big win.

If I were skating, under the heavy applause of the crowd, I'd take my victory lap, waving at people and collecting their roses.

God, I missed that.

An airhorn blared, yanking me back to reality. Chants of "Twin River sucks" echoed through the arena.

On the opposite side of the rink, Brodie picked up the puck and threw it into the stands. A little boy with red hair caught it and waved it above his head.

Totally in his element, Brodie grinned.

Coach made his way onto the rink and handed Brodie a puck painted maroon and silver. "Congrats, Brodie! You're our player of the game." As Brodie did a victory lap, Coach skated over to me. "Good game, Willow."

"I almost blew it by missing that shot, Coach." My lungs constricted, making it difficult to take a deep breath.

"Willow, you played well," he said. "And we came away with a win. Remember, hockey is a team sport. You have your entire team to rely on."

"Thanks." I knew he was right, but I was so used to being on the ice alone and having to execute every movement with perfection. It was ingrained in my DNA.

Preach patted me on the back as we made our way off the ice and toward the locker rooms. "Great job."

"Willow?" A girl with black braids approached me. She couldn't be more than twelve years old. "I...wow. I can't believe you're playing hockey. That is so cool."

"What's your name?" I asked, a wave of warmth flowing over my chest at the excitement in this girl's green eyes.

"Sarah. I'm a figure skater. I...you are such a great skater. How you took gold last year at Juniors Classic in Tucson." She let out a sigh. "I was there, you know. I handed you a white teddy bear."

The breath whooshed out of my lungs, and my eyes instantly stung. Last year, at Tucson...I'd torn my Achilles shortly after that. It'd been my last competition.

Sarah handed me a rose and smiled. "I hope you get back to it soon."

With shaking hands, I grabbed the flower, blinking back the tears burning my eyes. "Um. Thanks. I...hope so, too."

The girl hugged me, then hurried away.

Beaming, I practically floated back to the locker room, riding the wave of hope.

CHAPTER EIGHTEEN

Brodie

"Hey, it's the sequined goalie!" Eric pushed up from the couch where we'd been sitting, his drink sloshing over the rim of his glass.

I grabbed his cup and set it on the coffee table, then hopped to my feet. Willow ignored Eric's comment as she made her way in from the front door into the side hallway.

Nathaniel tackled Eric around the waist. Teddy joined in and tackled them both onto the couch, laughing and messing around. My cue to leave. I didn't have time for Eric's shit. He was getting as bad as Pax in harassing Willow for being on the team.

I cleared the two steps leading into the living room I'd been hanging out in, waiting for Willow to show up.

"Hey," I said, coming alongside her. "Thought maybe you wouldn't make it."

She shrugged, her long black hair a curtain over her shoulders. Usually, she wore it in braids, but now it was free. And it was pretty. Nice and shiny, and I caught a hint of coconut radiating from her.

"Didn't feel much like celebrating, you know?" She

stepped around me and headed toward the kitchen.

"Are you kidding me?" I followed her. "Your first game after having only been playing hockey a few weeks, and you blocked one of Matthew Halliday's shots."

She glanced over her shoulder, then veered into the kitchen. "Pepsi?"

She held up her hand and caught a can of soda without batting an eye. I leaned in and saw Landen sitting beside the fridge, giving out drinks. He nodded my direction, then held up a soda can, too. I shook him off, not wanting the caffeine right now, then followed Willow into the hallway, but it was away from the living room, which was fine by me.

"Some of the guys are frying fish outside. If you haven't eaten yet, you should totally get a plate. There's literally nothing better than fresh-caught lake perch."

She rubbed her stomach. "Fried fish does sound good. Maybe I'll try some in a bit."

As we walked down the hallway and farther away from the buzz of the party, my thoughts drifted to Pax. He was drunk and being more aggressive than ever with his smack talk about Willow almost losing the game for us. Normally, I'd cut someone like him out, but we had history. I needed to stand by him.

"Deke?" I asked as I hustled closer to her.

"What?" Willow whipped around, a smile filling her face. "You're seriously throwing a hockey vocab test at me? Now?"

"Gotta know this stuff." I shrugged and leaned against the wall in the narrow hallway.

"Yeah, yeah. So what's the big deal with this Twin River town? I don't remember such a big rivalry when I lived here."

"Yeah, back when you were eight?" I chuckled. "Twin River is way bigger than us. It's awesome when a small-town school beats the big ones. It's, like, total bragging rights."

"So beating Twin River is big, got it. That's why this place is packed." She nodded down the hall. "Preach's house sure is big."

It was, but right now, I was glad the fifty or so people here were confined to the living room area and there weren't many roaming around this end of the house.

Willow cracked open her soda, took a swig, then leaned back against the wall directly across from me. She wore a jean skirt, open-shouldered red shirt, and flip-flops. Her toned legs seemed like they went on for miles.

"Deke," I said again.

"That word's fake."

"It is not." I chuckled. "Come on. Deke."

She crossed her eyes at me.

I grinned. "A deceptive move or fake used to get around an opponent."

"Oh," she said, bonking her head back against the wall. "See, I'm never going to get this hockey thing."

"Sure you are. Give it a little time."

"I almost lost us the game, Brodie." She closed her eyes. "Shit."

"We won, Toe Pick," I said.

"What?" She leaned forward and cupped her ear.

I pushed off the wall and leaned toward her. Her bright blue eyes widened, and I palmed the wall right beside her head. Only about six inches separated us.

"We won, Toe Pick," I said, a little quieter since I was so close to her.

"Thanks to you," she whispered.

"Thanks to everyone on the team…including you."

She huffed and stood a little straighter, looking around. A swirl of coconut and citrus curled around me as I drew in her scent. It reminded me of the snack her gramps had brought down when we were training in her basement.

"Want me to get some orange slices to cheer you up?" I asked.

Her eyes darkened for a second, and her jaw tensed. Oh shit.

"I'm sorry. Dick of me to mention something your grandma used to do for you…"

"It's fine. Just stings a little. I'm…kinda missing her right now." She glanced to the side. "But Jessa tells me you know a little about that, huh?" she asked, her voice quiet.

What I appreciated was that she didn't have a pity stare when asking me. The awkward, *I'm not sure what to say* stance. I'd gotten sick of that over the last year and a half since my mom died.

"Yep. Mom." That was about all I got out before a lump formed in my throat.

"Sucks." Her gaze locked on mine.

Those blue eyes could see right through me. Right through my bullshit. The front I put on for everyone, except Preach, about how things were fine at home. About how scared I was Caleb would have another asthma attack and I wouldn't be there to help him. And about how freaked out I was that I might let my family legacy down by not getting on the Boston College hockey team.

Yet I didn't see any judgment in her gaze. It was like she really saw me as me. Not Brodie "Wind" Windom, son of the guy who owned half the town. Star hockey player.

Just me.

"Brodie," she whispered, her hand resting on my chest.

The warmth of her touch seeped through my shirt, sizzling everything inside me. I had no business standing this close to her. I'd sworn off drama. Coach said no fraternizing. And she was going to leave as soon as she got on a figure skating team. I didn't need that kind of heartache.

Yet I found myself stepping closer to her. To her warmth. "You're really pretty," I said.

"Hey, Brodie!" Preach's voice ripped through the hallway, and I pushed off the wall, instantly missing Willow's warmth.

Preach came around the corner and skidded to a stop. "Just the two I was looking for."

"What's up?" Willow straightened and took a sip of her soda.

"Air hockey!" He pumped his fist. "You two against me and Nathaniel."

"Be there in a second," I said, my heart drumming against my rib cage. I couldn't believe I'd told her she was pretty. What was I thinking? It was the honest truth, but still, I needed to back the hell away from the captivating Willow Covington.

Preach grinned and hustled away, yelling, "Nathaniel, get over here!"

I chuckled, then glanced back at Willow. "I got you something."

"What?"

I pulled the gift card out of my pocket. "Since I haven't been able to actually take you out for the coffee I owe you, I got you this."

"Coffee Cabin?" She held up the card.

"I owe you, remember?" I winked.

"Yeah, you do." She grinned and smacked my chest lightly, and I snatched her hand.

"There's that smile," I said. "I like that smile."

"Thanks, Brodie. For everything. All the training…" She held up the card. "I owe you lots."

"Americanos are my favorite." I tugged her hand gently to get her to follow me, then let it go. "Let's go kick some air hockey ass."

She followed me into Preach's four-season room. As usual, dog toys were scattered everywhere and clumps of fur mashed into a large cushion on the floor. His family had two great Danes. They were around somewhere, probably eating pizza or drinking soda out of someone's cup. The place was messy, but it was familiar. Like a second home.

"You're going down." Nathaniel stood tall and pointed at me as he bellowed. "Let's go!"

"You any good?" I asked as Willow and I went around the table to our side.

"Don't worry, I can hold my own. We had these and foosball tables at my training facility in Colorado. After my injury, if I wasn't rehabbing or at home with my host family, this was all I did in my spare time."

I laughed and pointed at Preach. "Oh, you guys are in so much trouble!"

Preach looked at me as if I'd sprouted a second head, but I just grinned.

"I'll take the left side," Willow said, setting up. She clearly knew what she was doing.

"Ladies first," Preach said, handing Willow the puck.

"Hah, Brodie can serve first," she said. "Best to let the weaker player start."

"Ohhhh." Nathaniel covered his mouth with one hand and then pointed at me with another. "Spitfire you got over there, Wind."

I hip-checked Willow, and she laughed, then I served it up.

As soon as the plastic disk hit the table, everyone else in the room faded away. The clapping and laughing morphed into white noise.

It was just me and the puck. Well, and Willow, defending the left side of the table.

She jumped right in and hammered the first two goals

past Preach and Nathaniel in back-to-back fashion.

Preach answered her last goal with a hit so hard, it bounced off the sides of the table four times before sliding into our goal.

"That's my boy." Nathaniel pointed at Preach, then nodded.

"Nice one, Toe Pick," I said, leaning into her. Tingles shot down my spine as my forearm brushed against hers.

"Totally your bad," she said, then stuck her tongue out at me.

The next point went on for an eternity before I finally slid one by Preach.

"Three to one," Teddy shouted from the front of the table. "The weak one scores!"

"Yeah, Puck Head," Willow said.

"Ice Princess." I jabbed her with an elbow, then looked up at Preach. "Are you going to serve it this century?"

He dropped the puck, and before I could even move my mallet, he shot the disc across the table. It sailed into the back of my goal with an audible click.

"Dang, Preach. All-star status over there," Willow said.

"Whose team are you on, Toe Pick?" I said, reaching for the disc.

I served up the puck so hard, it bounced off Nathaniel and Preach's side and rebounded directly into our goal.

"Damn it!"

"Own goal." Preach high-fived Nathaniel. "All tied up."

"Weak link." Willow laughed. "Just sayin'."

"Not only can she defend the goal, she can shut Brodie 'Wind' Windom up!" Nathaniel pointed at me.

I served up the puck, and we battled down to the wire.

"We only need one more score," Willow turned to me and said.

"We got this."

Preach dropped the puck, and it fired toward my side. I smacked it, and the thing zig-zagged across the table. Preach went to block it, but it blew by his paddle.

"Yes!" I tossed the paddle onto the table and scooped Willow up into my arms.

She curled her arm around my neck, then held up her free arm in victory. I hoisted her into my arms and raised my arm up as well.

"Damn it!" Nathaniel tossed his paddle and shoved Preach. "Dude. We choked."

"Yes. Yes, you did!" I yelled at Preach as Willow slid down my body.

The feel of her against me sent a shockwave straight down my spine. I dropped her and jumped back. Letting out a whoop, I gave her a high-five, hoping she couldn't tell what her body had done to mine.

Damn, this girl is dangerous.

CHAPTER NINETEEN

Willow

My worst nightmares had come true. I was back-to-school shopping instead of skating on an Olympic training team.

"Do you like this one?" Jessa frowned and bit her lip as she held up a flowery romper against her body.

At least I was hanging out with my best friend. It'd been a little over five weeks since I'd gotten cut by the skating team, and most of my so-called friends out in Colorado had dropped me like last year's skating costumes.

"It's cute." I nodded at Jessa. "You should get it."

Of all my skater friends, Aaliyah was the only one who texted me once in a while. No texts, calls, or even likes on my Instagram posts. Not that I posted many new pictures. I'd stuck to throwbacks of competitions or pictures of me and Jessa. No need to let anyone else know I was still struggling to recover from my injury.

School shoppers packed the store aisles. Moms trying to wrangle little kids and preteens rolling their eyes as they passed by clothing they deemed uncool. We had to drive almost an hour to get here.

Back in Colorado, there were loads of stores within a ten-minute radius. Not that it mattered. I couldn't afford to buy anything new anyways.

She flipped the hanger and held it against me. "I think it would look better on you. You should totally try it on."

"I'm good."

My phone vibrated, so I pulled it out of my back pocket.

UNKNOWN: Hey, it's Matthew from the Vikings.

"No freaking way." A streak of heat shot through my chest, and my cheeks instantly flamed hot as I showed Jessa my phone.

"Whoa!" Her gray eyes widened as she reached for my phone. "What is he doing texting you? Omygosh, he sent another."

UNKNOWN: Look. I'm sorry. I was a total jerk to you at the game.

"What do I do?" I all but squealed. I kind of wanted to block his ass, because he was a jerk. But here he was texting me? Apologizing? I wasn't sure what to think of that.

UNKNOWN: You're a good goalie. Do you forgive me?

I stared at the screen, my blood pumping through my body like a raging river.

ME: I don't tend to hold grudges.

UNKNOWN: Oh, good! I'll be in Woodhaven tomorrow. Wanna grab coffee?

"Dude. He just asked me out, I think," I said, showing Jessa.

My heart hammered in my chest, but whether it was from nerves or excitement, I wasn't sure.

"He sure did." Her voice cracked, and she jumped up and down. "Oh, wait. He's Twin River. You can't date him."

"I'm not going to date anyone, Twin River or Woodhaven."

She slouched. "You wanna get out of here that bad, huh?"

"No. No." I reached over the cart and rested my hand

on her shoulder. "It's not that. I just…I plan to get back to competing. I can't do that from here."

"Maybe you should just play hockey? Or…better yet, do both. Can you do that?"

I grinned. "You're so sweet. No. I can't. I…don't want to. I want to skate."

And I did. Sure, I was loving being part of a team, it was a different experience and actually it was pretty nice not having *everything* rest on my shoulders alone to do it all perfectly. But still.

UNKNOWN: Or not. I just thought maybe if you were up to it. I really am sorry.

ME: It's all good.

ME: Just shopping with Jessa.

UNKNOWN: Phew!

UNKNOWN: I thought you were ignoring me.

UNKNOWN: 😊

ME: Nope!

ME: Thanks for the invite, but I can't meet up with you tomorrow.

ME: I'm busy!

UNKNOWN: Next time.

My fingers started shaking as they hovered over the phone.

ME: Okay.

I slid the phone into my pocket again and faced Jessa. "That was weird."

"Matthew is cute, though." Jessa tossed the romper into her cart.

"Yeah." But not as cute as Brodie. *Dang it.* I did not just think that. "Back to us. This is *our* day. What's next?"

Jessa let go of the cart and yanked me into her arms.

"What was that for?" I asked, hugging her back.

"I'm just so excited to be going to the same school with

my bestie again!"

My stomach cramped at Jessa's excitement. While I was glad to be here with her, I was also struggling with the idea of not being out in Colorado, training for the Olympics.

"Preach told me that he and Wind are staying in town for their few days off from practice before school starts." Jessa grabbed a folded tank top and plopped it in the cart. "He asked if we wanted to hang this weekend."

I rolled my eyes, feigning disinterest. After that air hockey game at the party, specifically that wicked hot hug Brodie had given me…no. I needed to steer clear of him.

He ignited way too many warm, tingling feelings I didn't need to be dealing with right now.

"You want me to hang out with Wind outside of hockey practice? On purpose?"

"Come on," Jessa pleaded, pressing her hands together in front of her, like she was praying. "It's the last weekend before school, and you're not bogged down with hockey practice. We need to have some fun!"

It would be pretty fun seeing Brodie in a setting other than hockey or training. Though our training sessions were pretty hot. Literally and figuratively. That sweaty, sexy body of his—I shook my head, bringing myself back to the moment.

"Fine. Whatever you want to do, I'm in."

"Yes!" She scurried around the cart and gave me a hug.

My phone buzzed again, so I pulled it out.

BRODIE: Bar Down

I huffed, and Jessa looked at me. "Matthew texting you again?"

"No. Brodie. He's testing me with hockey vocabulary." I shook my head as a smile tugged at my lips. "He's such a dork."

BRODIE: Don't know it? You owe me coffee.

ME: I know it.

ME: Relax. I'm shopping.

BRODIE: ☺ Best not be googling it, Toe Pick.

ME: Bar down: when the puck goes in the net off the bottom of the crossbar.

BRODIE: Sauce.

ME: A pass that leaves the ice.

ME: To make it harder for someone to intercept.

"Yes! I so nailed that one."

Jessa laughed beside me and leaned over. "Dang, he really is quizzing you."

BRODIE: Nice. Have fun shopping.

BRODIE: I owe you coffee.

ME: Damn straight.

ME: 🏆

"Coffee, huh?" Jessa asked, her left eyebrow quirking up.

"If he stumps me, I owe him coffee. If I get them right, he owes me coffee." I smiled. "I think he really likes coffee."

"Oh, he definitely likes *something*." Jessa laughed.

"It's not like that, Jessa. He's uber-competitive and knows I can help the team win."

"Sure," she said with a wink.

"Hey, I'm curious." I pushed the cart to the side of the aisle. "How'd his mom pass away?"

"Terrible car accident almost two years ago. A drunk driver rammed into her, sent her over the edge into a lake."

"Oh my gosh." My stomach churned, and I clutched my chest. "She drowned?"

Jessa sagged against the cart and let out a sigh. "They say she died from the crash. It was bad. The driver is in jail for, like, ever."

"I can't believe it. That's really sad." My heart sank. I couldn't even begin to fathom losing my mom. Even though she hadn't been around much lately, I loved her with all of my heart. Losing her would be completely devastating.

"Don't tell him that I told you this, but he has a little brother who's sick. He's got terrible asthma that's always acting up. After they lost his mom, Wind took over taking care of him."

I frowned as we walked over to a new rack of dresses and halter tops. So he was captain of the hockey team, he had all of us to deal with, and on top of that, he had his brother and school to take care of. "What about his dad?"

"He's at work, like, twenty-four seven." Jessa shook her head. "Haven't seen much of him at anything since Brodie's mom died."

I never would have guessed Brodie had all that going on. How did he do it?

"Thanks for telling me." I let out a breath, still reeling from what I'd learned. "Um...you ready to head out?"

"Hey! Hey, that's her!" A little girl with fire-red pigtails tugged an older boy behind her in my direction. "Are you the goalie for the Falcons?"

"Um, yeah. I mean, yes, I am." This was so weird. Even when I was winning championships, it was rare that people recognized me off the ice.

"It's sooo cool that you made the team. You're the first girl ever to do that!" She clapped her hands together and jumped up and down, then glanced up at the skinny boy beside her. "This is my brother. He thinks you're awesome, too."

I took a deep breath as a massive smile crossed my face.

A bright shade of red colored his light-skinned cheeks as he shrugged. "I play goalie, too. Brodie coached me last year."

"That's awesome. He's a good coach," I said. "He's been helping me, too."

"One day, I want to be on the Falcons and beat Twin River just like you!" the little girl said. "I can't believe we're standing here with *the* Willow Covington!"

"Come on, dork, Mom's looking for us," the boy said as he dragged the girl away. "It was really cool meeting you."

"Great to meet the both of you, too."

I watched after them, frozen in place and totally out of breath. Talk about a rush. And that little girl. She was so cute.

"Would you look at that? I'm shopping with a hero." Jessa smiled and wiggled her eyebrows at me.

"Whew." I fanned my hot face. "That was…pretty cool."

"The town does love its hockey." Jessa chuckled as she guided us toward the checkout lanes.

The thought of Brodie losing his mom like he had jumped back into my thoughts. While I couldn't relate to losing a parent, I could relate to a parent working around the clock and being gone at a job out of town for months at a time.

Dad was gone from eight in the morning until eight at night, driving around and stocking stores in nearby counties with bread and other baked goods. Most weeks, he worked Monday through Saturday, only having the day off on Sunday.

But the thought of never seeing one of them again…it made my chest ache.

We pulled up to the line for one of the checkouts, and I reached down and rubbed the back of my heel. Per usual, it was sore.

"How is it?" Jessa asked.

"Not great." My Achilles tendon sure was angry about my most recent attempt at landing a Salchow.

"Don't worry, you'll get it back."

"Totally." A ping of doubt stabbed at my chest. What if I didn't? I was getting stronger and stronger every day, but what if…

No. I would be landing all my jumps by December and starting to send out some videos to coaches and hopefully nailing a tryout to get on a team. Level assessments were in January.

Figure skating was my future.

Nothing would *ever* change that.

CHAPTER TWENTY

Willow

MATTHEW: How's day one at WH going?
ME: WH?
ME: The White House?
MATTHEW: Woodhaven High
MATTHEW: 😂😂😂
ME: Oh, right!
ME: 😵
ME: It's going pretty well.
MATTHEW: I think you should transfer to Twin River...
MATTHEW: Just saying!
ME: Oh, do you?
MATTHEW: Then I could see you every day at school and hockey practice.

Matthew and I had been texting for the past couple of days. At first, he just seemed interested in apologizing for being such a jerk on the ice.

Then we transitioned to talking sports and life in general.

Things had turned flirty over the weekend. Well, at least on his end.

Most girls would be flattered to have Matthew Halliday

blowing up their text messages, but I couldn't ignore the sinking sensation in my gut.

He's not Brodie...

"Willow, over here." Preach waved from across the cafeteria.

He was sitting at a table near the back corner, close to a wall of windows overlooking a courtyard that some students were milling around in. Preach, Nathaniel, Teddy, and Brodie occupied four of the eight chairs surrounding the oval-shaped table.

I crossed the lunchroom on the outskirts of all the tables under the close scrutiny of some students. Being the new kid, even though I'd lived here before, totally sucked. I didn't know anyone but my teammates and Jessa, so I was thankful Preach waved me down, since my bestie wasn't here yet.

Preach tapped the chair beside him, so I sat next to him and flopped my reusable lunch box on the table before me. "Hey."

"How's the first day going, Darth?" Nathaniel asked.

"Darth?" I chuckled.

I pulled out an apple, an avocado sandwich, a baggie filled with pretzels, and a bottle of water.

Nathaniel sat up, his shaggy blond hair swooshing over his smooth, tanned forehead. "You're a figure skater who's crossed over to the dark side—hockey!"

"Weak," I said.

"You're an asshat." Teddy tossed a roll at him. "Oh, wait. Give that back. I'm starving!"

I chuckled as I unscrewed my water bottle, and I checked my phone for a message from Jessa.

ME: Where are you?

JESSA: On my way.

JESSA: See you in a min!

"How are the classes so far?" Brodie asked as he shook out his brown locks.

"English with Ms. Vang was good. Human biology seems tough."

"Who do you have for human bio? Mr. Todd or Mrs. Wilshire?" Teddy asked.

"Mrs. Wilshire." I popped a pretzel in my mouth.

"Oh, she's the best." He took a huge bite of a submarine sandwich.

I could feel Brodie's eyes on me, but I didn't look at him. It had been just under two weeks since our first game and that intense moment we'd shared in the hallway at Preach's party, where my body nearly combusted at Brodie's closeness.

That night flashed through my mind on repeat, especially the hug after the air hockey win. His cedar scent. His warmth. Part of me wished I'd just kissed him that night, but that would make everything complicated. First, we'd be breaking Coach Kurt's no fraternization rule and potentially introducing drama to the team, next it would destroy our friendship, and seeing as I only had a few people I considered friends in Woodhaven, I didn't want to blow that, and third, and most importantly, I'd be leaving soon. For the first time since I'd been kicked off the skating team, a flicker of hope had ignited in my chest. I could really make it back.

"You survived your first morning at Woodhaven High!" Jessa leaned over and wrapped her arm around me. After giving me a quick squeeze, she took a seat across the table next to Teddy.

"It's the first day of school, and I'm already getting asked to the homecoming dance!" Nathaniel flopped his phone onto the table and downed a carton of milk.

"It's two weeks away. You've got at least thirteen days to decide!" Teddy laughed and then pointed at Nathaniel, then

Preach. "Oh, but I got us a table at the restaurant."

"You guys start planning early," I said.

"Jessa, are we still going together?" Preach asked.

"Duh." She took a bite of a carrot and flipped her blond hair over her shoulder.

She'd told me that the two of them had an agreement. They'd always be each other's dance date, just as long as they weren't in a relationship with someone else.

"How you two aren't a couple still boggles my mind." Teddy laughed.

Preach and Jessa both scrunched up their noses.

"He's like my brother." Jessa dunked her carrot into a small Tupperware container of ranch dressing.

Preach nodded. "Yup, she's totally like my sister."

They fist-bumped each other from across the table and then laughed.

"Who are you going with, Willow?" Teddy grinned and wiggled his eyebrows.

"Well, I was going to ask you, but you know, Coach Kurt said no fraternization among the teammates."

Brodie, Preach, and Nathaniel burst out laughing. I tried to keep a straight face, but I didn't last long.

Even though I'd only known Teddy for a few weeks, it was obvious that he had it bad for a girl named Layla. She had been at the party, and they'd spent most of the night flirting. When we were on the ice, he talked about her constantly, but he still hadn't worked up the guts to ask her out yet.

"But for real, when are you asking Layla out?" I tossed a pretzel at Teddy.

He snagged it off his tray and ate it. "If we're going to play this game, you tell me who you're going to homecoming with, Willow."

"I might have an option." My cheeks burned. The one

person I wanted to go with wasn't an option. Part of me wanted to go with Jessa, but she and Preach had an agreement. Being a third wheel, even if it was just with two friends wasn't an option, either. Plus...Matthew had dropped a few hints that he'd be interested in coming to our homecoming; I just hadn't asked him yet.

"Options?" Brodie chimed in.

Nathaniel frowned. "Yeah, what do you mean by that?"

Jessa inhaled sharply and shot me a panicked look, nearly dropping her water bottle in the process. I'd told her about Matthew but swore her to secrecy. I didn't want the guys giving me a hard time, since Matthew was from Twin River. I wasn't even sure I was going to ask him yet.

"Nothing, it's no big deal." I waved them off.

Teddy got up and walked around the table, his brown eyes laser-focused on me.

"What are you doing?" I asked, sliding my legs around the seat.

"Teammates don't keep secrets." Teddy lunged for me, fingers splayed, ready to tickle me, but I jumped out of my seat and sprinted out of his reach.

He chased me around. "Spill it, Willow!"

I'd just done my third lap when Nathaniel's arm shot out and stopped me. "If one of our teammates has a boyfriend, he has to meet our approval!"

"Oh, and does that mean I get to approve of all your girlfriends, too?" I asked with an exaggerated eye roll. I struggled against Nathaniel's grip, which was light and playful but still held firm, then looked at Brodie. "A little help here?"

Brodie shrugged, a half smile filling his face, but I did notice he didn't seem as into this as the rest of the guys. His eyebrows were furrowed, and he was slouched over.

"What's it going to be, Willow?" Nathaniel still held me fast.

"Matthew! Matthew Halliday," I blurted out.

Literally everyone at the table gasped.

"From Twin River?" Nathaniel's jaw dropped. "You can't be serious. They're one of our biggest rivals!"

Brodie flinched but remained silent.

"I haven't officially asked him or anything yet."

The atmosphere had transformed from a lighthearted exchange to something much more serious.

"When did you two even start talking?" Nathaniel shook his head. "He was a huge ass to you during the game."

"Listen, I don't need a whole team of older brothers watching out for me." I put my hands on my hips. "I can take care of myself."

"Hey, I gotta head to class. See you all later." Brodie got up from the table, balancing his tray in one hand as he slipped his backpack straps over his shoulders.

Tightness spread across my chest. Did he dislike Matthew that much? Or was he mad I might go with someone who wasn't him? It wasn't like we could go together or anything, if he even wanted to.

But something was up, because I could still feel the tension that was rippling off him.

"I have to bolt, too." I threw my food back into my lunchbox and headed in the opposite direction.

This is not how I pictured my first day going...

I pulled out my phone once I'd found a little alcove with a bench.

The hall was all but deserted.

ME: You there?

ERICKA: In Ancient Civ.

ERICKA: What's up?

ERICKA: How's your first day?

ME: Things aren't going so great…

ERICKA: Do you need me to come and kick someone's ass?

ME: No…

ERICKA: Well, what's up?

ME: My teammates, well, one in particular, is pissed. They don't want me to bring this Matthew guy to Homecoming.

ERICKA: Why would they care who you go to the dance with?

ME: Well, he may or may not be the star player on our school's biggest rival team.

ERICKA: Willow!

ME: Would it help if I said he was really cute?

ERICKA: Maybe…

ERICKA: But even the hottest guy isn't worth ripping a team apart, right?

Damn, talk about a loaded question.

Sure, Matthew wasn't worth ripping our team apart, but what about Brodie?

I shook my head and chased the memories of Brodie's disappointed look away.

ERICKA: What are you going to do?

ME: Honestly, I have no clue.

CHAPTER TWENTY-ONE

Brodie

"**D**amn shame letting that girl on the team." Pax's dad, Frank, gripped my shoulder and stared down at me from beneath bushy gray eyebrows. Cigar smoke curled around me, making me cough. "Coach had no business doing that. You better keep them focused, Wind. No distractions, you hear? State, boy, we need another State win."

"Come on, Frank, the team is holding a perfect season with her in that goal," Mr. Wright, the town barber, said from the front row of the bleacher.

Pax's dad laughed, sending a nauseating cigar stench over me, strong as a tidal wave. There was a hint of liquor, too. I stepped back and turned my head slightly.

He grumbled, then made his way up the three stairs I'd just come down.

"Yo, Wind. Good job last night," someone from the crowd yelled.

I held up my hand and kept walking. Talk about living in a fishbowl. Sure, it was pretty cool knowing people everywhere, but yet not. It got old sometimes. And poor Caleb, he got pressure, too, and because of his health…

No. I wasn't going to go there. Tonight was about fun. Relaxing. We hadn't had practice today, so I got to hang with my little bro earlier. He was tucked safe and sound at Mrs. Armstrong's side for the game and then sleeping overnight at their house, too.

So it was time to turn off the worry and enjoy the game, because Mr. Wright was right. Willow had been a huge part in the fact that we were sporting six wins and zero losses.

The last two weeks had been great with stellar practices and three more wins. The team was clicking. Everyone except Pax and Eric had pretty much accepted Willow. She'd proven herself beyond measure—even our backup goalie, Izan, had commented a few times that she was the right choice.

Josiah was progressing and should be able to try out for the high school team in a few weeks. It might be interesting to see who made the starting position between him and Willow, if she was still around.

During a morning ice session last week, she'd landed what appeared to be a pretty big jump. She hadn't said much about it, but I could tell she was excited. It looked like she was moving ahead on her plan to get on a skating team again, and I just needed to deal with that.

She wasn't a hockey player. She wouldn't be on our team for much longer.

I stepped into the concession line and hugged my coat closer to me. It was cold tonight, and I'd totally not worn enough clothes.

Didn't matter. Tonight was a night for relaxing. The homecoming football game against Quails Hollow. They'd beaten us last year, so this was a big game. Needed this win.

"Ever try M&M's on popcorn?" someone behind me asked.

I turned to find Willow standing there, a smirk lifting the side of her mouth. No braids this time. Her long black hair curled in silky ribbons around her neck.

And those eyes.

Out from behind the goalie mask and beneath the stadium lights…the blue really popped, almost like it was on fire. Two weeks ago, at the first day of school, she'd announced she might go to the HOCO dance with Matthew Halliday, and I hadn't been able to get it out of my mind. I tried to tell myself it was because Matthew was from our rival school, but I knew it was more than that.

I was thinking about her as *more* than a teammate a little too much lately. The talent, the beauty, that exchange we had last month at the party, and that hug after air hockey—

"Fine, so you don't like M&M's. I was just sayin'—"

"No. Um…" I couldn't think with her staring up at me with those huge eyes. "What?"

"Graceful on the ice, but not so much with the words." She chuckled, and a soft pink dusted her cheeks.

"Graceful enough to score on you in practice the other day." I stepped closer to the concession window, thankful for the distraction that tore me away from her gaze. "Again."

She huffed as she shook her head. The long strands of hair shifted in a subtle breeze and brushed across her face. Before I could even think, I tucked the wild strands behind her ear.

She froze.

I yanked my hand back and whipped around again, heat steaming my cheeks and heart hammering like I'd spent the last hour running sprints. It did that a lot around her. Especially when the team was doing dry-land exercises and she was in only a sports bra and tight leggings.

I really needed to get whatever was going on with me under control.

I focused on the back of the head of the person in front of me. Only three more people until I could put in my order and bolt. Maybe I should just go now. I didn't need popcorn. I could come back after she was gone.

"What's wrong?" Willow asked. "You're acting all weird."

Wait, she was next to me now?

She was standing beside me, facing forward, but I could tell she was smiling by the way her cheek bulged. "You ticked off that I blocked your goal during our intersquad scrimmage yesterday?"

"The crease, what is it?" I asked to change the subject. I needed to make this about hockey. About the team. Anything other than how pretty Willow looked right now.

"Vocab test? Really?" She grinned as she shook her head.

"So you don't know it, then?" I nudged her.

"Four-by-eight-foot area in front of each goal in which opposing players may not stand unless they have the puck." She jutted out her chin in triumph. "Deke—defensive move or fake used to get around an opponent." And then she stuck out her tongue.

"Nice." I chuckled. It was the cutest thing when she did that.

"It's called studying."

"Too bad it doesn't help you guard your five-hole better."

"Puck Head."

"Ice Princess." Yes, bantering was much better. Safer. I could hide behind it, make it about hockey, 100 percent hockey.

Only one more person in front of me. At first I was happy, wanting to get out of here, but now that we were talking... And she smelled so good. She seriously gave off a scent of fresh ice. How was that even possible?

"For real, though, you should try M&M's in your popcorn. It's the best cheat treat ever."

"Cheat treat?"

"Um, yeah, we—when I was figure skating, with strict diets and stuff. We got cheat treats. That was mine."

I chanced a look at her and caught her scanning me from head to toe. Why the hell did that rev my engine so high?

"You're not really taking Matthew to our dance tomorrow, are you?" That came out of nowhere.

"I'm not sure that's any of your business." She huffed.

"But you can't…" My heart pounded so hard, it echoed through my head. I knew I had no right to say anything about the situation, but I couldn't stop. Matthew wasn't good enough for her. He was an asshat major. "He's…from Twin River High."

"Our rival, I know." She rolled her eyes.

"Not only that. He's a total dick."

"He's actually not. We've been talking a little…"

She curled some loose strands behind her ear as she mumbled something I couldn't understand.

"What was that?"

"Damn hair." She yanked out a pink stocking cap from her coat pocket and pulled it over her hair. "Why do I even bother?"

"Don't." I gently pulled it off. "It—your hair—it's really nice."

Her eyes locked on mine. They were wide and…was that longing? Maybe even searching, like she doubted what I'd said. Maybe I was searching for the hidden meaning or something.

What did I mean by saying that? I—well—*damn it*. She was hot, but I had no business noticing that. Okay, I could notice it, but what surprised me was how much I wanted to bend down and kiss those full lips. And smell her hair up close.

"Um…I—" I started.

"Next," someone shouted, and I whipped around.

Saved by the popcorn dude.

I spit out my order, including a bag of M&M's for my popcorn like she'd suggested, and rushed to the side for the pick-up. Hopefully, I'd get my grub before she was done ordering. I had to get out of here. Being near her melted my brain.

I sure didn't need my jacket anymore. I unzipped it and let it hang open to get some cool air up in there. It was not good what she was doing to my body. No one had ever affected me like this.

A brace-faced kid from behind the stand set my popcorn on the counter and said, "Hey, Wind. You gonna take us to State this year?"

"Gonna try." I grabbed my stuff and hustled away.

Willow hadn't made it to me yet, so maybe I could disappear without running into her again. Forget that whole intriguing and really awkward interaction I'd just had with her.

Shoving the bottle of soda in my back pocket, I dropped the M&M's in my coat pocket and zipped around the corner of the concession stand. It was darker here in the shadows, and I needed to calm the heck down.

I leaned against the brick and drew in a deep breath. The cool, popcorn-scented air filled my lungs, and I held it in there. Slowly letting it out, I opened my eyes.

"You okay?"

I shot straight at the sight of Willow standing in front of me. In one hand, she held a bag of popcorn and in the other a bag of M&M's.

"Cause you look like you just let me block one of your slap shots."

I coughed into my hand. "No. Um. I'm fine."

She eyed me as if she didn't believe a word I'd said, and she might have been right not to, because I wasn't all right. Stalking her on IG, talking to her, and what was with the touching her hair like that?

"There's something different about you," she said.

I went to step back, but I couldn't, since I was up against the concession stand wall. "Um, what?"

She brought the bag of popcorn to her face, then snagged a kernel with her tongue.

With. Her. Tongue.

Her freaking tongue.

"Nervous or something? It's not like anyone cares about this game, since it's not hockey, so what are you getting all worked up about?"

We were pretty hidden in the shadow of the concession stand, but still. I shouldn't be seen with her like this. Not off the rink. Just me and her. It would be nice, but it couldn't happen.

Coach would rip my captain's badge off if he thought we were messing around.

Her eyes locked on mine, and she stopped mid-chew. All noises around me vanished; it felt like a blanket of quiet draped over us. Like when I was alone on the rink, breathing in the cold air, listening to nothing. Quiet. Comfortable.

She was like the ice. Calming.

She was a solid goalie and all girl with her long hair flowing in the slight breeze, plus she was wearing a hint of makeup.

And that smell.

Her tongue jetted out again, but not to snag a kernel of popcorn this time. She licked her lips. Her nostrils flared, and she drew in a deep breath.

She eased toward me another step. As if she drew me in with her gaze, I leaned forward. That's when I zeroed in on her lips. They were shining now, the distant lights playing off them. I bet they were salty from the popcorn.

Screw it. I *had* to find out.

Easing forward, I cut the distance between us in half. Only six inches from changing everything.

Six inches from tasting the popcorn salt dusting her lips.

Six inches from opening a big can of problems.

Oh, but I wanted to kiss her. Big time.

I stopped. Her gaze shifted down a fraction, and she let out a slow breath as her eyelids hung heavy. I needed to step away now. Right. This. Second. We couldn't do this.

A blaring goal horn sliced through the moment like an ice bucket of water. Willow cursed and jumped back, her popcorn falling out of her hand and onto the ground.

The horn screeched again, and she dug into her back pocket.

Saved by the ringtone. My hammering heart didn't calm down and neither did my temperature, though.

"Hey, Matthew," Willow said into her phone.

Now my temperature was ice-cold.

Halliday was not calling her right now. This was not happening.

"Oh, I can't. I'm…at the game with Jessa." She showed me her back and leaned forward slightly. I couldn't hear her anymore, but that didn't calm me down at all.

"Sorry about that," Willow said as she hung up and turned around. "Dang it. I was craving popcorn!"

"That was Matthew, wasn't it?"

She nodded and glanced around.

"Don't go to the dance with him. He's a jerk. Maybe… we—I mean—the hockey team. Some of the guys are going." I took in a deep breath. "You just can't go with Matthew."

"Oh, I can't, can I?" She jetted out her hip and jammed her fist on it.

"Shouldn't. Er." Shit. This was all coming out wrong.

If I could ask her to the dance, I would. But maybe as a group we could go. That might be okay.

"Look. You don't get to tell me who I can or can't see." Her jaw ticked, and her nostrils flared. "I'm a strong, independent woman. I can decide what I want to do without you weighing in, Brodie!"

And with that, she stomped away.

Damn it. So much for me avoiding drama.

CHAPTER TWENTY-TWO

Willow

"**M**atthew won't be able to keep his eyes off you tonight."

"Thanks, Jessa." I spun around and smoothed out the fitted black dress. For a moment, I felt like I was back on the ice. Flutters in my stomach. Hands, slightly trembling. Getting ready to perform. Everyone's eyes on me, anticipating my new routine.

What I didn't admit was that I didn't care if Matthew liked it or not. The only guy I was hoping to impress was completely off-limits.

I was still upset with myself for that moment Brodie and I shared at the game last night. To risk losing my starting spot on the team by breaking one of Coach's cardinal rules was *not* worth it.

"Hey, Jess, will you take a picture of me in my dress so I can send it to Ericka?" I held up my phone.

"Sure!" She hopped up and aimed the phone. "How's she doing?"

"Good." My chest tightened.

"You miss her, don't you?" Jessa clicked the photo and

handed my phone back to me, a slight smile on her face, though it looked tinged with a little bit of sadness.

"Yeah, I really do. Her family was the best host. Ericka and I pretty much consider each other sisters at this point." I quickly sent off the picture, then tossed my phone onto the bed and faced the mirror again, meeting Jessa's eye. "It's still great to be back here with you, though. I'm excited for tonight. My first dance at Woodhaven!"

"I can't believe you're taking Matthew." Jessa grabbed her curling iron and wrapped a long piece of blond hair around it. "That takes some guts."

"He's actually really nice. I figure why not?" Brodie never once said he wanted to take me to the dance. All he did was harp on me about Matthew—and I certainly wasn't going to let him tell me what to do.

My phone dinged, and I picked it up from the bed.

MATTHEW: Can't wait to see you tonight.

MATTHEW: 😊

Jessa glanced over my shoulder. "Ahhh. Speak of the devil." She snatched my phone out of my hands. "Say cheese."

I reached out and tried to grab it back, but it was too late. Jessa had hopped onto her bed and out of reach. "Jess…"

She scrolled down as I jumped on the bed and tried to get my phone back.

"Ooh. A picture of him lifting weights." She pretended to fan herself.

I managed to grab my cell and plop down on the edge of her bed.

"You know that I'm all for you going to the dance with him, but…" Jessa sat next to me.

"But what?"

She shrugged. "He does play for Twin River. They're our biggest rivals. Won't that, ah, make it difficult?"

"Difficult?" I scrunched my nose.

"Yeah, you know, if you two start dating?"

"Not sure what the big deal is." I stood. "And hey, at least I won't lose my spot on the team."

Jessa opened her mouth but shut it before saying anything.

"You know I'm right. Plus, breaking things off with Matthew when I leave will be easy. A teammate, not so much." My heart twinged at the thought of leaving. And of not seeing Brodie again. It kind of took me by surprise, too—leaving hockey and a guy I wasn't even dating should be pretty easy. Skating was what I loved. What I wanted to do.

"Anyway," I said, changing the subject, "when did Teddy and Layla hook up?"

"Those two have been dancing around each other for years." Jessa headed over to the full-length mirror and applied another layer of mascara. "Are you excited about dinner? His dad owns the restaurant. He always hooks us up with tons of food when we eat there."

My black hair swung over my shoulders. Loose curls fell halfway down my back. I thought about Brodie tucking a lock behind my ear last night, making my stomach clench. His touch had set fireworks off in my system. *No. Stop thinking about him. Nothing can happen.*

Jessa adjusted her dress one more time before stepping back from the full-length mirror propped up in the corner of her room. "What do you think?" She turned in a full circle, her maroon dress flaring out from the waist.

"Beautiful. I'm glad you went with the halter top. It looks great."

She smiled and grabbed a small black clutch. "Thank you."

A second later, the doorbell rang.

Jessa grinned. "They're here."

She dashed out of her room and down the stairs. By the

time I'd caught up, her mother had already let Preach in. He stood in the entryway, wearing a sleek black tux with a fitted white shirt. In his hands, he held a maroon and silver corsage.

"Picture time." Jessa's mom held up her cell phone as Preach slipped the flowers over her wrist. Jessa grabbed a matching boutonniere from the small table beside the door.

Her dad came around the corner and smiled. "Aw. Look at my little girl."

"Dad." Jessa rolled her eyes, but she returned the smile.

The doorbell rang for a second time.

Jessa swung it open and grinned. "Hey, Matthew."

Matthew looked good in his hockey gear, but in a dark gray tux, I had to admit he was downright hot. His blond hair was short at the sides and longer at the top. Gel held it perfectly in place. His striking emerald eyes sparkled as he caught my gaze.

I inhaled deeply. *Maybe I can get over Brodie...*

"You look awesome, Willow."

"Thank you."

We swapped corsages and boutonnieres and took a few more pictures.

"We better get going, guys." Jessa kissed her dad on the cheek and hugged her mom. "Willow and I will be back by one."

"Be safe, and if you need anything, just call or text."

"Thanks, Dad." Jessa grinned and linked arms with me.

We headed into the chilly air. Luckily, Jessa and I had matching wraps.

"Here, let me help you with that." Matthew placed the material over my shoulders.

"Meet you at Taste of Rome?" Preach asked me and Matthew.

"Sounds good."

He helped me with the passenger side door to his black Ford SUV. The inside was immaculate, and it smelled like AXE body spray. Matthew might have been a little heavy-handed with the cologne, but maybe he was nervous.

A few moments later, he slipped into the driver's side and started up the engine.

"I'm really glad you asked me to the dance," he said.

I pulled my shawl around the seat belt. "Me, too."

"Preach seems really cool. I've played against him for years but never hung out. You know how seriously this town takes rivals." The corner of his mouth curved into a smile.

"Tell me about it. Some of the people who live here act like I'm committing treason by going to this dance with you."

Matthew scrunched up his face. "Screw 'em."

"Right? To make it worse, there's a few people who are pissed that I'm on the guys' team." I hadn't planned on opening up to Matthew, but it felt good. Like a weight being lifted from my chest. "It's only a handful from Woodhaven and a couple teammates who are super obvious about it, but seriously, why are they so fixated on the fact that I'm a former figure skater or, worse, that I'm girl? Why not worry about having the best players on their team? It seems like people are focused on the wrong things. You know?"

"Like I did. Which, for the hundredth time, I'm so sorry. I honestly can't believe I treated you like garbage on the ice the first time we met." Matthew kept his focus on the road, but he shook his head as he spoke. "The ones who are still giving you crap, they sound like a bunch of self-conscious douchebags."

"You're not wrong."

We both laughed.

A few minutes later, we pulled into the parking lot of Taste of Rome. Matthew, being the perfect gentleman, opened my car door and helped me out. Brodie was wrong about him being a jerk.

Preach and Jessa had caught up with us by the time we reached the door.

"Hey, guys. Over here." Teddy waved from a large table. Layla sat next to him in a beautiful navy dress.

After a few introductions, we all sat down. Glancing to my right, I noticed some empty seats. "Isn't it just the six of us?"

"Preach, Teddy, what up?" a familiar voice rang out.

Spinning around, my jaw dropped as I laid eyes on *him*. Brodie walked over to the table with Pax and Nathaniel flanking him.

I pulled my wrap around me tighter.

"Thanks for saving us a spot. We—" Brodie's mouth snapped shut as his gaze landed on Matthew. "What the hell are you doing here?"

Matthew grinned and nodded toward me. "I'm Willow's date."

He looked at me and then at Matthew again.

Brodie pulled out the chair next to me, and Pax and Nathaniel sat across the table. I could practically feel the tension settle over the group like a wet blanket.

"I'm Jared, and I'll be your waiter today. What can I get started for all of you?"

As soon as everyone rattled off their orders, Brodie dug into Matthew.

"So, Matt, how's the fourth-place team in the league doing?" Brodie elbowed Pax, who gave a nod of support.

"Oh, you know, wishing we had a goalie as good as Willow." He winked at me.

That response shut Brodie up for at least ten minutes.

The rest of dinner went slightly better. Preach, Matthew, and Teddy talked about an outdoor rink they played hockey at in the winter. Pax made childish jokes from time to time, but he also was incredibly focused on his soda. He'd slipped it below the table at least three times. *Is he getting drunk?*

Brodie sat back and listened, but he didn't add much to the conversation. Instead, I could feel his eyes on me. Sneaking glances when everyone else was talking.

Has Brodie been thinking about me like I've been thinking about him?

Because no matter how much it was against the rules, I couldn't stop fixating on him.

M usic blared overhead. Preach and Jessa swayed to the beat next to Matthew and me. Besides the awkwardness at dinner, the rest of the night had been perfect. Two juniors I hadn't recognized won Homecoming King and Queen. Teddy and Layla had been super nice and invited me and Matthew to a party at Layla's lake house after the dance.

"Woodhaven High, we've got one last song for the night." The DJ's voice rang through the gymnasium. "Grab your sweetie and let's end this dance right."

Matthew took my hand and spun me around before pulling me close. I fell into the moment as we swayed to the beat of one of Frank Ocean's slow songs.

Brodie and Pax hovered near the outskirts of the gym. Pax kept slipping a flask out of his pocket and taking sips—he wasn't even being discreet anymore.

I was about to turn away when Brodie caught my gaze. His stare actually made me flinch. I was here with a nice guy; I should be focusing on him. And besides, it was only one date. I wasn't going to marry him or anything. I wasn't sure I wanted to start dating anyone seriously, considering my plans to get back on a skating team.

The song ended a few minutes later, and Matthew took my hand. "Are you still up for Layla's party?"

My phone buzzed in my clutch. As I fished it out, a text from Gramps flashed across the screen, and only two words registered with me.

Ericka and *ambulance*.

CHAPTER TWENTY-THREE

Brodie

"You can't honestly be into that Vikings douchebag." I stomped into the deserted hallway right outside the gym. Willow had just hurried away from Matthew, her phone pressed to her ear, but the dickhead Matthew was, he didn't follow after her.

If he said something to upset her, I'd punch him.

Up and down, either way was empty. Only Willow stood, hunched over, near the lockers about twenty feet away. Her hand was pressed to her ear.

"Hey...you okay?"

She whipped around, her eyes filled with tears and the phone pressed to her other ear. "Shut up."

I skidded to a stop three feet from her, my heart instantly pounding, not from anger anymore but concern. And that was because of the fear in her eyes.

"I can't hear you, Gramps. What did you say?" She hunched over more.

The pounding bass spilling into the hallway from the gymnasium didn't do anything to help.

I grabbed her elbow and guided her down the hallway. It

was a little darker but farther away from the noise.

"Where? I don't know where that is. I—" She hiccupped as she started to cry. "Is she all right? Will she—" More sobs.

Her shoulders shook, and the sounds of her cries ripped a hole right through my chest. Someone must be hurt. Or— dead? Man, I knew that feeling. The tears, the crying, the… I rested my hand on her shoulder, then rubbed it across her upper back until my fingers went beneath her hair.

Hopefully, she found that as soothing as I had when I was freaking out over my mom dying. Dad had done that for me. I was hysterical, crying so hard I was almost going to puke. He'd directed me to a waiting room chair and sat with me. Tears streamed down his face as he sat there silently, rubbing my back.

It had worked, too. Not just that day, but the weeks to follow after her death. He'd done it for both Caleb and me. At least until he went MIA. I'd done it for Caleb plenty of times since then, and it seemed to work.

If only I had someone to do that for me these days.

Stepping closer, I tried to block out the thumping music still spilling in.

"Are they in the ambulance now?"

Oh no. An ambulance? Crap.

I towered over her by almost a foot, so I had to bend down a little. The nearest hospital was thirty miles away, but that didn't matter. I'd take her if she needed a ride somewhere.

Her eyes were wide and filled with tears.

Even tears streaming down Willow's face couldn't dull her beauty.

But no way could I leave her now; she needed me. Someone was on their way to the hospital. I had to help. She was a teammate, too, so—

Yeah, it wasn't that. I *wanted* to help her because she was

Willow. The girl I cared about. Tough, frustrating, annoying, beautiful, strong… I needed to be there for her.

I dug into my pocket and pulled out my phone to text Preach. I'd promised to hang with him and Pax at Layla's after party, but that was a no go now.

"Thanks for letting me know." Willow sniffled, then wiped the back of her hand beneath her eye. She shoved the phone into her little clutch thingy.

"What happened?"

She stared up at me for a breath; her eyes broke my heart. They were all bloodshot and red. So was her nose. "Ericka, my host family's daughter, she got in a car accident. I lived with them for two years in Colorado. She's a senior, too. She's like my sister, Brodie, and they're taking her to the hospital. It's serious. Really serious." Her chest heaved with a fresh round of sobs. "I just have to get out of here." Her voice cracked. "Um, Matthew drove. I can—"

"I can drive you." I offered her my hand. "We can go anywhere."

"You sure?" I hated how small her voice sounded.

Normally, she was all up in my face, bantering, and her voice was strong, confident. But this teary-eyed Willow…this was not okay. Not okay at all.

She nodded and slid her hand into mine.

I guided her down the hallway, and she stumbled along, walking in a daze.

The doors burst open, and Matthew stormed out. He looked up the hallway, opposite our direction, then at us.

He marched toward me. "What's going on?"

The doors burst open again, the music flooding in like a tidal wave. Preach, followed closely by Jessa, hustled through.

"You." Preach pointed at Matthew. "Get off this campus!"

I hadn't heard Preach yell that loud since he about

throttled one of our teammates for disrespecting his girl. And that was more than two years ago.

I came to a stop a couple feet from Preach, pulling Willow closer. She didn't resist, and for some reason, that gave me a warm feeling all through my chest. It was like she trusted me.

Matthew shoved Preach. "Get off me, man."

"What's going on?" I eased Willow behind me. "Preach?"

He pointed at Matthew, who stood there, legs bent, face red. "Found him in Coach's office."

"What?" Willow asked as she stepped from behind me.

"When you bolted out of the dance, he did, too, only not after you." Preach shoved him again. "I found him in Coach's office, looking at our playbook."

Matthew's jaw tightened. His glance went from Preach to Willow, then skimmed over me on its way back to Preach.

If that wasn't an admission of guilt, I didn't know what was.

"Matthew?" Willow's voice cracked as Jessa came alongside her. "Is that true?"

He stared at her, saying nothing.

I stepped forward, standing to my full height. He dared come into my school and use Willow to spy on us for his team?

I fisted my hands, and before I got the full thought through my head, my knuckles cracked against Matthew's cheek. A jolt of pain zipped into my forearm. Matthew's head jerked to the side, and his body followed, doing a full spin.

Stutter-stepping, he stayed on his feet as he brought his hand to his face.

Preach jumped in front of me and pushed me back. "Go."

Willow and Jessa were running down the other end of the hall toward the side exit. I chased after them, and we burst through the doors on the west side of the school. Just around the corner was the lot I'd parked in.

"What happened?" Jessa hugged Willow. "Is everything

okay with Gramps?"

Willow shook her head, and tears started streaming again. "Ericka. She's been in a really bad car accident. I need to get out of here. They're going to call me with an update as soon as they have one."

"Go." Jessa pushed Willow toward me, then jetted back the way we came. "No one saw you hit him, Wind—we'll cover."

Within two minutes, we were both tucked into my Tahoe, and I was revving the engine to life. "Where can I take you? Do you want to go home?"

She let out a breath. "No, not home. Just away from here... away from Matthew."

My stomach churned. Fucking Matthew Halliday. How dare he hurt Willow like this?

I knew he was an ass, a little bit of a player, but I never knew he was this jacked up. I hate that he hurt Willow. I pounded the steering wheel and let out a breath, willing my heart to stop hammering the air out of my lungs.

"I'm sorry, Willow. Matthew...Ericka." I shook my head.

"Just get me out of here," she said. "Please."

"You got it." No car in front of me, so I pulled forward and took a quick left, then right, and I was on Main Street.

"What about Pax? Won't he need a designated driver?"

I huffed. "Nathaniel's got him. His car is parked at home. He's safe."

She's always thinking about other people. I admired that so hard about her.

She sagged into her seat, staring out the window, suddenly appearing exhausted.

We'd been hitting the ice in the early mornings, training, and I'd been pushing her hard. And she fought back harder and harder each time with a fire in her eyes that rivaled mine.

But tonight...not so much.

This sad Willow really scared me.

"I'm sure she's going to be fine."

Tears streamed over her cheeks; she didn't even move to wipe them away. Her once nicely curled hair was all over the place, kind of matted and whipped around from the heat vent blowing warm air over us.

Again, she didn't move to fix anything.

She looked so pretty in her black dress. Hugging all her curves. When I'd seen her and Matthew together at the dinner table at Taste of Rome, I'd about shit a hockey puck.

Then again, I'd known he was going to be there, I'd just hoped she'd, for some reason, show up without him.

Willow wiped her cheeks with the backs of her hand.

I turned off Main Street and made two more lefts.

"Where are we going?" Willow's voice shook.

"You know how the ice rink is our place to bolt when we need to chill out, decompress?" I glanced over at her as I veered around the corner to Oak Street. "I've got another place that helps *almost* as well."

CHAPTER TWENTY-FOUR

Willow

"How is she?" I cradled the phone against my ear.

My host mother, Linda Foster, sniffled. "Punctured lung, broken collarbone, shattered femur, and she's got a pretty nasty concussion."

A solitary swing moved back and forth ever so slightly in the chilly wind that blew across the playground Brodie had driven us to.

"Oh my gosh. I am so sorry! But she's going to be okay, right? I mean—" A sob stole my voice. My eyes burned as I gulped through the emotions.

Linda sniffled. "She'll be fine, honey. She was very lucky."

I took a big, calming breath. "So then what about speed skating? How long will she be out?"

"At this point, at least several weeks. We'll have a better idea when the orthopedic doctors and other specialists assess her tomorrow morning." The emotion in Linda's voice cut through me like a razor-sharp knife.

I didn't know what else to say. The desperate and overwhelming sadness I felt when I got injured and when Grams passed away started to creep in.

"I wish I was out there with you all." I paced back and forth in front of the plastic barrier separating the grassy area from the mulched playground.

"I know you do, sweetheart. Listen, I have to go, but I'll call or text you with an update as soon as we have one."

I nodded. "Please tell Ericka that I love her, and I'm wishing her the speediest recovery of all time."

"I will, dear. Goodbye for now."

My lower lip started trembling as another round of burning tears bit at the corners of my eyes. "Bye."

A gentle breeze rustled the leaves of the giant oak tree next to the bench Brodie sat on.

"What did she say?" he asked.

"She got in a terrible accident. A drunk driver T-boned her." Tears dripped down my face and landed on the Boy's Hockey Woodhaven High sweatshirt Brodie had given me.

He flinched, and his jaw tensed. "Drunk driver?"

I nodded and faced the sky. "I can't believe this happened to her."

"Come here." He motioned for me to sit next to him on the bench overlooking the park.

"She has to have surgery, and her femur is shattered. She may never skate again." The words tumbled out of my mouth.

"She's a figure skater, too?"

"No, speed skater. She won silver at the Junior Speed Skating Championships last year."

"Oh man…" Brodie shook his head. "I can't imagine."

Pain shot through my Achilles tendon. I hadn't even done anything to make it hurt; it must have been sympathy pain for Ericka.

I sat next to Brodie and let my head fall into my hands as my elbows dug into my legs. A wave of fatigue slammed into me. My body felt instantly heavy, and my ears burned.

Brodie placed his hand on my back. "Can I do anything to help?"

"No…just keep her in your thoughts." I lifted my head and stared across the vacant playground. "It's hard to believe… just like that, in the blink of an eye, someone's entire life can change."

Brodie flinched again and pulled his hand away from my back. But instead of placing it at his side, he rested it on top of mine.

"Oh shit, Brodie," I said, suddenly remembering how his mom had died.

His nostrils flared, then he glanced skyward and drew in a deep breath. "When my mom was killed, it—it was like getting hit by a freight train. Me, Dad, Caleb, we were all shell-shocked. Completely lost. Unable to function. Dad is still struggling the most. He's drinking way too much, and he's constantly gone. He says he's got business trips, but I dunno. Shit is really difficult."

"I'm sorry. This has got to be so hard for you." I shook my head. "And here you are, taking care of me."

"I'm glad I can be here for you. I *want* to be here for you."

I wanted to be there for him, too. It had to be hard talking with people about his mom, but since he'd opened up to me about her tonight, I felt like I could ask. "What was your mom like?"

"Supportive. I remember that most about her. Always behind me, no matter what. Even when I fell flat on my face." He grinned and looked out over the park. "And her eyes. They were a pretty bright blue, and they always lit up when she saw me or Caleb. But all she had to do was give us *the* look with those eyes, and we knew we were up a creek."

"I bet you got in trouble a lot."

"A little." He winked at me, but a sadness dulled his bright brown eyes, and he slumped against the back of the bench we were sitting on. "Oh, and she smelled like roses. All the time."

"She sounds like an amazing person."

"She was. I miss her all the time."

My heart sagged, and it felt like a ten-pound weight in my chest.

"Life is really unfair." I shook my head. "It sucks."

"It sucks hard." Brodie shifted more, facing me full-on as much as he could, sitting beside me on this bench. "I did learn something through the shitstorm that followed my mom's death, though…"

"What?"

He got to his feet, still holding my hand. "Follow me."

He led me across the mulch and to the swing that was still moving in the wind.

"What are you doing?"

He got behind it and held the chains with his hands. "Have a seat."

"You learned to swing?" I sat and held on to the chains that ran up to a thick metal pole above our heads.

"Nope." Brodie placed his hands above mine and pulled me backward until my feet were off the ground. "I learned to live each day to its fullest. Tomorrow isn't promised. It helped me survive. I mean, I'm not reckless or anything, but I don't take anything for granted anymore."

"Makes sense." Warmth from how close he was holding me to him cascaded over me like warm bathwater. His sweet, woodsy scent was a balm to my aching heart.

"Ready?" he asked.

I nodded.

He let go of the chains, and I went flying through the chilly air.

"The other thing is I try to be honest with everyone. You know, say what needs to be said, live life with no regrets or whatever." He gave me another push that sent me soaring even higher.

Say what needs to be said…

I was glad he couldn't see my face as I cringed. I'd been keeping a huge secret from him: my feelings.

"Speaking of…"

I glanced over my shoulder.

Did he just read my mind?

Brodie caught the swing and slowed me to a stop. In one swift move, he spun me around, making an X above my head with the chains.

"Willow, I have…I mean, I—"

He shook his head and opened his mouth, but nothing came out. Instead, he pulled me forward until we were eye to eye.

Instead of waiting for him to finish, I reached up and wrapped my arms around his neck and pulled his face toward mine. With my feet still off the ground, our lips met.

Heat burst along my lips, carving a fiery path through my chest and pooling in my stomach. A wave of fluttering rippled through my body. He leaned toward me, opening his mouth. My fingers found their way into his silky hair, and I tilted his head.

The sweet taste of mint and chocolate tickled my tastebuds as I deepened the kiss. Everything around me melted away. The heat radiating off him chased away the chill nipping at the air, and I pulled him closer, wishing he wasn't holding the swing so he could wrap his arms around me.

Suddenly, the chains clanked, and I was sent flying backward.

"Oh my God! I didn't mean to let go."

Brodie took a step toward me, but I was quicker. I jumped out of the swing, then leaped into his arms.

He curled his arms around my lower back, securing me to him, and I melted against him, absorbing his heat, his comfort…him.

I leaned back slightly, still holding him close to see his reaction. Was he okay with this? I'd kind of tackled him without thinking it through, but after hearing what he said about his mom, not taking things for granted…

How could I not?

His gaze shifted to my lips, and he drew in a deep breath. "Willow…"

Our mouths crashed together with a spark, and he pulled me even closer. I wasn't sure how that was possible, but he did. His heart raced, thumping against my chest, and it turned into a drum duet because mine was pounding just as wildly.

The frigid air whipped around us, sending strands of my hair flying into Brodie's face, but I didn't feel the chill. All I felt was Brodie. His heat. His warmth. His mouth.

I kissed him deeper, drinking in his taste, his breath. It was everything I'd dreamed it would be. Gentle but urgent. I could almost taste the punch I'd seen him drinking earlier, but somehow, I took the kiss even deeper, needing to be closer to him. How he'd stood up to Matthew, and how he'd whisked me away after hearing about Ericka. Even how he'd opened up to me about his mom.

There was so much more to Brodie Windom than I could have imagined. He wasn't just the tough hockey player. No, he was different. Special.

And I wanted to get to know him better.

"Whoa," Brodie murmured against my mouth, then nipped at my bottom lip.

"Double whoa." I pulled back and grinned. "That was…"

"Awesome." He was still holding me, but his smile faltered. "What's wrong?"

He gently placed me back on my feet and led me over to the bench overlooking the little park.

"Willow, I like you." He twined his fingers with mine and shifted to face me more. "A lot."

"But?" I knew there was a but.

"But it's complicated. You know, with hockey and…you leaving." His eyes locked on to mine, the chestnut and amber swirls burning into my soul.

"You're right," I said. "Not to mention it's against the team rules. It could land us both in the penalty box."

"Shit," he said under his breath, and his shoulders sagged. Brodie lifted our hands and tipped up my chin. "So, what should we do?"

My heart sagged like his shoulders had a second ago as the realization of what we needed to do weighed me down. "I think there's only one option." I brushed my thumb along his bottom lip. "We shouldn't ever do that again."

CHAPTER TWENTY-FIVE

Brodie

"**M**atthew's lucky I didn't break his nose."

"I'm surprised you didn't, you hit him so hard." Preach shook his head. "I can't believe that jerk used Willow just to try and steal our playbook."

"Yeah, he's a total d-bag." I tapped my phone screen to open Willow's Instagram feed.

I hadn't heard from her since last night, but I sure hadn't forgotten that kiss. It pretty much occupied every second of every minute these last eighteen hours.

"I'm so about to crush your high score, *Ice Man*," Preach yelled from the floor. "You know that's a ridiculous gaming name, right?"

He was leaning against the foot of my bed, facing my TV while playing *God of War*.

"Suck it, man." I snatched my phone and scrambled to the end of the bed where I'd left my handle. "You're going down."

"And yeah, you should have broken Matthew's nose." Preach grinned. "But you still got him pretty good. I can't believe he did that."

"Poor Willow. Getting used like that."

"We tried to warn her about going out with him," Preach said. "What a jerk."

"Bombs away." Caleb screamed as he sprinted into my room. With one leap, he dive-bombed me on my bed at the same time he farted. "Stink bombs."

I half caught him to break his fall and then flopped onto my back. "Dude."

He started jabbing and punching my stomach. "I'm gonna get you."

I flipped him onto his back and started tickling his sides. That'd be the end of this dive-bomb mission of his. He instantly squealed, laughing his brains out. Squirming all around, kicking his legs, he about nailed me in the jewels.

"Yo. Settle." It was almost eight o'clock and time for bed. "You're gonna hurt something valuable."

He laughed and squirmed away.

"What's up, Limp Lungs?" Preach asked, never taking his focus off the TV.

Caleb laughed. "Beat his high score yet, loser?"

I palmed Caleb's face and shoved him away. He laughed and scrambled to the head of the bed and rested back. His chest was heaving pretty good, so I kept an eye on him.

"I'm fine," Caleb whispered and sagged against the wooden headboard. "Quit staring."

I narrowed my eyes at him but then gave him a soft smile. "Time for bed, Limp Lungs."

He punched my shoulder, then jumped off the bed.

"Wild little dude," Preach said.

"I'm not little," he yelled from his room down the hall.

"Pipsqueak," I said back.

"Hey."

"Bed. Now." I shook my head, but I couldn't help smiling.

Preach groaned and tossed his remote down. "Almost."

"I'm the king of the ice and of *God of War*." I kept playing as Preach flopped to his side on the floor.

"Mm-hmm. Well, Willow stopped *three* of your goal attempts at last week's practice, so let's get her in here and see if she can beat your top score. She probably could."

"As if." I slapped his shoulder, then grabbed the control and eased onto my stomach. Thanks to Preach, I was thinking about Willow yet again. Those kisses we'd stolen at the park... *Damn*. Last night, that accident with her host-sister back in Colorado had shaken not only her. It was a vivid reminder of the night my mom died.

And an even more vivid reminder about how quickly things could change.

I liked Willow, but we shouldn't start anything up. That was clear. And she'd agreed.

I hadn't told Preach we'd kissed—I didn't dare. He'd be all over me about breaking Coach's rule. Not that we were going to break it again, but still.

My phone pinged, but I stayed focused on the TV. I was close to breaking my high score. Plus, it was probably just Pax and Nathaniel sending me some ridiculous meme of somebody farting in someone's face.

"Ohhhh, IG message from Willow." Preach sat up, holding my phone close to his face.

"Shit." I tossed the controller down and tackled Preach around the shoulders.

We fell to the side, and my phone flopped onto the carpet. Preach grunted, then punched my stomach and flipped me off him. The next second he was on me, wrapping an arm around my neck. "Sleeper hold. I so got you."

I elbowed his gut, and when he flinched, I squirmed out. "Cheap shot."

I rolled away and grabbed my cell, then bolted out of my

room. My phone chimed again while I was booking it down the stairs to the main living room to get away from him. The sixty-five-inch flat screen was playing *F8*, right during the prison break, so I launched onto the leather couch to watch it.

Preach hollered, but then I heard his phone ring. It was his mom's tone, probably checking in on us. She'd mentioned a couple times that Caleb and I could crash at their place anytime if we were sick of roaming around this massive house alone while Dad was on work trips. It'd been getting pretty bad with Dad being gone so much; I might take her up on it soon.

With rap music and prisoners fighting blaring from my TV, I checked my IG.

New message from Willow.

WILLOW: Hey.

ME: How are you?

WILLOW: Not so good.

WILLOW: Ericka's in surgery right now. I'm going out of my mind.

ME: Crap. Okay. How long?

WILLOW: She's been under for almost two hours.

ME: She'll be fine.

ME: She's lucky to have you in her corner.

WILLOW: Thanks, it's been rough.

WILLOW: Distract me.

WILLOW: What are you doing?

ME: Watching F8.

WILLOW: #love

ME: You really aren't a frilly figure skater, are you??

WILLOW: Oh, I'm so much more…

WILLOW: Too bad you'll never know because all you ever want to do is quiz me on freaking hockey terms.

WILLOW: 😳😆

ME: Speaking of. What does deke mean?

WILLOW: Dork.

WILLOW: And I've seen F8 like twenty times by the way.

ME: That's it?

WILLOW: This year.

ME: Well damn, I'm impressed. Do you own it?

WILLOW: Yep.

ME: Put it on! I'm at the prison scene. We'll watch together.

WILLOW: BRB

I pressed pause so I wouldn't get too far ahead of her and rested back into the leather couch. Should I say something about the kiss? Or play it cool? Damn it. I told myself I wouldn't get involved with a girl this year so I could stay focused on hockey, but here I was, totally jonesing for more kiss-time with Willow.

WILLOW: Here. Damn The Rock is HOT!

ME: Typical.

WILLOW: 😵

WILLOW: How many times have you seen this?

ME: Too many to count.

WILLOW: You totally cried when you watched the scene where Brian and Toretto drive off after Paul Walker died during filming.

ME: Guilty. Every freaking time.

WILLOW: Me, too.

"Wicked." Preach landed beside me on the couch. "Love this part."

"What's up with your mom?" I asked.

"Just checking in." He grinned. "You know me, I'm kind of a wild one she has to keep tabs on."

I chuckled. Preach was basically any parent's dream of a kid. Never did anything wrong. Totally got good grades, didn't drink or do anything that could get him in trouble, and he volunteered at a homeless shelter, just to be nice.

"What's up with you and Willow?"

"What do you mean?" I asked, my heart suddenly racing.

Crap, did she tell Jessa about our kiss? But we'd sworn not to tell. What if the team found out? What if *Coach* found out?

"She just messaged you," he said. "Is it because of the whole Matthew thing?"

"Um, yeah. And her friend. You know?" I shifted slightly so he didn't have a good look at my phone. If she mentioned something about the kiss, I didn't want him accidentally seeing it.

I focused on The Rock kicking butt. The way he took those rubber bullets to the chest…the guy was a stud.

"I saw Matthew at The General Store yesterday. He was still sporting a black eye." Preach laughed and popped a couple Cheetos into his mouth, then passed the bag to me.

"He's an ass, and I might accidentally let one of my slap shots go wild at his face next week when we play them. But I do feel bad about giving him a black eye." I wouldn't actually ever do that, but the fiery hot anger over what he'd done to Willow ignited to life. My heart was pounding as hard as it was the night he'd done it.

Preach eyed me from the side, then focused back on the screen. "It was cool how you had her back, you know? Taking her outta there, then hanging with her during the Ericka stuff."

"Sure. She's…our teammate." I kept telling myself that was all she was. That was all she should be. I refused to get hooked on another girl only to be slashed down by her.

"You didn't get busted for the punch, though, right? He didn't rat?"

"Not that I can tell. He'd have to explain a lot if he did." I chomped on a few Cheetos and zeroed in on the screen. I had English Lit homework to do, but I so wasn't into it.

My phone chimed, and I picked it up.

WILLOW: Dude, that prison scene is the best.

ME: And that music.

WILLOW: What's your favorite song?

ME: Stand in the Fire - Mickey Thomas

WILLOW: Never heard of it.

ME: From Youngbloods.

WILLOW: I just watched that. You know…for research purposes.

ME: LOL. You loved it.

WILLOW: Meh.

I chuckled, and Preach eyed me, then focused on the screen again. "Who are you talking to?"

"Nobody, just…scrolling." I shifted to the side more. I probably shouldn't be chatting with her like this, but there wasn't any harm in getting to know her a little better, right? If this was all I could have with Willow, I'd take it. Sure, I'd much rather be kissing her, but that couldn't happen again.

ME: Your favorite song?

WILLOW: Small Town Boy by Dustin Lynch

ME: #WEAK

WILLOW: I know you are, but what am I?

ME: See if I train you anymore.

WILLOW: Hey Brodie?

ME: Yeah?

WILLOW: Thanks.

ME: For…?

WILLOW: Last night.

My stomach flip flopped. What should I say back? Did she mean the kiss? The swing, the—

WILLOW: The swing. Telling me about your mom…

My mouth went dry and my hands were so slick, a puck

would have slid right through my grasp.

WILLOW: For everything.

WILLOW: Oh, I gotta go. Ericka's mom's calling.

ME: Bye.

So…by *everything*, did she mean the kiss, too?

CHAPTER TWENTY-SIX

Brodie

"**D**id you hear about Pax?" Preach asked as he steered his Jeep onto the country road that'd get us to Eric's farm.

"Yeah, I called him." I shook my head, slouched into the leather passenger seat. "You know, to see if he was coming tonight. Guess where he was?"

"I'm not sure I want to know."

"Bud's Bar, picking his dad up."

"When?" Preach glanced at me. "It's not even seven o'clock right now."

"Three. He had to bolt right after school to get him." Man, Pax's family was a mess. His mom skipped out on them ten years ago with another guy. His dad couldn't hold down a job. Was addicted to opioids. And here I thought I had trouble with my dad being MIA. Not to mention Rita's last day was yesterday. Dad had fired her and George without even telling me.

"Dang. That is not good." Preach let out a long breath. "Think he'll come tonight?"

"Doubt it." I kind of hoped he didn't. Pax was my friend, but when things were really bad at home for him, he drank, and that never turned out well. And I was looking forward to a fun, relaxing night.

A twinge of guilt pulled at my heart. Pax had really been there for me in the past. I wanted to return the favor, but he could get pretty difficult to deal with when he was wasted.

"Well, I'm glad you decided to come tonight. Outside of seeing you in school a little and practice…you haven't been around much lately."

I let out a yawn and pulled my phone out of my back pocket so I could sit more comfortably. "Between early morning training sessions with Willow, school, homework, hanging with Caleb…"

"Well, the extra training Willow's getting is working, isn't it?"

"She's kicking ass."

"What's going on with your dad?" Preach asked.

"That's a great question." I shook my head. "The guy is *never* home, Preach. As in never. And if he is…"

"Not pretty, huh?" Preach let out a sigh. "I'm sorry, man."

"Check it." I tapped my phone to life and found the text I got from Miles. "Brodie. Your dad wanted me to let you know he won't be back from California today like he thought. Do you need anything?"

"Hold up. Your dad's *assistant* is checking on you?"

I clicked my phone off and tossed it on my lap as the ever-familiar vise started tightening around my chest. Dad couldn't even find the time to text me himself. Or even let me know what was up with the staff. Work was more important than Caleb and me. *Everything* was more important than us.

Thinking about it felt like a weighted blanket over my body, only the weight was too heavy, and it was suffocating me. And then there was Willow. I was completely wigging over her. It'd been six days since the kiss, that amazing, hot, intense kiss. I'd told her about Mom, helped her through the Ericka crisis, and then I go and kiss her like that?

We'd agreed it should never happen again, but I must be into torturing myself, because I couldn't stop thinking about it.

I drew in a breath and shook my head free of Willow thoughts.

"Hey, how's Willow's friend, the one who was in the accident? I forgot her name."

"Ericka. Actually, I just asked Willow about this earlier. The surgery went fine, but she's looking at a long recovery."

"How's Willow handling it?"

"She's pretty upset but hanging in there."

Preach steered the car onto the single-lane dirt road leading to Eric's farm. "Ready for Pine Valley on Wednesday?"

"Hell yeah." I clapped my hands, thankful for the distraction. "I smell a perfect season."

"Willow's really helped, huh?" Preach grinned.

Oh great. He just had to keep bringing her up. Dang it, I could *not* get her out of my mind.

"Sure has."

"Has she mentioned anything about getting back to figure skating?" Preach pulled up behind Nathaniel's blue Ford F150 and killed the engine. "Because she might actually beat Josiah if she decides to try out for high school."

"Yeah, um…" I shifted in my seat. Her on the high school team. I wasn't sure what to think about that. Sure, I wanted the best team possible, and if that meant having her in goalie, then I wanted her there. But one bummer…we'd still be teammates and couldn't date.

Not that she wanted to date.

Not that *I* wanted to date.

"She hasn't mentioned much. Something about January. Um…she needs to be all better by then." I reached for the door handle, my chest suddenly feeling even heavier.

Willow leaving…I didn't like thinking about it.

"Jessa said the same thing." Preach pushed open his door. "But to have her on our team through January would be great. Gives Josiah more time to heal up and get his mojo back. You know?"

"Yep." But it was also more time for us to get comfortable with her and then to have her leave. I couldn't afford to get too dependent on her. Plus, I was secretly worried about Josiah coming back. He wouldn't be in top form. There's no way we could win State with him only operating at half of his regular capacity.

We both met at the front of Preach's car, then started walking up the long drive. I could already hear laughing and music. Eric's farm was huge. Every year they put on this wicked-fun hay bale maze. And it seemed like each year it got more difficult to solve.

We were the test run for the maze before he opened it up to the public.

"Woo hoo!" I recognized Willow's voice immediately as we rounded the back of the main barn on the south side of Eric's property.

A massive bonfire roared, brightening the darkness. Jessa and Willow were sitting on the back end of a wagon filled with bales of hay, their feet dangling over the ledge. It was coming to a stop, but before it did, Willow hopped up, then jumped off, landing solidly on her feet.

She put her hands out, spun twice, then kicked her back foot out behind her into some kind of pose. I'd seen her do that on the ice after completing a routine, but I didn't remember what it was called.

Jessa clapped her mittened hands and jumped off the wagon as well. She pulled Willow into a big hug, and their laughter made me smile.

Seeing Willow happy was such a relief. She'd been through so much with her injury, Ericka, the whole Matthew thing. She was due for some happiness.

"Wonder what's going on there?" Preach said as we made our way toward them.

I shoved my hands in my front jeans pockets and relaxed my shoulders, hoping to come off as calm and cool.

I was anything but. My heart hammered, and my hands were clammy. The big smile brightened Willow's face, making her even more pretty than she normally was.

"Hey guys," Preach said, coming up to them. "What's up?"

"Hey." I nodded to Willow and then Jessa.

"Oh my gosh, Brodie!" Willow held her hand up. "Give me a high-five. Right now."

I did as asked. "Sure. Why am I high-fiving you?"

"I'm cleared!" she screamed and jumped up and down. "My PT cleared me. Full on cleared me for all the things!"

Willow was cleared? That meant she was even closer to leaving. It felt like someone had just kicked me in the balls.

"What's going on here, Ice Capades?" Nathaniel asked as he, Teddy, and Eric came up to the group. Amanda and a couple of her friends hovered nearby, and I could tell they were listening but didn't join the group.

"Willow's cleared one hundred percent from PT." Jessa hugged her again. "And she sent off a couple videos I made of her doing a routine to some coaches."

"Holy shit, Ice Capades. That's…wait. You're going to do both, right?" Nathaniel nailed her with a stare. "Hockey and figure skating. Because you can't leave us hanging."

"No. Yes. I mean. Yes. For now." The flames from the fire flickered off her big, blue eyes. Her lips shimmered as if she'd just put on some of that lip gloss she wore, and I couldn't help but stare. I'd kissed those lips once, and damn, I wanted to again.

My teammates fell silent, and the knot in my stomach twisted even tighter.

"Let her go back to her frilly skirts," Eric said. "I always knew putting her on the team was a mistake." Without another word, he stormed away.

"You know what? I'm in such a good mood, I'm not even going to let that asshat get to me." Willow jumped up and down. She was wearing a Woodhaven stocking cap, but her long black braids bounced against her chest as she moved.

Trevor, Landen, and Josiah came up to the group. "Let's hit the maze!"

The awkward silence dissipated as Willow grabbed my arm, forcing my hand out of my pocket, and said, "Come on, *Wind*!"

She tugged me along as we trailed the group. "You're awfully quiet."

The news of her getting one step closer to competitive skating again was amazing but also devastating… She made our team better, and damn, the thought of not seeing her every day, hitting the ice together, texting each other constantly, was truly awful.

We entered the maze, and she guided me around the first right turn. The bales were so high, barely any light from the fire bled in. A cool, crisp breeze toiled through, carrying the scent of apple, cinnamon, and burned embers.

I loved the smell of fall.

"I'm happy for you, Willow. So…it's really happening, isn't it?" I tried to hide the disappointment in my voice, but I wasn't sure if I succeeded.

"Yes. Yes. I mean, I hope so." She glanced at me, and she was still smiling. I hadn't ever seen her so happy. Well, that wasn't true. When she blocked my shot that first pick-up game we ever played together, she was pretty happy then.

"What's all this mean?" My mouth went dry and my hands started shaking, so I pulled my stocking cap down to try and keep them busy.

"I have to get on a team by at least January if I have any chance to take the level tests in time to work my way to worlds and then the Olympics."

"Why do you need a team?" I asked, then pointed to the left. "Let's try this way."

"I think the group stayed straight."

I shrugged. "I kind of asked Eric for directions."

"Cheater!" She playfully backhanded my gut, then grinned up at me. "And I need a team behind me to have access to the best coaches, trainers, PTs, and ice time. The two hours extra a day I get here, now, is fine. But I need to be at this for eight hours a day."

"Hard to do on your own. I get it." My heart palpitated in my chest. I wanted to be happy for her. I really did. This was her dream, and I wanted her to live it. I would never think of standing in the way of that. But she was talking about leaving…in less than three months. And that hurt like a bitch.

My phone bellowed the Muppets Manamana ringtone, and I pulled it out.

"The Muppets?" Willow asked.

"Pax."

Willow's shoulders slouched, and her smile faded slightly. "Kinda hard to match Muppets with *Pax*."

"Inside joke." I tapped the screen to make sure it wasn't a *respond now* text, and it wasn't. Just a gif of something, so I slid the phone back in my pocket.

"I don't get it, Brodie. Why are you such good friends with him?"

I let out a long, slow breath as I contemplated what to tell her. "He's had a tough life."

"And that excuses his asshat-ness?" Her jaw ticked, then clenched.

"Not even. But he…was there for me. You know. Um… when Mom died. Beside Preach, he was…he didn't leave me when the shit hit the fan."

"Oh," she said, barely above a whisper.

"His life is beyond messed up right now…so I can't leave him. I won't."

"You're a really good friend, Brodie. And I totally respect you for how loyal you are."

We took a right turn and ran smack into a skeleton, dripping with fake blood. "Whoa!" I spun away from it, taking Willow with me.

"Oh my gosh!" Willow grabbed onto me. "What the hell?"

"Come on!" I grabbed her hand and ran past the thing and deeper into darkness. "Eric's family really went all out this year."

My heart was still racing as we came to a stop. Willow rested against a tall bale of hay, her chest heaving. My heart was thumping wildly, but it wasn't because I was scared; it was because I was here with Willow. Alone. Just me and her. Like when we were at the park…

Willow grabbed my hand and, with a solid tug, pulled me to her. It was pretty dark here, with only the moon above us to light it up, but I saw her eyes. They scanned my face so slowly, it felt like a warm caress against my skin.

"Willow, are you sure we—"

She pushed up and swallowed my words with a kiss. Strong arms curled around my neck as her body pressed against mine. Even though she wore a thick hoodie, her heat seeped through, into my chest, triggering a spark of need that nearly knocked me over.

I put my foot out to steady myself, then I wove my arms around her waist and hoisted her against me. Nipping at her bottom lip, I smiled against her mouth as she then opened for me and tilted her head. It gave me full access to her, and I dove in.

She tasted like apple cider.

"Mmm," I hummed as I chased down every last trace of that sugary drink. Her fingers worked their way into my hair, pushing my stocking cap off. She tilted her head and stepped into me more.

I eased back, praying to God no one came by even while I knew I just didn't care, as the heat stormed through my body, tightening my spine. Tracing my hand down her spine, I followed her curves over her tight ass and pulled her to me.

She drew in a sharp breath but didn't back away. She felt absolutely perfect against me. She—

Something soft bumped my shoulder. Shuffling sounded above me, and I broke our connection.

A hay bale toppled just as I looked up, and it nailed me in the shoulder. Another tumbled, and I spun us out of its path just as one more landed on my back.

"Ah," Willow gasped.

We stumbled forward, but we both adjusted, somehow staying upright. "You okay?" I asked.

"I'm fine." She nodded and pointed to the hay bales around us. "But I think the Fates have spoken, huh?"

CHAPTER TWENTY-SEVEN

Willow

"Falcons! Falcons! Falcons!" everyone cheered on the bus. Brodie stood and leaned against the back of one of the brown bus seats. "Listen, guys," he said, then paused. "I mean, listen, guys and girl."

I smiled. "Thank you."

"This is our last league game. Our record is seven and zero. If we win, we'll have another perfect season under our belts, and we'll be Fall League champs."

"*When* we win," Teddy shouted.

"League champions!" Nathaniel yelled. He punched his fist into the air, bumping me in the process. "Seven years in a row!"

My teammates joined in, chanting, "League champs! League champs!"

Brodie raised his hands, and we quieted down. "Coach told me there's a scout for LSU here for the game."

My stomach tightened, and a flash of heat shot through my body. A scout?

"Yeah, baby!" Nathaniel yelled. "Coach Johns is mine. You all, just back away. I want LSU!"

Pax flicked his ear. "Like he'd come to see your sorry ass

flop all over the ice like a little Mini Mite."

Everyone started laughing, but my stomach hardened that much more. A scout. Watching… No pressure or anything. I knew the game was important to the guys, but this just kicked it up about one hundred notches.

The bus bumped along the side road that was taking us to the Pine Valley Ice Arena. I hadn't been to this rink yet, but according to the guys, it wasn't anywhere as nice as ours.

Nathaniel bumped me with his shoulder. "We're going to kick Pine Valley's ass today!"

"Yeah, we are!" I grinned.

I hadn't sat by Brodie on the bus. We'd kissed twice in the past couple of weeks, and honestly, neither one of us was handling it well. We'd had countless conversations that always ended up with us agreeing we had to stay just friends.

If we decided to be anything more, we'd have to hide it from everyone. Jessa, Preach, our families. That would suck, and if one person in Woodhaven found out, there was a good chance everyone would know by the morning. Small-town life at its finest.

Part of me wondered if I should just quit the team. Brodie and I could be together, officially, out in the open, and I could focus solely on figure skating. But, deep down, I didn't want to. I'd been cleared and working hard, but that didn't mean that I was going to get on a team tomorrow. I still had so much to do, and the extra ice time and team workouts were helping me get stronger.

I needed this team as much as they needed me.

Brodie's dimples floated through my mind. And his lips, those full lips and how they felt on my neck…

I wanted to keep kissing him, and I was pretty sure he felt the same way. But we had a major issue. We could not let our teammates find out, especially if I tried out for the

Woodhaven High team. The no fraternization rule would probably be set in stone for *both* teams. Not to mention, how could our teammates take either one of us seriously if we were sneaking around? It was totally backward, but if I was being honest: Brodie would probably be given a pass and I'd catch all the blame, no matter how my stat sheets proved I belonged in the goal.

"Did you hear Josiah hit the ice last week and started practicing?" Trevor said from the seat behind me. "Yeah, he just got cleared."

That pulled me out of my head.

I'd heard that he'd rocked physical therapy, but I didn't know he had gotten back on the ice already.

Would he be trying out for the Varsity team?

My thoughts drifted to Ericka. Surgery had been rough. Her femur was now held together with pins and screws. But, like me, she was a fighter. As long as her rehab went according to plan, she'd get back on the ice and hopefully be racing again.

Tryouts for the high school hockey team were next week. When I'd moved back here, I figured I'd be healthy enough to return to Colorado by the end of October, but I just wasn't there yet. Luckily, I had until January. That was plenty of time.

Single axels, toe loops, and salchows were mostly under control, but I really needed to nail at least a double for all of those jumps and not just once, repeatedly.

Jessa had been filming me at the rink a few times. The footage shocked me. I was so used to seeing myself fly through the air, making it appear effortless. Now, I looked like a clumsy new skater who was still getting her footing. There were positives, though. I'd gotten stronger and faster playing hockey in a few months than in nearly a year of physical therapy. I found myself feeling incredibly thankful that Brodie hit that wild shot over the boards back in August.

"So, you going out for the high school team?" Nathaniel asked me.

"I'm not sure yet." I did want to, but Josiah was back, so maybe he should take his place, and I could focus only on figure skating. That way, I wouldn't be leaving the guys high and dry when I got recruited or accepted into a new skating program.

"Why not?" His knees bumped into the seat in front of us.

"I don't even know if it's allowed." I'd miss the guys, except Pax and Eric, if I wasn't on the team. It kind of surprised me how much I liked these guys. Liked the team aspect of competition.

Nathaniel scrunched up his nose. "We don't have a girls' team. There are laws and stuff about that, right? They can't discriminate against you just because you're a girl."

"I think I'd have to get approval from the athletic director." I'd already started the process of being a girl on a guy's team with Fall League, so the athletic director probably wouldn't fight anything.

Nathaniel poked me in the leg. "You better get on that, Ice Capades."

Laughter erupted from the back of the bus, but when I turned around, all I saw were Brodie's dark brown eyes staring back at me.

Did he hear everything I said to Nathaniel?

Most of the guys had been cool with me joining the Fall League, mainly because Josiah was out and Izan wasn't ready to be starting goalie, but would that change now that their goalie for the last three years was all set to make a comeback? How rusty would he be? Had he been training at home or with another teammate, like Brodie and I worked together?

I raised my hand to the back of my neck and rubbed it on either side of my spine. My shoulders had hiked up to my ears, and I was starting to get a headache.

"Worried about the game?" Nathaniel asked.

"Nah." I focused in on a knot near the base of my neck.

"You lie." He scooted over until his back was against the side of the bus. "Spill it."

"Josiah."

Nathaniel nodded. "No use worrying about what you can't control."

I stopped rubbing my neck and brought my hands to my lap. As I cracked each of my knuckles, a sickening realization hit me. Josiah could beat me and take back the starting position as goalie. Then what? If I was backup, I wouldn't get nearly as much time on the ice.

As Nathaniel's attention shifted toward the guys in the back of the bus, I pulled out my phone.

ME: We need to up our practice sessions.

BRODIE: We can hit the rink before school every day from now until tryouts.

ME: I'll bring the coffee.

The buzzer sounded, and the fans in the arena erupted into cheers.

A few teddy bears flew onto the ice as well as the fans jumped up and down in the stands.

"Yes!" I left my goal and joined my team in the center of the ice.

Eric skated by me and growled, "You got lucky, Sequins."

"Epic job, Willow!" Preach high-fived me.

Teddy slapped me on the back and nearly sent me flying. "You did good!"

"She did great," Brodie shouted. He picked up my gloved hand and raised it in the air.

Adrenaline pumped through my body. I'd blocked nine attempts and kept my first clean sheet.

Coach Kurt joined us on the ice. "Excellent job, Falcons!"

We made a circle around him.

"It's a privilege to coach you kids. You all came together this season and ended up champions for the seventh year in a row!"

Everyone tapped their sticks against the ice.

"Our last game puck of the season goes to Willow Covington!" Coach handed it to me and smiled.

I held the cool rubber disc in my hands, and a rush of heat radiated through my chest. My chest swelled with pride, and a smile filled my face to the point my cheeks ached.

Figure skater *and* goalie. I never would have guessed, but now that I was here, holding the game puck, I knew I could do both, at least until I made a figure skating team. I could really help the guys. Help Brodie get to State and win it.

"Go take a celebration lap, Willow," Coach Kurt said. "You deserve it!"

I'd taken plenty of these in my skating career, but decked out in full goalie gear? My blades dug into the ice as I pushed off, tears stinging my eyes. I waved to our fans and held the puck above my head.

People were clapping; a few even stood and cheered loudly. Warmth spread through my chest as I continued to wave.

I picked up the pace, flying across the ice. The cameras flashing and people cheering transported me to my last competition. I'd won gold and taken the exact same victory lap.

As I rounded the bend, something took over me. Call it

instinct or a pure adrenaline rush, but I turned on my skates and started going backward. Closing my eyes, I pushed off and flew through the air. I didn't open my eyes until I landed the jump.

Fans gasped. My teammates gasped.

But no one was as shocked as I was.

Did I just land a double salchow?

CHAPTER TWENTY-EIGHT

Brodie

"**K**iller team this year, Wind." Coach Noah stood behind his desk and handed me the roster over the top of it.

Willow's name stood out as if it'd been printed in red. *Willow Covington, starting goalie.*

She'd done it. I wasn't surprised, though—she'd worked really hard. The strength and determination that radiated from her was inspiring. I couldn't help but be a little sad, though, that we were still teammates, which meant we couldn't date.

But one really great thing about her being on the team was that we had a real chance to have a stellar season. Josiah could continue to get stronger, so if Willow got called up to an Olympic training team and had to leave, he could step right in.

If she gets on a skating team? I was living in denial, wasn't I? Of course she would.

"She earned the spot." Coach came around the side of his desk.

He was a stocky six-foot-six guy with straight brown hair and a crooked nose he'd earned during his five seasons playing pro hockey.

"I know she did." I checked out the rest of the names, and it was everything I'd expected. She'd beaten Josiah out, fair and square.

"Having a girl on the team changes things, like it did for your Fall League, but you all did well with it, with a couple notable exceptions."

Pax and Eric.

"You're captain, Wind." He clapped his hand on my shoulder. "You're a senior. The team looks up to you, so how you handle things with Willow means something. They'll follow your lead."

"Yes, sir."

"I know Coach Kurt instituted a no fraternizing rule for the team over Fall League." He gave my shoulder a squeeze. "Make sure everyone knows that the rule still applies. Can't have anything come between you all. We have a tough schedule, and if your team wants to make it to State, you all have to be at the top of your games. No drama."

I nodded, my stomach sinking.

"Why don't you go hang that up outside my door for me? I have a couple calls to return." He winked at me. "One of which is to Coach Raymond from BC."

"Really?" The name of Boston's hockey coach caught my attention.

Coach Noah sat behind his desk again and grinned. "I'll let you know how it goes."

The paper in my hand started vibrating. Coach Raymond... Wow.

I hustled out of the small office and pulled the door shut behind me. If only I could have stayed in there to hear.

"What's the verdict?" Pax came up behind me and sucker punched my stomach.

I stepped to the side and snagged a tack from the bulletin

board beside Coach's office door and pinned the roster to the corkboard. "See for yourself."

"What. The. Hell," Pax yelled, and several expletives followed that nearly made my ears bleed.

"What's up?" Eric came up behind Pax and checked out the roster. "Shit."

"Guys. Chill." I elbowed him as I scanned the roster again:
Center: Nathaniel Baker and Jordan Wilson.
Right Wing: Ryan "Preach" Armstrong and Landen Jones.
Left Wing: Brodie "Wind" Windom and Jason Lopez.
Right Defense: Teddy Cook and Trevor Lee.
Left Defense: Pax Hunt and Eric Vang.
Goalie: Willow Covington and Josiah Brown.

Pax punched me in the arm. "This is bullshit, man. She is not better than Josiah."

"Are you guys saying Coach is wrong?" I faced off with him and Eric. "That he can't judge talent?"

"She's a girl!" Eric said.

"She made it, didn't she?" Nathaniel asked as he strolled toward us. Teddy and Preach were close behind him.

Preach hurried around Nathaniel and scanned the roster. "Yes! This team is going to rock it."

Nathaniel looked over Teddy's shoulder at the team line up while Preach came up beside me.

Pax jammed his forefinger on the roster. "This is bullshit."

I shoved him a couple of feet from the board toward the locker rooms. A few people peeked through the doorway that led to the actual lockers and showers, but I nodded them off.

"Look, man. You've got to knock this shit off."

"What's your deal? You getting in that little sequined skirt or what?" He shoved me, then charged out of the locker rooms into the hallway.

Streams of students were charging toward the doors since

classes were over, but I caught up to him near the water fountains beside the locker room entrance.

"She helped us nail a perfect season in Fall League, man. What's your deal?"

"Josiah deserves that spot!" Eric said, coming up beside Pax. "She's dividing us, man. Our hockey family. She's —"

"Helping us win," Preach said as he strode up, Nathaniel and Teddy close behind him. "You want State or not?"

My chest cramped at the mention of State. She'd probably be off training with a new figure skating team by then, but I didn't say anything. We had her now, and that was what mattered.

"Win State? We're not even going to be able to beat Twin River with her on the team."

"Screw you, dude. We *already* beat them with her in the goal!" Nathaniel said.

"That was a fluke," Pax argued.

"Hey, guys." Willow skidded to a stop when we all looked at her. "Um…everything okay?"

Pax stepped toward her, and I tensed, preparing to push him away if he got too close. "You only got the starting spot because Josiah was injured."

"You know what, Pax?" Willow stood tall, pulling her shoulders back and glared at Pax, then Eric. "You and Eric can both take a flying fuck off a cliff."

Nathaniel gasped and pointed at Willow. "Oh shit! Get it, Willow!"

"Grow up." She strode by him, knocking his shoulder, then shoved Eric by palming his shoulder, and tore down the hallway.

And I knew exactly where she was headed.

• • •

Gliding across the ice, Willow arched her back and her arms flowed smoothly through the air to an unheard beat. She wore Air Pods, so I assumed she had her music going, but I didn't even need to hear it.

She looked amazing out there. By the time I'd left the school and gotten to the rink, she'd already changed into her figure skating outfit.

The tight leggings hugged her body, the muscles rippling beneath the fabric. She flipped around, skating backward, her arms out. With the ease of someone who'd spent a lifetime on the ice, she jumped, flying through the air and spun. Landing on one skate, she kicked her leg out and brought her arms around, jumping into a spin.

She moved so fast, she was practically a blur. Round and round, until she raised her arms above her, stuck her foot out, and planted it into the ice. She came to a stop, arms out, back arched, then held the pose, her chest heaving.

I clapped, and she jerked straight. The open ice time had just begun, and only one or two people milled around the bleachers, getting their gear on to skate, but they'd stopped when Willow had landed her jump.

Captivated, like I was.

She pushed off, making her way to me, and I leaned on top of the short wall, watching her. Her cheeks were flushed, and my chest ached. She was so strong and graceful on the ice, it kicked me in the stomach that just as she'd made the high school hockey team, she'd be leaving us soon to go back to her figure skating world.

I glanced down at the ice as I clasped my hands together in front of me so they hung over the wall. The cool air curled around me, and I drew in a deep breath. Even though I wasn't on the ice, the smell and the chill were enough to calm and center me.

"Hey," she said, breathing heavy.

"That was incredible."

"Thanks." She smiled and gave me a nod. "What are you doing here?"

"I knew this is where you'd come after Pax and Eric were such assholes to you."

She huffed, and her jaw clenched. "They really are asshats. Don't they want a winning team? I just don't get it, Brodie. It's bullshit."

"And you shouldn't have to put up with it." I stood straight and ran my fingers through my hair. "I've talked to both of them a couple of times. Preach has, too. But maybe we should bring it up with Coach?"

"No. I'll *show* them I was the best choice. I can take their shit."

"As long as you have your figure skating to help calm you down…" I waited a beat for the sadness to fade from my voice before asking, "Was that one of your old routines?"

She nodded. "I won the Junior World Championships with it. Of course I didn't do all the jumps, but the ones I did felt pretty good." A smile curved her full, pink lips.

Her eyes lit up with a passion I recognized, deep in my core. Because I felt that way about hockey.

That was when it hit me like a slap shot to the gut. Figure skating was her true first love, and she'd always pick it first. Eventually, maybe even sooner rather than later, she *would* leave the team.

She'd leave *me*.

CHAPTER TWENTY-NINE

Willow

"Oh look, if it isn't Mr. Asshat," I yelled at Matthew Halliday as he stormed the goal.

The puck had gone behind the net, and he charged it, fire in his eyes. He darted around, moving the puck out of Pax's reach.

Oh shit. He flicked it my way, but I batted it down. The elusive black rubber disc shot to the side, and one of his guys passed it back a few feet. Matthew was there.

Damn, that guy was hard to keep track of.

He drew his stick back and slapped the puck. It shot at me like a bullet. I threw up my hand and kicked out my foot.

The slap of the puck hitting my leather sent a sting through my digits. I landed in the splits and bounced off the ice.

The crowd behind the goal gasped, and I heard a few moans. The guys on the team always did that, too, when I fell into the splits.

What was the big deal?

"I've got my stamps ready to send you this stat sheet, Matthew," I said as I hopped to my skates.

I tossed the puck he'd just attempted to shoot past me

onto the ice. The Twin River Fighting Pike captain huffed and skated away. I'd stopped every one of his shots tonight so far.

Served him right, too. It'd been nearly two months since I'd seen him at Homecoming, so it felt good to shut him down.

Nathaniel passed the puck to Brodie, and our captain worked his magic.

Moving the puck back and forth, so confident and sure, lit a spark of hope we might win this game.

Talk about a great start to the season. It'd been nothing but hard practices and scrimmages since I'd made the high school boys hockey team six weeks ago.

Brodie spun, keeping the puck close, then blasted into a sprint.

"Yes!" A breakaway. Brodie's specialty. "Come on, Brodie!"

Thwack. His slap shot flew by the goalie, and the crowd roared to their feet, shouting, stomping, and whistling. The noise was so loud I couldn't hear much else, but that didn't matter. All I had to do was keep an eye on the puck.

Nothing would get by me.

Absolutely nothing.

Matthew shouted something to his goalie. I couldn't make it out, but the tone in his voice was condescending and harsh.

He was the exact opposite of a team player. I couldn't believe I'd fallen for his crap.

With the loud *smack* of Matthew's stick hitting the puck, the game was back on, and his team advanced. My heart leaped to my throat. Adrenaline electrified the blood in my veins.

I was ready for this.

I'd show this team what I was made of.

Passing it to his left winger, Matthew charged forward.

Pax attacked. Matthew rammed his elbow into him, throwing him into the boards.

I shouldn't have smiled at my teammate getting hammered, but it was Pax...so I didn't feel quite so bad.

My shoulder still ached from when Pax brutally slammed me into the boards at practice the other day. It was nice to see him get some.

Instead of popping back up on his skates, Pax laid on the ice, causing the ref to blow her whistle and skate over to him. Teddy got there before her and helped him to his feet.

Coach shouted out onto the ice and then asked the ref for a time out.

I left the net, meeting up with everyone else near the player's box.

"You okay?" I smirked at Pax.

"What did you just say to me?"

"Dude, you hit me ten times harder at practice. I was just giving you a hard time."

Pax glowered at me.

Shaking my head, I turned my attention back to Coach Noah.

A few seconds later, the ref blew her whistle.

"On three, Falcons," Coach said.

We all put our sticks in and began counting, "One, two, th—"

Something slammed into the back of my calf and sent me flying forward. I bumped into Teddy, who barely budged, but that didn't stop me from hitting the ice, hard.

"Pax! What the hell is wrong with you?" Brodie shouted.

"Willow, are you all right?" Teddy asked, pulling me to my feet.

"Pax is done." Brodie pointed to the bench. "He just took Willow down."

"No way! I've already stopped twelve goal attempts! I'm the reason we're winning," Pax spat.

Coach pointed to the bench, his eyes narrowing in on Pax like a guard dog about to attack. "You're done! Eric, take his place and stay on Halliday."

The ref blew her whistle a second time. "Let's go!"

At the drop of the puck, Twin River took control and advanced on me.

Teddy charged Matthew, but the Fighting Pike defenseman was too fast. He whipped his stick back and hit the puck with so much force, I half expected flames to shoot out the end.

The puck slapped into my mitt, stinging my palm. Flipping my mask up, I glared at Matthew and gave him a wry grin. "Nice try, loser."

"What did you just say to me?" Matthew whipped off his mask and closed the space between us.

With the puck still in hand, I squared my shoulders. "I said, 'Nice try, *loo-ser*.'" I made sure to enunciate the last syllable. The buzzer went off, indicating we'd won the game.

Dropping his stick, Matthew shoved me with both hands. Completely surprised by the attack, I stumbled over my own skates and landed on my butt beside my goal.

Ugh, these pads. They still tripped me up. Heat steamed up my neck and pooled at my cheeks as I scrambled to my feet.

I spun around to face-off with Matthew, tossing my mask to the ice.

The ref blew her whistle and shouted, "Break it up!"

Brodie's gloved hand rammed into his chest, pushing the jerk-wad away from me. "I guess you didn't get enough last time."

Matthew's face turned bright red. "Get your hands off me."

No way. Brodie does not get to handle my fights.

Pushing Brodie out of the way, I dropped my gloves, planted my skates, and shoved Matthew with all my might.

"Bitch," he screamed as he fell back.

As his skates flew into the air, Brodie spun around, and his elbow rammed my shoulder.

Falling for the second time in minutes, I put my hands out to brace myself, but the flash of the overhead lights reflecting off Matthew's blades seared my eyes.

And then the cool, razor sharp metal slid along my steaming-hot cheek. I landed on my shoulder with a thud, thankfully keeping my head from smacking against the ice.

As I turned over, red splattered along the smooth ice. Gasps ignited around me.

"What?" I asked, my voice sounding small. Distant.

The ref pulled Matthew back and motioned for his coach to come get him.

My face throbbed. I eased my helmet up, and more blood splashed on the ice beneath me.

Wait a second, that was coming from *me*.

CHAPTER THIRTY

Brodie

Pushing up with one hand, Willow cupped her other one to her cheek as she made her way to her feet. The crowd gasped as red streamed down the front of her jersey.

My legs nearly gave out at the sight.

"Are you okay?" I reached for her cheek. She batted my hand away, giving Matthew one last glare. The color drained from his face as he stared at us.

Served him right, that son of a bitch! His ass better get suspended from some games for this shit.

"Willow—"

"I'm fine. Get out of my way." On wobbly skates, Willow pushed off toward our team's bench.

Coach met her on the ice with a towel. "I see stitches in your future."

I guided her to the bench and set her down carefully. "Where's your bag?"

She grunted and pointed to the side and behind her.

"You're a badass, Ice Capades," Nathaniel yelled from the ice.

I made quick work at getting her skates off and into her

bag, but after digging for a few seconds, I couldn't find her shoes. "Where are your shoes?"

"The ambulance is stationed out back." Coach handed her another towel, but this one was wrapped around ice.

"It's just a little cut. I don't need an ambulance."

"One's always here for tournament insurance reasons. *They'll* decide if you need transport. Are your parents here?"

"Yo, Wind," Preach said over the wall.

I bolted to him. "Can you take care of Caleb? I need to stay with Willow."

"Yeah, sure. No problem." He leaned to the side. "Nice one, Iron Willow!"

She huffed, and I let out a chuckle. She did kind of look like a boxer the way she threw down her mitts and was ready to take Matthew on.

"Um, no. My dad's at work, and my grandpa is at home. But please don't call him. I don't want him to worry." She grimaced, then hissed in a breath.

A wave of hot anger punched me in the chest. "Coach, they gonna suspend him for what he did to Willow?"

"Assessed a penalty, marked as not served." He shook his head.

"That's bull—"

"You know the drill. It was after the game, and it didn't lead to a full-on fight."

Yeah, yeah. I knew the drill all right. Still sucked.

"Let's get you up. Take it slow." I cupped her elbow and guided her away from the team bench. "Socks are going to have to do. I couldn't find crap in your bag."

She grinned, then flinched again. "Hey. No making me laugh. Or smile. Or talk."

I wanted to laugh, but I couldn't. I hated seeing her in pain. A blast of cold air stung my face as I pushed open the door for us. Snowflakes fell from the sky and landed on her lashes.

If she wasn't covered in blood right now, this might have been a romantic scene. But instead of romance, tears started to stream down her cheeks.

"Please don't cry." I eased my arm against her upper back and bent down slightly then said, "Hold on."

She draped her arm around my neck, and I hoisted her up, weaving my free arm beneath her knees. Clutching her to me, both from my need to take care of her and to keep her stocking feet dry from the snowy ground, I brushed my cheek against her forehead.

Warmth cascaded into me as she snuggled close. Damn, she fit in my arms perfectly.

Moving as gingerly as I could so I didn't jar her too much, I trekked across the lot to the ambulance parked near the back.

Coach emerged from the rink a second later and caught up to us. "Willow, I called your dad. He's going to meet you at the hospital."

"Maybe I can skip the ambulance ride. Can Brodie just drive me? Or better yet, I can call my mom. She—"

"I'll be the judge of that." A woman wearing a navy shirt and khaki pants gave Willow a warm smile as she stepped out of the back of the ambulance. "I hear you have a pretty deep cut. Let me give it a look."

I set Willow on the bumper of the ambulance but stayed close. The EMT gently nudged her chin with her gloved finger as I held Willow steady. Willow winced, and the gash started bleeding again.

"It appears to be pretty clean." The EMT stepped away from Willow. "Did you hit your head at any point?"

"No, I had my helmet on the whole time, and when I fell, I kept my head up."

After the woman conducted a few quick assessments, she gave Willow a nod. "I do not believe a transport to the emergency room is merited, but I can offer you one if you choose."

"That's way too expensive." She looked up at me from the shelter of my arm around her shoulder. "Can you drive me, Brodie?"

"Of course," I said, nodding to the EMT. "Thank you."

I got Willow tucked into my Tahoe under the close scrutiny of Coach as I told him our plan.

"Drive safely." Coach patted my shoulder. "Text me how things go."

I snagged a blanket from my trunk, then hopped in and threw it over her. "You warm enough?"

She rested her head back, still holding the towel of ice to her ashen face. "Getting there."

I fixed the vents toward her, then checked my surroundings before pulling out of the lot.

"I'm so pissed at Matthew, I could punch him. Again," I said.

"Get in line, buddy," she added.

Her eyes were closed, her head against the headrest. A tear escaped and tore a path down her smooth skin. I reached over and brushed it away. "It'll be all right, Willow."

She let out a breath, her nostrils flared. "Am I done playing for the weekend?"

"No. I mean, unless the doc says so, but you didn't hit your head, which is good. And I've played with cuts like yours, even worse. Once they're stitched up, you're golden." I glanced at her. "I mean, as long as you feel well enough. Josiah can fill in if you're not—"

"No way. I'm playing."

I grinned at her stubbornness, a warm feeling flooding

through my chest. "You're amazing, you know that?"

"Don't," she whispered.

"Don't what? Are you okay? Feeling sick?"

"No. I'm fine. I—" She squeezed her eyes closed for a second. "Don't say things like that. I'm not amazing."

"Yes, you are." I tucked the blanket closer to her neck, then brushed my knuckles along her skin. "And beautiful." Even tears, matted hair, and a swollen face didn't hinder her beauty. "And sexy—"

"Brodie. Stop," she whispered. "It's too…difficult. You're just so sweet and nice and thoughtful." Another tear escaped. "I hate that we can't be together."

It felt like someone kicked me in the stomach. I wanted to be with her, too. The two kisses we'd stolen haunted me. "Me, too, Willow. Me, too."

"**B**rodie!" Jessa stormed through the ER doors and directly to where I was sitting in the waiting room.

I'd been wasting space on the hard, plastic chairs for nearly an hour, waiting for an update. "She's still back there." I stood up, stretching my arms toward the tiled ceiling.

I hated waiting rooms. Hospitals, too. The bleachy, clean smell brought me back to being here when Mom was brought in. And then the times I'd been here with Caleb since. Each instance felt like a swift kick to the gut, and tonight was no different.

"I saw what happened on YouTube." Jessa stopped beside me, a whirl of grease and sugar smells plowing over me. My stomach roared with hunger.

That was when I noticed she was wearing a Sub Shop polo.

"You didn't happen to bring any subs, did you?"

She opened her big leather bag and pulled one out. "Thought you might be hungry."

"Lifesaver." I snagged the bag, then sat down in my seat and dug in. "I didn't want to leave in case she came out or her dad got here."

"He texted me; he's on his way. He was a few towns over making a delivery."

I nodded as I took a bite. I'd almost eaten half the sub with just a few bites.

"Freaking Matthew Halliday." Jessa plopped down beside me and fastened her long blond hair up with two pencils. "I'm just glad she didn't get injured so she can still skate. You know?"

My stomach dropped, and the bite I'd just taken tasted like dirt. I set the half-eaten sub on the bag that was on my lap.

"I got a pretty good video of her the other day, landing some doubles." She eyed me. "What's wrong?"

"Nothing." I took a drink of the now cold coffee I'd gotten from the cart that'd come by a while ago. "I'm glad, too."

"Yeah. I can tell." She nudged me. "She'll be fine. Willow's tough."

Jessa thought I was worried about Willow's injury, and sure, I was, but even more, I was sad. I hated the thought of Willow leaving. Of not seeing her every day. Sure, it sucked we couldn't be together, but at least I got to hear her laugh. Smell her coconut perfume.

"Jessie! Broda!" Willow wheeled through the ER automatic doors, a huge smile filling her face. "Wait." She giggled. "That's not right."

She looked up as if she was trying to see the orderly who pushed her wheelchair and pointed. "This is…Jaaaason."

Jessa put her hand over her mouth and chuckled. "She's

so loopy."

I set my food on the chair beside me and stood up, keeping Willow in my sights. She sagged against the wheelchair, smiling and laughing.

"She never could tolerate pain pills."

White gauze covered her left cheek, the tape going right up to her bottom lid. Hair had fallen out of her braids and shot out all directions. She was wearing a blue hospital top now but still had her leggings on that were under her pads.

"Here you go." The orderly handed Jessa a big plastic bag so full with the hockey gear inside, it was stretching the limits, nearly bursting through.

"Jessa. You're the bestest friend in the whole world." Willow laughed. "But you're kind of wavy and tilted. How'd you do that?" She pushed on the arms of the chair as if to get up.

"Oh my gosh," Jessa said, kneeling before Willow. "Stay put. I got all your stuff from your locker at the arena and what you came here in. Your phone's in there, too, and your dad is waiting out front with the car."

Her glazed-over gaze landed on me, and her smile widened. "You're my knight in shining armor."

Heat fused my cheeks as I stepped up beside her as the orderly pushed the wheelchair through the doors.

"Except I'm mad at you. You should have let me punch that turd Matthew right in the nose."

I chuckled. "Enjoy those painkillers, slugger."

Jessa pointed to a blue Honda. "There's your dad."

"That's him," Willow sang out, waving her hand.

Jessa hugged me. "Thank you for bringing her here! You're an awesome teammate and friend."

"Sure," I said, watching Willow. I didn't want to leave her. I couldn't invite myself over, though. Her dad and Jessa would take care of her.

But I wanted to watch over her. My breath whooshed out of my chest as a swirl of arctic air slapped me across the face. It was enough to drag me back to reality. Willow wasn't mine to take care of.

Like Jessa had just so starkly reminded me, I was her *teammate*. Maybe a friend, but nothing more.

"Jessa, are you coming to my house for a sleepover?"

She chuckled. "I'm going to come over and help you get situated."

"Situated. Situated. That's a funny word. Situuuuated."

"Let's get you out of this chair," the orderly said.

With Jessa on one side and me on the other, we each took one of Willow's hands as she stood up.

"Hey, honey." Her dad opened the passenger side door. "Thanks, Brodie and Jessa, for taking care of her."

"Daaaaad, how dooooo you know Broooooodie?" Willow said with a giggle.

He gave her a soft smile. "Sweetheart, it's Woodhaven. Everyone knows everyone."

"Feel better, Willow." I pulled her into a quick hug, then stepped back. "I'm glad you're okay. I'll text Jessa later and check on you."

"Thanks, buddy." She slapped her hands on my cheeks and pulled me close. "Come here."

Her lips crashed against mine. She tilted my head and dove into the kiss without restraint. As if on autopilot, I kissed her back.

I heard Jessa gasp, and I flinched back. *Shit.* "Um…she's out of it. I—we—"

"Mmm…that was nice, but the park was better." Willow swayed in the breeze, staring up at me with glazed eyes.

"The park?" Jessa asked, looking at me and then Willow.

"Probably just a doped-up loopy dream." *Lie*. Of course we'd kissed in the park. And at the Hay Bale Maze. And I'd wanted to kiss her every day since. But I couldn't let anyone know that. I had to try to cover.

Jessa arched an eyebrow. "*Riiiight*."

I might not have been very convincing…then again, maybe it was time to stop dancing around things and go for it with Willow. Tonight, being here at the hospital, her injury and that kiss—even if it was prompted by pain meds—was a vivid reminder of how life could change so quickly.

I'd told her I didn't want to take anything for granted that night on the swings when we'd first kissed. But I had been doing just that with Willow. I was wasting every second I had with her by hiding behind my fear. The fear of her leaving, the fear of our teammates finding out, not to mention the no-fraternizing rule.

Screw it. I liked Willow, and I wanted to be with her.

Rules be damned.

CHAPTER THIRTY-ONE

Brodie

It took talent to park a Land Rover sideways in a driveway without hitting the water feature. But Dad had done it.

Thank God Caleb was staying at the Armstrongs' this weekend because of the hockey tournament and didn't see this. I wasn't sure how I could explain it away like I had all the shit Dad had been pulling lately.

I eased the car around his and into the garage stall, then snatched the mail I'd gotten and hustled through the front door. "I'm home."

"Kitchen," Dad said.

I riffled through the mail as I made my way toward the kitchen. One item caught my attention because it had a huge red stamp on it that said FINAL NOTICE.

My stomach plunged.

I crept toward the kitchen, and I heard my dad say, "Hurry up, Brodie's home. Just shut it down. Get 'em off our backs."

Holding my breath, I slowed near the entryway to the kitchen to listen.

"Fix it, Miles—make this go away," Dad said, and then another pause followed.

He must be on the phone.

"Whatever, I have to go."

I heard what I thought was Dad's cell clanking against the countertop, and I drew in a deep breath as I took the final step through the doorway.

"Hey, kid," he said, then glanced behind me. "Where's your brother?"

"Armstrongs'." I leaned against the wall beside the center island.

There was a cup of coffee next to Dad and a small plate with some toast on it. Bags hung dark and heavy beneath his eyes, and his brown hair seemed grayer. More prominent streaks just above the ears.

He looked like a different man. A stranger.

Then again, I hadn't seen him in over a week. He'd not made any of my games this Thanksgiving break, nor had he shown up on Thanksgiving Day. I'd lied to Caleb and said he was away on a business trip, but I'd had no clue where he was. He'd texted me a couple times to say he wouldn't be home, but nothing other than that.

I plopped the envelopes in front of him. "Grabbed the mail."

He shoved the bundle aside, then reached for his cup.

"Coming to the game tonight?" I asked.

"Can't."

"We're in the championships."

"Of a *holiday* tournament. It's not a big deal." He grunted, focusing on the newspaper he was scanning on his iPad. He used to be *all* about my playing hockey, even the holiday tournaments. Came to every game with Mom, asked me questions about it, about school, about girlfriends.

But now…nothing.

And it wasn't just a holiday tournament. Sure, it might

not have counted against full season stats, but scouts watched them. They knew the teams that did well in these. *And* they sometimes came out to see them since it was on the holiday.

Dad didn't care about anything anymore.

I unfolded the envelope marked FINAL NOTICE, and when I held it up, it was shaking in my grip.

"Dad, what happened to Rita and everyone else?"

"Cut 'em loose."

"Are we getting new people?" I'd already known the answer since Rita was let go several weeks ago and nobody else came in to take her place.

"Don't need 'em."

"Yes, we do, or you need to come home and take care of us. I don't know how to cook anything other than mac-n-cheese and corn dogs. And Caleb needs—"

"Figure it out." He finally looked up, his brown eyes hard and cold.

Had I heard him right? Had he just told me to *figure it out*? Like I knew anything about cooking or taking care of Caleb.

"You gotta step up, kid. You need to help more around here."

The breath whooshed out of my chest. "But I— What do you mean?"

He shoved the iPad to the side. "There's more to life than playing hockey. Look after your brother while I try and keep things together here."

"Keep things together? You mean cooking dinner for Caleb, making sure he takes a shower once in a while and is doing his homework? Or take him to school every day? Because I'm already doing *all* those things." I held up the envelope. "Or are you talking about keeping the lights on? Is that my job now, too?"

"Shit." He reached over the breakfast bar table and snatched the envelope from my hand. "That's nothing. Oversight."

"Then what'd you mean by keeping things together?"

"Nothing you need to worry about." He stood so fast, the barstool behind him shuffled back. He grabbed it before it fell over, but the aggressiveness of how he did it had me stepping away.

There was a center island between us, but I could feel the anger palpating from him. It didn't make sense, though.

"Dad. What's going on?" My heart hammered away in my chest, and my fists formed tight balls.

"Nothing. It's fine."

"No, it's not," I said a little louder than I'd intended. "Things are *not* fine here."

"Watch it." He glared at me.

"Excuse me?" I could feel my pulse throbbing in my temples. "Did you even know I had to rush Caleb to the hospital last month for his asthma?"

"That kid is always—"

"Don't you dare finish that sentence, Dad." I yelled it that time as I stepped toward the counter that separated us. "He's sick."

"He's *always* sick."

"He didn't ask to have asthma. You think he likes being this way? Going to the hospital?"

"I have work."

"I have *school*. It's my senior year. And what the hell do I know about anything anyway?"

Dad stared at me, his nostrils flaring. "You've got it so rough." He raised his arms and waved to his surroundings. "Such horrible living conditions, how have you survived?"

"It's not that. It's—"

"Who do you think pays for that decked-out car of yours? Keeps your credit cards open? Provides a roof over your head any kid would dream of having?"

"You can have it all back. If it means you'd be around more, you can take it all away. You're *never* here. Caleb is always asking when you're coming home."

Dad huffed.

"He misses you. So do I. And then you let all the staff go and I find mail like this in our box? What the *hell* is going on?"

He stepped away but stumbled to the side enough that he had to grip the counter. I thought maybe something was on the floor there, but when I rounded the corner of the breakfast bar, there wasn't.

And then the stench of alcohol swarmed around me. I recognized that smell from parties, and it'd always made my stomach clench. Sure, I'd drank before, but after losing Mom to a drunk driver…I never touched the stuff again.

Dad, he had the opposite reaction. He drank all the time.

"Are you drunk?" I didn't see any bottles or anything on the kitchen counters or table behind him. "Who was that on the phone?"

"None of your business." He stumbled away toward the living room, which led to the hallway to his master bedroom.

"Dad." My voice ricocheted off the vaulted ceilings, and he stopped, but he didn't turn around. "Please."

His shoulders slouched.

I gulped through the fear preventing me from saying what I wanted to say. What I *needed* to say. "We lost Mom already." Tears burned my eyes. "We…we can't lose you, too. We need you."

"No, you don't," he whispered, still showing me his back. "You're better off without me."

"Don't say that. Of course we—"

"I have to go. California." He stood straight again and coughed. "Business."

"Dad. Wait—"

He stomped off and disappeared around the corner. A few seconds later, I heard the door to his room slam shut.

Silence.

He hadn't told me what was happening, but it was bad. I felt it in my stomach. Final notice mail. Dad drinking. Firing the staff.

The walls of the spacious kitchen closed in on me. Suffocating. It suddenly felt like Boston College and playing hockey for them was somehow slipping through my fingers. I mean, who would take care of Caleb? If we were getting final notices, who would pay for it?

Unless I scored a full ride. *But am I good enough?*

I flopped onto the couch and let the tears fall. The first tears since Mom's funeral.

Only I wasn't sure I'd ever get them to stop.

CHAPTER THIRTY-TWO

Willow

JESSA: I still can't believe you kissed him!
JESSA: In front of me and your dad!
ME: I know…
ME: Talk about humiliating.
ME: Thanks for not freaking out on me.
JESSA: Not going to lie, it was surprising!
ME: I wanted to tell you about the park, how I was feeling about Brodie, and everything else in between.
ME: I just didn't know how to do it.
ME: I'm so sorry!
ME: Do you forgive me?
JESSA: Of course!
JESSA: I thought something was going on before you laid one on him in the hospital…but I knew that you'd tell me once you were ready.
ME: You really are the best! Do you know that?
JESSA: Duh!
JESSA: ☺
JESSA: You're my best friend.
ME: And thank you for keeping it between us…for now.

JESSA: I totally get it, and don't worry, my lips are sealed.

JESSA: 🖤🖤🖤

JESSA: Love you!

ME: Love you, too!

I felt so much better after telling Jessa. It was like a huge weight had been lifted off my shoulders. I *really* was lucky.

My thoughts floated back to the hospital scene when I kissed Brodie. Sure, it might have been a loopy kiss, and I only vaguely remembered it, but it'd happened. We'd made it six weeks without kissing. We'd stayed focused on our sports. Trained hard. Hell, pushing the limits on my training was the only thing that kept me from throwing my goalie gear in the net and jumping on him during practice.

My thoughts were interrupted by a new slew of texts from Ericka.

ERICKA: Hey, babe!

ERICKA: Was just thinking about you…

ERICKA: How's everything going?

I'd called Ericka the day after I kissed Brodie. She'd been super supportive. Between her and Jessa, I'd struck the best friend gold mine.

ME: Pretty good!

ME: More importantly, how are you feeling?

ERICKA: A little better each day.

ERICKA: But not fast enough.

ERICKA: Six weeks off my feet is killing me!

ME: I know. It's horrible! ☹

ERICKA: How'd you get through it with your injury?

ME: You helped!

ME: 🖤

ME: Lots of crying, focusing on healing thoughts.

ME: And did I mention you?

ERICKA: I wish you were here.

ME: Me, too. Love you, girl! Stay strong. You'll get through this!

ERICKA: Hey, Mom's calling for me.

ERICKA: Gotta go!

ERICKA: Good luck at the game tonight!

ME: Thanks! Give Mom a hug!

I set my phone down, but it buzzed again just as I did.

BRODIE: Can you talk?

ME: Sure. What's up?

BRODIE: Come outside.

BRODIE: I'm in your driveway.

Holy shit. My heart thudded, then stuttered into a full-on pounding. I rolled off my bed, my mind whirling. The championship game didn't start for a few hours, so what was he doing here?

ME: On my way!

I threw on a stocking cap and hoodie and jammed my feet into my boots.

"Dad, Brodie stopped by quick. Be right back," I yelled as I bolted out the front door.

There was his black Tahoe, sitting between the small snowbanks that lined our driveway. The sun shone bright, searing my eyes, so I shaded them. I couldn't see very well through the tinted windows, so I just went to the passenger side and pulled it open.

"Hey!" I said, jumping into the seat. My cheek throbbed with the quick movement, reminding me to take it easy.

Brodie twisted in his seat and turned toward me, his eyes swollen and bloodshot.

"Oh my gosh. What's wrong?" My heart leaped into my throat as I grabbed his shoulder.

"Can we go to the park? Do you have time?" he asked, his voice low and trembling.

"Sure." I sent my dad a quick text and then grabbed the seat belt and clicked it in. "Are you okay? Is Caleb okay?" I reached over the console and grabbed his free hand.

He nodded as he maneuvered the car onto the street. "My dad freaked on me. I—I'm not sure what to do."

By the time we'd pulled into the lot at the park he'd taken me to that night of HOCO, when Ericka had been in her accident, he'd painted a word picture of what went down with him and his dad that made me cringe.

"He really said you'd be better without him?"

Brodie put the car in park and then scrubbed his face with both his hands. "I didn't know what to do. Or where to go." He swallowed hard, then nailed me with a gaze. "All I could think was that I needed to see you."

"Brodie," I said as I grabbed his hand again.

His skin was warm and clammy, his chest heaved, and fresh tears lined his beautiful brown eyes. I wasn't sure what to say. So I cupped his cheek and brushed my thumb below his left eye.

He leaned into my touch and closed his eyes briefly. My heart started pounding at the realization that here was this amazing guy, sitting before me, who was sweet, sensitive, and so very loyal. He was strong and an amazing athlete, but he had to carry so much on those broad shoulders of his. Way more than a seventeen-year-old should.

"Brodie." I pulled him into a hug. "I'm so sorry."

"I…I don't want to stay away from you anymore, Willow." He buried his face in my hair and drew in a deep breath. "I can't stop thinking about you. I want to be with you."

I felt the same way. My feelings for Brodie had been growing. I constantly thought about him. We texted and talked a lot on the phone. When we weren't, I found myself wondering what he was doing, worrying about him and Caleb, and hoping his dad could get his life together so they could be a family again. It was like my brain had been taken over by this adorable Puck Head.

"But the rule—"

"Fuck the rules." He eased back, then rested his forehead against mine. "Remember that night at the swings, what I said about not taking anything for granted? How things can change on a dime?"

I nodded. We both knew that pretty well, considering my injury and his mom dying.

Being this close to him, his scent swirled around me, tickling my stomach like it always did. But what he was saying…could cause trouble on the hockey team. And I knew for sure it would change our relationship forever. It could possibly ruin the friendship we'd been building since I first met him in August.

But here he was, asking me to do this. Being vulnerable with me. I hadn't been able to stop thinking about him, either, no matter what I'd tried. It was the end of November, and if one of the coaches I'd sent my videos to picked me up for their training team, I'd be out of here by January.

My time here in Woodhaven was limited—and I wanted to spend it with him.

"Say something," he whispered, his warm breath washing over me.

"Yes." I kissed him and then leaned back, heat flushing to my chest. "Yes."

He curled his fingers around the nape of my neck, cradling me so tenderly, it sent a wave of heat straight to my abdomen. He claimed my lips with an urgent need. Still, it was gentle but filled with emotion. Heat.

And he was right. Rules be damned.

...

Tied at zero. We had two minutes to do something or we'd get thrown into overtime.

The kiss Brodie and I shared in his car and our agreement to secretly date flashed through my mind. It sent shivers down my spine.

Focus, Willow!

You can think about Brodie after Woodhaven wins the game.

I bent my knees and smacked my stick against the ice. "Come on, Preach."

He took a shot, and it deflected off the goal. The crowd gasped.

"Let's go! Come on, guys!"

The other team's center charged the puck. Teddy threw his shoulder into him, but he raised an elbow and shoved Teddy onto his ass. That wasn't an easy feat, either, considering Teddy's size.

The center advanced on me. I gulped through the adrenaline rush nearly choking me and gripped my stick.

He crossed the centerline, ice spraying from under his skates. Eric attacked the puck. Sticks clashed, but it didn't stop him. He laid Eric out flat.

The space between us closed.

Less than ten feet.

The unstoppable center brought back his stick and slapped with a deafening *thwack*.

It felt like time stopped as the puck flew through the air. I could almost count the rotations as my eyes focused on the vulcanized black disc. Dropping to the ice, my knees pressed together, I held out my glove and said a silent prayer to the hockey gods.

The puck hit my glove with such power, it moved my hand back several inches. Digging my skates into the ice, I leaned into the momentum and forced my glove forward as a scream burned its way through my throat.

No way was he going to score.

Not on my watch.

Push it, Willow!

Finally breaking through the momentum, I fell forward, the puck safely tucked in my glove.

I'd done it. I'd stopped it. I might have broken my fingertips, but it was worth it.

People leaped to their feet, cheering and punching the air.

In front of me, the center stood with his mouth agape. His blue mouth guard hanging low, he tapped his stick on the ice and dipped his head at me, a major sign of respect in hockey. Pride swelled deep in my chest.

With only twenty-seven seconds left on the clock, I passed the puck to Brodie. "Get a goal already, would ya?"

"Nice stop, Toe Pick." Our eyes locked for a moment, and he winked, then he charged forward. He glided across the ice with a grace and power that few possessed.

My heart hammered at each push of his skates, each shift in direction as he charged.

Twelve seconds.

Brodie passed to Preach, who wove around a defender. Preach hoisted the puck, avoiding the steal, then back-passed it to Brodie.

And then he charged the goal in typical Brodie "Wind" Windom fashion.

Three seconds.

Brodie dodged a check, spun, and set himself for the shot.

"Yes," I yelled. "Come on, Brodie."

In one swift motion, he hit the puck with such force that I thought his stick had broken.

The goalie dropped to his knees, but he was too late. The puck slammed into the back of the net with such force that it bounced back out and landed in front of the goalie.

The buzzer sounded.

The crowd erupted with cheers and applause. I slid my mask off, careful not to hit my stitches.

I snapped my head to the right, to where I'd seen Gramps sit down before the game had started. He stood there, waving maroon and silver pom-poms.

Grinning, I waved back with both arms as I coasted toward the team.

"Oh my gosh. No way!" I said. Next to him stood my dad. He was still in his work uniform, which meant he must have found someone to cover the second half of his shift. He normally had Sundays off but was asked to come in today to cover for someone who'd called in sick. He waved at me and smiled.

Pride burst through my veins as I joined the guys.

Eric wacked Brodie on the back and held up the puck.

"You did it, Willow." Preach pointed at me, then he and Teddy skated toward the group of players.

Brodie looked over at me and nodded. "We won!"

The cheers were almost deafening.

Eric rammed into my shoulder and shoved Brodie into the group. "That goal was freaking epic!"

My cheek ached from smiling. We'd won the tournament! I pumped my stick in the air as I followed the team to the player's box.

"Nice job, Willow. Excellent goal, Brodie." Coach patted us both on the back. "I know we usually pick one MVP per game, but you both get to split the honor tonight."

"Thank you, Coach!" All the extra practices and training with Brodie on and off the rink had paid off.

Clutching the puck to my chest, I held it there until Coach told us to head to the locker rooms. Talk about an amazing day. First, Brodie and I decide to start up dating in secret. Then this epic win and MVP honor…

I touched my hockey puck to Brodie's as we started making our way off the ice.

He grinned and brushed his mitted hand against mine. My stomach clenched as if his bare skin were touching mine.

Brodie and I brought up the rear of the team gliding across the ice to the exit. Just as we stepped off the ice, I felt a tug on my jersey. I turned around, Brodie by my side, to see what was up.

"Willow!" a little girl with curly brown hair exclaimed. "Will you and Brodie please sign my puck?"

She thrust a gold permanent marker and a puck into my hand. My cheeks flushed as I reached for the offerings with shaky fingers. I'd signed plenty of autographs while figure skating, but for hockey?

If the girls on the skating team could see me now. I was sporting a nice war wound on my cheek, I was decked out in goalie gear and playing hockey, and now I was signing an autograph!

"We'll catch up with you all in a few minutes," Brodie shouted to the team.

I scribbled my signature on the top of the puck and handed it to Brodie to do the same. "Do you play hockey?" I asked her.

"Squirt League. I wanna be like you!"

I ruffled her hair and smiled. "Then you will be! Keep at it."

"Here you go." Brodie put the top back on the marker and handed it to the little girl.

Her grin, missing her two front teeth, was absolutely adorable.

"Thank you so much," she squealed as she clutched the puck and held it up to her chest. "Can I ask you a question?"

"Absolutely."

I figured she'd want to know what it was like playing on a guy's hockey team, but instead she blurted out, "Are you two boyfriend/girlfriend?"

Two hours into our secret relationship, and we'd already been outed. Were we really that obvious?

CHAPTER THIRTY-THREE

Brodie

The thunk of the lights clicking on and warming up rattled through the empty arena.

I drew in a deep breath of the cool air and closed my eyes. I loved coming here before the hustle of everything filled the place. And I loved it even more now that it included Willow Covington. Meeting her here for practice had become the highlight of each morning.

The only tricky part had been finding someone to come over to the house at five o'clock in the morning to watch over Caleb and help get him to school. Thank God for babysitting services that took credit cards.

The lights had warmed up enough that I started making my way between the bleachers to the rink, clutching my bag close to me. I slid over the ice, heading to the team bench, when I heard a door creak. I dropped my bag on the bench and leaned over the short wall.

Hopefully it wasn't anyone coming early, because I wanted to steal a few kisses from Willow while we were practicing. Couldn't do that with the guys around. We were eleven days into our secret relationship and so far doing pretty well keeping it hidden.

"Hey!" Willow jumped onto the ice and slid a few feet, keeping perfectly balanced.

"What's up, Toe Pick?" I said, and she laughed.

"I think I like Ice Princess better. Well, Princess, because well…" She curtseyed. "You're my prince."

I laughed, and it echoed through the arena. She covered her face with her hands and laughed, too, as she made her way to me. When I stepped onto the ice, her eyes widened and she dropped her bag, gave a quick look around, then leaped into my arms.

Cinching her legs around my waist, I held her tight, my arms around her butt. There was nothing better than being held by Willow. She came in and planted a whopper of a kiss on me.

"Missed you," she whispered as she feathered kisses along my neck.

"You just saw me last night." I shifted, rested her on the short wall, and stepped into her more.

"Well, that was twelve whole hours ago."

I touched a kiss to the tip of her cold nose. "Are we practicing or…"

"Practice." She patted my chest. "I'm so excited, Brodie. I have to show you something."

She jumped down, then grabbed her bag and hustled to the team bench. A flash of white caught my attention. She'd pulled out her figure skates.

"Um…thought I was slapping shots at you?" I leaned forward, resting my elbows on my knees.

"I was practicing the other day."

"When?"

"You were hanging with Preach a couple days ago, I can't remember. Anyway. I came up here during open ice." She stood and pulled off her sweats and hoodie.

She was wearing a sequined skating outfit of some sort. Nothing as flashy as those I'd seen her compete in, but not too far off. Even had the tights on and everything.

"What's going on?" My stomach twisted into a knot seeing her in the skating outfit. I wanted her so much to focus on hockey. Yeah, it was selfish of me, but I couldn't help myself. We were now in the second week of December, and she'd said she'd have to get on a team by January.

That meant our time together was seriously limited. But if she loved hockey enough, maybe she wouldn't leave?

"I can't wait to show you, Brodie. I'm so excited, I can't even…" She quickly laced up her skates as I did mine. "Will you video me?"

She was holding out her phone to me when I looked up. "Um…sure."

What the heck was going on? The same fire I'd just been thinking about was in her eyes, but it was for figure skating.

"We're facing off with Roger the Right Hand of God in a few weeks. We really should—"

"What is up with that nickname?" she asked. But then: "Just give me a few minutes and we can practice." She hopped up from the bench, then kissed my cheek. "Brodie. I'm so excited."

I could tell, and I wanted to be, too, I really did, but it was like she was slipping through my fingers. These three and a half months had been amazing. I didn't want it to end. Ever.

She hunched over and powered through a few laps, a smile filling her face the entire time. Each push was strong, focused. The skating outfit hugged her fit body, highlighting her curves, her strength. She was beautiful. Sexy.

"Watch!"

She flipped around so she was skating backward. Her

arms were out, her skates expertly crossing over each other, and she was picking up speed. One great push from her powerful legs bolted her into the air. She pulled in her arms and kicked her leg around, then brought it close to her other one as she flew through the air, spinning.

With the grace of a swan, she landed on her skate, her other leg kicking out, and then she turned, stabbed her toe pick into the ice, and stopped, her hands in the air, her back arched, and a smile filling her face.

She'd nailed it.

I applauded her as the realization hit me like a hockey puck to the forehead. A training team would definitely pick her up. She would leave me.

"Yes!" She whooped and zoomed toward me. "Did you see that?"

She didn't slow down, so I widened my stance and opened my arms, knowing what she was going to do. With another solid push, she leaped into my arms. I caught her and coasted back slightly. Glancing over my shoulder, I glided around toward the middle of the rink.

"I did it, Brodie. I did it. A double axel! And not just one. I landed that jump and a few others *multiple* times, *multiple* days in a row, all with minimal discomfort!"

"That's…great. Really great." My gut churned as I held her tighter to me. I didn't want to let her go.

"So, will you video me?"

I eased her to her skates. "I thought you sent out videos already?"

"Oh, I did." She slouched slightly. "I got two rejections, but there are a few out still. And there's this new company opening up in Miami. I was talking to Ericka earlier, and she said she heard about it at the rink yesterday."

"Miami, huh?" The weight on my chest got even heavier.

That was really far away.

"I'm still looking into it, but there isn't much online about it yet. I want to know who the coach is." She held up her phone. "But I was hoping to get another video made up in case it's a go."

"Sure. Yes." I accepted it and cleared my throat. I couldn't have her hearing or seeing my disappointment. She was so happy. And to come back from the injury she'd suffered, that was a huge feat.

She quirked her eyebrow up and then smiled. "You good?"

"Yes. Yes. Great." I gently shoved her away from me. "Loosen up a little again. Then go for it."

My stomach plummeted. Not only was Willow going to leave, it was actually my fault. I was the one who'd offered to train her so she'd be on our hockey team. All because I wanted to win so badly. I'd trained her hard. Pushed her. And now her dreams were coming true, which was everything I wanted for her; I did. I just never expected to feel this way about her.

And now my time with her was quickly coming to an end.

CHAPTER THIRTY-FOUR

Willow

"**A**re you ever going to tell me why they call Roger the Right Hand of God?" I leaned over, resting my hands on my thighs as I gasped for air after that last drill.

"Come on, Princess! Let's go." Brodie slammed his stick on the ice, totally ignoring my question.

He'd set two orange cones out, fifteen yards apart. I'd lost track how many times I'd skated back and forth as Brodie timed me on his iPhone. I needed a rest.

"Again," he said, clapping his hands together.

"Need a breather," I said with a gasp. "Tell me about Roger."

Brodie remained in the middle of the rink, his hands on his hips. He was wearing jogging pants, a long-sleeve Wolverines Athletics shirt that hugged his chest and biceps. I was already breathless, but him standing there, looking all statuesque, made it even harder to breathe.

"Right Hand of God. Just a nickname we gave him because he's so good."

"Not as good as you."

"We jockey back and forth in the record books." He let out

a long breath. "Right now, I've got the lead scorer record by one. And he has a slap shot almost as lethal as mine."

"Hence the extra hard slap shots you hammered at me earlier." I nodded and leaned forward. "I'm ready."

He blew his whistle, and I blasted out of my starting position.

My skates dug into the ice, and I pushed even harder. Lungs burning, I zeroed in on the final cone in front of me. By the time I reached it, my legs felt like jelly.

"Better." Brodie glanced up from his cell phone.

"Are you serious?" I crouched and tried to catch my breath.

"You beat your old time by a second and a half."

His lack of enthusiasm wasn't lost on me.

I struggled to get back upright.

"Is something wrong?" I skated to him and reached my arms around his neck.

He shook his head.

"Do you want to watch a movie later tonight?" I stood on my toes and kissed him on the cheek.

Brodie pulled back. "I can't. I'm hanging out with Preach."

"Oh. All right." I let my gloves fall to the ice and pulled off my helmet.

"What are you doing?" Brodie looked at my gear and then back at me.

My pads came next. I threw them across the ice, and they slid until they bumped against the boards.

"Willow?"

I jumped up and wrapped my legs around him.

"Whoa." He held on but didn't meet my lips for a kiss. "For real, what are you doing? We're supposed to be practicing."

"We only have twenty minutes left, and since you're going to be hanging out with Preach tonight..." I dipped my head and met his lips. They were cold from being in the rink for the last hour and a half.

He returned my kiss with a sense of urgency and intensity I hadn't experienced with him yet. Curling his hands around my butt, he held me flush with him. That simple movement stoked the embers simmering to life deep in my core.

Fastening myself to him even more, I tilted his head, my tongue dueling with his as we got lost in the kiss. I vaguely remember him gliding across the ice as I was tackling his mouth, but we came to a stop.

He stepped over the threshold, into the penalty box. His hands shifted to my waist as he sat down on the bench. My legs fell astride him, sending a streak of heat scorching through my abdomen. I settled atop him, basking in his warmth as I took the kiss deeper.

Combing my hair away from my face, he eased my head back and peppered kisses and nips along my neck.

Goose bumps stormed down my spine, and I couldn't hold back a shiver. It wasn't from the cold, not one bit, but Brodie pulled away slightly.

"This okay?" His hot breath caressed my skin.

"There's nobody I'd rather be in the penalty box with than you."

I buried my hands in his silky hair and leaned back, giving him even more access. He tasted like mint, and his woodsy scent fused with me as I breathed him in.

I might be leaving soon, so I was going to take advantage of every single minute I had with this amazing guy. And by the way he was clinging to me, he must be thinking the same thing.

CHAPTER THIRTY-FIVE

Brodie

The shrill ring of my phone ripped me out of the dark depths of sleep like someone threw a bucket of ice water on me.

I rolled over and slapped at the phone sitting on my bed table. It wasn't Preach's ring or Willow's, so it didn't matter. Only sleep mattered.

"Hello?" a slurred voice called out. "Brodie!"

Wait a second. That was Dad's voice. I sat up, shoving the covers off and snatching my phone. I'd accidentally answered the call in my fuss to silence it.

It was an unknown number, though. What the heck?

Clearing my throat, I sat up more. "Hello?"

"Son. It's me."

"Dad?" I kicked my feet over the side and planted them on the soft carpet. "What's wrong? Where's your cell?"

He coughed into the phone so loudly, I had to pull it away from my ear.

"Come get me." His voice cracked, and I heard murmuring over the airwaves. "I'm at the station."

"Station? As in—"

"Yes, damn it, the police station. Get down here *now* and grab the checkbook out of the safe. You'll need to post bail for me."

My stomach plunged, and the air knocked out of my lungs as if someone slapped a puck to my chest.

"Brodie," Dad yelled.

"I'm here. I—safe—what's the code?" I asked as I put him on speaker and opened a note on my phone to write it down.

He rattled off four numbers.

"Wait. What? Slow down—"

The phone clicked.

"Hello?" I said.

No answer.

"Dad?"

Silence.

"What the hell?"

I hopped to my feet and hurdled the pile of dirty clothes next to my dresser to get to my closet. I dug around the laundry basket and grabbed my sweats and yanked a hoodie from the hangers.

"Oh crap." Caleb was here. I couldn't leave him.

Maybe Willow could come—no. As much as I would love to call her, I didn't want her to have to explain to her dad at five o'clock in the morning that she had to help me with Caleb because my dad was in jail. I'd call Preach. The Armstrongs were almost like surrogate parents to Caleb. They'd understand.

I'd text Willow later once I figured out what the hell my dad was doing in jail.

I dialed Preach's number as I hustled to Dad's room and into his closet where the safe was.

"This better be good," Preach said, his voice cracking.

"Can you meet me at the police station?"

"What?" His voice came through loud and clear that time.

I rattled off what little I knew as I punched the code into the safe. He said he'd meet me there, and I hung up.

Hopefully, I'd heard the numbers correctly and the safe would open. I turned the knob and it clicked. I yanked open the heavy door.

Piles of cash nearly filled the thing. "Son of a bitch." I'd never seen so much money. Beside the stack on the right, there were three checkbooks. I grabbed them all and shoved them in my hoodie front pocket.

While in the closet, I snatched a Wolverines stocking cap to cover my unruly hair. No time to brush my teeth, though, so I snatched some gum off his dresser beside the closet door.

I bolted to Caleb's room and cracked the door open. The kid was zonked out, lying on his belly, his left arm perched behind him, and his mouth wide open.

The humidifier was going full steam beside the bed, and tissues littered the floor. Damn stuffy nose. The kid was getting a cold again.

"Caleb?" I said, trying to see if he'd hear me.

Good. He didn't. I snuck to his bed and swaddled him up in his blankets, then hoisted him into my arms. The quilts would keep him warm.

With the coordination of a newbie skater, I got Caleb tucked into the Tahoe, and then I hopped into the front seat.

Watching over my shoulder as I turned on the engine, my sleeping-like-the-dead brother didn't even flinch. Maybe I'd catch a break, and he wouldn't know what happened.

As fast as the icy roads allowed, I sped to the police station. It had snowed overnight, but I hadn't noticed. I was too busy messaging Willow until I could hardly keep my eyes open.

I steered the car into the station lot. It was empty except

for Preach's black Jeep, so I pulled in beside it. He jumped out and came to my side of the car.

"What's up, man?"

His dragon morning breath rammed into me like a steamroller. "Can you come sit in here and watch Caleb? He's sleeping."

"Sure." He opened my front door. "What's—"

"Don't know any details yet."

"Go find out what's going on," Preach said, then slid into my seat. "I got him."

I charged up the five steps leading to the front entrance, then pulled open the door and hustled to the front desk.

A lady with long brown hair and an officer's uniform leaned over the front desk. "Hi."

The five chairs in the small waiting room were empty, so I went with it. "I'm here for Ken Windom."

The lady leaned back, disappearing from my sight, so I stepped in closer. She came around the corner from behind a half door that was still swinging.

"You okay, kid? Oh. Hi, Brodie. I'm Darla."

Damn small towns. I hated that everyone knew me.

I nodded. "My dad's here?"

"Unfortunately." She leaned to the side and followed my line of sight.

"Kid brother's in the back. He's sleeping. Preach is with him."

"Oh, got it." Her hazel eyes softened. "Sorry, Brodie. Not exactly what you need to deal with right now, huh?"

Oh great. What'd she know that I didn't? I nodded and stepped farther into the waiting room, toward her desk, as she went back around the corner to her seat.

"Here are his checkbooks." I handed them over and realized how bad my hands were shaking. "I didn't know what to bring. He said something about bail?"

"I'll go get things taken care of. Here are his personal belongings." She handed me a manila envelope from across the desk. "Be right back."

My freaking dad was in the slammer. My severely asthmatic brother was in the backseat of my SUV at an ungodly early hour. And…it was negative fifteen degrees out. It was like I'd fallen into a nightmare or something.

I didn't need this shit.

Darla came out from behind the counter. "Hey, Brodie." She eyed me. "Everything okay with you? I mean…are you and Caleb doing all right?"

"Um…yeah?"

"Your dad was in a bad way last night. He got in a fight over at Bud's Bar. Officer Banks charged him with disorderly conduct."

A fight?

I'd never seen my dad put his hands on anyone. Drunk or not.

Plus, I didn't even know he was in town. I thought he was at a business meeting out of state. But I didn't tell her that. No need for Child Protective Services to get involved with us.

"We're fine. The Armstrongs have been watching out for us." I gulped through the lie.

"If you're ever *not* fine, you can come here. You know that, right?"

My gut clenched at the concern softening her gaze. She was worried about me and Caleb. That was nice of her but scary, too. My dad must have really done something bad. "Um. Thanks."

She dipped her head at me, then stepped through the short swing door back to behind the counter while I stood here in the middle of the empty waiting room. My heart was hammering so hard I could almost hear it echoing off the walls that felt like they were closing in around me.

A few minutes later, Darla stood from behind her computer and held up Dad's checkbooks. "Here you go, Brodie."

"Do I have to sign something?"

She shook her head. "He'll sign himself out. You're not eighteen."

"So…"

"He's almost processed out." She nodded toward the chairs against the far wall of the small waiting room.

"I'll wait outside." I whipped around, busted through the doors, and hustled down the steps.

Preach rolled the window, and I tossed the checkbooks onto the passenger side seat. "Sounds like he's coming. Thanks for being here, man."

"Sure."

I stepped back from the car to give Preach room to get out when I heard the station doors open again. "Now what?"

I whipped around, and Dad thundered down the steps. "Let's go."

His foot slipped out from beneath him on that last one, and he landed flat on his butt just below the bottom step. Swear words streamed from his mouth that were so colorful, a sailor would have blushed.

"Dad." I hustled toward him.

He waved me off, then hopped to his feet. He put his arms out as if trying to keep his balance.

A wave of liquor-scented air washed over me as he faced me. Dang, was he still drunk? His cheeks were gaunt and his eyes bloodshot.

It was like it wasn't my dad or something.

Tears stung my eyes, but I swallowed them back.

"Let's go home," he said, carefully navigating the icy sidewalk.

"What happened?"

He ignored me as he made his way toward the driver's side of the car. "Give me the keys."

"I'll drive," I said, looking at Preach as he worked his way out of the driver's side seat.

Dad glared at me. "I will drive my own goddamn car, kid. Give me the keys."

"No." I shoved my hand in my front pocket. "You're drunk."

He turned around and stomped toward me. "You ungrateful piece of—"

"Dad." I widened my stance, preparing for him to slam into me as Preach came to my right side. "What are you doing?"

Dad's jaw clenched, and so did his fists. Holy fuck, was he going to hit me?

"Daddy?" Caleb's tiny voice streamed around my irrational father.

I stepped to the side, then spun around Dad so I was between him and my brother. Preach did the same. No way was my father going to drive, and no freaking way in hell was he going to do anything to my little brother.

"Dad. Stop. What's going on?"

He collapsed to his knees on the snow-covered sidewalk, wailing. "It's over. It's…this…it's too much."

"What is, Dad?" I couldn't believe no one was coming out from the station for how much noise he was making.

Caleb's tiny hand filled mine. He hugged the blankets around him and looked up at me. "What's wrong with Daddy?"

"Not sure, buddy." I wiggled our joined hands. "Get back in the car. I'll take care of him."

Dad looked up from his sprawled position on the frigid sidewalk. His tear-filled eyes widened, his nostrils flared, but then as quickly as that happened, his face went stone-cold. His jaw clenched, and his eyes narrowed.

His attention was on Caleb's hand, which was in mine.

Two long breaths passed without a sound. It was like everything around us went silent.

Then he stood, turned, and started walking away. He didn't even have a jacket on.

"Dad?" I yelled.

He took off running.

"Dad," I yelled again and looked down at Caleb.

Tears filled his eyes, and he started shaking. "Brodie?"

I hoisted him into my arms and tucked him into the backseat of the car. Dad turned the corner at the end of the block and fell out of sight.

He was gone.

He'd abandoned us.

CHAPTER THIRTY-SIX

Willow

"Willow! Brodie! You made it," Preach called out. Laughter filled the air as we approached the crackling bonfire.

I fought the urge to grab his hand.

We'd been secretly dating for almost a month. It was exciting and kind of nice having something that just the two of us shared, but at the same time, it sucked. I wanted to hold his hand in public. Kiss him in front of other people. Go to the movies and share popcorn.

Brodie and I had decided that a couple of weeks after the season ended, we could start to date for real. But would we even be together then? Or could we maybe try long distance?

I shook the worries from my mind. Tonight was about having a good time with Brodie, Jessa, and my team.

"Drink?" Skylar, a junior on the basketball team, asked as we walked by.

"I'm good, but thanks."

Brodie shook his head, and we kept walking.

We'd each brought a big reusable bottle filled with water.

Pax stumbled over to us. "Brodie, I didn't think you'd make it."

"Whoa." Brodie grabbed onto his shoulder to steady our teammate. "How much have you had to drink?"

"Just a couple beers." Pax grinned. "And some Jager."

"Take it easy," Brodie warned him, letting his hand fall.

Pax turned his attention toward me. "You two came together?"

"Brodie gave me a ride."

He narrowed his gaze on Brodie and then turned toward me.

"You know, Sequins, I give you a hard time, but you're actually not half bad in the goal."

"Exactly how much have you had to drink tonight?" I asked with a chuckle.

"I mean it. I swear." He somehow lost his footing, even though he'd been standing still, and nearly fell over.

"Wow. Thanks, Pax." I didn't know if he was serious or if it was the alcohol talking, but damn, Pax had actually given me a compliment. I looked up at the sky, just to make sure I didn't see any pigs flying around.

"Damn, big guy. Never thought I'd hear you say that," Brodie said.

Pax let out a loud belch.

"I think you need to get some water," Brodie added.

Pax grumbled something before turning and heading to an open cooler.

"Good thing he's too drunk to suspect something," I whispered, my heart suddenly banging against my rib cage. Maybe we shouldn't have come together. What if people, sober people, made assumptions? Started talking? Shit... what were we thinking?

"Nah, but even if he did, he's so lit he won't remember

anything tomorrow," he said as we made our way to Preach and Jessa.

The fire roared as Teddy and Nathaniel threw on two more big logs.

"Hey, you two." Jessa gave us both a big hug.

She and Preach had come up to Bear Lake early to help set up for the party, which gave me the perfect excuse to ride with Brodie.

"Fire's awesome," Brodie said as he and Preach clasped hands and bumped chests.

A loud cheer echoed off the partially frozen lake.

"What was that?" I asked.

Jessa rolled her eyes. "Just the Twin River kids trying to throw a better party than us on the other side of the lake. Anyway, we've got hot dogs, stuff for s'mores, and soda on that table over there."

Preach motioned to the folding tables set up across from the fire.

"Looks like Pax decided to bring his own drinks." I looked over my shoulder and caught my teammate laughing so hard, he tripped and fell over his own feet.

"I thought he was going to cut back?" Jessa asked. "Especially during hockey season."

Preach shook his head. "I've already talked to him a few times about it, but I think we may need to have some kind of an intervention."

Brodie nodded in agreement.

"Come get some food with me." Jessa took my hand and led me toward the tables.

I grabbed a skewer and two hot dogs. "You want to get the buns?"

Jessa nodded. "Onions and ketchup?"

I normally loved onions on my hot dog, but the thought

of kissing Brodie later with onion breath made me cringe. "Skip the onions tonight."

She scrunched her nose. "You love onions."

My heart rate kicked up a notch. "Um, just…not craving them as much lately."

Twenty minutes and two hot dogs later, Jessa clapped her hands together. "Everybody, come on over to the fire. We're going to play a game of *Never Have I Ever*."

A few of the guys grumbled, but Preach shut them down immediately.

Everyone grabbed a chair from a big pile next to Eric's dad's truck.

"Rules are simple—we'll go around the circle, one at a time, and make a never-have-I-ever statement. If you *have* done said thing, you take a drink. If you *haven't* done said thing, you don't do anything."

Brodie and I settled in chairs next to each other. I prayed no one would ask a question that would somehow out us. Or ask something embarrassing… That would totally suck. Heat flooded to my cheeks. Thank goodness it was dark.

"I'll go first. Never have I ever"—she gave a dramatic pause—"sang along to a Justin Bieber song."

Teddy and Nathaniel burst out laughing and took a sip of soda.

"Ryan Anderson, don't you lie!" Jessa laughed as she pointed to Preach.

"Ohhh," Nathaniel sang out. "Jessa used your real name, Preach. She's serious!"

He brought a hand to his chest. "I'd never!"

"Need I remind you of the sixth-grade talent show?" Jessa countered.

"Ohhh…right…" Preach chuckled and took a big sip of his water as the rest of the people at the party started singing

"Love Yourself."

Pax stood and moved his chair next to Jessa. "I'm next."

Brodie tensed, watching his friend very closely, almost like he was ready to jump up and help him or something.

Pax started laughing. "Never have I ever had a hangover."

Most of the people around the fire, Brodie included, took a sip. Preach and Jessa didn't, and neither did I.

Teddy was up next. "Never have I ever forged my parent's signature on something for school."

"Teddy," Jessa gasped as he took a drink.

"What? They didn't want me to go on the Six Flags field trip in ninth grade, and there was no way I was going to miss that!" He threw his head back and laughed.

Over half of the people around the fire took a sip.

Eric cleared his throat and stood up. "Never have I ever kissed someone and then lied about it."

My mouth went dry, and I dropped my gaze to the ground.

Brodie's boot-clad foot flinched.

There was no way I'd ever take a drink in front of anyone in response to this question.

Thank goodness Brodie didn't take a sip, either.

"Eric," Lizzie, a junior with curly red hair said, "you sleeze!"

The game continued for thirty more minutes. Both Brodie and I asked silly questions that would in no way lead our friends and teammates to believe we were an item.

Darrion, a sophomore on the field hockey team, was next. "Never have I ever hooked up with someone in Bear Lake."

Eric laughed so hard he spilled his beer. "Bottoms up, Wolverines."

Brodie fidgeted nervously next to me, but he didn't take a drink.

"Brodie 'Wind' Windom, don't you dare lie about your epic pants-off dance-offs with Gretchen in the lake!"

Brodie coughed and then took a small sip of his water.

My shoulders slumped. We hadn't talked too much about our previous relationships, but I'd heard about Gretchen from a couple of people at Woodhaven High. She was this super stunning junior from Twin River.

Brodie nudged my foot with his. A subtle move, but one that almost erased the mental image of him having sex with Gretchen in the lake.

"That concludes our first game." Jessa smiled. "Now, go get some more food!"

Once everyone got up, Brodie gave the back of my jacket a tug.

Without a word, we backed away from the group and disappeared into the woods. He led me by the hand away from everyone, weaving between trees, and the darkness enveloped us, hiding us away from everyone. I couldn't even hear voices anymore.

"I'm sorry you had to hear that crap about me and Gretchen like that," Brodie said.

"I mean, I figured you weren't still a virgin, but you know, it was a bit shocking to hear that you and she hooked up like, right here. She is a *rival*, after all."

"Yeah, well, why do you think I was so against you dating Matthew?" Brodie stopped and leaned against a tall tree. Slouching, he kicked at the snow and glanced off to the side. "I learned the hard way to steer clear of those Twin River people."

"Have there been, you know, more?" I asked quietly. I wasn't sure if I wanted to know, but after finding out he had, it made me curious. It wasn't like we were even close to having sex, but still…

"Only Gretchen and Sydney."

"I haven't. I mean…had sex with anyone," I admitted.

Brodie grabbed my hand. "I'd never pressure you or anything."

"I know." I squeezed his hand. "I'm glad you told me, though."

Without another word, Brodie tugged me into his body. His gaze met mine, triggering a firestorm in my belly.

I wove my arm around him, then jumped in front of him, but stayed in step as I walked backward. Almost felt like I was skating, we were so in tune.

A smile curved his lips as he cupped my face, keeping perfect time with me. "You are so beautiful."

Pushing me up against a tree, he touched a kiss to the side of my cheek.

The full moon overhead filtered through the trees, lighting the space around us. His eyes locked on to mine. Flecks of copper glowed as he stepped into me.

We were both wearing thick jackets, along with stocking caps and gloves, but that didn't stop the heat emanating from him. It seeped into me, sending my heart into race pace.

His lips brushed mine as he leaned into me even more, igniting a whole new set of fireworks in my abdomen.

"I hate that we have to keep this secret…" I said as he nipped at my bottom lip. "But it's worth it." He responded by wrapping his arms around my neck and pulling my body flush with his and claiming my lips.

Kissing him deeply, I got lost in the moment. Only Brodie and I existed. Out here, in the woods, away from everyone who would totally freak out if they saw us together.

Brodie nipped at my lower lip and traced kisses down my neck. Tilting my head, I gave him even more access. Goose bumps claimed my skin, but it wasn't from the arctic air swirling around us. It was his touch. His closeness.

Him.

Heat stormed through me as my hands navigated the front of his jacket. If only I could wish it gone. My breathing hitched as he nipped at my earlobe, and a jolt of electrified tingles flooded my chest. "Brodie."

He eased back and looked down at me, his lips shiny and swollen. His fingers clasped the zipper of my jacket, and he paused, as if silently asking me for permission. My hammering heart stole my voice, so I gave him a nod.

Ever so slowly, as if teasing me, he lowered the zipper a few inches. Peeling back the fabric, he dove in and kissed a trail along the newly exposed skin where my V-neck shirt sat beneath my jacket.

His eyes widened as he tugged the zipper down all the way. With his forefinger, he trailed the skin along the neck of my shirt, leaving a trail of goose bumps in its wake. I let my head fall back against the tree and closed my eyes as his hands drifted down my body and settled on my upper thighs.

Heat coursed through me. Each searing kiss along my collarbone sent me further into oblivion. I yanked down his jacket zipper, and, thank God, he wasn't wearing a sweatshirt. The tight gray Woodhaven athletic shirt hugged his pecs like a second skin. I ran my hands over his chest, basking in his warmth. "Brodie," I said, my voice raspy.

His hand moved up and squeezed. "You have the best ass in the entire universe."

I raked my fingers down his chest and grabbed him by the belt.

Brodie let out a moan as I reached around and squeezed his butt. "Yours isn't too bad, either."

I pushed off his jacket, tossing it to the snow. I wanted to feel more of him against me.

He unzipped mine the rest of the way and tossed it beside his.

He tugged at my shirt and trailed kisses down the V-neck shirt I was wearing. His tongue swirled under the edge of my bra, sending my body into overdrive.

"Come on, just a little bit farther," someone whispered loudly.

Brodie and I froze as the crunch of broken twigs, and a fit of laughter filled the air.

Pax and Julia, a sophomore with pretty blue eyes and long brown hair, crashed through the woods, not thirty feet from us. He couldn't catch us here. He'd ruin us. More specifically, me.

Heart racing, I grabbed my jacket and tossed Brodie his.

He held a finger to his lips and motioned for me to follow him away from Pax as we put our jackets back on. Talk about bad timing… After sneaking through the darkness a few minutes, Brodie spun around, weaving his hand around my waist, and pulled me to him. My heart rate ramped right back up there.

"That was hot as hell!" Brodie said, grinning, then pressed a kiss to my mouth.

"What? Almost getting busted by Pax?"

"No! Kissing you was hot!" He offered me a sexy grin and tucked a strand of hair behind my ear. "You're amazing, Willow."

"You are, too. And that ass…"

We both started laughing.

"You head back to the party first. I'll come in a minute. Then we won't look like we were messing around in the woods." I winked.

Brodie grinned and then slapped me on the butt. "Can't have that now, can we?"

CHAPTER THIRTY-SEVEN

Brodie

"I can't believe we're in Twin River!" Willow said as she sipped her hot cocoa from the thermos cup I'd brought. "Isn't it sacrilegious or something?"

I laughed and steered the Tahoe onto Wildflower Street. "Tinted windows, no one will see."

"Really? So they won't see this?" She leaned over the console and pressed her warm lips to my cheek. Then my neck. Behind my ear.

A jolt of heat shot straight down my spine as she nipped at my earlobe.

"You're gonna make me crash," I said, scanning the road for a spot to park, because I wanted to take this a little further.

Hopefully she did, too.

Her lips grazed my ear, and she let out a quiet sigh. Warm breath brushed against my neck, and my spine tightened. Damn, she tripped my trigger.

Badger's Park. Perfect.

I steered the car into the dark, empty lot and pulled into the farthest parking spot.

"I thought we were going to tour the lights?" Willow whispered.

"In a bit." I put the gear into park and grabbed her thermos. She giggled as I put it in the cup holder. "I need more of you first."

She nodded, then leaned toward me. I cupped her face and met her halfway, claiming her lips with an urgency that almost scared me. When it was just me and her, together, nothing else mattered. Crap with my dad. School. Her leaving. None of it.

The only things that existed were her lips. Her tongue. Her soft skin. Her fresh, clean citrus scent fused with me. Locks of her hair tickled against my face as she leaned more into me.

"Do you trust me?" I whispered against her mouth.

She moaned a yes.

I moved my seat back while I stayed connected to her addicting mouth. Once it was far enough back, I disconnected with her and gave her a wink.

I sat up straight, then burrowed my hands beneath her. She squealed with laughter. I hoisted her up and brought her to my side of the car.

"Thank God for big seats," she said as she sat astride me. "Wow."

I pulled her in for a kiss. Her body formed to mine as she leaned into me. "This okay?"

"More than okay." Her fingers combed through my hair, and I reached down to recline the seat more. "Oh my gosh."

I claimed her mouth again, sliding my hand over her tight butt to pull her closer to me. She suddenly flinched, then looked up. "Crap. Someone's coming."

A flash of light beamed through the Tahoe, and my hammering heart cranked up that much more. Just when things were getting hot...

I glanced over my shoulder, and sure enough, a car was pulling in.

Laughing, she scrambled back to her side of the car and cupped her hands over her cheeks. "Dang, Brodie."

Hopefully, she meant that in a good way. I righted my seat and put the gear in reverse. "Right back atcha, Princess."

She chuckled and buckled her belt as I drove the car out of the lot, the ice-packed snow crunching beneath the tires.

"I need an ice-cold drink instead of this steaming hot cocoa." She grinned and fanned herself with her hand.

"Same." I reached over and twined my fingers with hers.

I steered the vehicle onto the main drag. Every year, Twin River had a community light show. Sure, they were our rival town, but it was cool how they did this to raise money for the food pantry. Usually, I was here with Preach, Pax, and Nathaniel, but this time, it was just me and Willow, and I was totally good with that.

"This is cool," Willow said, looking out her window. "Annie's Coffee Shop. Look at that. So cute."

"Maybe once the season is done, you and I can come here, you know, out in the open, officially dating." I kissed the back of her hand.

"Deal," she said. She didn't smile, though, and her voice carried a hint of sadness.

"What's up?" I asked.

"Nothing. Just…wish we could openly date now, you know? Not have to hide it. Just come here and have a coffee date."

"Well, I did lose those two coffee bets. You still have the gift card I gave you?"

"I totally do." She grinned.

"There you go. We can go, and it'll be under the cover of me owing you for my bet I lost."

"True. I totally creamed you."

"You totally surprised me," I said. "In lots of ways."

"That Sydney girl, she really ruined you for figure skaters, huh?" Willow sagged into her seat more, resting her head back.

That stopped me cold. "How'd you find out?"

"Small town, gossip, you know… Or Jessa."

I cracked a smile. "Ah…she and Preach could write my autobiography."

"You know, not all figure skaters are the same."

"Yeah, you sure showed me that."

She wasn't watching the lights out the window anymore. She was solely focused on me. If I didn't have to watch the road, I would have been happy to get lost in her big, blue eyes.

"You don't talk much about her or your past girlfriends."

"Not really wanting to talk about that stuff with my current girlfriend, you know?"

"Girlfriend?" She sat up.

"Secret girlfriend?" I said, more like a question. We hadn't really talked about official titles.

"I like the sound of girlfriend." She closed her eyes and let out a sigh. "I like it a lot, Brodie."

"Good. Me, too. And as for Sydney, she was fake. More after me because my name is on the Ice Den sign and stuff like that. I just didn't catch on. I figured since she loved the ice and was a pretty good skater, she'd get me." I shook my head. "So not the case."

"Yeah, well, figure skaters and hockey players are kinda like vampires and werewolves…never got along. We always ragged on you guys for being puck heads." Willow pointed out the window. "Oh cute, look at that snowman of lights."

"Yup, that's the Ice Cream Shack. Wicked awesome malts," I said. "I'll bring you here, too. Oh, and in Clover, there's another ice cream place." I couldn't wait to bring her everywhere, out in the open, after…well, if she was still here. *Shit.*

I hated that the thought of her leaving to go back to figure skating always popped into my mind. *No. Not now.* I was going to enjoy every second I could with her.

"I was so wrong about hockey players, though. You're not just a bunch of brutes."

"No, we're a brute squad." I laughed.

"Wait, what?" She scrunched up her nose.

I clutched my chest, pretending to be offended. "It's a *Princess Bride* reference! Only one of the most classic movies of all time. My mom loved that movie."

"That's really sweet." She smiled.

"Anyway, back to the brute or, as you say, puck head, stuff— we're not so bad…" I poked her shoulder. "You're a hockey player now, too, you know."

She picked up her thermos and took a sip, looking out the windshield. She'd positioned her long hair around her neck, so it all lay on her chest, shiny and soft. Her skin reflected the barrage of lights we were driving by, giving it a subtle glow.

A smile curved her full lips. "I am a hockey player, aren't I?"

"Hell, yeah." I nodded, a twinge of hope that my dream of her staying here to play hockey instead of leaving for figure skating pulsing through my chest. "Have you ever thought of focusing on hockey? I mean, maybe trying to get a scholarship or something, you know, to a four-year college?"

"No. I've always just expected to skate. Make the Olympics." She let out a sigh. "It's always been skating. But it's almost Christmas, and a team hasn't picked me up yet."

"Have you heard from any more of them?"

"Got another rejection email today, after school. I just don't get it. I thought for sure…" She rubbed her thighs with her hands and shifted in her seat. "Time's running out, Brodie."

More hope sprung in my chest, but it was quickly followed by a pang of guilt. I shouldn't be wishing for her dreams to not come true because I wanted her to stay here in Woodhaven. "But there's time. You still have some videos out and you're landing your jumps more and more."

She nodded but kept her focus on her fingers, picking at the nail polish.

"But…with hockey," I said, my heart pounding. I wasn't sure I should say this, because it was more selfish talk, but…I had to. "You should think about it. The scouts are looking at you as well as some of the other players."

Willow sat up a bit straighter. "Seriously?"

"Seriously."

"It *is* nice being on a team. Figure skating is pretty much a solo gig. We're always kind of watching over our shoulders to make sure someone isn't going to push you down so they can have your spot."

"Pretty catty, huh?"

"Some. And here, on this team—other than Eric still giving me grief—it's not like that." She grinned. "It's fun being on a real team."

"You've got choices, girl." If only she'd choose me—er—hockey. Maybe she'd consider Boston College? Or one nearby. It'd be amazing having her here for good.

I wasn't sure I should go that route, though. I was already hooked on her, big-time, but she was getting so strong. She was consistently landing some pretty wicked jumps again. It was wrong of me to want her to stay back, giving up her dream.

Ah hell. I wasn't sure what to think other than I really, really liked her and was glad she was in my car right now, with me, holding my hand. That was all I needed…for now.

CHAPTER THIRTY-EIGHT

Brodie

"**I** am *not* eating corn dogs and hot sauce for Christmas Eve dinner." Caleb threw the frozen package on the floor and stomped his foot.

"That's enough, Caleb." I couldn't blame the little guy, but frozen packages—totally dangerous.

"Where's Dad?" Caleb yelled, his face getting red. "It's Christmas Eve. I want real food."

I snatched the package off the floor. "Did you *not* see the burned-to-a-crisp pan in the sink? I tried to cook a turkey."

Caleb stuck out his bottom lip, and his eyebrows pulled together. "That's why it stinks in here?"

I chuckled. "I suck at cooking." Corn dogs were one of my favorites, but I was getting sick of them, too.

"Where's Dad?"

"I don't know."

An ache gave way in the back of my throat as I pulled my little brother in for a hug.

I'd gotten a text from our dad yesterday, but it was random. Something about coming home for Christmas dinner, all the fixings in tow. Then again, pretty much everything he'd said lately had been all but worthless and totally unreliable.

It was nearly seven o'clock on Christmas Eve. That jerk wasn't showing up.

I let out a long breath and opened a text to Preach. Maybe we should just crash over there for the rest of Christmas break. The Armstrongs were always offering. They knew things were rough… They just didn't know how rough. Plus, I couldn't keep lying to Caleb. I didn't know where our father was.

And he was right. He couldn't keep eating this crap food.

"Hey, guys," Dad yelled as he paraded through the kitchen entryway.

I let out a gasp.

"Daddy!" Caleb bolted around the kitchen island corner and directly into Dad's open arms.

He'd had to drop a bag in order to catch my little brother, but he'd done it. Even if he'd had to stumble back a little. I was at the ready to jump in and catch him if he'd fallen.

Instead, I leaned against the side of the center island, watching.

Dad's normally crisp business shirt was wrinkled, like it'd been crammed into a gym bag for two days. His brown hair was noticeably grayer along the temples. And he hadn't shaved in several days.

My heart thudded wildly in my chest.

The bag on the floor wasn't food. It was a couple of wrapped presents.

Great. What were we going to eat? There wasn't crap in the cupboards or fridge, not that it mattered. I mean, even *I* could cook better than he could.

An ache bloomed at the base of my skull and pulsed a steady beat until it pooled at my temples. I needed to figure this out. Talk with Dad or something. I couldn't keep doing this.

"...Brodie?" Dad said, stepping toward me.

In his hands, he held a wrapped box.

"Sweet," Caleb yelled as he dropped to the tile floor. "Can I open it now, Daddy? Can I?"

"Sure, kiddo." As he drew near, the stench of liquor rolled over me. My stomach clenched with such a force, I had to cough to cover.

I could *not* believe this shit. I stepped toward him and stared him eye-to-eye since we were the same height. My heart hammered and my hands went slick.

"You're drinking?" I whispered as I checked on Caleb. He was out of range, too focused on tearing the paper off his gift. "And you drove here?"

"Only a couple. I could pass a sobriety test." He rested his hand on the center island as he eyed me with a glazed look. I could knock him over with a hearty sneeze; there was no way he could pass a sobriety test.

"Where have you been for the last two weeks?"

"Working." He shoved my gift into my stomach. "You're welcome."

Anger bubbled just under the surface of my skin, threatening to erupt at any moment.

I tossed the present on the center island without looking at it and stepped back. "We're leaving."

"You are not going anywhere." He grabbed my arm.

I spun around and shoved him. "Get your hands off me."

"Brodie?" Caleb's tiny voice trickled in from behind me.

"Come here, kiddo." Dad squatted down and opened his arms to Caleb. "Brodie's upset. He'll get over it."

Caleb didn't move.

"Pretty sad when your own son won't come to you when he's scared, huh?" Brodie asked.

"You ungrateful—"

"*Son*. Yeah. I'm ungrateful. I'm a jerk to think our dad should be with us, *sober*, on Christmas Eve." I backed up, putting my hand out for Caleb to take.

"Don't be mad, Brodie," Caleb whispered to me. "Daddy's here."

"That's right, kiddo." Dad focused on Caleb. "I'm here."

My hands trembled, and my face felt like it was on fire.

"For how long? Until you need another hiatus from life for a two-week bender?"

He glared at me, but he didn't say anything. Instead, his cold, hard eyes softened. His tense jaw loosened. He glanced at the table where my gift was thrown, then closed his eyes and took a deep breath.

"What's it going to be, Dad?"

"I can't do this." He shook his head and stepped back.

"Or *won't*?" I yelled.

Tears lined his eyes, and his nostrils flared. "I can't do this…" He took in a hitched breath. "… without her."

It felt like someone rammed a hockey stick through my chest and directly into my heart. Tears instantly stung my eyes, and bile tainted the back of my throat.

Without her.

"Daddy?" Caleb asked, easing out from behind me.

I put my hand on my brother's shoulder, keeping my focus on my father. "I can't, either, Dad." My voice cracked, and Caleb hugged me around my waist and buried his face in my stomach. My heart pounded so loud, I couldn't hear my thoughts to try and figure out what to say or what to do next.

And then Dad sobbed. Full on, face in his hands, shoulders shaking sobs.

I knelt before Caleb. "Hey, buddy, run up to your room."

Tears filled his eyes.

My heart shattered into a million pieces. This wasn't fair.

He didn't deserve to be dragged into my dad's crap.

"Go on. I'll be right there," I whispered and brushed my knuckles along his cheek, trying to keep my own tears at bay. I had to be strong for Caleb. He needed me to take care of things.

Dad must have gotten him a teddy bear because he hugged one I'd never seen before to his chest and nodded as he backed away, out of the kitchen.

I shifted around and, still on my knees, shuffled to Dad. He was on his knees now, too, his hands covering his face, sobbing. The scent of alcohol wrapped around me again, nearly choking me, but I brushed it off.

Maybe this was it. Maybe he was ready to change his ways.

I'd Googled a little bit about alcoholism, not that I was sure he had it, but *something* was wrong with him, so I'd started there.

What I'd seen scared the shit out of me, but it didn't have to be fatal. Dad could come back from it. We all could.

"Dad?" I whispered as I covered the last few inches to him. "Dad."

"It's too hard."

"I know," I said, squatting down. I wasn't sure what to do other than sit there in front of him, willing my heart to stop jackhammering my ribs. I drew in a deep breath and slowly let it out, then rubbed my sweaty hands on my jeans. "I miss her, too."

He sobbed even harder. "It's my fault."

"No. Dad." I gulped. "It was an accident. The ice—"

"We fought. We were arguing about—" He sobbed even louder. "It's all my fault."

My chest ached as if someone had stabbed me with a rusty steel blade. Tears streamed down my face, burning a fiery trail through my skin. The drunk driver crossing into

Mom's lane was *not* Dad's fault.

"Brodie?" Caleb asked from behind me. He must have snuck back in.

"Caleb, just stay there," I said, not looking at him. "Dad. Come on. It's going to be okay."

"No. It's not. It's *not* okay," he yelled.

I bolted back and to my feet. He reached for the countertop and pulled himself up, then staggered to the side.

"Dad—it's not your fault."

He charged me, but he stopped with about an inch between his nose and mine. "You don't know shit."

Caleb started crying. "Why are you yelling at him, Daddy? Brodie didn't do anything wrong!"

I backed away, reaching for my little brother. "It's all right, buddy. Everything is going to be just fine." It was a lie. I knew it. My dad knew it. But Caleb couldn't find out.

Dad looked beside me as I grabbed for my brother's hand. He held his breath. Just stared at Caleb, almost like he couldn't see him.

Dad's face darkened, and a vein bulged along his neck.

Fear crept down my spine, leaving a cold chill behind.

"Please calm down, Dad." I stepped back, staying between Caleb and my dad. I didn't know what was going to happen next, but the look on his face—

"No," he yelled so loud, his voice echoed around us. And then he turned and bolted out of the kitchen.

In the next breath, I heard the door to the garage swing open, then slam shut. It slammed so hard, the walls vibrated and a picture across the kitchen crashed to the floor.

"Brodie. What's wrong with Daddy?"

I heard a crash outside. "Holy shit!"

"You just said a naughty word," Caleb said.

"Sorry, buddy," I said as I hoisted Caleb into my arms and

hustled to the kitchen window. Dad's car had rammed into the water fountain in the front yard.

Headlights coming up our driveway drew my attention. It was so dark out I couldn't tell what car it was, but I hadn't been expecting anyone.

What if it's the police?

Would he get arrested again? Get sent to jail?

"Hold tight, buddy." I cuddled Caleb close to me and booked it to the front door, then pulled it wide open.

The frigid air slapped my exposed arms and instantly stung my lungs. Dad's car lurched forward, directly toward the oncoming SUV.

"Watch out," I yelled.

The approaching car swerved, narrowly missing Dad's. A horn blared from a black Lexus.

That was Preach's dad's car.

The driver's side door swung open, then Mr. Armstrong jumped out, shouting after Dad's car.

But it kept going, no taillights.

Preach hopped out of the passenger side and hustled toward me. "Brodie."

I hugged Caleb closer as a shiver raked down my spine. It was pitch black and freezing, and here I stood, in a T-shirt, holding my baby brother to me after Dad had driven away, intoxicated, and narrowly missing ramming into the Armstrongs.

Mr. Armstrong hurried up the walk and ushered us all inside, out of the freezing temps. "You okay, kid?"

Tears stung my eyes, and fear nearly choked me. I couldn't even answer.

"Sean Wright saw your father weaving all over the road while they were driving home from dinner and called me. We came to check on you guys."

Small-town living for the win. I was genuinely thankful he and Preach were here right now.

Caleb bawled and reached for Mr. Armstrong. I let him go along with the tears that'd been building. Tears that I'd been holding in for months. For years, actually.

"Come here, son." Mr. Armstrong hugged me to him while holding Caleb. Preach put a hand on my shoulder and stood next to us in silence.

I didn't know how long I cried into my best friend's dad's shoulder, but I didn't care. What else could I do but just let it out? My dad was a drunk, wasn't he? He needed help. But he obviously wasn't ready or, worse, didn't want it.

And it wasn't good.

I could handle it, but what about Caleb? He was just a kid.

Hell, I was technically still a kid. Seventeen. I couldn't legally do anything. But if Dad was AWOL…what'd that mean for me?

Eventually, I leaned back and wiped my eyes, then grabbed Caleb's hand. He kept his face buried in Mr. Armstrong's neck, though.

Mr. Armstrong looked at me, his square jaw tight and his eyes narrowed. He had the same look Preach did when he meant business. "Pack your bags," he said. "You're staying with us."

CHAPTER THIRTY-NINE

Willow

"**M**om! You're home." My throat grew thick with emotion as I tossed my practice bag on the floor just inside the front door and ran to her.

"Hey, honey." She embraced me in a big bear hug, and we stood there in the middle of the living room for I didn't know how long. It was so good to have her here for Christmas Day. I'd missed so many holidays with them while I was living in Colorado.

The scents of turkey cooking and the glow of the lights surrounding me made me smile. It felt like a real Christmas. An actual family Christmas. Did I really want to go back to a skating team, if anyone offered, and be away from family again? Miss this?

"Oh, honey, I missed you, too!" Mom kissed the top of my head.

"I thought you weren't coming home until the weekend," I said, releasing my hold on her.

"Come on into the kitchen and have a seat."

I looped my arm through hers, and we made our way into the kitchen. She tapped on one of the chairs around the already-set-for-Christmas dinner table, then stepped away, clasping her hands in front of her.

My stomach flip-flopped as I sat down. "Everything okay?"

"Hal, Willow is home. Can you come join us?"

What's happening? My heart started racing and my mouth went dry.

Dad strode into the kitchen and stood beside Mom.

"Honey," my mom said, "your dad and I have some good news."

Good news? I'd kind of been expecting them to tell me they were splitting up or something. Mom had been gone a ton, and when I'd heard Dad talking to her over the phone, it wasn't super awesome.

"After my next contract is over, I'll be moving back home. Permanently."

"Are you serious?" I leaped out of my chair and threw my arms around Mom. Tears instantly stung my eyes. Mom was going to be home. Here. With me and Dad and Gramps.

Together.

I released one of my arms and pulled Dad in on this hug. We were going to be a family again. Tears of happiness freely flowed as I hugged my parents. This was the best Christmas present ever.

The feeling immediately vanished once I realized that she would probably be moving home right around the time I would be leaving…if I'd be leaving.

Warring emotions tore through my chest. The joy of my family reuniting slammed directly into the pain of having to miss it, again.

Dad eased out of the hug and looked at me, a big smile filling his face. "We're going to start looking for a house or an apartment in a few months."

"That's amazing." I wiped the tears from my face and sat

back down in the chair. My legs kind of felt like jelly after hearing this good news. Living with Gramps was incredible, but I knew my parents would be happy to have their own place, and they'd still see him all the time. Woodhaven was a small town; chances were we'd only be a ten-minute car ride away.

"What about a job, though? The hospital here is still closed."

My mom smiled. "A new community clinic is being built in Woodhaven, and I've already talked to the doctor who's opening it. I think he's actually got a son on your team, Nathaniel? Anyways, it looks like I'm going to get a job working for him."

"Oh my gosh. That's amazing!" A worry cramped my stomach. "Wait a second. Um…it's just, you two normally fight a lot. Are you sure it's a good idea for us to all move into a new place together? What if you decide you hate each other?"

Dad shook his head. "Willow, we've been going to virtual counseling, and through a lot of hard work, we figured out a lot of our issues."

"Counseling? Why didn't you tell me?" How had I not noticed that? Then again, I had been pretty focused on school, skating, hockey, and Brodie. I felt bad for being so stuck in my own world that I hadn't noticed what was happening around me.

"Yes, online with a licensed therapist." My mom put her arm around my dad's waist. I couldn't remember the last time they'd shown any type of PDA. "It's been really great."

"But why didn't you tell me?" I asked.

"We wanted to see how things were going to progress before we mentioned it to you. Plus, you didn't need anything else on your plate. You've had a lot going on."

I shifted in my seat. "Oh, I guess that makes sense."

"We still have a lot to work through, but we feel really happy about the future." My dad kissed my mom on the cheek, and she nodded.

It felt like my heart swelled three sizes bigger and a fuzzy blanket of warmth wrapped around me.

"The gas station had some!" Gramps shouted as he came in from the garage, holding up a tub of vanilla ice cream. "Can't have apple pie a la mode without the mode."

"Let's eat," Mom said.

Within a few minutes, we were all seated at the table for our first Christmas dinner as a family in two years. My eyes burned with tears of joy. My cheek with the scar ached, and I couldn't stop smiling. I reveled in the lack of tension that was normally present when we were all together. Instead, a feeling of contentment settled over the kitchen, and I sighed.

"Oh, wait!" I pulled out my phone from my back pocket and put it on selfie mode. "Say, 'Merry Christmas, Ericka!'"

I snapped the photo and sent it to Ericka, then clicked my phone off.

"How's her recovery?" Gramps asked as he plopped a pile of mashed potatoes on my plate.

"She's nailing her physical therapy." I scooped up some green beans, so ready to dig in. "And taking things one day at a time."

"Like you have, honey." Mom smiled at me, then nodded to Dad.

"Oh yes. Well. You know, we haven't had a chance to tell Willow *all* the news yet." Dad looked at Gramps. "Do you want to do the honors, Dad?"

All the news?

"Your coach from Colorado called, Snowflake," Gramps said.

The breath whooshed out of my chest so violently, I dropped my fork. It clanked against my plate, then flopped onto the tabletop, splattering the gravy I'd just poured onto my potatoes. "Oh my gosh. What did she say?"

My heart hammered in my ears, and my hands started shaking.

"She said your physical therapy reports are good, and she was very pleased with your videos."

My heart nearly jumped out of my chest, and I clutched the edge of the table.

"She wants to set up a virtual meeting to talk about your options."

"My options? Seriously?" I pushed back out of my chair and jumped up and down. "For real?"

"For real." Gramps laughed as I embraced him.

"I don't even know what to think right now." As my heart rate started to drop back to normal, I felt a bit of ice join the warm sensation this news had given me. "I mean, they dropped me. And…I didn't even send them a video. Mostly because I was mad at them. So how'd they see it?" My voice started shaking like my hand. Thoughts flew through my mind on fast forward.

They'd dropped me, and now they wanted to talk to me? Did they want me back? Did I *want* to go back to them?

"It's just a virtual meeting, honey," Mom said.

"I know." I fanned my steaming hot face and nodded as I paced the floor behind Gramps's chair.

I couldn't wait to tell Brodie, Jessa, and Ericka. Though… maybe now wasn't the right time to tell Brodie? I jammed my hands into my hair as my hammering heartbeat stole my breath. I wanted to, but what if nothing ever came of it? And he was a little upset by the fact that I could be leaving soon to return to skating. He'd even brought up possibly trying to play hockey instead of figure skating. My phone buzzed in my back pocket.

"I'll be right back." I snuck around the corner to see who it was from. Oh, good. It was Brodie. I hadn't heard from him yet today, other than our regular good morning text and a few heart emojis.

BRODIE: Merry Christmas! Sorry I'm just getting to text you now.

BRODIE: Crazy eighteen hours.

ME: Merry Christmas to you, too! I was worried about you. How are you?

BRODIE: Well...I've got some news.

I gulped.

Me, too...

ME: What's up?

BRODIE: Caleb and I are staying with Preach now.

ME: Wow!

ME: Is that a good thing?

ME: Are you okay?

BRODIE: Yes and yes.

BRODIE: We got here late last night.

BRODIE: This was the first I could get away to text you. I'm sorry.

BRODIE: Can I call you later when I can get away from Caleb and Preach?

ME: Perfect!

ME: ♥

BRODIE: ☺

I held the phone to my chest, my heart suddenly racing. Something big must have happened for the Armstrongs to take Brodie and Caleb in so suddenly.

I rested my head back against the wall and let out a slow breath, my mind racing through what could have happened.

Maybe Caleb had an episode or something. Or maybe Brodie's dad. I squeezed my eyes shut and brought my phone to my chest. Hopefully, Brodie's father was all right.

Here I was having an amazing Christmas Day, and Brodie must be dealing with something devastating. One thing I knew for sure, though. My good news would have to wait.

CHAPTER FORTY

Brodie

"**B**rodie, help me! He's gonna get me!" Caleb came into the kitchen screaming, his hands in the air.

But a smile filled his face. We'd been living at Preach's now for about five days or so, and Caleb hadn't been sick once, was laughing more, and seemed so much happier.

I darted around the kitchen table and scooped him into my arms, then blasted down the hallway in time to see Mr. Armstrong chasing us.

"*Rawrrr*!" he roared, his voice rattling and deep like he was trying to imitate a monster. "I'm going to get you, Caleb!"

Caleb squealed and tightened his hold on me. I dove onto the leather couch.

"Incoming!" Preach yelled as he landed on top of us. He started tickling Caleb, and I rolled off, going for Caleb's feet.

"Tickle fest!" Mr. Armstrong said and poked at Caleb as well.

Laughter echoed off the high ceiling, and I couldn't help smiling. I was so thankful for Preach's family taking us in. It was nothing permanent, but Mr. Armstrong said that Caleb and I were welcome to stay as long as we needed while Dad worked through his issues. Talk about a fifty-ton weight off my shoulders.

"Yo!" Nathaniel yelled and joined in on the pile.

Caleb squealed some more, and I eased back. The rest of the team filed in for our annual Holiday Classic Championship pregame dinner. Including Willow.

I hadn't seen her much these past few days because I was getting settled in here with Caleb, and man, she was a sight for sore eyes in her fitted, long-sleeve Wolverines shirt and jeans. Her long black hair was back in her trademarked braids, but she was wearing some eye makeup today, showcasing those gems.

If only I could get up and give her a hug and kiss. But I couldn't. And that totally sucked. So I gave her a quick wink instead. Maybe later we could steal away for a kiss or two...

"What's up, Little Man?" Nathaniel yanked Caleb off the couch. "Need a rescue?"

"Airplane!" Nathaniel and a few of the guys took Caleb out with the sounds of airplanes following after them.

Damn, I had awesome friends. They pretty much all knew I was living here with Preach now, but not once did I feel like they were pitying me.

"Dinner's almost ready!" Mrs. Armstrong shouted from the kitchen.

"I better help her," Mr. Armstrong said and hustled out of the room.

"I brought garlic bread," Teddy said, lumbering after Mr. Armstrong.

Pax plopped onto the leather chair next to the couch. Preach and Willow launched themselves onto the couch next to me.

"You getting all settled?" Willow asked.

I nodded.

"Hey, Sequins," Pax said as he focused on his phone. "You ready for Roger the Right Hand of God tonight?"

I hated that Pax called her that, but over the past few weeks, it'd actually become less derogatory since he'd eased up on her a little. It was obvious he kept her at arm's length, but he didn't rag on her as much. He was probably starting to accept that she was a vital part of this team. Finally.

Willow faced me more and grinned. "So, you and Caleb hanging in there?"

"I haven't seen Caleb this happy in a while. It's going really well."

And it was true. He was like he was when Mom was around, and he, Mom, Dad, and I were a real family. We needed that more than anything right now, as the anniversary of Mom's death was just a few weeks away.

"That little dude is stoked. He's wearing me out!"

I laughed and socked Preach on the shoulder. He really was the best friend.

"Who's ready to kick some Milwaukee Knights ass?" Nathaniel yelled as he jumped onto Pax.

Teddy came thundering in, straight toward the Pax and Nathaniel pile. "It's on!"

"Waiiiiiiit!" Nathaniel rolled off Pax onto the floor in front of the couch.

Teddy landed on Pax with a loud grunt. Pax groaned, pushing at Teddy, but nothing was moving that mountain. More laughter bounced off the walls surrounding us, and I rested my head back.

Willow poked my shoulder, then glanced toward the hallway. "Where's the bathroom, Preach?"

"Down the hall. First door on the left."

Willow got up, then as she passed behind the couch, she flicked my shoulder. I watched after her as she walked down the hallway, thoroughly enjoying the view.

I pushed up from the couch and said to the guys, "I'm gonna make sure Caleb's breathing all right."

Preach nodded, then looked at the TV screen. *ELF* was playing, and even though this was one of my favorite movies, I bolted. I'd rather sneak some Willow time.

I went through the kitchen in case anyone was watching, then came at the bathroom hallway from the other direction. I passed by the office doorway, and Willow grabbed my wrist. With a solid tug, she yanked me into the room.

In the next instant, her mouth was on mine.

I spun us to the side, and she pinned me against the wall beside the door. "How are you?"

"Better now." I dove in for another kiss, heat spreading through me like a wildfire. I'd missed her kisses. Her scent. The feel of her against me.

"Really. I can't believe what's happening with your dad." I'd been able to sneak away on Christmas Day for a while and was able to call her and tell her everything that'd happened Christmas Eve. She'd been the first one I'd wanted to call, the one I trusted with my secrets, the one I knew would be there for me.

We hadn't had a chance to be together since then, though.

She kissed my lips, then pulled away, slightly. "I'm glad things are going better, Brodie. Really. Because I've been dying to tell you something."

I hugged her close, just happy to have her in my arms again, and said, "Fire away."

"My former coach, the one from Colorado, reached out to me to talk about possibly returning to the team." Her smile widened.

My stomach dropped. "Um...wow." I hadn't been expecting that. The news effectively doused the flames her kisses had stoked.

"I just, didn't…with everything going on with you, I wasn't sure how to tell you my great news when you were hurting so much."

She was leaving me, wasn't she?

I pulled her into a hug, and I buried my face in her long hair so she couldn't see the sadness I knew was showing through on my face. Tears stung my eyes as I drew in her coconut scent, fusing it in my senses.

"I'm so happy for you," I choked out, but inside it felt like my insides were getting shredded by a dull knife.

CHAPTER
FORTY-ONE

Willow

"Looks like the Wolverines really put the *period* in third period," one of Roger's teammates said, then threw his head back and laughed. Bright orange hair poked out from under his helmet. The guys on his team came up alongside him, laughing and patting him on the back.

The anxiety and pent-up anger from missing Roger's goal earlier in the game exploded to the surface as I threw down my stick. "You want to say that again to my face?" I lifted my chin, challenging him.

Carrot Hair took two strides until his padded body bumped mine. Easily five or six inches taller than me, the fullness in his cheeks and his thick neck indicated that he had at least fifty pounds on me. "You think you can take me?"

Pushing my shoulders back, I narrowed my eyes. "I *know* I can."

He brought his arms back and shoved me.

As I glided backward, keeping my balance, I said, "That's all you got?"

The boy with the bright orange hair charged me, but unlike Brodie or Roger, he wasn't very agile. His skate clipped my stick that I'd thrown down. Flat on his stomach, he let out a grunt, and I couldn't help chuckling.

He pushed up and snatched one of his buddy's sticks. "You're dead." He swung his hockey stick and whacked me in the back of the leg, just above my hockey skate.

Searing pain ripped up my calf, and I crashed to the ice. I flopped onto my side and grabbed my leg.

Towering over me, Carrot Hair's lips curled into a wicked smile the devil would have been envious of. Brodie flew by me in a blur and slammed into the orange-haired winger just as he was about to slam his right skate down on my leg.

The kid landed on his back with a grunt and slid a few feet away.

The ref promptly awarded Carrot Hair a penalty for fighting and slashing. Luckily, the ref had only been a few feet away from us, and Brodie didn't get charged with anything.

"This is bullshit!" the winger said as he skated away. His coach pulled him off the ice and laid into him as he sat red-faced on his team's bench.

Teddy helped me to my feet. Wincing, I fought back the urge to cry. It literally felt like someone had stabbed a hot poker into my calf.

"You okay?" Brodie asked, coming to a stop in front of me.

I tried putting an equal amount of weight on my skates. Pain shot down the back of my right leg. Panic seized my heart as I zeroed in on where the pain was. It wasn't my Achilles, but it was close. Hair prickled on the back of my neck as a rush of adrenaline coursed through me. I could have been hurt. As in seriously hurt.

That would tear away all the progress I'd made toward getting back on a figure skating team. Holy shit.

"Willow?" The urgency in his voice rose.

"Ah. I'm fine," I lied and then drew in a long breath to try and calm down my thrashing heart.

"He clipped you just above your bad ankle, didn't he?" Brodie looked down at my skate and then back up at me.

My chest started to rise and fall rapidly again, and the room felt like it had tilted sideways. That asshole hadn't hit my ankle, but he had been close. Thankfully, the skate protected my Achilles well enough. Damn, that was close.

"I'm fine. Come on. Let's show these jerks what's up!" My voice quavered, but I managed to punch him in the shoulder, as if everything was fine.

We were down to two minutes in the third; we had to make something happen ASAP.

The guys headed back to center ice, and the whistle blew. Brodie and Preach dominated the power play, and each attempted a shot as the seconds ticked away on the scoreboard. The goalie caught one in his glove and blocked the other.

Even with a power play, Roger and his team were so good, we couldn't get a goal. The score was tied at one.

Fifteen seconds left on the clock.

It was now or never. Someone had to score or we'd head to overtime.

That's when it happened. The substitute for the jerk who had whacked me hip-checked Brodie into the boards. On the other end of the ice, defenders blocked Teddy, Preach, and Nathaniel.

With the flick of the wrist, one of the wingmen passed the puck to Roger.

Gulping, I swallowed the anxiety. *You've got this, Willow. You've blocked ten of his shots. The one that got by you was a fluke.*

Roger passed the puck to his wingman. Both burst forward with astounding speed, leaving Pax and Teddy in the dust.

The crowd chanted, "Five, four, three…"

Roger's teammate passed him the puck. He was less than ten feet away from me. A smirk settled on his lips as he pulled his stick back.

I braced for the worst as my bruised calf tensed.

Dropping to my knees, I thrust my blocker out to intercept the puck barreling through the air.

I caught the edge of it, the impact stinging the back of my wrist. The puck hopped off my gear and shot straight up. With a loud *ding*, it rebounded off the top of the goal.

And tipped backward, sailing above my head.

Into the net.

Bzzzzzzzz.

They'd scored.

A second buzzer rang, indicating that the game was over.

That was it.

We'd lost.

I'd allowed Roger the Right *Freaking* Hand of God *two* goals. *Two.*

Sinking to the ice, I pounded my fist. My stomach knotted, and a wave of heat steamed up my chest. I should have stopped that. Tears stung my eyes as I hit the ice again.

Both teams left their benches. Roger's guys hoisted him into the air, while our guys entered the rink silent, heads down.

Eric skated right at me. "That is your fault, Sequins!" He pointed his stick at me. "Josiah should have been in goal, and you know it!"

The anger that had been boiling just below the surface exploded. "Eric, why don't you shut the fuck up and sit down!"

His eyes went wide.

I hopped up to my skates. "You're always going on about how much better Josiah is than me. Well, guess what? Coach didn't feel that way, and he has the final say. I blocked twelve shots today. Yes, I let in two, but I didn't see you stopping Roger before he scored. You let him by you more than you stopped him today."

Eric's mouth fell open, but he didn't say anything.

"That's what I thought. Stop coming for me if you can't back your bullshit up!" My heart hammered, and my hands went slick beneath my gloves. I hadn't cussed that much in a long time, but I'd had just about enough of Eric's shit. I'd proven myself over and over, and he was just bigoted asshat.

Pax skated beside me, saying, "Leave her alone, Eric."

Whoa. Had I heard Pax right? First the drunken compliment and now he was defending me? As in Pax Hunt, the previous leader of the anti-Willow coalition? My heart actually stopped for a full beat, maybe two as I watched him coast away from me, toward Eric, then bump shoulders with him.

Pain pulsed in my calf, ripping me from the alternate plane of existence I'd stumbled into. I pushed off, gliding across the ice toward the door. Most everyone was already off the ice and marching toward the locker rooms.

Brodie stayed back, nodding at the last of our teammates as they passed by.

"You okay, Willow?" he asked, handing me my blade guards.

"Did you just hear Pax? Or did I hallucinate?"

"I did." He looked up at the ceiling of the rink and squinted.

"What are you doing?"

"Waiting for it to rain frogs or something?" Brodie gave me a lopsided grin.

"They'd probably make it past me, too," I muttered as I threw on my guards, then stepped over the threshold of the door onto the soft mats. I wanted to take my skates off and chuck them against the wall, but that wouldn't do anyone any good, including me. I had to deal with the fact that I missed a block that cost us the game.

Brodie nudged me with his elbow, and his big brown eyes greeted me when I looked up. "It's gonna be okay, Willow."

We were about twenty feet from the locker rooms. I just wanted to get these pads off and take an hour-long hot shower.

"Willow! Willow Covington," an unfamiliar voice called out.

Turning around, my eyes landed on a woman in a black tracksuit jacket with a logo I didn't recognize. She had short silver hair and light blue eyes.

"Deena Polanski," she held out her hand for me to shake. "I'm the head coach of the Miami International Skating Center that's opening next month." She wasn't exactly bubbly, but she appeared pretty excited to talk to me.

I glanced up and down the empty hallway, then shifted my focus back to her. My knees got a little wobbly, so I was thankful Brodie was next to me.

"Hi. It's, um, it's nice to meet you." I shook her outstretched hand and nodded, my heart pounding deep in my chest. I'd heard about the new program opening in Florida, but I didn't know much about it yet. Everything was being kept pretty hush hush, including who was or wasn't getting a possible invite.

"Nice job out there." A slight smile curved her bright red lips.

"Um...thank you."

"I flew up here, directly after seeing your video. We'd like you to come try out for a spot on our team."

My mouth suddenly turned arid, and my hands started shaking. Had I heard her right? Did she really just offer me a tryout for her team? But I hadn't sent her anything. Hell,

I hadn't known who the head coach of this mysterious new training center opening in Miami was yet, and here she stood, before me.

She grinned and handed me a tote. "I've included information about our state-of-the-art training center and a few goodies."

It was everything I could do to remain upright because my legs had officially turned to jelly.

Speechless, I opened the tote to take a glance. There was a matching jacket, a water bottle, and a folder filled with papers. Talk about things happening at the last minute. I'd needed to get on a team by January to have any chance of testing through the levels and competing in Worlds this coming year. And now, two teams were looking at me.

"Tryouts are this Saturday," she said. "And if things go well, like I think they will, I expect we could start working together shortly after that."

Brodie stiffened beside me, but I couldn't look at him. Not yet. I wasn't sure this was actually happening. Maybe I'd hit my head in the goal and I was unconscious.

Because I had actually been starting to wonder if any team would want me. It was almost the end of the year, and time was running out. Even though I'd been training on my own, I was falling behind my competition without a proper coach and facilities.

"Is that something you'd be interested in?"

"Um, yeah. I mean, yes, ma'am." My pulse thudded in my ears. "I…I'll talk to my parents as soon as I can."

"Are they here?"

"No. Dad's at work but will be home in a few hours. You could stop by then."

"Perfect. I have the first flight out in the morning, so I have plenty of time tonight." Deena handed me a business card.

"My cell is on there if anything comes up."

Blood pounded through my head, drumming in my ears. My world tilted slightly as I smacked my lips, searching for some moisture. Any moisture. Was this happening? As in really happening right now? This fast?

Saturday was only five days away. What about the hockey team? What about Brodie? No. I needed to chase my dreams. If anyone should understand that, Brodie should.

I finally looked up at him, and his jaw was tight. He looked straight ahead with unseeing eyes. Thankfully, the rest of the team hadn't witnessed this. Mostly just Preach, Jessa, and Brodie knew I was doing hockey only until I could get back to figure skating.

"It was great meeting you, Willow. See you soon," Deena said.

"Thank you. You, too." I shook her hand again, hoping mine wasn't too sweaty, and watched her walk away. I didn't recognize her name, so I'd have to look her up and check out her skating history, but the fact that she'd personally come up here to freezing cold and very snowy Wisconsin from Miami must be a good sign.

I dropped my helmet to the padded ground and slapped my cold hands on my steaming cheeks. Tears spilled out as I drew in a shaky breath.

"So that just happened," I whispered, my breathlessness stealing my voice.

Brodie stared down at me, his nostrils flaring and his cheeks flushed. His jaw was tense and his forehead crinkled.

I fanned my face, willing the tears to dry and said, "Brodie?"

"You're leaving…" He faced the ceiling and let out a breath. "It's happening. You're…leaving."

I grabbed his arm and wiggled it, urging him to face me. My heart was weighed down with a somber heaviness, replacing the excitement that had lightened it. "It's just a tryout. I haven't made the team."

"But you will." His voice was clipped. Tense. "Of course you will—you deserve it. You've earned it."

"We don't know that." I fisted my hand in the front of his jersey. "We don't know that."

He closed his eyes and sniffled. "We should…you should get home. Sounds like she wanted to meet your parents."

"Brodie. Wait." I held tight to his jersey. "Please don't say anything to anyone."

"What do you mean?" he asked, looking at me with genuine concern. "We can't keep this from the team. I can't keep this from Preach." His voice ricocheted off the cement walls.

"We don't know anything other than I've been offered a tryout. Let's not bring anything up because if it doesn't work out, then we've riled them up for nothing."

"But Preach? I can't—"

"Just until after tryouts. I might not make the team, Brodie." I rested my palm on his chest. He was still wearing his hockey pads beneath, but I swore I could feel his heart hammering through the layers of protective gear.

My heart cramped at the thought of leaving him. Leaving the team. I'd come to really love these guys. And Brodie…he, and the team, had really won me over. I liked hockey.

But figure skating…it'd been my entire life for so long. And now I had a chance to get back to it.

I had to take that chance.

CHAPTER FORTY-TWO

Brodie

The Ice Den wouldn't work as my church today. I needed to be at Jackson Pond.

I needed to feel the fresh, ice-cold air stinging my lungs. Bundled up in my Gore-Tex jacket, I hopped onto the ice.

My home.

My church.

I pushed off nice and easy, warming up my legs, breathing in and out. Letting the frigid air cleanse the junk from my mind.

My soul.

After a few strides across the ice, all that was left was the thought of Willow. Willow Covington. She'd come at me out of left field. I'd had my senior year all planned out: focus on hockey, get on the BC team, and no distractions. And four months into the school year, I was secretly dating and completely falling for Willow.

My dream of playing hockey for Boston College felt like it was slipping through my fingers, too: I hadn't heard anything further from their coach, Coach Raymond, since he'd spoken with my coach, Noah. And Caleb and I were living with Preach, no clue where tuition money might have to come from someday.

Not to mention, I was keeping Willow's figure skating tryouts secret, hiding it so my best friend and teammates wouldn't find out.

Everything about us broke the rules, yet, while I skated on this uneven ice with the splash of the setting sun bouncing red rays of light through the air, everything about her felt right.

Even through the darkness of Dad's issues and Mom's death, Willow was real. The intensity with which she played hockey, battled off all those slap shots and backhands from Right Hand of God, and then the crap Pax, Eric, and even some of the town had thrown at her, she'd handled it all with grace.

The grace of a figure skater and the guts of a pro hockey player.

Yet she was going to leave me soon to go back to figure skating. I'd known all along it was going to happen, but each day she'd not been picked to join a skating team, my disappointment for her warred with my hope of her sticking around to play hockey that much more.

Until two days ago, when that Deena Polanski showed up after our loss to the Knights and offered her a tryout. And even worse, the tryout was in four days.

I might only have four days left with Willow. A hockey puck to the forehead would have hurt less than the thought of Willow leaving.

My skates hit a bump, and I was so lost in my thoughts, it laid me out flat. The ice hit my stomach, stealing the air from my lungs. I slid, my arms out in front of me, a look even Superman himself would have been jealous of.

"Um…are you okay?"

I flopped onto my stomach, and there stood Willow decked out in a green jacket. Her long braids spilled out from beneath a bright pink stocking cap that had a fuzzy poof on the top. She'd totally snuck up on me. I glanced at where my car was parked, and sure enough, hers was there, too.

"Did you hit your head or something? Should I be worried?"

"You surprised me. I'm fine." I flopped onto my back, the air finally making its way into my cramping lungs.

"Good," she said, then launched herself on top of me.

Her warm mouth found mine, but her nose was frigid. I might have to work on warming her up.

I hugged her close as I tilted her head to take the kiss deeper. She'd promised to show up if she could get away, but she hadn't been here when I'd arrived. It was okay, too, because I needed some alone ice time to process what'd happened after the game on Sunday.

Her scent and her heat curled around me as I tilted her head for more access. Her kisses were addicting, and my chest ached at the idea of walking the halls of Woodhaven and not seeing her. Hopping on the ice for drills and her not being there, kicking everyone's ass.

She leaned up and grinned, her lips shiny from our kiss and her eyelids hanging heavy over her blue eyes. I loved that look.

I kissed the tip of her nose. "You're cold."

"A little. Let's skate!" She touched a kiss to my mouth, then got up, and we jumped into a few laps of the pond.

"You doing okay?" I asked.

"Yep. Almost all packed up to leave on Friday."

I nodded, unable to say what was really on my mind. That I wanted her to tell me we'd be all right. That we weren't going to break up. And, as unfair as I knew it was to hope for, that she wanted to stay in Woodhaven and play hockey.

But I couldn't. I only had a few days left with her before

she headed to her tryout. I couldn't believe how fast this was all happening.

"You've worked really hard for this, Willow... I know they'll both want you."

The sound of our blades scraping against the ice calmed my racing heart. Skating always centered me. Even when my life was in complete chaos.

"I'm not getting my hopes up," Willow said, breaking the silence. "Well, I am a little, but I'm also scared to. Especially with my Colorado team. They'd bailed on me...didn't believe in me. I'm not sure I could go back to them if they offered." She sped up a little. "I was glad you texted me to see if I could sneak away for some ice time. I remember skating on this pond when I was a kid."

It was weird to think that she'd lived here before I'd moved here and knew about this rink. I chased her for a couple more laps until she blasted ahead of me, then whipped around, skating backward.

"You want to keep going or are you ready to declare me Queen of the Pond?"

"As if." I skated a little faster, but she sped up, too. It took some serious talent to skate backward that quickly.

She cupped her hand around her ear. "What's that? I didn't hear you quite right. Did you say, 'Willow Covington is the Queen of the Pond'?"

I chuckled. "Yeah, yeah. Willow Covington is the Queen of the Pond."

As we slowed to a stop, she bowed and waved to an imaginary audience. "Thank you, thank you very much."

"You are legit one of the fastest hockey players I've ever met."

"It's a lot easier when I'm not wearing all those goalie pads."

"I bet." I eyed her fitted black pants, hugging each curve of her sexy, toned legs. Damn, I was going to miss her.

We locked eyes, and she bit her lower lip. My body heated enough that I thought I might have to take off my jacket. "Come here."

She offered me her hand but stayed skating backward. She pulled me close until we were doing our own little dance in the middle of the pond. I tucked her head to my chest and held her close, *needing* her close. How she suddenly became my anchor in this world threw me for a loop. But her leaving soon was more of a slap shot to the face.

"I wanna tell you something, but I'm not sure I should," I said.

She went to look up, but I kept her face tucked to my chest. "You okay?"

"Yes, and you're a lot of the reason. You know that?"

"I feel the same," she said, hugging me tighter.

We'd come to a stop in the middle of the pond. My heart hammered so hard, I was sure my voice would come out shaky if I tried to talk. But I had to. I had to tell her how I felt. I'd learned a hard and fast lesson about leaving things unsaid after losing Mom so suddenly.

Even though I might lose Willow to figure skating, I had to say it.

"I'm really falling for you, Willow."

Her body tensed, and then her grip on me tightened. Snow started drifting around us, and a sense of peaceful quiet settled over us. I rested my cheek on the top of her head and let out a contented sigh. I'd said it. I felt it, it was true, and now I'd said it.

"Me, too, Brodie."

Warmth washed over me as she said each word. She cared about me, was falling for me, too. A ping of sadness burst this little bubble of peace with Willow when I realized our time was seriously limited.

"I hate that you might be leaving in a few days...for good." Fuck, I hated keeping this information from Preach and the rest of the team. It felt like I was betraying them.

"I may not make it. And if I do, you have Josiah."

"But you *do* want to make it, don't you?"

"Yeah. I mean, yes." She nodded. "It's my dream. I've always wanted it."

It felt like there might be a but coming, but there wasn't. She just kept skating, and I just held her. I was going to as long as I could.

"Everything was always so crystal clear to me until I moved here." She paused, and I tightened my hold on her and sent a silent prayer up to the skating gods that she might be reconsidering. "Now, things are a little murky. I mean, I love hockey and the team. It's a real team—well, other than a couple guys who weren't so welcoming at first. Plus, my mom is moving back here, and I really like hanging with Gramps."

My mouth went dry as I waited for her to bring up us.

"And then there's...you."

I let out a breath of relief.

"I really like you, Brodie."

"Enough to maybe stay? To consider a different path for your future?"

She let out a sigh, and I felt her ease away slightly. I leaned back to look down at her, but she did, too. My skates flew out from beneath me, and for the second time that day, Willow lay atop me.

"Shit, sorry," I said, my right butt cheek throbbing.

She let out a sad laugh and nodded, her bright blue eyes reflecting the sunshine bouncing off the ice. She was so close to me, our noses almost touched, and her coconut scent wrapped around me, but since we were outside, it was mixed in with a gentle hint of pine from the trees surrounding the rink.

"You know, at the Ice Den. When you first batted that wild puck down." I shook my head as I brushed some snow off her rosy cheeks. "Right then and there—I was yours."

"Really?" She cocked her head to the side.

I nodded, cupping her face. Her nose was bright red, and so were her cheeks. We probably needed to get into a car pretty soon and warm up. But all I could think about was kissing her again.

"Hey, guys." Preach sprayed us with ice as he stopped beside us. "What's going on?"

"Ah…um," Willow said, looking up.

"Wicked wipe out," I finished for Willow.

"Dang, you guys sure end up tangled in each other a lot," Preach said with a laugh as he started skating away. "If you weren't teammates, I'd say you were doing it on purpose."

We both let off a nervous laugh as we scrambled to our skates.

Damn, that was close.

CHAPTER FORTY-THREE

Willow

I'd been in Miami for two days, testing, going through evaluations, and today, the last day, we were with our families, taking a final, in-depth tour of one of the most prestigious, state-of-the-art facilities I'd ever skated in.

"Here is our heated, Olympic-sized pool." Deena opened a glass door. We followed her through, inhaling the humid air.

In front of us was a beautiful pool with inviting water. What I wouldn't have given to slip into it after the last hockey game. Finishing up with a dip in a hot tub.

"It's perfect for cardio and rehab." Deena continued walking. "We have a sauna, steam room, and of course, three hot tubs.

"Locker rooms on your left and right. Now, if we head through here," she said, exiting a second set of glass doors, "we'll visit the physical therapy clinic."

Two rows of ten treatment tables were lined up on the right side of the room. On the left side were ten treadmills, seven stationary bikes, and at least a half dozen elliptical machines.

Five women were lined up in the back, all wearing

matching black shirts and khakis. Behind them were lockers and shelves stuffed with athletic equipment from yoga balls to jump ropes.

"This is our physical therapy staff. They work around the clock and are able to address any of your needs."

The women stood with smiles on their faces and their hands clasped behind their backs.

"And that concludes our tour of the Miami International Skating Center." Deena grinned. "Let's head back to the conference room, and I'll be able to answer any final questions you have now that you've all been here a couple of days."

Nearly forty of us entered the conference room. Most skaters had at least one parent or guardian present, but a few of us had two. I was so glad it worked out for Mom and Dad to both come with me. All this had happened so quickly, my head was still whirling.

Skating at the highest level had been my dream since I was a kid. I'd had a taste of it, the lifestyle, even medaled at the World Junior Figure Skating Championships two years ago, then got injured and was thrown into something so unexpected. A team of hockey players I once deemed puck heads had shown me a whole different world of competitive sports and teamwork.

A world I didn't hate, either.

This facility was perfect, and it had everything I needed to get back to 100 percent. There was no doubt I'd reach the World Championships and then the Olympics if I was on this team.

Then there was Brodie. I knew that I couldn't make a decision about my future based on a guy, especially someone I was secretly dating. But, damn, I cared about him, a lot. The thought of never getting to kiss him again felt like a skate directly to the heart.

Like my heart was being torn in two.

What the hell was I going to do?

Skating, what I'd wanted all my life, was on one side and hockey, a sport I'd come to love and excel at, was on the other.

As we moved farther into the conference room, I noticed rolling chairs sitting behind a massive mahogany table, in front of each one a tote bag, like the one Deena had given me after the Holiday Classic Tournament.

"Please feel free to ask your questions, hit the restrooms, or grab a snack and a drink." She motioned to a long, thin table pushed against the wall in the back of the room. It was overflowing with fresh fruit, bagels, cream cheese, and bottles of water and juice.

As parents began rattling off questions, I excused myself and went to the back to grab a bottle of water and some pineapple.

"Hey," a girl with shiny blond hair whispered from beside me. "What do you think of this place? Pretty amazing, huh?"

I turned toward her and nodded. "Definitely." She looked familiar, but I couldn't quite place her face.

"Not sure if you remember me, but we met two years ago at the last Junior Championship. You won gold. Your routine was amazing. Inspiring, really." The girl extended her hand. "I'm Shayna, Shayna Holland. I was one of the flower kids. You got a million roses and teddy bears that day."

"Wow. That's awesome." Dang, she was young. Thirteen at the most. I shook her hand. "It's super nice to meet you."

"When I heard that you might be training here, I got really excited." She bit into a piece of apple. "You're, like, my hero."

Now I felt practically ancient sitting next to her. Every year of a skater's life was like two normal years. Most skaters aged out in their mid-twenties. I only had seven or eight years left—and that was pushing it. That meant one or two shots, max, at the Olympics.

"Do you have any tips on landing a triple axel? I'm just really struggling," Shayna said.

"Back scratch spins are everything. Practice them and you'll feel more comfortable in the air. You'll rotate more efficiently and be less likely to go crooked, which makes it harder to land," I said.

"Holy smokes! I'd never thought of that. Dang, you're brilliant! Can you be my coach?" She gave me a big smile, which warmed my heart.

"Thank you." Wow. This girl was really sweet. Her blond hair was pulled into two braids, then piled atop her head. It looked like she was ready to hop on the ice and compete because she had all her performance-style makeup on. Her skin was flawless, and her smile filled her face.

"When I heard about your Achilles…I can't even…" She exhaled as she shook her head. "It's really amazing, that you're recovered and all. A lot of times when that goes, well, you know." She slid her finger across her throat.

A phantom ache shot through my ankle.

"Well, it took a lot of hard work." And it had. But today, in the final round of assessment, I'd nailed almost all my jumps.

But it sure felt different to be on the ice without all my goalie gear on.

"Sorry. Sometimes I talk too much. Like, right now." Shayna shook her head. "Officially shutting up!"

"Don't apologize," I said.

Her cheeks turned bright red. "Fair point. I better go sit back down."

"It was nice meeting you, Shayna."

"You, too." She rushed back to a chair next to a woman wearing a black dress.

I slipped my phone out of my pocket and snuck a quick peek.

ERICKA: You've got this!

A smile tugged at my lips.

JESSA: Good luck!

JESSA: 💪

I have the best friends…

BRODIE: Kick ass today!

BRODIE: 😵

And the best boyfriend.

My palms were suddenly damp.

What if he breaks up with me after I move down here?

What if Jessa slips up and tells Preach where I am?

All of the lying had been weighing me down, but it was the only way.

As the questions wrapped up, I piled a few more pieces of fruit on my plate and then headed back to the chair between my parents. If I got accepted to the team, no more pizza parties after games with the guys. It'd be back to a strict nutrition plan and full days of training.

No more seeing Brodie in the hallways. Sneaking kisses.

No more Nathaniel joking around with me.

No more team pregame pasta dinners at Taste of Rome.

Deena stood up and straightened her jacket. "If that's everything, please feel free to explore. We have one final dinner scheduled for tonight. Decisions on the team will go out in a few days."

"This place is pretty impressive." Dad looked around.

"Easily as nice as Colorado," my mom said, nodding.

"If not nicer," Dad added.

I swallowed a piece of pineapple and took another sip of water. Colorado. After seeing this place…no way could I go back there, if they even offered. Which it didn't seem like they were, since I'd never heard anything after they'd requested my medical records.

"Can we head back to the hotel before dinner? I'm pretty beat. It would be nice to just chill out for a bit." I needed some time to rest and think things through.

"Of course." My parents pushed back from the table and grabbed the bags in front of them.

As we made our way out of the conference room, I fished my phone out of my pocket.

BRODIE: How'd tryouts go?

BRODIE: Did you nail the double axel?

BRODIE: How's the facility?

A sad smile tugged at the corners of my mouth. I couldn't stop thinking about the team and Brodie as I went through my routine. The rush that I used to get from landing jumps had been replaced by standing in goal, deflecting and catching slap shots, snap shots, and wrist shots from guys twice my size. It was a lot less painful, too. Minus the whole stitches on my cheek incident.

ME: Everything's going well.

ME: But I miss you.

ME: And the team.

ME: Minus Eric.

ME: 😝

BRODIE: When do you find out?

ME: Few days.

"Willow?" Mom draped her arm around my shoulder. "Earth to Willow?"

"Oh, my bad. I was just checking in with Brodie." I dropped my phone into my back pocket. We were almost to the elevators that led to the garage where we'd parked.

"Willow. Mr. and Mrs. Covington," Deena said, hustling toward us. "May I have a word?"

"Everything all right?" my dad asked as he took my mom's hand in his.

"Yes." She waved us to follow her into a smaller conference room off to her left. "Come on in." She shut the door behind my dad, who was the last to enter.

The room was small, with a six-person wooden table and plush leather chairs. The wall of windows overlooked one of the indoor skating rinks.

I wasn't sure if I was supposed to sit, so I just stood beside my mom, my heart hammering.

"Whew." Deena patted her chest and took in a quick breath. "You guys hustled out of there quickly."

"Oh, sorry. Yes," I said. "I just wanted to get to the hotel to relax a bit before dinner."

"Great." She offered me a wide smile that made her light blue eyes shine. "Because I wanted to let you know. The decision about your acceptance to the program has already been made."

My heart stopped.

I grabbed Mom's hand and drew in a breath.

"Willow Covington, on behalf of the Miami International Skating Center, we would like to invite you to join our team."

"Oh, honey!" Mom dropped her hold on my hand and hugged me. I kept my focus on Deena to make sure she wasn't joking or something. Or that maybe I wasn't dreaming all this up in my mind.

Dad stepped forward and offered his hand to Deena to shake. "You have a real nice facility here. It's an honor to have you coaching our daughter."

My mouth went dry, and my heart started beating again with a vengeance, almost stealing my breath. I got in. I was accepted. Tears pricked at the backs of my eyes.

"Honey?" Mom released me from the hug and gripped my shoulders.

"I...I can't believe it!" I gulped for air, suddenly feeling light-headed. "Really?" I looked at Deena.

She nodded, her smile getting impossibly bigger. I leaped at her and wrapped my arms around her. "Thank you so much."

"You've earned it," she said, hugging me tightly. "We will accomplish great things together, Willow Covington."

Pride swelled in my chest, but only for a few seconds.

How was I going to tell Brodie and the hockey team I'd come to love that I was leaving?

CHAPTER FORTY-FOUR

Brodie

"Team meeting, five minutes," Pax yelled as he stood on the locker room bench, then glared at me. "Outside."

"What the hell, man? It's, like, fifteen degrees out there," I said.

"Wear a jacket." He hopped down from the bench, then nudged me with his shoulder as he strode by.

What the heck was wrong with him? Preach shrugged as he shut his locker, and Teddy, behind him, rolled his eyes and then bit into a candy bar.

"PDA!" Nathaniel said.

"Um, what?" Teddy asked.

"Pax Drama Ahead." Nathaniel chuckled.

Josiah grabbed a large parka from the locker next to me. "Nice work on the ice today."

"Thanks." He tugged on a stocking cap. "What do you think Pax wants?"

I shrugged as I snagged my bag from the locker and slammed it shut. By the clip to Pax's voice, something was definitely up. I wasn't sure what it could be, though. We were just over five weeks before the first rounds of regionals began, and the team was humming. We were so ready to kick ass at State.

I checked the locker room to make sure everyone was out, then busted through the door, hustling down the hallway and seeing the tail end of Preach and Teddy heading outside. A blast of arctic air swept through the hallway along with some flurries. Dang, was it snowing again?

I checked my phone to see the time. Willow had texted that she'd landed and her parents were going to drop her off here on their way home from the airport. I couldn't wait to see her and hear how everything went. Even more, I couldn't wait to kiss her. She'd been so busy, we didn't get to even text very much.

The door slammed shut right when I got to it, so I pushed it open, saying, "Thanks a lot, guys."

Pax glared at me and thrust his phone into the air. "So, how long have you guys been dating behind our backs?"

I gulped, and my bag slid off my shoulder. On Pax's screen was a picture of me and Willow at Jackson Pond on New Year's Day, kissing next to my car.

"Shit," I said.

"Oh, hey, guys." Willow rounded the corner, then skidded to a stop, her eyes wide and her jaw open. "What's going on?"

"Shit, Brodie! You lied to us?" Preach yelled. "To *me*?"

Josiah gasped. So did Nathaniel and Teddy. Preach had sworn. He'd actually said a cuss word. I could count on one hand how many times I'd heard him use profanity. He had to be really pissed.

My heart hammered in my chest and my mouth went dry.

"Is this true?" Preach pointed at me, stepping toward me. "You and Willow? Hooking up? Tell me—"

"They have been." Pax flipped his phone in our direction again. "My cousin totally busted them!"

"How did you get that picture?" I growled.

"Doesn't really matter, asshole," Pax said. "But my cousin snagged it when he drove by the pond. What else are you guys hiding? Huh?"

"I saw them in Clover, once, too," Teddy said, shaking his head. "At the ice cream shop."

My heart pounded. And here I thought we'd be safe in Clover.

"The practice sessions. The pond. Excuses as to why we couldn't hang." Preach's voice reverberated off the arena brick wall behind us. "All lies?"

"Preach. I can explain. Let me—"

"Save it." He showed me his gloved palm, then pointed at Willow. "I can't believe you guys did this to the team."

Oh shit, he was going to tell Coach, wasn't he? Preach was a stickler for the rules, which was exactly why we hadn't told him. Why we hadn't told anyone. We'd been so careful…

"Wait, Preach, don't. Please don't tell," I said.

Willow just stared at me. Her mouth open. Her eyes wide. She didn't deserve to be called out like this. The hurt I saw ripped through my chest.

Shit.

"Is that why you wanted her on the team so bad? Because you were getting in her pants?" Pax yelled.

"Fuck you, Pax!" Willow yelled.

Before I could register the thought, I fisted my hand and slammed it against Pax's cheek.

He spun and flopped onto the snow-packed ground, groaning.

I pointed at him. "Stay down."

"That bitch ruined everything," Eric added.

"Oh, shut up, Eric. You're a sexist pig, and the only one ruining *anything* right now is you," Willow said.

Preach tackled me around the waist, and I was down. He'd caught me off balance, and the next thing I knew, I was on my back, and he was putting all his weight on me.

I actually thought he was going to hit me, but then someone yelled, "Hey."

I recognized that voice as Preach's dad.

"Brodie," he yelled. "Preach. You guys out here?"

"Brodie?" Caleb yelled, coming out from behind Mr. Armstrong.

I shoved Preach off me, and he didn't give much of a fight. He was probably as confused as I was as to why his dad and my little brother were here.

So much was going on at once, I was having trouble keeping everything straight.

"Caleb?" I hopped to my feet and opened my arms for him to come to me.

"Dad?" Preach stood and brushed the snow from his arm. "You okay? Is Mom okay?"

"Yes. Fine." Mr. Armstrong waved me to him. "Brodie. Come with me now. Ryan, follow behind us."

Oh crap. Mr. Armstrong was using Preach's real name. Something was up, and that made the hairs on the back of my neck stand on end. Caleb seemed fine, so it couldn't be him, but the strained look on Mr. Armstrong's face didn't help calm my thrashing heart down at all.

I hoisted Caleb into my arms and hustled after Mr. Armstrong. Willow followed close behind.

Thank God Mr. Armstrong hadn't noticed Pax on the ground.

The chatter from the rest of the team faded away. The fear surging off Preach's dad nearly plowed me over.

"I parked right next to you," Mr. Armstrong said. "We've got to move fast. Give him to me." He pointed at Caleb. "I'll buckle him in while you get your stuff out of your car."

"What's going on, Dad?"

"Just do as I say, and hurry. Ryan, get your car and be ready to follow us. Brodie, pull everything from your car that you want to keep."

"What's happening?" I asked as I handed him my baby brother. He reached for me, but I forced a smile. "It's all right, buddy."

Mr. Armstrong held my brother and tucked his head to his neck. "Asset seizure. Police are on their way to your house. I got a tip from a buddy."

"Oh my gosh." Willow gasped from beside me.

I reached for her, and we ran toward my car. I hadn't seen her since Friday before she'd left for Miami, and now, instead of sneaking away to spend some time alone with her, we were in the freezing cold, running to empty out my car, an entire team feeling betrayed behind us. But I couldn't worry about that right now.

Mr. Armstrong's Lexus was right beside mine, still running.

"Why are the police involved?" I asked.

"That's just how it all works," he said. "The bank is seizing your father's assets. They'll come take this car soon, so we might as well get what we can from it."

"I don't understand," I said as I opened the glove compartment and center console and grabbed everything I could shove in my pockets and hold in my arms.

With Willow's help, we emptied my car in under five minutes and threw everything into the back of the Lexus. I crawled into the backseat to sit beside Caleb, and Willow followed me in.

Caleb grabbed my hand, then focused on the screen affixed to the back of the seat in front of him. He was wearing headphones and watching a Minions movie. I turned and looked between the seats and out the front window. The snow flurries zoomed toward the car, but they blurred out of focus.

I was tired.

It was cold.

And I just wanted to forget today ever happened.

But no. I was going to go to my house, which hopefully wasn't seized already by the U.S. Marshals. The house I'd lived in for eight years. I'd loved that house until Mom died, then I'd hated it. But now that it might be taken away, I loved it again.

First the team busted me and Willow, now this. My fucking life was falling apart. No, it was being ripped apart at the seams.

"Can I see your phone a sec, Willow?" I didn't even know where mine was right now. Probably stuck in my bag in the back of the car.

She unlocked it, then handed it to me, and I typed a search for *seizure of assets*. The results weren't good.

"That means Dad's broke, right?" I said, adjusting the heat vents to hit Caleb more.

"Rumors have been flying for a while now, I've been hearing things, but I didn't want to believe it. Just figured he was struggling with your mom's death. Drinking. Making wrong choices."

"What happened?"

"He stole people's retirements. They caught him at the international airport about an hour ago, son. He was trying to flee the country."

"What? He was…he was leaving…the country?" My stomach bottomed out. Bile stung the back of my throat. I hadn't heard anything from him since Christmas Eve, but to leave the country? I had to have heard wrong.

Mr. Armstrong nodded. The final turn to our long driveway was coming up.

Dad was going to leave us? Leave Caleb? Just run away? Not even say goodbye?

"He's sick, son. It may have started out as grief over losing your mom, but it quickly turned into addiction. He's out of control."

"But…"

"Just hang with me a few more minutes. Stay strong a bit longer." He nodded as he focused on the road ahead. "Think quickly. What do you need from the house? Does Caleb have all the prescriptions he needs? Medical records in a safe…"

"Got most of his medicine at your place. I'll grab everything I can get my hands on, though." My head was spinning. "I don't remember the safe code."

"Does he keep it anywhere?"

"Wait. I think I might have it on my phone. I—I saw lots of cash in there before." I gulped, remembering when I'd dug in the safe for bail money that time he'd been thrown in jail. "Like…a lot of cash, Mr. Armstrong."

"Leave it. Just take medical records or important stuff like that, birth certificate, social security cards…"

"And clothes, I need—Caleb needs some more—"

"We got that covered. Don't forget something that reminds you of your mom. That's important. Don't want to lose anything like that in all of this."

"Oh my gosh, Brodie," Willow whispered.

I gulped. I was losing everything, wasn't I?

At least I had Willow with me. And hopefully Preach could forgive me for lying. But what about Boston College? Where would we live? What would happen to us?

Tears stung, but I blinked them back. Like Mr. Armstrong said, I needed to hang in there a few more minutes. I needed to be strong for Caleb.

Willow's phone in my hand chimed, and I looked down.

An email message preview filled the screen.

From someone named Coach Deena Polanski: *Welcome to the team! You're all confirmed for your January 11th arrival. Flight information attached. So pleased you accepted our offer.*

CHAPTER FORTY-FIVE

Willow

"I can't believe you didn't tell me." Brodie paced back and forth in front of Preach's house.

We'd just gotten back from emptying out his house into Preach's and Mr. Armstrong's cars. The second the car stopped, he'd jumped out and run to the front of the house. The snow had picked up, morphing into huge, fluffy snowflakes, but they weren't pretty like I normally thought.

Nothing about my return to Woodhaven today had been pretty.

I closed my eyes and took in a slow, deep breath, trying to calm my heart down. "I came right to the Ice Den to tell you. This wasn't anything I could just send over text. Then I walked into the Pax Hunt Shit Show."

"Why couldn't you have told the team? Now they're going to know I lied to them again!" Brodie's eyes narrowed in on mine, the amber flecks that usually sparkled weren't visible under the pale moonlight.

"Because I wanted to tell my boyfriend first!" I argued. "You, Brodie. You were all that mattered to me once I got off that plane."

"Well, what does it even matter if you're leaving?" He shook his head. "They're already feeling betrayed, but this is going to gut them."

I opened my mouth but then shut it. I didn't know what to say or even what I *could* say at the moment. So much had happened over the past few hours. His dad was in jail. He was basically homeless, not a possession to his name except what he was able to pack into Mr. Armstrong and Preach's cars before the authorities arrived.

Yes, I had asked him to keep the tryout to himself for a few days, but I hadn't expected things to move so quickly. I thought I'd have more time.

Plumes of white burst from his mouth, he was breathing so heavily in this frigid air. The snow crunched beneath his boots as he marched back and forth before me.

"You said you weren't even sure anymore, and now you're all of a sudden going? What the hell happened?"

"I can't help it. They want me down there right away." My shoulders slumped, and tears stung my eyes. "Y-you always knew this might happen."

"But you were really starting to love hockey. The team. I thought…" He let his head fall into his hands. "Maybe you'd stay…"

Tears blurred my vision, and my body sagged beneath the weight of his sadness—and mine. I couldn't blame him for being so upset, to find out I was leaving Woodhaven in a matter of five days by seeing an email scroll over my phone… and after what went down with his father.

That was about as horrible as it could have gone.

"You know what hurts the most, Willow?" Brodie's eyes were glassy. "That you didn't even talk to me about it first."

"I'm so sorry, Brodie. The timing…everything happening so fast. This wasn't something I could just call up and tell you or text you."

"You could have *tried*."

"I know that," I said, defeated. "And I should have. But you know, I also don't need your permission to make decisions that impact my life."

"Of course not." Brodie let his arms fall to his sides. "I just thought you'd talk to me about it. Tell me what you were thinking. You'd seemed interested when I brought up playing hockey and some scouts checking you out as well. And then… you go away on Friday, come back on Sunday, and bam, I find out you're leaving me."

"You were looking at my phone. You weren't supposed to find out that way." I knew the excuse was weak, but I needed to make the decision on my own or I was afraid I'd talk myself out of it. Not because of my relationship with Brodie, but because of the way I felt when I played hockey. Joy, pure joy.

Brodie shook his head. "I should have known you'd leave me. Abandon the team when we need you most."

Talk about a sucker punch to the stomach. "You don't mean that, Brodie."

"Don't I?"

He'd known since day one I was on target to get back to skating. I'd never held that back. Then again, I hadn't intended on falling for him. And I knew he was hurting—over a lot more than just his chances of winning State being in jeopardy.

But this hurt me, too. It wasn't like I'd made this decision lightly. My heart was breaking, too.

"I sure as shit mean it, Willow. Because it's exactly what's happening." He turned away from me and tugged on his Wolverines stocking cap. "Why did I let this happen? Why did I let you in? I knew it'd burn me. I knew it'd end this way."

His voice was full of anguish. A pain I hadn't heard him express before.

"Brodie, I—I love you! I never meant to hurt you. I'm so sorry."

Brodie spun around, but he didn't say anything. He just looked at me with those big brown eyes. I'd said the three words, the three words I'd never said to a guy other than my dad or grandfather, and he was speechless. Couldn't return my words.

He didn't love me, did he? And now that I was leaving…

A jolt of pain struck my heart like a lightning bolt, and I stepped back at the sensation. He didn't love me. And I'd just told him I did.

Heat flushed up my chest and pooled at my cheeks. "Brodie, please."

"Please what, Willow? Please don't be pissed? Please don't be upset?" Tears poured from his eyes, but he batted them away and glared at me. "My life is so fucked up right now, this just—I'm happy for you, really. This is your dream. You should go chase your dream."

A wave of nausea stormed through my stomach. Hot tears scorched a path down my face.

"What about us?" A sob caught in my throat. I could barely get the question out.

"Us?" Brodie shook his head. "I can't even think about this right now."

"We talked about giving the long-distance thing a try. I still want that. I know you care about me—"

Brodie wiped the tears off his face. "I can't do it, Willow."

Pain coursed through my veins. I reached for him, but he pulled back. "But you said—"

"Yeah, well, a lot sure has changed in the last five hours, hasn't it?" He glanced over his shoulder toward Preach's house. "Look. My dad just got busted, my baby brother is inside, crying his eyes out, and my girlfriend is leaving me."

"Brodie," I whispered.

"I need to get inside and be with my brother. I can't do this, Willow. I can't do long distance. I can't…" He batted away the tears streaming down his face. "I really am happy for you. Good luck in Miami. You're going to kill it."

"It's not, Brodie. Just…before you decide, let's think about it. We can—"

"No, Willow. I'm sorry. It's better this way." He stepped toward the house. "I'm sure Preach'll drive you home. Thanks for your help tonight. I—thanks."

Without another word, he walked into the house.

I covered my face with my mittened hands and sobbed. He'd just walked away. Left me standing out here in the dark. Alone.

No, no, no!

This isn't how things were supposed to happen!

An icy wind cut through my jacket, chilling me to the core. I was supposed to be happy right now. All my hard work had finally paid off. I'd won a spot back on an elite skating team.

Instead, I was in tears, in the snow, having been dumped by the greatest guy I'd ever met.

"Hey, Willow." Preach came up beside me, his hands shoved in his jacket pockets.

I barely remembered getting into his Jeep, but as I started thawing out from having been outside the last half hour talking with Brodie—no, getting dumped by Brodie—I realized we were almost to my house.

"Thanks, Preach."

He nodded, but his jaw ticked. He hadn't said a word to me the whole drive.

"I really am sorry," I added. "I didn't mean to leave the team high and dry like this."

"I get it. You've always been a figure skater, Willow." He

sighed. "I...can't believe you guys hid this from me." He gripped the steering wheel with both hands and stared forward. "From Jessa."

"We felt like we had to."

He huffed and steered the Jeep down Manchester Street.

"He broke up with me anyway," I said, my voice cracking. To say it out loud was like a slice to my heart.

"Just keep in mind," Preach said, "it's been kind of a rough night for him, you know?"

"And it hasn't been for me?"

"I don't know, Willow, did your dad just get arrested? Did everything you own, except what you were able to throw in a car, just get seized?" Preach's jaw tensed as he looked pointedly at me, then back at the road.

"Shit..." Of course he was right. Maybe...if I talked to Brodie tomorrow, things might look different for him?

"Look. I'm sorry. I'm still pissed off about the lying." Preach maneuvered the car through a small pile of snow at the base of my driveway and pulled in. "Maybe things'll shake out."

"I'm not so sure." I rested my head back, the full effect of what'd happened today and my fatigue slammed into me like a two-by-four to the chest.

"I'm not, either. The guy's been through the ringer. Just coming off the two-year anniversary of his mom's death. First it was his mom getting killed by that drunk driver. Then, within a year of that, his dad started falling off the rails." Preach pounded the steering wheel. "I can't believe everything that's happened."

Neither could I. Everything got so messed up. "I didn't mean to hurt him. Or the team."

"I know. And I'm happy for you about getting an offer. But...are you sure you can't stay and goal for State first?"

I shook my head. "Against the liability agreement I signed. Can't chance an injury."

"But you've gotten nothing but super strong being on the hockey team."

"I know, but that's how it works in this world. It's all or nothing." My eyes burned with unshed tears.

"But it's what you want, right?"

"Yes. It's all I've ever known." My voice cracked. "All I've ever dreamed of."

And in five days, I'd be gone. Probably wouldn't see them again—or at least not any time soon.

Preach let out a long breath and nodded, then reached over and took my hand.

It was finally starting to hit home how much I'd truly miss these guys.

CHAPTER FORTY-SIX

Brodie

"**S**o, you're drowning your sorrows with cheeseburgers and chocolate malts, huh?" Preach sagged into the plastic chair across from me while Caleb jumped into the ball pit.

A red ball popped out of the open door and rolled across the tile floor, but I just left it. I had no energy today. Everything in me felt heavy.

"We had to get out of the house. The little guy needed to move."

"And it had nothing to do with the fact that Willow left for Miami today…" Preach stole one of my fries and stuffed the whole thing in his mouth.

How heavy and sad I felt today had *everything* to do with Willow leaving. She'd gone. Caught her plane to Miami today at noon. I'd heard the day and time from Preach after he'd gotten the info from Jessa.

Willow hadn't returned to school other than to do withdrawal papers. Seeing her on Tuesday in the office as I passed by felt like a kick to the balls. She was smiling, her eyes were bright, and she seemed…happy. She'd gotten everything she'd wished for.

I can't believe she's gone.

It'd been five days since I'd found out my dad was a thief and would be heading to prison.

A swirl of anger clenched my stomach. So much shit had gone down on Sunday, I felt like I'd been walking around in a dream or something. No, a nightmare.

"Well, you know you were a dick for lying to us all, right?" Preach took one of my cheeseburgers and opened it up.

"I know." I was thankful he was forgiving me. Things weren't quite the same with us yet, but it felt like he was on his way.

I was just stuck on the fact that Willow left me. Left the team. "You can't fault her, you know," Preach added.

Caleb squealed, and a few more red balls came out of the doorway.

"You okay in there, Limp Lungs?" I asked.

"Mm-hmm. Come in with me!"

"Hang on a sec, buddy," I said, then looked at Preach. "What do you mean?"

"You can't tell me you wouldn't jump at the chance if the NHL came calling for you."

I snagged my soda and took a swig. He wasn't wrong. It hurt so damn much. I'd let her in. And the exact second that my life fell apart, she'd left. It felt like everyone left me when I needed them. First, my mom was killed. Then, a year later, Dad checked out on us, I'd tried dating a couple times, and they ended miserably. Willow was different, though. A true athlete, nice person, and real.

And yes…she'd never lied to me about her true intentions of returning to an elite figure skating team.

But I'd still fallen for her.

Hard.

It was my senior year, a Friday night, and here I was in this empty McDonald's play area with my best friend eating burgers. Basically, a homeless orphan.

Oh, and to make things worse, we'd totally lost our game last night. The team wasn't the same without Willow. Josiah did the best he could, but...he wasn't Willow.

"This freaking sucks." I flopped onto my chair again and slammed my drink down.

"You need to chill, man," Preach said.

"I am." I took in a deep breath. "I am."

"Yeah, *sure* you are." He lifted an eyebrow. "Willow."

I scowled.

"Willow Covington," he said as he jumped out of his chair.

"You're an asshole." I charged him, but he ducked out of the way and hid behind the back of the slide.

Caleb started laughing, then said, "Willow. Willow. Willow."

"You guys suck." I stormed the ball pit.

Caleb saw me coming, and his eyes widened. He loaded up on balls, and as soon as I leaned into the doorway, he threw one at me.

It didn't even make it to the doorway, but he laughed. "No. No."

"I'm so getting you," I said.

Preach shoved my back, and I fell into the ball pit, then he dove in and tackled me around the waist.

"Let me just reiterate, for the record, you're a dick for dating her behind our backs," he said.

"I know, Preach. Again: I'm sorry." I threw a ball at him.

"But...I can tell you love her." Preach flopped onto his back and tossed a ball into the air above him. "'Cause you *never* would've put the team in jeopardy if you didn't."

When Willow had said those three words on Sunday, when we were out in the front yard of Preach's house, I wanted to say them back. More than anything. But I couldn't. I knew I was losing her to skating, so I couldn't put myself out there, say the words for the first and last time.

But just because I hadn't said them didn't mean I didn't love her.

Because I knew I did.

I loved Willow. As in, I totally loved her. "But look where it got me."

"Was it worth it?"

I smashed my hand into the balls and flopped onto my back, unsure how to answer that. Was falling in love with Willow and then losing her worth it? Worth the pain I was in now? The bad spot the team was in? Was it worth lying to my best friend *and* my whole team?

"I don't know."

Caleb launched himself at me and about kneed me in the balls.

"Dude. Watch where you're kicking." I tossed him a few feet from me.

He squealed, laughing. That made me feel good, because ever since all this crap with Dad went down and Willow stopped coming by, he'd been so sad and a little more sickly than normal. Damn cough. But he was looking better today.

"Have you talked to her since Sunday?" Preach flopped onto his back beside me.

"No." I just couldn't bring myself to. She'd texted me a couple times, the last one being last night, saying that she'd miss me and wished me well.

I'd opened her texts a couple of times to reply but deleted them. It just freaking hurt too much.

"She came straight from the airport to tell you about the offer. Then that crap with Pax and then your dad…"

"I know. She said all that." I scrubbed my face with my

hands. "I just thought…"

"That she'd choose hockey." Preach grinned and stole one of my fries. "I'd be lying if I hadn't hoped the same thing."

"She was good, wasn't she?"

"It defies logic how good she was—considering she picked up a brand-new sport and excelled at it her senior year of school." Preach laughed, then nailed me with a brown-eyed stare. "She is seriously something else."

That she was. I sure did love her, but it didn't matter. She was in Miami, and I was here. If everything worked out the way I'd been planning on my whole life, I'd still be going to Boston College next year. And she'd be traveling the world, working her way to Olympics status.

She must be so happy right now. She was headed back to the ice, competing for gold medals instead of dealing with puck heads, as she called us, and stitches in the cheek.

"Remember that night she got that cut on her cheek?" I asked.

"She is such a badass."

"Dude. Potty mouth." I punched his shoulder. Preach never swore, never did anything off the straight and narrow, but twice now, within two weeks he'd sworn.

Preach nudged me with his elbow. "So what are you gonna do?"

"Nothing. It's over. Focus on winning State and making BC's team—like I'd planned all along. Only thing that's different is that I *really* need a scholarship now."

"From what Jessa says, Willow's really upset with how things turned out." Preach shook his head. "She never meant to hurt you."

I knew that. Willow wasn't mean or vindictive. But I was just so hurt. She was gone now, and anyway, I couldn't do long distance even if I could move past her leaving. Those kinds of relationships never lasted. It'd lead to even more hurt than I was feeling right now.

Caleb twitched and took in a ragged breath.

"Is he wheezing?" Preach sat up.

"I'm not sure… He's been doing this on and off all afternoon." I rubbed his back. Caleb coughed. His whole body flinched, and his eyes popped open. And then his shoulders relaxed, and his eyes closed.

"That's plain freaky," Preach said. "Is he okay?"

I pressed my palm to his forehead. "Doesn't feel warm. But that was weird. His inhaler wasn't working super well earlier."

"Brodie?" Caleb looked up at me from my arms. His chest started heaving as he gasped for air. His jaw tensed.

"Let's get your inhaler." I scooped him into my arms and made my way to the table, Preach close behind me.

"Should I call Dad?" Preach asked.

I snatched Caleb's inhaler from my jacket pocket, and he took a hit from that. "No. Let's give this a second."

I rubbed his back as he sat on my lap. "Breathe, Little Man."

"Do you think Daddy is okay?"

I kissed his temple and hugged him close. I didn't know what was happening with Dad, but I wasn't really sure what to say. So I just rocked with him and said, "Yeah. He'll be fine." I had to lie—for both of us. If I didn't, I'd totally lose it.

The thought of losing another parent…that wasn't something I could handle.

CHAPTER FORTY-SEVEN

Willow

"**A**gain!" Coach River shouted from across the ice. "Your arms are too sloppy."

Closing my eyes, I headed back to the center of the ice and started my new routine over for the eighth time. What I thought would be the best time of my life was turning into anything but. The nonstop schedule. The strict nutrition. And the girls… Here I thought Pax and Eric were catty to me when I'd joined the hockey team. They were sweet in comparison to some of these girls.

As I glided across the ice, arms held out as gracefully as possible, I thought back to the team. The guys I'd left behind. Or, in Brodie's words, *abandoned*. That word had haunted me each day since he'd said it.

I'd checked their stats from the regionals that started this weekend, and I had to do a double take. They'd barely made it to the State Competition. I wasn't able to watch more than a period of the game last night, but it was enough to see things were not going well.

Kind of like they weren't going well here.

Preparing for my first jump, I flipped around backward

and held my foot out.

Brodie.

I dug my toe pick into the ice, but my timing was off. Tripping over my own skates, I hit the ice. Hard.

"Willow, where's your head?" Coach River yelled. "You're all over the place."

"Sorry, Coach."

"I think we should call it for today." She made a note on her clipboard, her lips forming a tight line.

I picked myself up off the ice and skated toward the door leading to the locker rooms.

Every part of my body ached, especially my Achilles. Not the sharp, biting pain from when I tore it, but more of a sore, nagging sensation that I had a feeling would be with me as long as I was training and competing.

The locker room was abuzz with skaters. Twenty of us had accepted the invite to join.

Nikki, a girl from Indiana, gave me a shrug. "You'll get it back."

"Thanks." But did I *want* it back? Something was missing since I'd returned to figure skating full time. The rush, the comfort I used to get from nailing a routine, just felt muted somehow. I plopped onto the wooden bench separating the lockers and tugged off my skates. After wiping them down, I put on the guards and set them in my locker.

A hushed voice floated through the air from the next row over. "If she keeps falling, I'm totally taking her spot. I can't believe the coaching staff ranked her at number two. I mean, she's been away and playing *hockey*! What kind of figure skater does that?"

Heat flashed up my neck and spilled across my face.

I stomped over and came face-to-face with two girls who had been doing incredibly well on the junior circuit. "*This* kind of figure skater does that."

They looked at me in horror, mouths agape.

"I got hurt. Hockey made me stronger, and it improved my reflexes." I knew I didn't need to justify myself to these girls, but standing up for myself felt good.

"Reflexes? Is that why you keep falling on your ass?"

I whipped around. "Ariel. I was wondering when you'd show up."

A girl who had nearly beaten me in the last competition I skated in looked me up and down.

"How's the Achilles?" She grinned.

"Good. How's that silver medal from the Junior Championship? Oh, wait. You got a bronze. My bad."

A scowl replaced her smug grin.

"Wow, how I didn't miss this." I turned and stomped back to my locker, my heart hammering so hard, I heard it echoing around my head.

Of course, not all the girls were like Ariel or the other two. Janae and Liv were both really nice. We'd had lunch together every day.

But, man.

The mean girls on the ice sure didn't waste any time trying to take control. Had I been like that? Not really, though I had looked down my nose at hockey players. A ping of sadness stabbed at my chest at how I'd first reacted to Brodie when he'd asked me to cover the goal for Josiah that day back in August. *Me? Hockey?* What a jerk response. And boy, had they proved me wrong. They were tough, but not puck heads, like I'd always thought they were.

And, sure, at first, they were a little apprehensive of me. But except for Pax and Eric, the team had really welcomed me in. They weren't like these backstabbing princesses here hoping I'd fall down so they could move into my spot. Hell,

I'd even begun to win over Pax and Eric before I left.

As I got changed, my thoughts drifted to the team I'd left behind. Teddy's massive grin and his ability to take out just about any defender who approached him. Nathaniel and his fast footwork and all his joking around. He was a really talented skater. Pax… Oh Pax. Even though he was a major jerk at times, he was still a solid defender.

Brodie.

The guy who had taught me everything I knew about being a goalie. The guy I'd kissed in secret every spare chance we got those few weeks we'd secretly dated. The guy I'd fallen in love with… I missed him so much it hurt, but I also missed the rush of blocking those pucks firing at me.

I missed the guys teasing me, calling me Ice Capades. My tears stung as I remembered Nathaniel always calling me that. They were like my brothers.

And I missed my family.

I slammed my locker shut and turned the lock.

Crap.

I screwed up.

I'd been forcing this. Figure skating at an Olympic level had been my dream for so long, I'd never even entertained a life without it. But I'd changed, and I knew what I needed to do to fix things, but I had to get to my room first.

Practically sprinting, I rushed back toward my dorm and swung open the door.

Where'd I put my phone?

Coach Polanski had a strict rule about phones. They weren't allowed on the rink or in our lockers. She viewed phones as distractions.

Excitement raced through my body and caused my fingers to tremble as I tore through my room, trying to remember where I'd set it.

There it is!

I grabbed it from my dresser, then plopped to the floor and leaned against the wall beside it.

My trembling fingers flew across the screen as I searched for Coach Noah's phone number. I tapped on his name and held my breath as the phone started to ring.

Ring.

My heart hammered.

Ring.

"Hello?"

"Coach Noah? It's me, Willow. I made a huge mistake. I want back on the team." I just threw it all out there, no pleasantries, no nothing.

And then it was silent.

I gulped, heat crawling up my neck. He didn't want me back. *Shit.* What if the team didn't want me back? What if—

"We need you, Willow, but the choice isn't just up to me anymore," he finally said. "If you want back on, it needs to be a team decision."

I was screwed, then. The team hated me. Brodie hated me. He hadn't replied to any of the three texts I'd sent him after we'd broken up. He rarely posted much of anything on social media these past six weeks. Jessa said he didn't seem to smile as much as before and didn't do much other than school, hockey, and hang with Caleb.

"Can you be back here this Friday for our first State game?"

"Yes." As I cradled my phone, a huge weight I hadn't even realized was there since I got to Miami finally lifted off my chest. Because he wouldn't ask that if he didn't think the team would agree, would he?

Didn't matter. Even if they didn't vote me back on, I didn't want to stay here. I was more than just skating, and hockey showed me that. And I *wanted* more than skating, too.

I wanted to be part of a real team. A team that didn't have teammates trying to stab me in the back. And college. What if I went to a regular four-year college? Maybe I could even study coaching.

"I'll be there, first thing Friday morning."

"Good. Then we'll bring it to a vote."

CHAPTER FORTY-EIGHT

Brodie

"I think I'm gonna puke," Trevor Lee said as he stood from his seat on the bus.

He'd never been to State. I remembered my first time here, and I'd felt like puking then, too.

My phone vibrated in my pocket, so I pulled it out to find a message from Preach's dad.

MR. ARMSTRONG: All good here, Caleb's tucked in the car, and we're headed your way for tonight's game.

ME: Any word on Dad?

MR. ARMSTRONG: He's good, kid. Safe, getting the help he needs. Don't you worry.

ME: Thanks.

It'd been just over seven weeks since my dad had been arrested. All things pointed to a super-long stay in prison, so the Armstrongs had started the process of maintaining custody of Caleb and me. What had started out temporary over Christmas was turning into permanent, especially for Caleb. I'd be eighteen soon, so I'd be fine to stay wherever, but Caleb was only eight.

I glanced out the window to my right and looked at the

massive hotel. The billboard sign read WELCOME, HOCKEY PLAYERS!

This town, much like Woodhaven, loved their hockey. Coach Raymond was here, and I had a meeting scheduled with him for later this afternoon, before the first game. Mr. Armstrong was pretty sure he was going to offer a scholarship, but I didn't want to get my hopes up. At this point, I couldn't afford to go to college unless I got a full ride. Dad had all but cleaned out our accounts.

An overwhelming heaviness landed square on my chest, and a lump lodged in my throat. If I didn't get some kind of hockey scholarship, college wasn't an option for me any longer. This tournament, this team, and Caleb, this was all I had.

I eased off the cushioned seat after everyone had passed by. I followed Teddy as he lumbered along the aisle. Preach was laughing; I could hear it before I even got out of the bus.

"Come on, guys, gather up." Coach waved us to him just outside the bus exit. "Nonstarters, grab the bags and meet us in the lobby."

I glanced at Preach, and he shrugged. Usually, Coach was all about us going in together. Why would he ask the nonstarters to carry our stuff?

"Come on!"

Preach, Josiah, Nathaniel, Teddy, Pax, and I chugged along behind Coach, up the stairs and toward the double door entrance. Two doormen opened the doors, and I nodded to them as I walked by. "Thanks!"

Inside, the floors were marble. Up ahead was the main desk where there was a line, three people deep, at each station. To the left, there was a grand stairwell up to the second floor.

"Right this way, guys." Coach Noah waved us to follow him down a side hallway. The sign above the opening of the hallway read CONFERENCE ROOMS.

"What the hell?" Pax said from behind me. "What's going on?"

"No idea."

"Some captain you are," Nathaniel said, grinning at me.

It was only noon, so we had five hours before the first game, but usually we all met as a team, all of us, so this didn't make any sense.

"I know. It's scouts!" Teddy bumped into me as he pulled off his cap. "Maybe we're all getting scholarships."

"That makes sense." Pax huffed. "You and I are juniors, dipshit."

"Oh…" Teddy laughed. "Just kidding. Yeah, then I have no idea."

We followed Coach around the corner. He pulled open a door to a small conference room called the Biola Room and held it open as we passed by.

"Holy shit," Nathaniel said, but I couldn't see why since I was last in line to enter. "Ice Capades."

My heart stalled out. Literally freaking stopped.

Then my stomach hardened like I'd swallowed about fifteen hockey pucks. Nathaniel called *Willow* "Ice Capades." Did that mean…?

I stepped into the room, and at the front of it, near a podium, Willow stood.

"Listen up, guys. We only have this room for a few minutes." Coach pulled the door closed behind him and stood in front of it. "Willow has something to say."

I found the first seat I could, and the rest of the team filled the remaining seats. We were all facing the front, where she stood, but nobody uttered a word, and she hadn't yet met my eye.

She was wearing leggings, a long Woodhaven Hoodie, and her long black hair was in her trademark braids. Beneath the lights above her, her blue eyes lit up as they scanned each of the players. The pink scar beneath her eye crinkled as she smiled tentatively at me.

God, I'd missed that smile. It stole my breath, to the point where I had to look away. What was she doing here? My mind blanked after that. I couldn't conjure up another coherent thought.

She cleared her throat and shifted her weight. Resting one arm on the wooden podium beside her, she stood tall.

"I made a mistake. Um…a few of them," she dodged, glancing quickly at the coach. "And I'm here…ah…" She cleared her throat, glanced at me, then scanned the room. "I love hockey. I love you guys."

"Yes!" Nathaniel yelled. "I knew you'd miss us. Well, me, anyway."

Willow smiled, a light blush coloring her cheeks. "Once I got to Miami, I realized it wasn't my dream. Yeah, I love figure skating, but it's not who I am anymore. All I could think about when I was down there was this team, playing hockey with you guys—and winning State!"

I glanced at Preach, who sat beside me, and he looked at me with wide eyes. My gut clenched like I'd been sucker punched. Nathaniel watched Willow with a grin filling his face. He seemed fine with all this. Pax's jaw was gritted shut and eyebrows furrowed, so I wasn't sure what he was thinking. Teddy watched Willow up there with wide eyes, but he was nodding and smiling. But Josiah, his reaction caught me by surprise the most. He was grinning and nodding as he looked at me.

"Also, I owe you all an apology. Especially you, Brodie." She hit me with her blue-eyed gaze. "I asked you to keep my tryout a secret. I wasn't sure anything would come of it, so I didn't want it to get out. He wasn't comfortable with doing that, you guys, but he did it for me anyway." A few of the guys threw understanding looks my way.

A sense of relief loosened the tension in my neck and back. Damn, she was laying it all out there, wasn't she?

"Then I up and left you all," Willow continued. "I know that wasn't fair to you, and I'm sorry. I…I wanted to stay with you all. But I had to go down to Miami. I had to try. For me. Little did I know, though, that once I did, I'd realize my dreams had changed. You guys are all a huge part of that. I couldn't have realized that without seeing it through, though."

Silence filled the room, so I was sure everyone could hear the blood raging through my body. Thudding in my ears. My heart banging against my chest. My cheeks heated as I fisted my hands beneath the table. She was here. Standing before us, the team she'd abandoned.

But she hadn't abandoned me.

She was here now.

"Willow's asked to play goalie this weekend." Coach pointed at her. "Which means you guys have a decision to make."

"Yes! So much yes!" Nathaniel yelled.

Pax punched his shoulder. "Shut up, asshole. Let Coach talk."

"You'll each get your vote. You guys decide, as a team, if you're wanting her to start as your goalie in tonight's game."

"Hell to the yes!" Nathaniel jumped up and ran over to Willow. He wrapped his long arms around her, nearly knocking over the podium in the process. "I knew you'd be back, Willow. I just knew it. I vote yes!"

"Ooph," Willow said with a massive smile on her face.

"For real, Willow? You're okay with giving up figure skating?" Teddy asked.

She nodded, the smile filling her face even more. She

looked at peace with herself. With her decision.

"I vote yes," Teddy said as he nodded, then looked at Josiah. "But I think Josiah's vote should count for double or triple. It's his spot."

"I don't know, Sequins." Pax shook his head. "That was some fu—messed-up crap you pulled on us. And with Brodie…" He trailed off, looking surreptitiously over at Coach. "Not cool."

"I get why she left, though," Teddy said, clearly trying to get us off the unsaid subject of our secret relationship. "She was—"

"Let me finish, dude." Pax flipped Teddy off. "I vote yes."

I whipped my head around at that one, along with Coach and the rest of the guys. Pax wanted her on the team? Holy shit. I knew he'd been coming around to the idea of her, after resisting it pretty violently in the beginning, but to be one of the first ones to say yes now?

"Dang," Preach whispered beside me.

"Josiah?" Coach asked.

"I'm honestly all for it," Josiah said. "Willow. You're the shit. I wanna win, and to tell you the truth, I'm not all that thrilled about facing off against Roger the Right Hand of God when I'm this rusty."

"Josiah and I will be here next year," Pax said. "You'll nail it then, man."

Nathaniel chuckled, then fell to the floor beside Willow in a fake faint. "I think I just saw a pig flying by the window. Did you guys see it?"

Pax flipped Nathaniel off, then dipped his head in Willow's direction. "Sorry for being such an asshat."

Willow wiped a tear away from her eye, then looked up at me.

"Come on, Brodie. Make it unanimous," Preach said.

"Because you know I'm a yes."

I noticed my teammates weren't saying anything about my and Willow's dating, probably because Coach was in the room. But, for the most part, they all seemed to be over the fact that she'd up and left us.

Weren't they hurt by that? I mean, she'd up and left.

Then again, she did just show up here and make a plea to the team. She'd left Miami and had obviously been in touch with Coach before doing this. That took guts. This girl wasn't scared of anything. She took charge when she needed to.

But was I okay with her playing goalie again? This was State, after all. She hadn't been practicing with us for seven weeks like Josiah had been.

"Well, Brodie?" Coach said. "What's it going to be?"

CHAPTER FORTY-NINE

Willow

Eyes laser-focused, I prepared for the Jupiter Bulldogs' leading scorer. He raced down the ice, nailing Pax in the chest with his elbow.

Bringing his stick back, he slapped the puck so hard, I was sure flames would shoot out the back.

The puck zinged toward the lower right corner of the net. Falling to my knees, I dove to the right, desperately trying to block the shot.

The *thawck* of the net told me I had missed.

I banged my gloves on the ice. "Damnit!"

"Come on, *Ice Capades*, get your head in the game." Nathaniel winked as he skated by me.

The ice usually calmed me. Centered me. But today, it left me feeling jittery and uncertain. Brodie had voted yes to allowing me back on the team, but we'd broken from the meeting and I hadn't been able to get him alone before the game. I wanted to talk with him one-on-one, to see if he'd truly accepted my apology and understood I was asking for more than just his forgiveness.

I knew I'd made the right choice leaving Miami, but it was

hard not to let the nagging voice of doubt in the back of my head break through: *You'll never make it as a hockey player. You'll never get into a college. You should have stayed in Miami.*

The puck shot down the ice. Preach attempted to sling one in the other goalie's five-hole.

It ricocheted off his glove and landed right in front of Brodie.

In a split second, he brought his stick back and slapped a shot right over the goalie's right shoulder.

The crowd erupted into cheers that people back in Woodhaven could probably hear. Relief swept over me. We were finally back in the lead with under a minute to go.

Stay focused.

I knelt and put my palm to the ice.

Eyes closed, I counted back from three, focusing on calming my heart.

Once my eyes opened, the rink appeared crisper.

Side to side, I moved, loosening up and preparing for the Bulldogs to attack. They wouldn't go out without a fight, but neither would we.

A quick fake out let the Bulldogs' forwards break away from Pax and Teddy.

Both guys dipped their heads down and chased after the Bulldogs' offensive line.

The left wing tried to catch me off guard by taking a shot from more than fifty feet away.

I caught it in my blocker and checked the clock.

"Denied," Teddy shouted.

Hell yeah, I knocked that down. "Yes! Come on, guys! We got this!"

It took nearly the entire game, but I finally felt like I'd found my rhythm.

The team, me included, had been struggling on the ice all

night. It was almost like we'd only just played a game or two together before we'd gotten here. We were making mistakes that had cost goals and possibly the game.

Another shot came whizzing at me. I snatched the puck out of the air, then dropped it in for Preach.

"There you go, Willow! That's our goalie," he said, giving me a nod.

As the guys skated down the rink, Preach passed to Nathaniel. He brought back his stick and slapped the puck. It bounced off the top of the goal.

"Good try, guys," I shouted.

Almost there!

"Ten, nine, eight," the crowd counted down the remaining seconds left in the game.

Brodie and Nathaniel continued to attack the other team's net. The goalie blocked Nathaniel's shot but failed to scoop it into his catcher. With the puck loose on the ice, I could practically feel the panic emanating from the other goalie.

Scrambling to get back into his defensive stance, the guy was too slow. With the flick of his wrist, Brodie shot the puck above the goalie's left shoulder. As the buzzer sounded, the crowd erupted into thunderous applause. They chanted Brodie's name as he lifted his arms into the air, celebrating our three-to-one win. Hats from around the rink slid across the ice, acknowledging his hat trick. A few stuffed animals and roses made their way onto the ice as well.

State Championship, here we come!

Even though Brodie and I weren't together, I was proud of him. With all the drama going on in his life, he deserved a great game. There were loads of scouts and coaches in the stands watching a number of the guys playing this weekend, but a solid performance at State would all but guarantee Brodie a scholarship. I heard he even had a meeting with

Coach Raymond from Boston College lined up. Rumor was he was going to land a scholarship. Which, like me, would be the only way he'd be able to afford going to college. His dad had not only lost all his money, he'd cleaned out Brodie and Caleb's college accounts as well.

The scored goal replayed in my mind.

The game had been too close for comfort.

We were disjointed.

If it hadn't been for Brodie's and Preach's goals, we would have been screwed. As in, booted from the State tournament in the first round and completely missing out on having scouts watch our games.

"Can we talk?" I asked as Brodie stepped off the bus. My phone buzzed in my pocket.

I knew without checking that it was either Jessa or Ericka. I'd been texting with them on the bus, trying to work up the courage to do this.

He slouched and stepped forward as if he was going to walk right by me, but he said, "After. Right now, it's time for our postgame grub."

Preach stepped off the bus next and glanced at me, then to Brodie. "Look. Give me your stuff. Go talk. Figure it out." He eased my bag off my shoulder, and Brodie handed him his. "I'll save you a seat, but I can't promise Teddy isn't going to eat all the food in the buffet."

Brodie nodded and I chuckled, then Preach grinned and strode away, leaving us alone. "Let's walk," I said.

Silently, he followed me as we strolled around the side of the hotel. I pointed to a little patio I could barely make out in the darkness, and we made our way there. The silence was heavy, laden with questions, anger, and whatever else was going on. Hopefully one of those things was love. Because I loved him, and he needed to know it.

"I'm sorry, Brodie. I really am."

"I know you are." He offered me a slight smile but then looked down at his feet again, and his shoulders were slumped.

"But…" I sat down on the bench and let out a sigh. "I hurt you."

He shoved his hands into his jacket pockets and remained standing. "Everything just got so fucked up."

"It's showing on the ice. We almost lost tonight."

"Well, you've been gone for almost two months." He faced skyward, and I saw a white plume of air slowly release from his mouth. "I'm sorry. That was a dick thing to say. We all sucked out there."

"It was ugly." I pulled my hat down more to chase away the chill settling in over us. It wasn't just from the weather, either. "There's no chance for us, is there?"

He shifted to face me, then sat down, keeping a few inches between us. All I wanted to do was curl up under his warm arm and breathe in his sweet, woodsy scent.

"Because I love you, Brodie. I really do."

"What if you leave again? What if another training team approaches you? And—"

"I won't, Brodie. You have to understand, though, that I needed to go to Miami to find that out. If I would have stayed because of you, I could have really ended up hating you. Wondering, *what if?*" My heart started hammering. "And that wouldn't be fair to you or me."

"You're right." His head hung low, and his shoulders curved forward. "God, I missed you, Willow."

My heart stung, like a knife had pierced it. "I missed you,

too. So much."

He finally looked at me. His brown eyes, in this dim light, were dark, almost black. The distant lights from the hotel didn't do much to eat away at the dark void out here, but I caught a hint of a smile curving the corner of his mouth.

"That speech…in front of the guys and Coach." He shook his head. "That took balls, Willow."

"I was shaking in my hockey skates." I nudged his shoulder. "But I meant every word. I really am sorry. For everything. I just hope you can forgive me."

"I can," he said, his voice a whisper.

My heart stopped for a beat or two, then kicked into high gear. "You can?"

He nodded. "I mean, I'll be going away to Boston College in the fall…to play hockey for them." His grin widened as he grabbed my hand. "But until then—"

"Wait, what?" I turned more to him.

"Talked with Coach Raymond. They offered me a full ride." Tears lined his eyes.

I threw my arms around him and squeezed. "Brodie. Oh my gosh! That's amazing!" I leaned back and looked into his eyes.

He pressed his cool lips to mine as he held me close. A flash of heat stormed through me, and it didn't take more than a few seconds, kissing Brodie, to warm up my body. Tilting my head, he took the kiss deeper as he got reacquainted with my mouth.

It felt like home, being in his arms right then and there.

I didn't care if he was leaving for Boston in the fall; we'd make this work. After what we worked through, nothing would break that up.

He eased back, keeping his cold nose to mine. A flash of light ignited beside us, and we both turned.

Flood lights kicked on, bouncing their illumination off a massive ice sculpture of a hockey player, taking a slap shot.

Brodie chuckled.

"What?" I kissed him again, then nuzzled his neck so I could inhale more of his scent.

"Hockey. Brought us together, then we broke up. And now it's brought us back together." He cupped my cheeks and tilted my head as he gazed at me. "I love you, Willow Covington."

Tears streamed down my face as I closed my eyes, basking in the three words. They warmed my chest and felt like a blanket wrapping around me. "I love you, too."

Brodie stood up and offered me his hand. "Let's get back to our team."

CHAPTER FIFTY

Brodie

"I'm shutting you down, Right Hand of God," I yelled, pointing my stick at Roger.

"Nice one." Preach tackled me into the boards, slapping at my helmet.

I'd just scored, tying the game up at one.

One minute left on the clock.

Sixty freaking seconds to score one more goal and become repeat State Champions.

One.

More.

Minute.

The crowd screamed so loudly, I could barely hear anything else.

Except Coach. There was no missing his voice. "Focus. Get back into formation. Pressure. Pressure. Pressure."

He barked a few more orders to Pax and Teddy.

Stay focused, Brodie.

Willow slapped her stick, and I pointed at her.

"Defense," she yelled. "Keep it going."

She'd really shown up in a huge way. First on that Friday

appearance, then after we'd nearly lost on Friday, pulling me aside. That girl, she was so strong. Tackled things head on. And I was thankful for that because I knew I was a stubborn guy. I'd almost lost her because of it.

But now that we were back together, and the team was on board with everything, we were truly a team now. Everything was out in the open and we were dealing.

Nathaniel met in the center for the drop. The ref regarded each of them and then dropped the puck. It hit the ice, and Nathaniel slapped it to me.

I dipped and deked, keeping the puck close. I needed to run down the clock.

Then Roger, the Right Hand of God, charged me. I could almost see the fury in his eyes. Willow had stopped all fifteen of his shots. His right winger was the only one who'd gotten one past her. I knew how hungry he was to get one by Willow. To tie us. Force us into extra time or, even worse, a shootout.

They were damn near unstoppable in shootout situations.

"You're going down, asshole." He dipped his shoulder to ram into me.

I braked, spun, and lifted the puck over his stick, then flipped it to Preach. A quick spin had me in the open, and I went up the left side.

Moving past their defenders, Preach did his dance.

Roger cut him off, swiping his feet, and Preach fell hard. I lunged for the puck, took it with me when I turned, then pulled back for another shot.

Let's make this the game winner!

Out of nowhere, a shoulder rammed into my side. Right below the rib protectors.

The crowd groaned—even louder than I had.

The air burst from my lungs and my head snapped back. Lightning struck through my mind, but I rolled, punching whoever had taken me down in the chest.

It was enough to get him off me, and I was on my skates again. Gasping.

Where was that puck? I checked the clock.

Thirty seconds.

"Breakaway," someone yelled.

Shit, break—

The Right Hand of God attacked our zone, skating faster than one of his slap shots.

And no one was near him.

Willow stiffened, her knees bent. I charged, the last of my energy powering through my quads. The ice scraped beneath my blades as I sped toward Roger. No way was he going to score on us.

I'd get to him.

Or Willow would block it. I had to trust her.

The deafening crowd faded. Everything around me vanished as I zeroed in on the puck. My lungs burned. Sweat chilled my back.

Five feet.

I pushed harder.

Three feet.

Almost to him.

He took his swing. The slap of his stick hitting the puck vibrated through my bones. His signature sound for how hard he smacked that thing.

It was aimed for just above Willow's shoulder. The same spot he'd scored on her last time they'd faced off.

Oh shit.

Willow's glove shot up.

The clap of the puck hitting her leather pocket echoed through the arena. She snapped the mitt shut. She'd done it. She'd blocked his shot!

Roger bellowed and kept charging.

"Willow!" Pax yelled as he checked Roger out of the way. "Here!"

She dropped the puck onto the ice and passed it to him. He swerved around the goal, then blasted toward me. I tapped the ice. He flipped it to me. I spun, taking the puck with me.

Fifteen seconds!

Cheers radiated through the air.

Focus.

I deked and weaved. Blasted down the ice. I flipped it to Preach, then he found me down the ice.

"Go! Brodie! Go!" I heard Willow's voice above everything. Only her voice could register with me right now. It was like the sound fueled my tired legs. My burning lungs.

My heart exploded as I pushed forward.

Five!

"Come on, Brodie!" someone yelled.

Four!

I spun, taking the puck with me.

Three!

My lungs burned.

Two!

I pulled my stick back and slapped that puck with everything I had.

The black disc flew through the air. A blunt force rammed into my shoulder, but I stayed focused on the puck as I landed on the ice.

It was on target.

The goalie's glove reached out to bat it down.

He missed.

The puck smacked against the net.

Buzz!

I pushed off the boards and hopped to my skates.

We'd won.

We'd won State.

We were State Champions again.

The crowd went nuts, throwing crap onto the ice.

Goose bumps puckered my arms and prickled my neck as I skated to the middle of the rink. I ripped off my helmet and tossed it into the air along with the rest of the team. Tears stung. My throat tightened.

We'd done it.

We'd won.

Despite all the shit happening around us, we'd done it.

I raced toward Willow and was the first one to make it to her. I tackled her to the ice. Her laughter filled the air. Preach landed on us next. After that, I couldn't tell who was next; I only felt the weight building.

I pressed my hands against the ice to try and block some of the weight from Willow. This close, I could clearly see her.

Tears flowed.

A smile filled her face.

She was laughing.

"We did it, Brodie," she yelled.

"Sure as shit did."

"Hand of God my ass," Pax yelled. "That guy had nothing on you, Willow!"

Pax of all people, cheering for Willow. I never thought I'd see the day. She squeezed her eyes shut and screamed as loud as I'd ever heard her.

The weight atop us lessened, and I shifted slightly. Her eyes popped open, and her smile widened.

I grabbed her mask and pulled her head up off the ice slightly so she could see me, and I could rest my head against her mask. "I love you, Willow Covington. I love you!"

She froze. Her eyes wide. "I love you, Brodie Windom!"

Someone grabbed me by the back of my jersey, pads and all, and yanked me off her. And then I was airborne, hands poking into my back.

I lifted my legs so I wouldn't slice anyone with my skates, and then I was thrust atop Nathaniel, Pax, and Preach's shoulders.

Willow squealed.

Teddy, Josiah, and Trevor had hoisted her up on their shoulders, and they were skating toward me.

"Willow," I yelled, reaching for her.

"Wahoo!" she screamed, punching the air with her fists. "We did it. *Wolverines forever!*"

We all collided and made a mess of people, but our teammates held us both up, still.

"Okay," Preach yelled to me. "*Now* you two can date."

EPILOGUE

Five Days Later

Brodie

"I so needed this alone time before the party!" Willow leaned into me as we skated around Jackson Pond.

No training.

No hockey vocab testing.

No slap shots.

Just me and her, leisurely skating around Jackson Pond, and not at all worried who might see us. We were free to date. Free to be together.

And we were.

It was freezing out, and flurries settled over us, but that didn't matter. I had Willow in my arms again. She held me close as we danced along the outskirts of the pond to our own song.

"Have I said lately how glad I am that you're back?"

"Not in the last ten minutes. I was starting to wonder if maybe you weren't anymore." Willow winked.

She was wearing a pink stocking cap with a white poof on top. Her bright blue eyes drew me in, and I just had to kiss her again.

"I'm glad you're back," I said, then brushed my lips against hers. "I'm glad you're back. I'm glad you're back, infinity."

Her hold on me tightened as I got reacquainted with her mouth. It'd been five days since State, so yeah, I'd kissed her a few times since then, but never enough. I'd never get enough of her.

She giggled against my mouth. "I feel like I'm dreaming."

I curled a strand of her silky black hair behind her ear. Her big blue eyes were dilated and her lips shiny. I was addicted to that look. And thanks to scholarship offers at nearby schools in Boston, I'd be able to see her like this all the time still.

She'd gotten calls from Boston College, the University of Wisconsin-Madison, and the University of Boston, but she'd chosen the University of Boston. It would have been great to have her at the same school as me, but she wanted to take the better offer.

"We should start heading to Bear Lake for the victory party, huh?" Willow said between kisses. "They're probably waiting for us."

I bent my knees slightly, then hoisted her up. She cinched her legs around me and took control of the kiss. She felt like home. Her fresh ice scent, her warm mouth, and strength surrounded me.

She was my anchor.

We coasted to the edge of the rink, and I fell back into a bank of snow. Her giggle echoed off the trees surrounding the pond. She wasn't even phased by the cold air and flurries. She just smiled and cuddled up against me.

"Hey, I haven't told you yet! Mom and Dad found a cute little apartment close to the Ice Den, and it's only a block from Jessa's house," she said. "They say we can move in next month."

"Sweet. Does that mean your dad found a job?" I asked.

"He's got an interview with something that actually might use his finance degree, finally!" She propped her chin on my chest and looked up at me. "I haven't seen him smile this much in a long time. Him *and* Mom."

"I'm glad."

"Have you heard from your dad after yesterday's visit?" She brushed away some flurries that'd landed on my face.

"Yeah, he called and said good night to me and Caleb. It's so weird. I mean, I never thought I'd go visit my dad in jail." I closed my eyes and sagged against the snow as I drew in a breath of the cool air. "But even in the orange jumpsuit, he looked better. Weird?"

"No." She shook her head. "I'm glad you went to see him and that he called. I bet that made Caleb really happy."

I nodded, happy that he was getting help and that we could still see and talk to him, but super sad it took him landing in jail to get said help. "He said he watched the State Championship."

Her head perked up. "Really?"

"Yep. Saw my winning goal, even." I couldn't help the smile filling my face. "It was cool to talk about hockey with him again."

"I'm proud of you for going. I'm not sure I would have been able to."

"He's family," I said, then hugged her tight.

"So what's next?"

"Absolutely nothing other than dating you and everyone knowing that we're together." I kissed her cheek. "Starting with the State champs party!"

We hopped to our feet.

"Shall we, Toe Pick?" I grabbed her in my arms and spun her, finally putting her back down.

She looked up at me with a huge grin. "After you, Puck Head."

Acknowledgments

I wish I could specifically name every single person who's come alongside me during this writing journey, but the list is so very long. I will try to name a few here, though. Super Agent Nicole Resciniti, thank you for your tireless work. I can't tell you how thankful I am for you. Super Editor Stacy Cantor Abrams and team. There were several editors who worked on this book, and I'm so thankful for you all.

My sweet hubby, Charlie. Thank you for your endless support, your willingness to brainstorm with me and give me hugs and chocolate when the world just isn't quite right.

Kelsey and Chloe Evans. Thank you for all your help with the high school side of things. It was fun getting to chat with you guys about all this. You're so sweet and fun. Thank you!

To everyone at Entangled and Macmillan who has played a part in the creation of this amazing story. I love how the story turned out, I love the cover, and I love your dedication to helping create an amazing product.

To Michele Trent and Beth Cowles, thank you for your friendship. Thank you for being there for me during the ups and downs that come with the world of publishing. I couldn't imagine life without you two. Thank you to my Trail Sisters and the Snot Rocket trail running group, for logging all those miles on the trails and taking amazing adventures with me. They help fuel my creativity, and I so enjoy your company!

To the beta readers who took the time to read through

early drafts for us and offer up amazing feedback.

And finally, to the fans of Willow, Brodie, and the whole Woodhaven High crew, thank you from the bottom of my heart for your support and enthusiasm. We hope you enjoyed reading *In the Penalty Box* as much as we enjoyed writing it.

XO ~Lynn

In the Penalty Box came together with the help of countless individuals. First and foremost, I'd like to thank Lynn Rush, my amazing coauthor, for agreeing to write a book with someone she'd only met online! Ha-ha! I'd also like to thank our superstar agents Nicole Resciniti and Jennifer Wills.

If you read the first draft of this book, you'd be amazed at how far it's come and how much better it is now compared to back then! This is thanks to our fantastic editors, Stacy Abrams and Judi Weiss.

To Liz and everyone else at Entangled Publishing, thank you for believing in this story!

Another round of thanks goes out to our incredible beta readers, especially our hockey experts! Colin McDermott, A.J. Simmons, Anna Webb, Travis Parisi, Robbie Shapiro, and Myles Bible—you are all so amazing, and we are beyond grateful for your help!

Thank you to Andrew Cole-Bulgin and Fiona Simpson for always believing in me! I'm here today because of both of you.

On a personal note, I want to thank my husband, Lee Roy. Your encouragement to follow my dreams means the absolute most to me! I love you and everything you do for me and our family. Sweet Bella Rose, you inspire me to achieve my goals! Thank you, my darling, smart, and inquisitive daughter!

To my parents, thank you for raising a daughter who loved to read and write! What a fine example you set for me! Bella Rose is following in my footsteps, and I could not be more proud! I'm so grateful for your love and wisdom!

To my mother-in-law and father-in-law, thank you for all of your encouragement, support, and for watching Bells! Thanks to your help, I'm able to meet my deadlines!

To my Street Team members, thank you! You do so much for me, and it is appreciated more than words can express!

I also want to thank my friends. I've known some of you for years, others, only a few months. But each of you holds a special spot in my heart! It's inevitable that I left someone off the list—I always do and then feel terrible about it afterward, so I'll apologize in advance! I feel very blessed to have such incredible friends, and please know that the following people are all amazing! Especially Lynn Rush, Ali Novak, Alex Evansley, Rachel Meinke, Ariana Godoy, Jordan Lynde, Sarah Ratliff, Zara Ali, Katarina Tonks, Elizabeth "Lizzie" Seibert, Peyton Novak, Kristi McManus, Ravendra Patel, Eve Martaa, Michelle Hayes, Rob Shapiro, Tracy Wolff, Rusty Marcum, Anne and Mark Casadei, Kim from Read Your Writes Book Reviews, Katie Prouty, Angela Sanders, Chelsea Hjalmarson, Lindsay von Arx, Lauren Magnatta, Kelly Frey, Hannah Matthews, the AVL Mops Crew, Meg Summers, Noreen Bruce, Sarah Phillips, Suzanne Correnti, Kristin Polk, Darci Simer Yahnke, Yetta Williams, Beth Revis, Nora Carpenter, Rachel Hylton, Meg Cook, The Overworked Moms Writer Club, Sprinters United (Writing) Group, our Friday Night IG Live Crew, my Komixx Family, and my WattFam. Your support is worth its weight in gold!

No matter if we see each other weekly or we haven't been in the same state or even country in years or we've never met in person, you are all appreciated and loved.

A huge thank-you to our sharp-eyed proofers! You all helped more than you could ever know! Wow! Thank you, Kathleen "Chip" Haley, Fiona Simpson, Heather Nelson, Jodie Zellmer, Lauren Johnson, Melissa Chandler, Amanda-Victoria Sumrall, Sarah "Roooomie" Coyer, Elizabeth Johnson, Jeanna L. Blume, Brianna Williams, and our author friend and hockey enthusiast, Rob "Robbie" Shapiro!

To my readers and reviewers, thank you! I've always wanted to be an author. You made it possible and for that, you will always have my gratitude!

—Kelly Anne xoxo

Loved Woodhaven? Then you won't want to miss taking a trip to their rival town, Twin River, with the Twin River High series—all three books coming soon!

The goth girl covers up a major secret
for the school's hot quarterback...

The genius and the brooding soccer star make
a mutually beneficial deal...

The new girl pretends to have it all,
with the boy who actually does.

Fun and drama abound in the
halls of Twin River!

Coming Soon!

Don't miss Kelly Anne Blount's sweet and hilarious rom-com, available now!

New York Times bestselling author Rachel Harris returns to YA with a passionate, emotional romance perfect for fans of Sarah Dessen or Huntley Fitzpatrick.

BY RACHEL HARRIS

Look up the word "nerd" and you'll find Lily Bailey's picture. She's got one goal: first stop valedictorian, next stop Harvard. Until a stint in the hospital from too much stress lands her in the last place a klutz like her ever expected to be: salsa dance lessons.

Look up the word "popular" and you'll find Stone Torres's picture. His life seems perfect—star of the football team, small-town hero, lots of friends. But his family is struggling to make ends meet, so if pitching in at his mom's dance studio helps, he'll do it.

When Lily's dad offers Stone extra cash to volunteer as Lily's permanent dance partner, he can't refuse. But with each dip and turn, each moment her hand is in his, his side job starts to feel all too real. Lily shows Stone he's more than his impressive football stats, and he introduces her to a world outside of studying. But with the lines blurred, can their relationship survive the secret he's been hiding?

New York Times bestselling author Julie Cross's sexy, relatable hockey series is perfect for fans of Miranda Kenneally.

OFF THE ICE

Claire O'Connor is back in Juniper Falls, but that doesn't mean she wants to be. One semester off, that's what she promised herself. Just long enough to take care of her father and keep the family business—a hockey bar beside the ice rink—afloat. After that, she's getting the hell out. Again.

Enter Tate Tanley. What happened between them the night before she left town resurfaces the second they lay eyes on each other. But the guy she remembers has been replaced by a total hottie. When Tate is unexpectedly called in to take over for the hockey team's star goalie, suddenly he's in the spotlight and on his way to becoming just another egotistical varsity hockey player. And Claire's sworn off Juniper Falls hockey players for good.

It's the absolute worst time to fall in love.

For Tate and Claire, hockey isn't just a game. And they both might not survive a body check to the heart.

For every book nerd who's ever crushed on a guy from afar, this sweet contemporary romance will be sure to melt your heart.

The
BOOK
WORM
CRUSH

LISA BROWN ROBERTS

Shy bookworm Amy McIntyre is about to compete for the chance to interview her favorite author, who hasn't spoken to the press in years. The only way to win is to step out of the shadows and into the spotlight, but that level of confidence has never come easy.

The solution? A competition coach. The problem? The best person for the job is the guy she's secretly crushing on...local surfer celebrity Toff Nichols.

He's a player. He's a heartthrob. He makes her forget basic things, like how to breathe. How can she feel any confidence around *him*?

To her surprise, Toff agrees to help. And he's an excellent teacher. Amy feels braver—maybe even brave enough to admit her feelings for him. When their late night practices become less about coaching and more about making out, Amy's newfound confidence wavers.

But does Toff really like her or is this just another lesson?

Let's be friends!

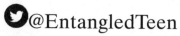@EntangledTeen

@EntangledTeen

@EntangledTeen

 bit.ly/TeenNewsletter

entangled teen

an imprint of Entangled Publishing LLC